ROBERT LOUIS STEVENSON

The Annotated

TREASURE ISLAND

Introduction and Notes by
Simon Barker-Benfield

WITH ILLUSTRATIONS BY LOUIS RHEAD

FINE & KAHN
New York

For Nancy Needham

FINE
KAHN

Published by Fine & Kahn, LLC
322 Eighth Avenue
New York, NY 10001

Introduction, Notes, and Robert Louis Stevenson biography
Copyright © 2014 by Simon Barker-Benfield

Stevenson, Robert Louis, 1850–1894, author.
[Treasure Island]
The annotated Treasure Island / by Robert Louis
Stevenson ; introduction and notes by Simon Barker-Benfield ; with
illustrations by Louis Rhead.
pages cm
Includes bibliographical references.
LCCN 2014934735
ISBN 978-1-937075-01-9

1. Treasure Island (Imaginary place)–Fiction. 2. Treasure troves–Fiction.
3. Pirates–Fiction. 4. Sea stories. I. Barker-Benfield, Simon, writer of
supplementary textual content. II. Rhead, Louis,
1857–1926, illustrator. III. Title.

PR5486.A2B37 2014   823'.8
QBI14-600105

Designed by Lisa Chovnick

Printed in the United States of America
on acid-free paper.

Fine & Kahn and the Fine & Kahn colophon are registered trademarks.

QT   10   9   8   7   6   5   4   3   2   1

Contents

PART IV

The Stockade

PART V

My Sea Adventure

PART VI

Captain Silver

Introduction

In the 1750s Bristol was the United Kingdom's second-largest port.

ONE FRIGID DAY in early March 1758, just before the sun rose over the port city of Bristol in the west of England, an early riser would have seen figures on a two-masted vessel preparing to raise anchor. Of the 26 people on board, 19 were pirates who had criminal records established with considerable effort in Caribbean, Atlantic, and Indian waters.

As the anchor came up on the schooner *Hispaniola*, the faint sounds of a work song trailed over the water: "Fifteen men on the dead man's chest . . . Yo ho ho, and a bottle of rum."

We know all this because the principal narrator of *Treasure Island*, Jim Hawkins, tells us or we can figure it out from the details he mentions.

What Hawkins does not mention is that it was slow work raising an anchor by hand—we know this from modern efforts with replica vessels—and that before a vessel reached the open sea, it faced a tricky, three-hour, seven-mile run down the River Avon. In the 1750s the Avon had 45-foot-high tidal ranges at Bristol, smelled foul, and challenged mariners with unreliable winds and tight turns

through the Avon Gorge, as it flowed down to the Severn Estuary and the Bristol Channel. Most vessels had to be towed both up and down the Avon.

This annotated edition of *Treasure Island* aims to fill in other gaps in the narrative and provide what writers for movies call the "back story" to some of the details mentioned in the tale.

The tale itself has found many new generations to entertain since it was first published in 1883. It is about a quest. It involves a journey and danger. There are good people and bad people, and one person who is both. It all sounds simple enough in the hands of a storyteller like Robert Louis Stevenson. But there is also a backdrop to the story, filled with information about another long-ago age that Jim Hawkins could take for granted but that is new to most of us.

The 1750s of *Treasure Island* were roughly the midpoint in what some British historians call "the long 18th century," a period that began in 1660 and lasted until 1832 or so. Historians find it a convenient framework for examining political, social, and cultural changes in Britain. It is also convenient for plotting changes in the world of the buccaneers, privateers, pirates, sea rovers, filibusters, and picaroons, an era that lasted roughly from the death of the callous and audacious Welsh sea-raider Henry Morgan in 1688 to the hanging of the murderous pirate Rhode Island–born Charles Gibbs in 1831.

The British in the Caribbean of that era made a distinction between *privateers*, who had government licenses (letters of marque) that authorized them to make attacks on the enemy of the day, and *buccaneers*, who did not and therefore were pirates.

Morgan sued two London publishers for calling him a buccaneer rather than a privateer in their

Henry Morgan led profitable attacks on Spanish towns in the Caribbean; he later became Sir Henry, deputy governor of Jamaica, and a rich buyer of plantations.

1684 translation of A. O. Exquemelin's *Bucaniers of America*. They publicly apologized. Since then the terms seem to have been conflated by writers describing the Caribbean marauders of that century, along with *freebooter, filibuster, sea rover,* and *pirate.*

During the long 18th century, pirates were vividly in evidence in the Caribbean Sea and the Pacific Ocean, and in the Atlantic Ocean, the Red Sea, the Indian Ocean, and the South China Sea.

The Caribbean—which in *Treasure Island* is the *Hispaniola*'s destination—had long been plagued by the legal and illegal raiding of seaborne commerce by crews from England, the Netherlands, France, and Spain, countries that were at war with one another at various times throughout the 1500s, 1600s, and 1700s.

The death of Morgan—one of his doctors, Sir Hans Sloane, was still alive in the 1750s—provides a convenient break between the more-or-less licensed Caribbean privateers of the 1660s and 1670s and the Golden Age of the pirates who followed them, which lasted until 1725 or so.

The term "Golden Age" needs to be used carefully with respect to whom, to where, and in what period it applies.

The historian Marcus Rediker applies it to those he calls "Anglo-American pirates" who "plied the oceans of the globe" between 1715 and 1725. Their numbers, according to contemporary estimates, ranged at any one time between 1,000 and 2,000, with one group of pirates claiming the number reached 2,400. The numbers drop off into the low hundreds after 1725 as British Royal Navy patrols and at least 400 pirate executions—but more likely 500 to 600—took their toll, according to Rediker.

Meanwhile, Chinese pirates, for example, also had their own "Golden Age" in the early 1800s, and it dwarfs the Anglo-American version. Historian Dian Murray estimates that "by 1805 a confederation of seven fleets, 2,000 junks and between 50,000 and 70,000 pirates" was based in Kwantung province.

By the time the *Hispaniola* sailed, the Golden Age had been over for almost 30 years, but as a way of life, the prospect of making one's fortune and living outside the constraints of ordinary society as a pirate still had attractions, even for members of the Royal Navy.

In 1748, just ten years before Jim Hawkins set sail, the ship's company of HMS *Chesterfield* mutinied with the intention of setting themselves up as pirates. One of the mutiny's leaders apparently was a refugee from that Golden Age, like Long John Silver and his men: John Place, the *Chesterfield*'s carpenter's mate, was accused of having

Admiral Benbow

THE INN THAT Jim Hawkins's father operates is named for Vice-Admiral John Benbow (1653–1702) of the Royal Navy, a successful pirate hunter in his younger days, who became a popular hero when he attacked a French fleet, even though the captains of the other ships in his squadron declined to support him.

The event took place during a series of clashes with a French fleet off Santa Marta on the Caribbean coast of modern Colombia between August 19 and August 24, 1702. Benbow, in his flagship, the *Breda*, made repeated, close-in attacks on the enemy fleet, but only two of his captains, George Walton in the *Ruby* and Samuel Vincent in the *Falmouth*, joined him. The others hung back, in spite of Benbow's repeated orders to stay in formation with him and "behave themselves like Englishmen."

Gun crews on the *Defiance* were so frustrated by the inaction of their commander, Richard Kirkby, that they "cried out they had as good throw the guns overboard as stand by them," or so the ship's boatswain, Thomas Mollamb, testified later at the court-martial. Mollamb also testified that Kirkby kept dodging behind the mizzenmast or dropping down to the deck whenever there was gunfire.

Drink seems to have played a role in the unfolding debacle. On August 19, at the beginning of the fight, Captain John Constable of the *Windsor* came aboard the flagship drunk. On the *Greenwich*, a second lieutenant, John Codner, noted in his journal on August 22 that his captain, Cooper Wade, was drunk and "had been so every day since we first began to engage the enemy."

The crew and officers of the 50-gun *Ruby* fought well. She was badly damaged on the fourth day

Admiral John Benbow.

after the French had been sighted. The ship was ordered by Benbow to make its way back to Jamaica for repairs. Later, at about 3 a.m. on Monday August 24, Benbow's right leg was shattered by a "chain shot" fired by an enemy ship.

A chain shot–two small cannon balls linked with a chain–was designed to disable a sailing ship by cutting through the rigging used to secure masts and sails, and by damaging the sails themselves. The objective was to make it more difficult to keep the ship moving and so turn it into a stationary target. Chain shot was also highly effective against people.

Benbow was taken below to have his wounds treated. He then insisted on being taken back up onto his quarterdeck and placed in a cot so he could continue to direct the fight.

Later that morning Kirkby of the *Defiance* came on board the *Breda* to urge that Benbow give up the battle. Benbow summoned the other captains to hear their views, a common practice in the wartime Royal Navy. Wade of the *Greenwich*, Constable of the *Windsor*, and Thomas Hudson of the *Pendennis* signed a document called "a consultation and opinion"–drafted by Kirkby–giving their reasons why the British fleet's attack on the French should be called off. Also signing the document were two other captains, Samuel Vincent of the *Falmouth* and Christopher Fogg, captain of Benbow's flagship, both of whom had fought bravely.

This formal opinion argued that the British ships were in disrepair and the men tired; ammunition was low, and the winds were too variable to be relied on. The captains recommended that the British fleet continue to follow the enemy fleet and, if sailing conditions improved, try another attack.

Not trusting that enough of his captains would follow him if conditions did improve, Benbow ordered the squadron to return to its base in Jamaica, where he had his captains imprisoned until they could face a court-martial.

Kirkby and Wade were sentenced to death and were shot on board HMS *Bristol* the following year. Constable was found guilty of disobeying orders and of drunkenness, and was dismissed from the Navy. Hudson died before he could be tried. Vincent and Fogg were found guilty of signing the advisory document and also sentenced to be dismissed. But Benbow declared they had fought well, and the two returned to naval service. The two had signed the paper advising against continuing the fight because they felt that if Benbow were to fight on without the other four captains he would likely be captured by the French.

Benbow did not long survive the battle. His leg did not heal well. In addition, the admiral who had presided over the court-martial wrote, the "malady, being aggravated by the discontent of his mind, threw him into a sort of melancholy which ended his life." He died in November 1702.

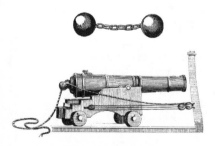

Chain shot and gun. The chain connecting the balls cut through rigging and damaged sails and caused great damage to the human body.

served with the pirate Bartholomew Roberts in the early 1720s.

In 1761, three years after the *Hispaniola* returned from Treasure Island, the crew of the Bristol privateer *King George* mutinied as part of a plan to turn pirate in the East Indies. The plan ran aground in a Spanish bay, where about 100 members of the crew promptly disappeared. Four of the ringleaders were convicted, and three were acquitted.

And 50 years after the *Hispaniola* returned from Treasure Island, the Caribbean saw another surge in seaborne violence. The Spanish territories in the Americas were establishing themselves as independent nations, and licensed picaroons were beginning to attack cargo vessels, ostensibly in their names. Charles Gibbs eventually didn't even bother with the fig leaf of a bogus or near-bogus privateering commission. He was hanged for burning to death a captured crew, among other acts.

The treasure that the crew of the *Hispaniola* sought was serious money: 700,000 British pounds sterling, or enough to buy a fleet of 11 duplicates of HMS *Victory*, the 104-gun battleship best known as Admiral Horatio Nelson's flagship at the 1805 Battle of Trafalgar. The order to build Victory was given the year after the *Hispaniola* returned, and *Victory* now remains, almost 250 years later, a commissioned ship of the Royal Navy and a link to those days. Today, according to Bank of England calculations, 700,000 pounds would be worth about 131.4 million pounds sterling, or about $200 million.

MONEY

In the 1700s money was not measured in today's decimal system. In 1750 British coinage—gold, silver, and copper—was divided into three groups or categories: *pounds, shillings,* and *pence* (one of the plural forms of *penny*). There were 12 pennies in a shilling, and 20 shillings in a pound.

People carried coins of different values and names, all based on the pounds-shillings-pence system. There was no one-pound coin, but several coins called guineas; there were 21 shillings in a *guinea*. In 1750 British coins consisted of:

HMS *Victory*, Admiral Horatio Nelson's flagship
at the 1805 Battle of Trafalgar.

Gold coins: five guineas, two guineas, one guinea, and half-guinea. The coins were called guineas because at one time the gold used to mint them came from the Guinea Coast of West Africa, sometimes called the Gold Coast (present-day Ghana). The value of one gold guinea was set at 21 silver shillings by the government in 1717, and the gold guinea was minted until 1816 when the *sovereign*, a one pound coin, was introduced.

Silver coins: *crown* (equivalent to five shillings), *half crown* (equivalent to two shillings and sixpence), *shilling, sixpence, fourpence (fourpenny), threepence, twopence*, and *penny*. Some verbal usage could baffle foreigners. For example, a half-crown piece could be referred to in different ways, including "half a crown," "two shillings and sixpence," and "two-and-six."

Copper coins: *halfpenny* and *farthing* (a quarter of a penny).

There was also paper money in circulation, issued by banks, but the notes were for large sums. Until 1793 the smallest banknote issued by the Bank of England was for ten pounds, roughly half a year's wage for some sailors.

The pounds-shillings-pence division of British coins, based on an ancient system of counting in twelves and twenties, continued to confuse foreigners accustomed to the decimal system until 1971, when Britain adopted the decimal system for its coins and paper money.

THE STEEP SLOPES OF BRITISH SOCIETY

Who had pennies, shillings, and guineas had a lot to do with the contours of British society at that time.

Squire Trelawney, the character who pays for the expedition to Treasure Island, is one of the major figures in this tale. In small rural districts of Britain, *squire* was an informal title for a major landowner.

Squire Trelawney was one of about 15,000 country gentlemen whose families in the 1750s occupied the upper slopes of British society—but not the highest slopes, which were occupied by "peers of the realm." The local squire was an influential person in his immediate area but usually not outside it.

The highest slopes of society were occupied by a handful of aristocratic families of great wealth and national political power. "Handful" is the operative word. In 1760 there were, in a country that numbered about 6 million people, just 181 peers, and they had titles like the Duke of Devonshire and the Earl Temple. These men (the grand titles were inherited by the oldest son, not the oldest child) typically were the largest landowners in their counties. Between 1700 and 1800 just 1,003 people held peerages—that is, had titles, in order of rank, of duke, marquis, earl, viscount, and baron. Some individuals held more than one title.

Good-natured, honest, but slightly dim, Trelawney would have been a substantial landowner in his district and would likely have rented some of his land to tenant farmers. He was probably a local magistrate at some time in his life, one of 8,400 in 1760 in Britain, concerned with road maintenance, licensing pubs, collecting taxes, and presiding over some criminal cases. The local squire likely controlled who was chosen to be in charge of his local church. He might also sit in Parliament at some point in his life.

Fore-and-aft rigging.

Square rigging.

The collective name for country gentlemen like Trelawney was the *squirearchy*; in many cases, their roots in their communities went back for generations.

But care needs to be taken when we try to precisely parse the structure of British society in Trelawney's day. It is a trap for the unwary. There were lords without broad acres, sirs with land but not much money, or much money and no land, misters like Trelawney who were richer than sirs, and misters in the towns who were richer than many lords, sirs, or squires, and so on.

"YOU NEVER IMAGINED A SWEETER SCHOONER"

Those words are spoken by Squire Trelawney, and he is talking about the *Hispaniola*, which he has bought to carry him on his treasure-hunting expedition.

The *Hispaniola* was a topsail schooner—a vessel with at least two masts, carrying primary sails arranged "fore-and-aft" and square topsails above them (see illustration, p. xiii). Two important ways of rigging a vessel are reflected in the terms "fore-and-aft" and "square sail."

On the *Hispaniola* both primary sails were four-sided but not square-shaped. In order to catch the wind, the tops of the two sails were attached to spars called *gaffs* and the bottoms of the sails to spars called *booms*. The booms were longer than the gaffs. Both gaffs and booms were attached to their respective masts by equipment that allowed the sails to swing from side to side as needed in order to harness the wind as efficiently as possible. The mast nearer the stern was taller than the mast ahead of it.

Hispaniola also had *square topsails* rigged above the fore-and-aft sails; they hung from spars called *yards* that looked like crossed *t*s on the masts. The topsails were also four-sided but smaller and more or less oblong in shape. And here is where the terminology can get confusing. "Square" sails have nothing to do with their shape; the term refers to the way they hang from a mast. The yard they are attached to is in turn attached at a right angle—square—to the mast. (For more on rigging and its implications for speed and handling, see note 4 on p. 56.)

We don't know exactly what the *Hispaniola* looked like. However, several sources provide some guidance.

In 1755 Britain's Royal Navy sold the *Sharke*, a 201-ton vessel built in 1732 that was probably rigged as a schooner, according to Karl Heinz Marquardt, an authority on how schooners developed between 1695 and 1845.

Two original technical drawings of the vessel survive in the archives. They label her a *sloop*. Marquardt notes that in the merchant navy the term applied to vessels with a particular one-masted rig, but that in the Royal Navy the term was a flexible one and was used describe its smallest vessels, which might have varying rigs.

The archives show a vessel with two masts, angled back like those of many schooners. She looks to have been about 75 feet long. (See illustration, below.)

"The *Sharke*'s topsail-schooner rigging plan I designed resulted from the positioning and declination of her masts, which differ from other types of rig," said Marquardt.

The *Hispaniola* was a 200-ton schooner, and her voyage took place in 1758, three years after the *Sharke* was sold. As historian David J. Starkey has pointed out, "redundant naval vessels" were purchased by privateering ventures. Were the two vessels the same? We don't know, but the faded drawings in the old archives provide a clue to how the *Hispaniola* might have looked.

Another clue is the *Sultana*. Built in Boston in 1767, the *Sultana* was purchased for the Royal Navy and sailed to England in 1768. After her service was over, she was sold in 1773 for 85 pounds sterling, at which point she disappeared from view. Recreated in 2001 from the original

1. Ship's counter
2. Mainsail
3. Main mast
4. Main boom
5. Gaff on main mast
6. Peak
7. Truck
8. Masthead
9. Main topmast
10. Fore topmast
11. Crosstree

12. Yard arm
13. Foremast
14. Forestay
15. Jib
16. Jib boom
17. Bowsprit
18. Bobstay
19. Cutwater
20. Deadeye

21. Backstay
22. Backstay
23. Fore sail
24. Shrouds
25. Chains
26. Rudder
27. Waterline

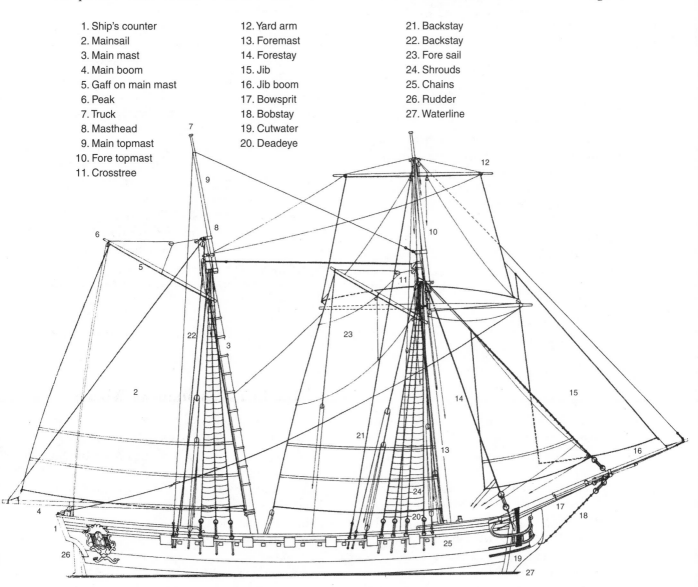

The 201-ton *Sharke*.

19th-century brigantine.

Royal Navy dockyard survey, she is now docked at Chestertown, an 18th-century Maryland port town, and accepts passengers in the summer.

At almost 53 tons burthen, the original *Sultana* was smaller than the *Hispaniola*'s 200 tons (*burthen* is explained a few paragraphs below). The *Sultana* had a 52-foot-long deck, was 16 feet wide at her widest point, and carried 2,010 square feet of sail. She had a hold converted into living space for the crew, and a brick stove and a galley. In 1768 she carried a crew of 25 and could make 10 knots. She crossed the Atlantic twice in bad winter weather.

Another source is a draught of a schooner-rigged privateer, also from 1768, by Swedish naval architect Fredrik Henrik af Chapman. At 93 feet, 9 inches long and almost 24 feet wide, the privateer was big enough to carry supplies for 100 men, including a one-month supply of water.

It is important to remember that *schooner* refers to the *rig* of a vessel—the ways its sails and masts are arranged—and not to a vessel of any particular shape or size. A vessel could start out as a schooner and then be re-rigged. Chapman, for example, designed the yacht *Amphion*, which started life as a 110-foot-long, 22-foot-wide schooner in 1778. She was later converted into a *brigantine*, which meant she had two masts, with a big square sail on the forward mast and a big fore-and-aft sail on the second mast (see illustration, above). An 18th-century *bark*, with a hull designed for carrying cargo, could be fitted with any number of rigs, including a schooner's.

By 1757 some Baltimore-built *clipper schooners* were 80 feet long. They were narrow and had a big sail area, including a square topsail on the foremast.

A best guess is that at 200 tons the *Hispaniola* was large for a schooner of the 1750s, so she might have been 70 feet to 90 feet long.

The squire's use of the word *ton* needs to be read carefully. Ton is used here in the sense of *tons burthen* or *tons burden*. It is a term based on using a formula to calculate the cargo capacity of a vessel and not a measure of weight, as it is on land.

The word *ton* by itself is also a trap for the unwary, depending on the context and when in time the word is used, and whether the ship owner needed a big number or a smaller number.

A ship owner might use *measured tons* when negotiating with a shipbuilder for a new vessel, then calculate how much he could load aboard it using *cargo tons*, also known as tons burthen or tons burden, which would be more than measured tons; he could then argue with officials trying to charge fees and taxes by using *registered tons*, which were less than either measured or cargo tons.

For example, the 1740s ship *Susannah* of London was registered as being 100 tons but was described as being about 180 tons burthen, or a little smaller than the *Hispaniola* and its 200 tons.

Overall, in the 1700s, according to historian John J. McCusker, two registered tons equated to about the same as three measured tons, which equated to about the same as four cargo tons or tons burthen.

DR. LIVESEY'S MEDICAL WORLD

Another important figure in the story is Dr. Livesey, and he too opens a window, through the eyes of Robert Louis Stevenson, into the Britain of *Treasure Island*.

Dr. Livesey was both a doctor and a local judge. As the story tells us, he had served with the British army in the 1740s in the Flanders region of what is now modern Belgium, which suggests he also had skills as a surgeon. At a time when most medical practitioners were not held in high social esteem, the fact that Dr. Livesey had been

Yo-Ho-Ho, and a Bottle of Rum!

THE PIRATES LIKED THEIR RUM. So did a lot of other people. In 1770 Americans drank an annual average of four gallons of rum per man, woman, and child, not counting the enslaved population of the colonies. One explanation for its popularity in North America is that rum was a cheap source of calories.

American rum consumption pales in comparison with that in the British West Indies, where white adult men averaged 21 gallons per year or seven one-ounce shots 365

Big three-roller mills ground the juice from sugar cane and were powered by cattle, horses, windmills, and water-power.

days a year. In the late 1760s a gallon of Barbados rum cost on average less than two shillings, or less than two day's pay for an ordinary seaman in the Royal Navy.

In Jim Hawkins's day, rum also was used in the slave-buying business as a form of currency. For example, in 1767, in what today is Ghana, a Captain William Taylor assembled a cargo of enslaved people and paid 130 gallons of rum for each man, 110 gallons for each woman, and 80 gallons for each young girl. Cider, gin, beer, and

brandy were also used as currency with the West African sellers of slaves, but rum was king.

Alcohol was part of the daily shipboard rations of the Royal Navy for both officers and men. Beer was the standard issue for alcohol rations for non-officers until 1831; if beer was unavailable, other drinks, including rum, could be substituted. The first recorded issue of rum on a Royal Navy ship was in 1655 in Jamaica.

In the days before refrigeration, beer tended to go bad within a few weeks, and it was heavy and bulky: beer for a few hundred men, each entitled to a gallon a day, took up a lot of cargo space on an extended voyage. So substitutions for beer were allowed. Navy regulations dating back to 1731 established the formula "a pint of wine, or half a pint of brandy, rum, or arrack, hold proportion to a gallon of beer," according to Royal Navy historian James Pack.

Rum was a bonus product for 18th-century sugar planters in the Caribbean, the center of rum production, because it was mostly made from molasses, a waste product created when making sugar. Molasses was also shipped in bulk to New England rum makers.

When rum has a high alcohol content it can be a powerful poison. John Reading, 24, boatswain's mate on Captain James Cook's *Endeavour*, got hold of a partially full bottle on August 27, 1769, drank it at one sitting, and died the next day. Alcohol depresses the human nervous system and too much can cause the body's respiratory system to stop working.

Rum was a killer in the 18th century in more ways than one. Figures in one 1781 estimate by the abolitionist William Fox suggest that–based on the life expectancy of a typical enslaved West Indian sugar worker–one person died to produce 450 pounds of sugar. Since rum is a by-product of sugar making, that person also died to produce between 11 gallons and 66 gallons of rum, depending on the island where the sugar was produced.

appointed a magistrate indicates that he was well-respected and supported by local leaders like Squire Trelawney.

The fictional Dr. Livesey was by no means the first doctor to become entangled in the affairs of pi-

rates, buccaneers, and privateers. In the real world of the 1750s, Sir Hans Sloane was still alive in London's Chelsea district, the same Hans Sloane who in 1688 had treated one of the greatest raiders of them all, Sir Henry Morgan. When the young Sloane saw him, Morgan had retired to his sugar plantation in today's Morgan's Valley in Jamaica and was drinking too much. Sloane described the soon-to-be-dead, 53-year-old Morgan as "lean, sallow-eyed, eyes a little prominent, belly jutting out." Sloane later donated the core collection that established the British Museum in London.

Accounts left by successful 18th-century rural medical practitioners tell us that they worked hard. Writing in the 1740s, a Doctor Kay noted that on just one summer's day he rode 12 or 14 miles to treat 11 patients suffering from ailments ranging from fever to "a very sore stinking leg." Charles Darwin's grandfather, Erasmus, a successful country physician, estimated he rode 10,000 miles a year. He also fathered 14 children and wrote poetry. And the money could be good. A capable country doctor could earn 500 pounds a year, enough for him to live like minor gentry, and some earned much more.

The most effective medical training in Livesey's day was available at Scottish and Dutch universities. To add to their skills, some medical practitioners, whether university graduates or not, spent part of their careers working in hospitals, the army, or the navy.

A more typical entry into medicine at that time would have been via a seven-year apprenticeship to an apothecary. An apothecary in Livesey's era mixed medicines, gave advice, and performed a broad variety of medical services. There was minimal regulation of the practice of medicine in the 1750s and ineffective regulation of entry into it. The result was that men and women flocked into the medical business.

Reform and regulation as we know it today came in the next century, along with that familiar figure in British medicine, the general practitioner or GP, of which Dr. Livesey was a prototype.

THE *HISPANIOLA*'S HOME PORT: BRISTOL

Trelawney, Livesey, and our hero, Jim Hawkins, set sail from the port of Bristol, in southwestern England. Mostly a city of narrow streets and densely packed, old-fashioned buildings, it was famous for its mile-long quay and the sledges used instead of heavy wagons to transport unloaded cargoes. Bristol was surrounded on three sides by an anchorage created by the River Avon, the smaller River Frome, and their junction.

Bristol is seven miles inland from the estuary of the Severn River, the Bristol Channel, and the open sea beyond. The Avon's fast current and the lack of wind where the river banks were high and the river narrow meant vessels large and small needed to be towed to and from the port. A small vessel like the *Hispaniola* might make do with one towboat. Larger vessels might need as many as ten towboats with 150 rowers.

Although Bristol's port was awkward to use, its location and facilities were useful enough that Bristol had ties to Ireland and its farms and to the British and Continental ports that face the North Sea and the English Channel.

Bristol made things, everything from soap to copper wire. There were coal mines just outside town, and the coal was used in Bristol furnaces to refine sugar; make glass for bottles and windows; work copper into plates that were then used to sheathe ship bottoms; work lead into pipes and iron into anchors; and boil animal body parts from the slaughter yards into soap.

Bristol traded with Scandinavia and the Baltic, and with the ports of the Mediterranean. The city and its manufacturers, merchants, and mariners were equally familiar with Africa and its slave exports, the West Indies and its sugar, and British North America and its tobacco.

Bristol may have been fortunate in its prosperity, but it was not fortunate in descriptions provided by writers who visited the city and wrote about it in the 1700s. Someone who wrote under the name "An Irish Gentleman" passed through Bristol in 1752 and reported that "the town is but disagreeable," while another writer, Horace Walpole, thought it "the dirtiest great shop I ever saw." Through the years visitors found the floating filth in the harbor both impressive and noteworthy. But not everyone

The port of Bristol.

sneered at the town: the river scenery was "delicious to the eye," we are told by one visitor in 1759, and offered views of "agreeable villas of the merchants of Bristol."

Underpinning its role as a port and manufacturing center was Bristol's role as a trading center for the immediate region around it, which used the Severn, the Avon, and the Frome rivers to ship out its produce and ship in the products it needed.

Even the largest freighters could reach Bristol and use the cranes on the wharves in the city center, thanks to tidal ranges of up to 45 feet.

Bristol was an expensive port to use. There were fees, tolls, and taxes. Fees were charged for rowers, pilots, and the use of port cranes, and tolls were levied—it cost five shillings for the *Hispaniola* to enter the port. There were also customs and excise duties to be paid. The relatively high cost of using Bristol's harbor facilities helped Liverpool to the north overtake Bristol in the later 1700s as Britain's second port.

Bristol was at the junction of five main roads. By 1750 most of them had good surfaces for a limited distance from the city, although the tolls charged to pay for road improvements were greeted with riots in some areas.

The volume of traffic around Bristol could be high. In the week ending June 2, 1765, one toll booth just north of Bristol counted 259 coaches, 11,759 horses, 491 wagons, 675 donkeys, 722 carts, and 206 drays passing through it.

All that traffic has left its mark. Just southwest of Bristol is the village of Wrington, where an intriguing survival of the ancient road system leads to the coast. In 1969 a local historian reported that next to the Paradise Motel visitors could still see, side by side, 75-yard stretches of three versions of one of the major roads to Bristol—today's A38—dating back to the early 1700s. They included the remains of the original coach road. The ruts were so deep they had survived the rains of 250 years.

Mrs. F. A. Neale, a historian, reported, "The old coach road, up the hill, being unsurfaced, was worn very deep into the ground by sheer usage. It also became very wide, as coaches and wagons drove further and further over the verges in an effort to avoid the ruts in the center."

The 18th century saw the first concerted, broad-scale effort to improve Britain's roads since the departure of the Roman legions and their highly developed road-building skills 1,400 years before.

Organizations called "turnpike trusts" raised money from road users and investors to improve and maintain roads. The turnpike trusts were controversial, and the way some people reacted to them should help dispel any notion of the English of the 1700s as docile, deferential, and polite. There

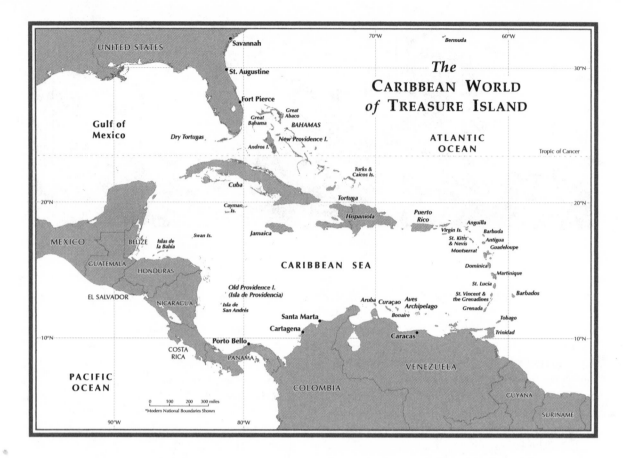

were riots near Bristol and elsewhere. People who once had used the public highways for free did not want to pay for improvements they didn't need to move their cattle or pack horses.

If people inland could be turbulent, some on the coast could be casual about which laws they chose to observe and equally turbulent if challenged. These were the smugglers. Smuggling was a big business, with as many as a thousand people helping with a single landing of cargo, and with smuggling communities willing to use cannon against revenue officers. The British maintained armed forces to intercept them, to the great good fortune of Jim Hawkins and his mother, as we later learn.

THE BUCCANEERS: OUTSOURCING WAR

The word *buccaneer* surfaces a number of times in *Treasure Island*. It is a term that repays a little ex-

ploration. The buccaneers were also called *filibusters* and *freebooters*; they called themselves *the brethren of the coast*. The Spaniards whom they attacked called them *piratas*.

In the beginning, at the heart of the buccaneers' raiding was the centuries-old concept of legally seizing enemy property because you had a government license (a letter of marque) to do so.

When commissioned as privateers by governments, they received no pay but instead made their living from the enemy property they captured, which led to the term "no purchase, no pay." The word *purchase* in the 1660s meant "catching prey."

The glory days of the Buccaneer Era were the years 1655–1671, when as many as 1,200 to 1,500 mostly English-speaking privateers used Port Royal, Jamaica, as a base and as a market for selling the goods they took from Spaniards.

What is surprising is how few privateers there

were, given the damage they caused in an enormous arc from Venezuela in South America to St. Augustine in Florida. The historian Peter Earle estimates that in 1671 Henry Morgan assembled something over 2,000 men in 38 vessels for his successful attack on Panama, "nearly every English and French privateer in the West Indies." Yet even this is not a very large force, compared to, for example, the one hundred privateering vessels that the single French port of Dunkirk kept at sea at one time during the early years of the Anglo-Dutch war with France (1701–1713). There were other French ports in the privateering business then, as well as British and Dutch ports.

Morgan recruited from the Port Royal contingent and from the thousand or so men available on French Tortuga off the north coast of modern Haiti. Among those joining up were some of the roughly 100 cattle hunters working on Tortuga and Haiti, the *boucaniers* who gave us the name *buccaneer*. (See "Buccaneers and Boucaniers" on p. xx.) Those crews that did not have a privateer commission—a government license—were provided with one by Morgan, who had been given authority to do so by Sir Thomas Modyford, the governor of Jamaica.

Between 1655 and 1671 the Caribbean privateer and buccaneer crews successfully sacked and looted cities in modern Nicaragua, Cuba, Colombia, Panama, Mexico, and Venezuela. Their overall score was 18 cities, 4 towns, and more than 35 villages, some attacked as many as eight times. The numbers are a commentary on how thinly defended the Spanish settlements were.

The Atlantic coast of what is now the United States was certainly not beyond their reach. One group under Robert Searles, alias John Davis, attacked St. Augustine in Spanish Florida in 1668, killing at least 60 people, holding women for ransom, and taking prisoner anyone who looked black or Indian for later sale as a slave. A Father Sotolongo protested the abductions but was told that the raiders were acting within the terms of their commission.

In 1682 St. Augustine was attacked again, this time by buccaneers who included a nine-year-old boy. The attackers were driven off by the Spanish garrison and the local Timucua Indian militia. The buccaneers then headed north, looting the Mission San Juan del Puerto on modern Fort George Island near Jacksonville, Florida, and Mission San Felipe on neighboring Amelia Island. They used the mission churches as latrines.

Another attack, in 1684, by 11 Anglo-French crews under one Captain Jingle, resulted in the attackers being taken prisoner and sentenced to work on the unfinished stone fort at St. Augustine. The fort they helped build is still there.

After the 1670s the buccaneers became less significant for Jamaica. Some of their targets had been attacked so often there was not much left to steal. More important, the Port Royal merchants were making more money by smuggling goods and slaves into Spanish territories than they were from the buccaneers. The Spanish government prohibited their American colonies from importing goods from non-Spanish sources, but Spain did not have the resources to deliver what their colonies wanted. The Port Royal merchants were happy to fill that vacuum in return for Spanish colonial silver.

As a result, Jamaica shipped out so much bullion it was likened to a silver mine that required no miners or digging. And now the buccaneers, with their thieving, were hurting relations with the Port Royal merchants' Spanish colonial customers, and the raiders lost the political cover they had previously enjoyed. They were pirates and "regarded simply as a nuisance," according to two historians of the city, Michael Pawson and David Buisseret.

Port Royal, with its densely packed brick houses, may have been the richest town in British North America before an earthquake demolished the port in 1692.

PRIVATEERING: NEW OPPORTUNITIES

Making money legally by privateering was a concept that was alive and well in 1757 when the first global war, the Seven Years' War—in America known as the French and Indian War—broke out. Privateering was once again a big business with at-

Buccaneers and Boucaniers

How the buccaneers got their name is a story that has been told often. The name was originally given to the little bands of non-Spanish hunters who lived outside Spanish law and established themselves over the years on the nearly empty north coast of Spanish Hispaniola, the island shared today by Haiti and the Dominican Republic. They killed the local small horses for their tallow fat. They hunted wild cattle for their meat and hides, as well as pigs. They dried the meat to preserve it using the *boucan* technique of the Arawak-speaking Taino Indians and became known as *boucaniers*.

Given the opportunity, they also took to piracy, and the name *boucanier*, reworked into the English *buccaneer*, became applied to the crews that used—among other islands and coasts—the island of Tortuga off Hispaniola and later Port Royal, Jamaica, as bases. The crews recruited from those adrift in the multi-national Caribbean world of the 1600s included sailors without ships, runaway slaves, log cutters from Belize, escaped convicts, political prisoners, laborers escaping from their indentures or contracts, and failed tobacco farmers from Barbados.

During the period when the buccaneers were becoming less important to Jamaica, their first chronicler, Alexandre Olivier Exquemelin, published in 1678, in Dutch, the first edition of his best-selling account of his life with the buccaneers. It was the book that firmly fixed exotic buccaneers in the public imagination.

He called them *aventuriers* ("adventurers") in the title of the edition he arranged for his French readers. An English edition was published in 1684, with the title *Bucaniers of America*. The spelling *buccaneer* became standard, and the book in one form or the other has been in print ever since.

tractive profits to be made, and in the fictional world of *Treasure Island*, one year into the war Squire Trelawney was in Bristol trying to assemble a crew from sailors who had plenty of options.

Trelawney was competing for sailors with four main groups: investors who outfitted government-licensed private man-of-war vessels (also called privateers) for cruises in search of enemy merchant cargo ships to capture in order to sell both cargo and vessel; captains of armed merchant ships who obtained a similar privateering license that allowed them to capture enemy merchant ships if the opportunity arose while going about their normal business; and the Royal Navy. Crews working for these three categories of employer shared in the money made from capturing enemy shipping, although in differing proportions. The fourth group competing for crews were the ordinary merchant ship owners just trying to go about their normal business

In 1758, the year Squire Trelawney was trying to find a crew, the Royal Navy was looking for men and would end the year adding 10,000 new hands to its vessels. This may not sound like many people, but one estimate suggests that there were only 80,000 civilian seamen and fishermen in the entire British workforce at the beginning of the war. The navy already had increased its seagoing manpower by about 30,000 by the time the squire arrived in Bristol. During the war nearly 185,000 sailors and marines would serve in Britain's Royal Navy.

Britain and France and, later, Spain targeted enemy commerce and did so at very little cost to their taxpayers. The British government expanded the number of vessels it could send into the fight by granting licenses to enable private ships to legally attack enemy trading vessels. The system had the advantage of costing the government nothing but adding greatly to its armed seagoing forces.

It was a system with roots in the Middle Ages and one that would last until 1856, when the more powerful governments on the planet agreed to end it. One government, the United States of America, declined to join in the ban, although it did do so later. In the meantime, the Confederate States of

America licensed privateers to attack Union vessels during the American Civil War.

In the 1700s, the system found enough favor with the British government that in order to encourage privateering ventures it agreed in 1708 to forgo its share of the money made from ships captured, and France soon followed suit.

HELP WANTED:
SAILORS FOR PRIVATEER SHIP

We do not know whether the squire tried advertising in the Bristol newspaper, but certainly some Bristol-based privateer captains did so during the Seven Years' War. Sample advertisements from a 1756 edition of the Bristol paper include Ezekiel Nash, who was looking for 200 men for the *Caesar*, 360 tons; Robert How, who sought 250 men for the *Lyon*, 360 tons; and William Burch, who needed 120 men for the *Tygress*, 200 tons.

The *Caesar* found the men it needed, and her men needed all their fighting skills. In one encounter, they fired 700 cannon rounds and 8,000 musket shots, and threw 30 hand grenades. The *Lyon* returned to Bristol with two prizes. We do not know how the *Tygress* fared, but she did sail looking for opportunity.

In addition to advertising for hands, captains dangled incentives in front of potential recruits. The year after the *Hispaniola* sailed, the privateer named the *Hawke* was offering advances of 11 guineas to get men to sign on, the equivalent of about four months of wages and food on board a Royal Navy ship.

Privateer captains also competed with merchant vessel captains, who carried a variation of the privateering license in case they came across an opportunity to take a prize; thus they could offer their crews regular wages plus a chance of a bonus.

Overall, during the war, 253 Bristol vessels received one of the two variations of the letter of marque license that allowed them to attack enemy shipping, and they claimed 81 prizes, more than any other British port outside of London.

In wartime Bristol, captains competed for crews with advertisements like these, which appeared in *Felix Farley's Bristol Journal*, September 11–18, 1756.

The Royal Navy, according to one of the leading naval historians of the period, N.A.M. Rodger, offered volunteers better odds of doing well from prize money than did a privateer.

IF ALL ELSE FAILS: THE PRESS GANG

The navy also had another recruiting tool as a backup: shortfalls in manning navy ships could be met by forcibly drafting men into the service, a common practice in many countries in that era. In Britain the legal authority to seize civilians for military service, called *impressment*, was used both by the army and the navy. The term was often shortened to *press*.

When it needed men, the navy sent out "press gangs" under the command of a junior officer in port cities and also onto merchant ships to seize men who did not have documents—known as *protections*—that exempted them from seizure.

The *Hispaniola*'s pirates were not the only hard cases working out of Bristol. In 1759 in Cardiff, 32 members of a navy press gang tried to seize 70 members of the crew of the privateer *Eagle* of Bristol, who were in a pub. The crew organized itself for battle, gunfire broke out, and the press gang retreated with one dead and four men seriously wounded.

And in 1760 when HMS *Winchester* in New York harbor sent a detachment of seamen to board the *Sampson* of Bristol, the *Sampson*'s crew fired two volleys into the ship's boat and killed four of the 14 men on board.

In March 1758, the month the *Hispaniola* sailed for Treasure Island, she shared Bristol harbor with the privateer *St. Andrew*, 300 tons, which soon left with a crew of 140 men. They returned from her cruise in November, ready to enjoy the prize money from the 15 vessels the ship had taken.

THE PIRATES' LONG REACH

During the voyage Long John Silver tells Jim Hawkins that his parrot was "at Madagascar, and at Malabar, and Surinam, and Providence and Portobello. She was at the fishing up of the wrecked plate ships" (p. 81)—all places associated with pirate activity in the so-called Golden Age of Piracy.

MADAGASCAR

Madagascar, located 250 miles off the Mozambique coast of East Africa, was one of several islands where, especially between the 1690s and 1720s, British and other pirates who attacked shipping in the Indian Ocean took on food and water.

Madagascar is big. The world's fourth-largest island, it would fit between New York City and Jacksonville, Florida, with 45 miles to spare.

The preferred anchorage and base for pirate crews, according to a historian of piracy on Madagascar, Jan Rogozinski, was a circular, well-protected bay on an island close to the well-watered northeastern shore of the main island. This is St. Mary's Island, also known as Île Sainte-Marie, Nosy Sainte Marie, and Nosy Boraha (the latter in the Malagasy language).

The pirate settlement in the bay was spread between a mini-island called Ilot Madame at the entrance, suitable for cleaning, or careening, a vessel's hull; a smaller island in the center of the bay called Isle des Forbans, or Pirates Island; along the north shore of the bay; and around the corner to where the village of Ambodifotatra is located.

In 2000 archaeologists led by Barry Clifford and John de Bry arrived at the bay hoping to find Captain William Kidd's *Adventure Galley*, abandoned by him in 1698. Instead they found the wreck of the pirate Christopher Condent's Dutch-built *Fiery Dragon*. It had been abandoned and set on fire by Condent in February 1721, still with some residual treasure—a few gold coins—on board.

Connoisseurs of the workings of today's global economy may be surprised to learn of Adam Baldridge and his fortified store located on Isle des Forbans. Baldridge, financed by Frederick Philipse of New York City, set up shop in 1691. Philipse would send out from New York arms, ammunition, clothing, liquor, and the supplies needed to operate sailing vessels. Robert C. Ritchie has documented voyages during which Baldridge would fill Philipse's ship for the return voyage with enslaved people for resale in New York, as well as gold, silver, jewels, silks, and other goods taken by his pirate customers, plus some of his pirate customers themselves who wanted a discreet passage home. Off the North American coast a returning ship might be met by another Philipse vessel that would transfer the high-value luxury items for sale in Hamburg, Germany, where prices were better than in New York.

THE MALABAR COAST

For at least 2,000 years the Malabar Coast of southwestern India had attracted resident foreign merchants from Europe, Africa, the Middle East,

South Asia, and China—and pirates to prey on them.

The attractions included spices, especially black pepper, popular in Europe since Roman times and worth its weight in gold because transportation was so expensive; also sought after were gems, including diamonds and pearls, and textiles.

The 1500s and 1600s brought traders and cargo vessels from Portugal, France, the Netherlands, and Britain to the Malabar Coast and other parts of India. The 1700s saw the ultimate in trade competition: French and British traders recruited military forces to evict their competitors and assert political control. The Battle of Plassey gave the British control of a major portion of northeastern India the year before the *Hispaniola* sailed, and they expanded into southern India in the years that followed.

Where Was Treasure Island?

THERE ARE TWO KNOWN Treasure Islands in the West Indies. The first, Isla Tesoro, is part of the Rosario islets near Cartagena, Colombia; it's tiny, less than 500 acres, and sandy. It is also in the area where a Spanish ship, the *San Jose*, and its cargo of gold and silver bullion sank in 1708 after being ambushed by a British squadron.

The other Isla Tesoro is part of Venezuela's Aves Archipelago, whose reef-like islands are so low and small that a French fleet of ten warships sailed straight into them one night in May 1678 and sank with the loss of 500 lives.

Then there is the third one.

Billy Bones, the drunken pirate who enters our story on page 1, recorded Treasure Island's location in his account book using both latitude and longitude. The numbers in Bones's account book–latitude 62 degrees, 17 minutes, and 20 seconds and longitude 19 degrees, 2 minutes, and 40 seconds (see p. 49)–are both precise, yet they keep their secrets, omitting information needed to calculate which of four possible locations they refer to.

It would have been helpful for Bones to have noted if the latitudes he recorded were north or south of the equator and also where the starting point or "first meridian" of his longitudes was. We are used to measuring longitude from the observatory at Greenwich, now part of London. Greenwich did not become the standard longitude 0 for British chart makers until 1767, long after Flint was dead. Before that the starting point could be St. Paul's Cathedral, also in London, or a coastal feature called The Lizard in the far west of England. French chart makers used as many as five starting points for longitude 0. With a choice of seven longitudes 0 between the charts of just two countries, he could have been in one of 28 locations.

If for the sake of convenience, we use Greenwich as the site of longitude 0, Bones could have been plotting a place that was 44 miles from the Swedish coast in the Baltic Sea's Gulf of Bothnia; 98 miles south of Iceland; 517 miles north of the coast of Antarctica; or 327 miles north of another part of the coast of Antarctica. (For more detail on why we are faced with these four choices, see note 8 on p. 49 for a discussion of latitude and longitude.)

Given the relative lack of opportunity for profitable piracy in these four chilly zones, what Billy Bones and Co. were up to in plotting the coordinates of Treasure Island remains a mystery.

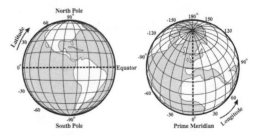

The intersections of vertical lines of longitude and horizontal lines of latitude create a grid that helps travelers locate their position on a map.

SURINAME

The Suriname is a river in northeastern South America that gives its name to today's Republic of Suriname. In the 1700s Suriname was a rich Dutch sugar colony on what had been called the Wild Coast and was known for its profitability and the opulence of its planters. It was also known, even in that tough corner of the world, for the harshness of its plantation life and, not surprisingly, for its large population of escaped slaves who had established new free lives in the deep forests.

Even in a rough age, the plantation owners and overseers were remarkable, in the words of the historian Charles Boxer, for their "sadistic cruelty, pigheaded selfishness, and short-sighted cupidity."

One result was a series of revolts by some of the enslaved workers. Today six groups of their descendants—the Saramaka, Djuka, Matawi, Paramaka, Kwinti, and Aluku—still maintain their political identities in Suriname's back-country rain forest, practice customs brought over from Africa, and account for some 10 percent of the country's population. Some moved to neighboring French Guiana after a civil war in Suriname. But how long these Suriname communities will continue to survive is an open question, according to two historians of the groups, Richard and Sally Price. Their forest areas, guaranteed by treaty in the 1700s, have been opened to development, including logging, mining, and the creation of a lake for hydroelectric power.

PROVIDENCE

Silver is referring to Nassau on New Providence Island in the Bahamas. The place was a rendezvous for pirates until 1718. That was the year when ten were hanged. Sanitation at Nassau during its pirate days was so bad that arriving mariners could smell the place before they saw land.

New Providence Island was settled tentatively by the English in 1648 with a group of Puritans, 70 strong. But not many stayed. The island became another place where pirates could refit. An obliging governor of this privately owned English colony was willing to issue a privateering license to legalize their activities, especially after Jamaica became less hospitable after 1670. Punitive attacks by Spanish and French forces did not stop Nassau from being repopulated between attacks.

When Captain Vincent Pearce arrived at Nassau in 1718, just ahead of the new governor, there were about 500 pirates in the settlement, of whom 209 surrendered and accepted pardons under a new piracy law.

The new governor was the former privateer Woodes Rogers, who arrived with instructions to restore order and build up the little colony. He had the legal authority to try pirates using a tribunal without a jury, execute those he found guilty, and issue pardons. He was backed up by soldiers and warships. Initially Rogers was successful, but some of the pirates escaped, Blackbeard among them, and others went back to their old ways; there were many hundreds of places in the Bahamas for them to hide.

New Providence later became a refuge for British loyalists fleeing the American Revolution; a base for Confederate blockade runners during the American Civil War; and a staging area for bootleggers smuggling liquor into the United States during Prohibition.

The other Providence Island with a link to pirates and to Britain is sometimes for clarity called Old Providence; the modern Isla de Providencia, it is located 145 miles off the coast of Central America. About six miles long and four miles wide and hilly, Old Providence started out in the 1630s as a settlement for English Puritans who were part of the same movement that created the Puritan settlement in Massachusetts. However, things here did not work out well as they did in New England, and Providence became a base for privateers.

PORTOBELLO

Portobello, sometimes spelled Puerto Belo, was famous as the transshipment point on the Caribbean coast of Panama for silver mined by the ton in Bolivia and also as a smuggler's haven. In other words, it was a magnet for trouble.

Organized and fortified in 1596 and 1597 to replace nearby Nombre de Dios as Panama's Caribbean port, the little settlement was protected at various times by as many as five forts of varying size.

The defenses may have discouraged some attacks, but the town was captured with some regularity. It was sacked in 1601 by William Parker; in 1668 by Henry Morgan; and in 1680 by John Coxon, Peter Harris, and others. In 1739 a British vice-admiral, Edward Vernon, took the town, held it for ransom, and destroyed its fortifications. One of his officers, Lawrence Washington, renamed his Virginia estate Mount Vernon in his honor; it was later inherited by his half-brother George.

The reason for Puerto Belo's existence was silver. The silver was mined in modern Bolivia, then shipped up the Pacific coast before being taken overland to Portobello and finally to Spain by armed convoy. In addition to its role as a silver port, Portobello was a point of entry for illegal cargoes, ranging from soap to pots and pans, writing paper, and clothing delivered by British and other merchants.

The smuggled cargoes were the basis of an informal and illegal trading system that delivered what the official system could not, and by the early 1700s it was bigger than the official one. Henry Kamen, a student of the Spanish Empire, estimates that "without smuggling the Spanish colonies would have collapsed."

The Spanish colonies were also legal and illegal importers of enslaved people. One estimate is that between 1658 and 1729 some 97,000 slaves were delivered by Dutch merchants alone to Portobello, Cartagena in modern Colombia, and Veracruz in modern Mexico. Also active in this trade were the British, French, and Portuguese.

The destruction of Portobello's defenses by Vernon was followed after some years by the ending of the fleet convoy system. In operation since the 1500s, the little settlement emerged briefly from obscurity when in 1819 the freelance soldier and talented con man Sir Gregor McGregor briefly occupied the town. Some of the fortifications still exist.

THE WRECKED PLATE SHIPS

At 2:00 a.m. on July 31, 1715, the full force of a hurricane drove 11 of 12 vessels of a Spanish convoy onto the Atlantic coast of Florida, leaving a debris trail of 700 bodies, broken ship parts, and tons of silver bullion that stretched from modern-day Fort Pierce north for 30 miles to Cape Canaveral and possibly beyond. One ship alone, the flagship *Nuestra Señora de la Regla*, carried more than 100 tons of silver coins and bars.

To get a sense of the modern value of the lost treasure, in 2007 a salvage company reported recovering just 17 tons of mostly silver coins from a 1641 wreck, or less than one-fifth of the 1715 *Regla's* silver cargo. The estimated value of the 2007 treasure find was about $500 million.

It was silver that gave the plate ships their name: *plate* is the English adaptation of the Spanish word for silver, *plata*.

The 1715 loss sparked a financial crisis for the Spanish government, prompted a major salvage effort by the authorities, and attracted swarms of freelance looters, who at one point numbered some 3,000 men in 14 very crowded sloops.

Nearly 300 years later some of the treasure from known wrecks of the 1715 convoy remains to be found. As recently as 2003 a gold jewelry box from the wrecked fleet, containing two emerald rings and a gold chain, was found in 12 feet of water. In addition, the locations of five of the wrecked ships remain unknown.

The shore on which the fleet had been wrecked was a familiar one to the Spanish garrison in St. Augustine 137 miles to the north. Sebastian Lopez de Toledo, overseer of the royal works, led the first group of rescuers, militia made up of refugee Yamassee, Guale, and Apalachee Indians, and they organized shelter for the survivors and a water supply from shallow wells that were found 250 years later by archaeologists.

Some 1,500 Spanish men, women, and children

had survived the storm. The last of the women and children were rescued on September 10 by vessels sent from St. Augustine to the north and from Havana, Cuba, to the south, which allowed the officers to concentrate on the salvaging the bullion,

One-ounce silver coin "cobs" recovered from the 1715 wrecked "plate ships" off the Florida shore.

first on their own and then with help from Havana. The children had been so tormented by the clouds of biting insects that some parents buried their children up to their necks in the sand to reduce their misery.

The officers needed all their powers of concentration. Their sailors looted dead bodies and pilfered what they could pick up. A church official from St. Augustine attempted to lay claim on the bullion for the Royal Commissary of the Holy Crusade, an organization that was an important source of income for the Spanish crown. And then there were the pirates.

The first group, 300 men in five vessels, led by Edward Jennings, arrived in November. They attacked the Spanish camp and its 60 guards at what is today's Sebastian Inlet State Park and made off with silver that was being washed to remove corrosive saltwater and stored. One often-repeated account has it that Jennings returned for a second

helping, but that account is apparently incorrect, according to a specialist in Spanish Florida's history, Professor Eugene Lyon. Nevertheless the salvage professionals sent in by Havana managed to retrieve, by one estimate, 80 percent of the government's bullion.

But most of the private shipments of valuables were still missing, and they attracted swarms of would-be treasure hunters, including the celebrity pirate Blackbeard, according to his biographer Angus Konstam. The looters at one point established their own settlement on the shore, fortified in regular military fashion with earthworks and four cannon, until driven off by the Spanish authorities.

The loss of a convoy was a catastrophe for the Spanish government. For many decades the Spanish government relied on silver—and some gold—from its mines in Latin America for 15 to 20 percent of its annual income, and that treasure was delivered to Spain in sporadic armed convoys like the 1715 fleet. The bullion did not stay in Spain. It was used to pay the people who had lent money to the Spanish government.

AND TODAY

Today pirates are still to be found where ships are vulnerable. The International Chamber of Commerce's International Maritime Bureau reports that 297 ships were attacked in 2012. Bureau warnings of areas in which mariners must be careful include the Malacca Straits; the Singapore Straits; the Indonesian archipelago; and the coasts of Nigeria, Benin, and Togo. Increased naval patrols reduced attacks off Somalia in 2011.

As another example that some things do not change very much, the Bureau is located at 26 Wapping High Street, in London, by the River Thames, not far from the former Execution Dock where pirates by tradition were hanged. (For more on Execution Dock and its location, see note 12 on p. 92.)

TREASURE ISLAND

A Scale of 3 English Miles.

Foremast Hill

10
10

Strong tide here

ye
Spye glass
Hill

14

Cape
of ye
Woods

Mizzenmast Hill

Haulbowline Head

North Inlet

Spring

Swamp

The Bulk of treasure here

Swamp

Graves

White Rock

Skeleton Island

Foul Ground

Spi Cove

Spye glasse opens clear of N:

South a bout N:B:

Glass going

Treasure Island
Augst 1750: J.F.

Given by above J.F. to Mr. W. Bones Maste of ye Walrus
Savannah this twenty July 1754 W. B.

TO

S. L. O.,

AN AMERICAN GENTLEMAN

IN ACCORDANCE WITH WHOSE CLASSIC TASTE

THE FOLLOWING NARRATIVE HAS BEEN DESIGNED,

IT IS NOW, IN RETURN FOR NUMEROUS DELIGHTFUL HOURS,

AND WITH THE KINDEST WISHES,

DEDICATED

BY HIS AFFECTIONATE FRIEND, THE AUTHOR.

To the Hesitating Purchaser

If sailor tales to sailor tunes,
*   Storm and adventure, heat and cold,*
If schooners, islands, and maroons,
*   And buccaneers, and buried gold,*
And all the old romance, retold
*   Exactly in the ancient way,*
Can please, as me they pleased of old,
*   The wiser youngsters of today:*

—So be it, and fall on! If not,
*   If studious youth no longer crave,*
His ancient appetites forgot,
*   Kingston, or Ballantyne the brave,*
Or Cooper of the wood and wave:
*   So be it, also! And may I*
And all my pirates share the grave
*   Where these and their creations lie!*

PART I

The
Old Buccaneer

Chapter One

The Old Sea-dog
at the Admiral Benbow[1]

SQUIRE TRELAWNEY[2], DR. LIVESEY[3], and the rest of these gentlemen having asked me to write down the whole particulars about Treasure Island, from the beginning to the end, keeping nothing back but the bearings of the island, and that only because there is still treasure not yet lifted, I take up my pen in the year of grace 17—and go back to the time when my father kept the Admiral Benbow inn and the brown old seaman with the sabre[4] cut first took up his lodging under our roof.

I remember him as if it were yesterday, as he came plodding to the inn door, his sea-chest following behind him in a hand-barrow—a tall, strong, heavy, nut-brown man, his tarry pigtail[5] falling over the shoulders of his soiled blue coat, his hands ragged and scarred, with black, broken nails, and the sabre cut across one cheek, a dirty, livid white. I remember him looking round the cove and whistling to himself as he did so,

1. Vice-Admiral John Benbow of the Royal Navy was a popular hero who inspired rollicking ballads and whose name has been appropriated by the owners of countless pubs and inns. (For more, see the introduction, p. ix.)

2. An important local landowner and former navy officer. (For more, see the introduction, p. xi.)

3. A physician and local magistrate. (For more, see the introduction, p. xiv.)

4. The ideal sabre (also spelled saber) is a light cavalry weapon that has a slightly curved blade with a single edge; it functions as both a cutting and a thrusting weapon. The challenge is to find a saber, or any sword, that effectively combines both capabilities.

A curved blade works best for making a slashing attack and is easier to handle instinctively in the confusion of a fight. A straight blade is best for a thrusting attack; the point creates penetration wounds that are generally more lethal than slicing wounds.

5. Tar was found everywhere on a ship, including on the hands and clothes of the crew. Derived

from pine tree resin, tar was used to waterproof canvas and cordage, clothing, and headgear. It was inevitably transferred accidentally onto the hair of crew members, some of whom braided their hair into pigtails. Several accounts suggest, without citing sources, that seamen intentionally used tar as a hair dressing. How they then removed the stuff from their hair is not mentioned.

6. A capstan is a type of winch, which on an 18th-century vessel was powered by human muscle, used to raise an anchor or do other heavy lifting. (See illustration, p. 78.; also see note on p. 77.)

7. The handspike was a general-purpose wooden lever several feet in length.

8. See the introduction, p. xv.

9. On many merchant ships, crew members who were not officers had their quarters at the front end of the vessel between the bow and the first mast, or *foremast*. Saying someone "sailed before the mast" was a way of saying he was an ordinary mariner, not an officer. This area of a vessel was also called the forecastle (pronounced *foh'k'sill* and sometimes spelled *fo'c'sle*), and the seamen bunking there were known as *forecastle hands*. (For more, see note 3 on p. 74.)

10. The *mate* was the second-ranking officer on a merchant navy vessel, next to the master or commanding officer. The mate was in charge of navigation and organizing the work of the crew and so was accustomed to exerting authority. Larger vessels might have more than one mate.
    Technically a *skipper* is the master of a merchant ship, fishing vessel, or other small craft, but the term is used informally to refer to a ship's captain or master. The word probably was borrowed in the 1300s from the Dutch word *schipper*, derived from the Dutch *schip*.

11. Country people often called the passenger coaches that they preferred to have carry their correspondence the *mail*, but sending letters this way was against the law in the 1750s. It was illegal to send letters by any means other than through the Royal Mail service's expensive monopoly or,

and then breaking out in that old sea-song that he sang so often afterwards:

"Fifteen men on the dead man's chest—
Yo-ho-ho, and a bottle of rum!"

in the high, old tottering voice that seemed to have been tuned and broken at the capstan bars.[6] Then he rapped on the door with a bit of stick like a handspike[7] that he carried, and when my father appeared, called roughly for a glass of rum.[8] This, when it was brought to him, he drank slowly, like a connoisseur, lingering on the taste and still looking about him at the cliffs and up at our signboard.

"This is a handy cove," says he at length; "and a pleasant sittyated grog-shop. Much company, mate?"

My father told him no, very little company, the more was the pity.

"Well, then," said he, "this is the berth for me. Here you, matey," he cried to the man who trundled the barrow; "bring up alongside and help up my chest. I'll stay here a bit," he continued. "I'm a plain man; rum and bacon and eggs is what I want, and that head up there for to watch ships off. What you mought call me? You mought call me captain. Oh, I see what you're at—there"; and he threw down three or four gold pieces on the threshold. "You can tell me when I've worked through that," says he, looking as fierce as a commander.

And indeed bad as his clothes were and coarsely as he spoke, he had none of the appearance of a man who sailed before the mast,[9] but seemed like a mate or skipper[10] accustomed to be obeyed or to strike. The man who came with the barrow told us the mail[11] had set him down the morning before at the Royal George,[12] that he had inquired what inns there were along the coast, and hearing ours well spoken of, I suppose, and described as lonely, had chosen it from the others for his place of residence. And that was all we could learn of our guest.

He was a very silent man by custom. All day he hung round the cove or upon the cliffs with a brass telescope;[13] all evening he sat in a corner of the parlour next the fire and drank rum and water very strong. Mostly he would not speak when spoken to, only look up sudden and fierce and blow through his nose like a fog-horn; and we and the people who came about our house soon learned to let him be. Every day when he came back from his stroll he would ask if any seafaring men had gone by along the road. At first we thought it was the want of company of his own kind that made him ask this question, but at last we began to see he was desirous to avoid them. When a seaman put up at the Admiral Benbow (as now and then some did, making by the coast road for Bristol),[14] he would look in at him through the curtained door before he entered the parlour; and he was always sure to be as silent as a mouse when any such was present. For me, at least, there was no secret about the matter, for I was, in a way, a sharer in his alarms. He had taken me aside one day and promised me a silver fourpenny[15] on the first of every month if I would only keep my "weather-eye open for a seafaring man with one leg" and let him know the moment he appeared. Often enough when the first of the month came round and I applied to him for my wage, he would only blow through his nose at me and stare me down, but before the week was out he was sure to think better of it, bring me my fourpenny

in some cases, by private messenger. However, many people paid coach drivers to carry their letters disguised as parcels, as parcels were legal. The royal postal service used relays of riders–post riders–carrying leather satchels filled with mail. It was only in 1784 that a service of fast official mail coaches with armed guards was established.

12. Another inn farther along the coast, possibly named for King George I or George II.

13. Brass was not always used for making the barrels of telescopes. Mahogany was common. Often the telescope was a single long tube, maybe three feet long, rather than an instrument that could be extended using multiple "draw" tubes. A sea officer commonly would use a strap to sling his telescope over his shoulder before climbing to the masthead to get a better view.

14. In the 1750s Bristol, in the west country of England, was the United Kingdom's second-largest port after London, and prosperous. (For more, see the introduction, p. xvi.)

15. A silver fourpenny was a coin. (For more on British coinage of the 1750s, see the introduction, p. x.)

piece, and repeat his orders to look out for "the seafaring man with one leg."

How that personage haunted my dreams, I need scarcely tell you. On stormy nights,

"If you do not put that knife this instant in your pocket, you shall hang at the next assizes."

when the wind shook the four corners of the house and the surf roared along the cove and up the cliffs, I would see him in a thousand forms, and with a thousand diabolical expressions. Now the leg would be cut off at the knee, now at the hip; now he was a monstrous kind of a creature who had never had but the one leg, and that in the middle of his body. To see him leap and run and pursue me over hedge and ditch was the worst of nightmares. And altogether I paid pretty dear for my monthly fourpenny piece, in the shape of these abominable fancies.

But though I was so terrified by the idea of the seafaring man with one leg, I was far less afraid of the captain himself than anybody else who knew him. There were nights when he took a deal more rum and water than his head would carry; and then he would sometimes sit and sing his wicked, old, wild sea-songs, minding nobody; but sometimes he would call for glasses round and force all the trembling company to listen to his stories or bear a chorus to his singing. Often I have heard the house shaking with "Yo-ho-ho, and a bottle of rum," all the neighbours joining in for dear life, with the fear of death upon them, and each singing louder than the other to avoid remark. For in these fits he was the most overriding companion ever known; he would slap his hand on the table for silence all round; he would fly up in a passion of anger at a question, or sometimes because none was put, and so he judged the company was not following his story. Nor would he allow anyone to leave the inn till he had drunk himself sleepy and reeled off to bed.

His stories were what frightened people worst of all. Dreadful stories they were—about hanging, and walking the plank, and storms at sea, and the Dry Tortugas,[16] and wild deeds and places on the Spanish Main.[17] By his own account he must have lived his life among some of the wickedest men that God ever allowed upon the sea, and the language in which he told these stories shocked our plain country people almost as much as the crimes that he described. My father was always saying the inn would be ruined, for people would soon cease coming there to be tyrannized over and put down, and sent shivering to their beds; but I really believe his presence did us good. People were frightened at the time, but on looking back they rather liked it; it was a fine excitement in a quiet country life, and there was even a party of the younger men who pretended to admire him, calling him a "true sea-dog" and a "real old salt" and such like names, and saying there was the sort of man that made England terrible at sea.

In one way, indeed, he bade fair to ruin us, for he kept on staying week after week, and at last month after month, so that all the money had been long exhausted, and still my father never plucked up the heart to insist on having more. If ever he mentioned it, the

16. The Dry Tortugas are seven small sand and coral reef islets, surrounded by shoals, about 70 miles from Key West, now a national park.

The first European known to have seen the group, in 1513, was the Spaniard Ponce de Leon, who named them Las Tortugas–Spanish for "the turtles"–because of the large number of turtles found there. Sailors in need of fresh meat found turtles to be good eating, not least because they could be captured easily, loaded on board, flipped on their backs, and kept alive for a long time with minimal effort. There is no fresh water on the Tortugas, thus they are the Dry Tortugas. They are a hazard to navigation, because they are low-lying and thus hard to spot in a storm or at night. They are the site of hundreds of shipwrecks.

The Dry Tortugas are located in the area known as the Florida Straits, through which Spanish bullion convoys from Central and South America moved, and so they attracted the attention of pirates and buccaneers, as well as smugglers.

17. The "Spanish Main" is often used as a general name for former Spanish-controlled territories in Central and South America facing the Caribbean Sea. From the late 1600s to the early 1800s the term also included the sea itself. More precisely, the Spanish Main refers to the north coast of South America bordering the Caribbean that is modern-day Venezuela, Colombia, and Panama.

In the 1500s, 1600s, and 1700s, the Main was a target for commerce raiders and smugglers from France, the Netherlands, and Britain. In the early 1800s the area began exporting its own pirates and privateers to attack cargo vessels in the Caribbean.

The eastern portion of the Main included the ports of Rio de la Hacha and Santa Marta, both on the Caribbean coast of modern Colombia and both favorite targets of seaborne raiders. The western section included the towns of Portobello in modern Panama and Cartagena in modern Colombia, both on the Caribbean coast of those countries, and both also popular with raiders.

In the early days of the exploration and colonization of the Americas, Spanish sailors called the area Tierra Firme and gave this name to one of the two fleets in the Spanish convoy system between Spain and the Americas. One convoy, the New Spain fleet, went to Vera Cruz in modern Mexico. The other, the Tierra Firme fleet, in the

17th century went to Cartagena and Portobello in the western section of the Main.

18. A hawker travels the countryside selling goods that are small enough for him to carry.

19. Folding up part of the brim of a hat was called *cocking a hat*. Some people folded up or cocked the front of their hat; some folded one or both of the sides, while others cocked three sides. Given the fashion of his day, the captain was most likely wearing a hat cocked on three sides.

20. It was the fashion in the 1700s to powder one's hair or wig. A common powder was white flour, although fancier powders, some colored and scented, were also used. Powder also had by law to contain starch, although the law was often ignored.

Livesey wore a wig that required powdering (see note 8 on p. 21), and keeping it powdered was a tedious process. The wig was smeared with sticky grease; the powder would have been pumped or dumped onto the wig while Livesey held a protective cone over his face so he could breathe.

Powdering natural hair as opposed to wigs was equally tedious. Some army regiments required their men to wear their hair in a 15-inch-long queue or pigtail. Keeping a queue in a satisfactory condition was a laborious, hour-long ritual involving a bag of white powder, a powder puff, wax or grease, and soap. Wrote one English soldier in his memoirs of service in the British Army:

> *A large piece of candle grease was applied first to the sides of my head, and then to the long hair behind. After this, the same operation was gone through with nasty, stinking soap, the man who was drenching me applying his knuckles as often as the soap.*

After the grease was worked in, the hair was pulled tightly back with a ribbon "so tightly that individual hairs were liable to spring out again with an almost audible snap," then sprinkled with powder.

captain blew through his nose so loudly that you might say he roared, and stared my poor father out of the room. I have seen him wringing his hands after such a rebuff, and I am sure the annoyance and the terror he lived in must have greatly hastened his early and unhappy death.

All the time he lived with us the captain made no change whatever in his dress but to buy some stockings from a hawker.[18] One of the cocks[19] of his hat having fallen down, he let it hang from that day forth, though it was a great annoyance when it blew. I remember the appearance of his coat, which he patched himself upstairs in his room, and which, before the end, was nothing but patches. He never wrote or received a letter, and he never spoke with any but the neighbours, and with these, for the most part, only when drunk on rum. The great sea-chest none of us had ever seen open.

He was only once crossed, and that was towards the end, when my poor father was far gone in a decline that took him off. Dr. Livesey came late one afternoon to see the patient, took a bit of dinner from my mother, and went into the parlour to smoke a pipe until his horse should come down from the hamlet, for we had no stabling at the old Benbow. I followed him in, and I remember observing the contrast the neat, bright doctor, with his powder as white as snow[20] and his bright, black eyes and pleasant manners, made with the coltish country folk, and above all, with that filthy, heavy, bleared scarecrow of a pirate of ours, sitting, far gone in rum, with his arms on the table. Suddenly he—the captain, that is—began to pipe up his eternal song:

"Fifteen men on the dead man's chest—
Yo-ho-ho, and a bottle of rum!
Drink and the devil had done for the rest—
Yo-ho-ho, and a bottle of rum!"

At first I had supposed "the dead man's chest" to be that identical big box of his upstairs in the front room, and the thought had been mingled in my nightmares with that of the one-legged seafaring man. But by this time we had all long ceased to pay any particular notice to the song; it was new, that night, to nobody but Dr. Livesey, and on him I observed it did not produce an agreeable effect, for he looked up for a moment quite angrily before he went on with his talk to old Taylor, the gardener, on a new cure for the rheumatics. In the meantime, the captain gradually brightened up at his own music, and at last flapped his hand upon the table before him in a way we all knew to mean silence. The voices stopped at once, all but Dr. Livesey's; he went on as before, speaking clear and kind and drawing briskly at his pipe between every word or two. The captain glared at him for a while, flapped his hand again, glared still harder, and at last broke out with a villainous, low oath, "Silence, there, between decks!"

"Were you addressing me, sir?" says the doctor; and when the ruffian had told him, with another oath, that this was so, "I have

21. The system for administering law was based on visiting judges from the capital who dealt with the more serious cases not addressed by the local magistrates called justices of the peace. The judges presided over quarterly courts called Quarter Sessions. The formal progress on foot of a visiting judge in his robes, wig, and buckled shoes from his official lodging to his court room to open the session was an event of high pageantry.

The assizes system for administering the laws of England was established in 1166 and lasted until 1971, when their jurisdiction over civil and criminal cases was shifted to other courts.

The system called for some judges to preside over cases in the capital, London, while other judges traveled around the country presiding over cases in selected towns. The country was divided into "circuits," and judges were assigned to different circuits. In the 1750s there were six circuits. The system played an important role in establishing national laws in place of local law or custom.

The word *assize* comes from the 13th-century French word *assis*, from the verb *asseoir*, which meant "sit," "settle," or "assess."

only one thing to say to you, sir," replies the doctor, "that if you keep on drinking rum, the world will soon be quit of a very dirty scoundrel!"

The old fellow's fury was awful. He sprang to his feet, drew and opened a sailor's clasp-knife, and balancing it open on the palm of his hand, threatened to pin the doctor to the wall.

The doctor never so much as moved. He spoke to him as before, over his shoulder and in the same tone of voice, rather high, so that all the room might hear, but perfectly calm and steady: "If you do not put that knife this instant in your pocket, I promise, upon my honour, you shall hang at the next assizes."[21]

Then followed a battle of looks between them, but the captain soon knuckled under, put up his weapon, and resumed his seat, grumbling like a beaten dog.

"And now, sir," continued the doctor, "since I now know there's such a fellow in my district, you may count I'll have an eye upon you day and night. I'm not a doctor only; I'm a magistrate; and if I catch a breath of complaint against you, if it's only for a piece of incivility like tonight's, I'll take effectual means to have you hunted down and routed out of this. Let that suffice."

Soon after, Dr. Livesey's horse came to the door and he rode away, but the captain held his peace that evening, and for many evenings to come.

Chapter Two

Black Dog Appears and Disappears

IT WAS NOT VERY long after this that there occurred the first of the mysterious events that rid us at last of the captain, though not, as you will see, of his affairs. It was a bitter cold winter,[1] with long, hard frosts and heavy gales; and it was plain from the first that my poor father was little likely to see the spring. He sank daily, and my mother and I had all the inn upon our hands, and were kept busy enough without paying much regard to our unpleasant guest.

It was one January morning, very early—a pinching, frosty morning—the cove all grey with hoar-frost, the ripple lapping softly on the stones, the sun still low and only touching the hilltops and shining far to seaward. The captain had risen earlier than usual and set out down the beach, his cutlass[2] swinging under the broad skirts of the old blue coat, his brass telescope under his arm, his hat tilted back upon his head. I remember his breath hanging like smoke in his wake as he strode off, and the last sound I heard of him as he

1. Europe went through what is known as the Little Ice Age between 1300 and 1850. During this time the glaciers advanced, growing seasons shortened, and harvests failed. The coldest cycle was between 1680 and 1730. In the winter of 1683/84 there was sea ice off the English and French coasts. Several times between 1695 and 1728 Inuit in their kayaks were seen near the coasts of the Orkney Islands off the coast of Scotland. In 1756 most of Iceland was surrounded by ice for 30 weeks.

2. A cutlass is a sword short enough for fighting in the restricted, crowded spaces found on board ship; it has a strong blade and a protective hilt. Blades range from 14 to 28 inches long and typically are slightly curved.

3. Tallow is animal fat, solid or otherwise, made from fat that has been collected or rendered from the remains of a cow, sheep, or pig after the edible cuts of meat and the usable bones have been removed. "Rendering" is a process whereby the animal remains are combined with water in a pot, then boiled so that the fat is dissolved, floats to the top, and is collected for later use, including the making of soap.

Tallow was one of several substances applied in the 1700s to the bottoms of vessels in order to deter slime-producing bacteria found in sea water. This slime is an environment that attracts seaweed, teredo worms, and barnacles, which attach themselves and can grow to the point that they slow a vessel down. A hull in this condition is known as fouled. Tallowing a hull did not work well but was regarded as better than nothing. (See note 5 on p. 97.)

turned the big rock was a loud snort of indignation, as though his mind was still running upon Dr. Livesey.

Well, mother was upstairs with father and I was laying the breakfast-table against the captain's return when the parlour door opened and a man stepped in on whom I had never set my eyes before. He was a pale, tallowy[3] creature, wanting two fingers of the left hand, and though he wore a cutlass, he did not look much like a fighter. I had always my eye open for seafaring men, with one leg or two, and I remember this one puzzled me. He was not sailorly, and yet he had a smack of the sea about him too.

I asked him what was for his service, and he said he would take rum; but as I was going out of the room to fetch it, he sat down upon a table and motioned me to draw near. I paused where I was, with my napkin in my hand.

"Come here, sonny," says he. "Come nearer here."

I took a step nearer.

"Is this here table for my mate Bill?" he asked with a kind of leer.

I told him I did not know his mate Bill, and this was for a person who stayed in our house whom we called the captain.

"Well," said he, "my mate Bill would be called the captain, as like as not. He has a cut on one cheek and a mighty pleasant way with him, particularly in drink, has my mate Bill. We'll put it, for argument like, that your captain has a cut on one cheek—and we'll put it, if you like, that that cheek's the right one. Ah, well! I told you. Now, is my mate Bill in this here house?"

I told him he was out walking.

"Which way, sonny? Which way is he gone?"

And when I had pointed out the rock and told him how the captain was likely to return, and how soon, and answered a few other questions, "Ah," said he, "this'll be as good as drink to my mate Bill."

The expression of his face as he said these words was not at all pleasant, and I had my own reasons for thinking that the stranger was mistaken, even supposing he meant what he said. But it was no affair of mine, I thought; and besides, it was difficult to know what to do. The stranger kept hanging about just inside the inn door, peering round the corner like a cat waiting for a mouse. Once I stepped out myself into the road, but he immediately called me back, and as I did not obey quick enough for his fancy, a most horrible change came over his tallowy face, and he ordered me in with an oath that made me jump. As soon as I was back again he returned to his former manner, half fawning, half sneering, patted me on the shoulder, told me I was a good boy and he had taken quite a fancy to me. "I have a son of my own," said he, "as like you as two blocks, and he's all the pride of my 'art. But the great thing for boys is discipline, sonny—discipline. Now, if you had sailed along of Bill, you wouldn't have stood there to be spoke to twice—not you. That was never Bill's way, nor the way of sich as sailed with him. And here, sure enough, is my mate Bill, with a spy-glass under his arm, bless his old 'art, to be sure. You and me'll just go back into the parlour, sonny, and get behind the door, and we'll give Bill a little surprise—bless his 'art, I say again."

So saying, the stranger backed along with me into the parlour and put me behind him in the corner so that we were both hidden by the open door. I was very uneasy and alarmed, as you may fancy, and it rather added to my fears to observe that the stranger was certainly frightened himself. He cleared the hilt of his cutlass and loosened the blade in the sheath; and all the time we were waiting there he kept swallowing as if he felt what we used to call a lump in the throat.

At last in strode the captain, slammed the door behind him, without looking to the right or left, and marched straight across the room to where his breakfast awaited him.

"Bill," said the stranger in a voice that I thought he had tried to make bold and big.

The captain spun round on his heel and fronted us; all the brown had gone out of his face, and even his nose was blue; he had the look of a man who sees a ghost, or the evil one, or something worse, if anything can be; and upon my word, I felt sorry to see him all in a moment turn so old and sick.

"Come, Bill, you know me; you know an old shipmate, Bill, surely," said the stranger.

The captain made a sort of gasp.

"Black Dog!" said he.

"And who else?" returned the other, getting more at his ease. "Black Dog as ever was, come for to see his old shipmate Billy, at the Admiral Benbow inn. Ah, Bill, Bill, we have seen a sight of times, us two, since I lost them two talons," holding up his mutilated hand.

"Now, look here," said the captain; "you've run me down; here I am; well, then, speak up; what is it?"

"That's you, Bill," returned Black Dog, "you're in the right of it, Billy. I'll have a glass of rum from this dear child here, as I've took such a liking to; and we'll sit down, if you please, and talk square, like old shipmates."

When I returned with the rum, they were already seated on either side of the captain's breakfast-table—Black Dog next to the door and sitting sideways so as to have one eye on his old shipmate and one, as I thought, on his retreat.

He bade me go and leave the door wide open. "None of your keyholes for me, sonny," he said; and I left them together and retired into the bar.

For a long time, though I certainly did my best to listen, I could hear nothing but a low gabbling; but at last the voices began to grow

The next instant I saw Black Dog in full flight.

higher, and I could pick up a word or two, mostly oaths, from the captain.

"No, no, no, no; and an end of it!" he cried once. And again, "If it comes to a swinging, swing all, say I."

Then all of a sudden there was a tremendous explosion of oaths and other noises—the chair and table went over in a lump, a clash of steel followed, and then a cry of pain, and the next instant I saw Black Dog in full flight, and the captain hotly pursuing, both with drawn cutlasses, and the former streaming blood from the left shoulder. Just at the door the captain aimed at the fugitive one last tremendous cut, which would certainly have split him to the chine[4] had it not been intercepted by our big signboard of Admiral Benbow. You may see the notch on the lower side of the frame to this day.

That blow was the last of the battle. Once out upon the road, Black Dog, in spite of his wound, showed a wonderful clean pair of heels and disappeared over the edge of the hill in half a minute. The captain, for his part, stood staring at the signboard like a bewildered man. Then he passed his hand over his eyes several times and at last turned back into the house.

"Jim," says he, "rum"; and as he spoke, he reeled a little, and caught himself with one hand against the wall.

"Are you hurt?" cried I.

"Rum," he repeated. "I must get away from here. Rum! Rum!"

I ran to fetch it, but I was quite unsteadied by all that had fallen out, and I broke one glass and fouled the tap, and while I was still getting in my own way, I heard a loud fall in the parlour, and running in, beheld the captain lying full length upon the floor. At the

4. *Chine*, which means spine or backbone, derives from the medieval French *eschine*, which in turn was modified from the Latin *spina*.

5. A stroke occurs when there is an interruption in the supply of blood to the brain–typically, when a blood clot blocks a blood vessel that delivers blood to the brain or when there is a rupture in the wall of a blood vessel.

same instant my mother, alarmed by the cries and fighting, came running downstairs to help me. Between us we raised his head. He was breathing very loud and hard, but his eyes were closed and his face a horrible colour.

"Dear, deary me," cried my mother, "what a disgrace upon the house! And your poor father sick!"

In the meantime, we had no idea what to do to help the captain, nor any other thought but that he had got his death-hurt in the scuffle with the stranger. I got the rum, to be sure, and tried to put it down his throat, but his teeth were tightly shut and his jaws as strong as iron. It was a happy relief for us when the door opened and Doctor Livesey came in, on his visit to my father.

"Oh, doctor," we cried, "what shall we do? Where is he wounded?"

"Wounded? A fiddle-stick's end!" said the doctor. "No more wounded than you or I. The man has had a stroke,[5] as I warned him. Now, Mrs. Hawkins, just you run upstairs to your husband and tell him, if possible, nothing about it. For my part, I must do my best to save this fellow's trebly worthless life; Jim, you get me a basin."

When I got back with the basin, the doctor had already ripped up the captain's sleeve and exposed his great sinewy arm. It was tattooed in several places. "Here's luck," "A fair wind," and "Billy Bones his fancy," were very neatly and clearly executed on the forearm; and up near the shoulder there was a sketch of a gallows and a man hanging from it—done, as I thought, with great spirit.

"Prophetic," said the doctor, touching this picture

with his finger. "And now, Master Billy Bones, if that be your name, we'll have a look at the colour of your blood. Jim," he said, "are you afraid of blood?"

"No, sir," said I.

"Well, then," said he, "you hold the basin"; and with that he took his lancet and opened a vein.[6]

A great deal of blood was taken before the captain opened his eyes and looked mistily about him. First he recognized the doctor with an unmistakable frown; then his glance fell upon me, and he looked relieved. But suddenly his colour changed, and he tried to raise himself, crying, "Where's Black Dog?"

"There is no Black Dog here," said the doctor, "except what you have on your own back. You have been drinking rum; you have had a stroke, precisely as I told you; and I have just, very much against my own will, dragged you headforemost out of the grave. Now, Mr. Bones—"

"That's not my name," he interrupted.

"Much I care," returned the doctor. "It's the name of a buccaneer[7] of my acquaintance; and I call you by it for the sake of shortness, and what I have to say to you is this: one glass of rum won't kill you, but if you take one you'll take another and another, and I stake my wig[8] if you don't break off short, you'll die—do you understand that?—die, and go to your own place, like the man in the Bible. Come, now, make an effort. I'll help you to your bed for once."

Between us, with much trouble, we managed to hoist him upstairs, and laid him on his bed, where his head fell back on the pillow as if he were almost fainting.

"Now, mind you," said the doctor, "I clear my conscience—the name of rum for you is death."

6. *Lancet* is an old name for what is usually called a scalpel today.

Dr. Livesey is performing a phlebotomy or venesection, a procedure that was common in the 1700s and into the middle 1800s. Called "breathing a vein," the procedure involved making a small cut to let a quantity of blood out. There was a common belief, dating back to Greek and Roman times, that some ailments reflected the presence of too much blood in a patient's body, and that therefore the ailment could be treated by reducing blood volume.

One of the ailments that supposedly could be treated by opening a vein was apoplexy, better known today as stroke. Also supposedly amenable to bloodletting were fevers and headache. Bloodletting was a popular remedy, and people sometimes requested it be done even when there was nothing wrong with them, as a sort of tune-up for the body. Drawing too much blood was, of course, dangerous: George Washington was thought by some to have been bled to death in an attempt to help him during his last illness. Note that Livesey tells Jim that he has drawn enough blood from Billy Bones to "keep him quiet awhile."

7. This was one of the names given to the mostly French and English raiders who attacked Spanish ships and settlements in the Caribbean and the Americas in the 1600s. (For more, see the introduction, p. xviii.)

8. Staking one's wig was an expensive bet. At one time a fine wig could cost as much as a year's earnings for a skilled person who made a good living from a trade.

Livesey would recognize the big, full-bottomed wigs used by judges in British courts today, and the small, neat wigs made from horsehair that are worn by the lawyers who appear before them.

Wigs that allowed men to appear with luxuriant cascades of shoulder-length human curls became the height of fashion in the 1660s in Britain. At first, fashion wigs were an "unutterable peril" and "godless emblems of iniquity," according to a chief justice of Massachusetts. By Livesey's day, wigs were part of the accepted order of things, as much a symbol of status as a white collar and tie would be 200 years later, and came in many styles.

Bill Severn, a historian of wigs and hair, reports

that when Virginia backwoodsmen, wig-less and with unkempt hair, marched on Williamsburg in 1775, bewigged townsmen of Williamsburg barricaded their doors against people who looked "so savage." Going wig-less became associated in Britain in the 1790s with the French Revolution and the mass killings that accompanied it. Some parents in England refused to send their children to schools taught by men who did not wear wigs.

Wigs were made of human hair, hair from the tails of young cattle, North African sheep's wool, and goats' hair, from horse hair, vegetable fiber, yak hair, and, of course, hair taken from the occasional corpse. Even sailors wore wool wigs at one point.

By the last decade of the 18th century, wigs had started to fade from fashion, and a 1795 tax on hair powder helped speed their departure from fashionable heads.

And with that he went off to see my father, taking me with him by the arm.

"This is nothing," he said as soon as he had closed the door. "I have drawn blood enough to keep him quiet awhile; he should lie for a week where he is—that is the best thing for him and you; but another stroke would settle him."

Chapter Three

The Black Spot

ABOUT NOON I STOPPED at the captain's door with some cooling drinks and medicines. He was lying very much as we had left him, only a little higher, and he seemed both weak and excited.

"Jim," he said, "you're the only one here that's worth anything, and you know I've been always good to you. Never a month but I've given you a silver fourpenny for yourself. And now you see, mate, I'm pretty low, and deserted by all; and Jim, you'll bring me one noggin of rum, now, won't you, matey?"

"The doctor——" I began.

But he broke in cursing the doctor, in a feeble voice but heartily. "Doctors is all swabs,"[1] he said; "and that doctor there, why, what do he know about seafaring men? I been in places hot as pitch,[2] and mates dropping round with Yellow Jack,[3] and the blessed land a-heaving like the sea with earthquakes—what do the doctor know of lands like that?—and I lived on rum, I tell you. It's been meat and drink, and man and wife,

1. A swab was a mop made from strands of old rope that had been untwisted. It is used here in the sense of a useless person, good only for mopping a deck. It is also used as a term for a drunk.

2. Derived from pinewood tar, pitch was used as a protective coating for hulls and for waterproofing the fiber oakum used to seal the seams of decks and hulls. It has to be applied in a melted state–hence, "hot as pitch."

In the 1750s pitch was made by boiling tar, a process that was a crude form of distillation. Tar was extracted from short lengths of pinewood by heating them in an airtight tar kiln until only charcoal was left. Tar was used as a protective coating for cordage and for waterproofing canvas. The words *pitch* and *tar* sometimes are used interchangeably.

3. Slang for yellow fever, a disease caused by a virus spread by infected mosquitoes. Symptoms include high fever, muscle pain, vomiting, bleeding from the eyes and other body openings, kidney failure, and liver failure, which causes jaundice. Jaundice turns the skin yellow, hence the name. More than half of the 43,000 troops sent from Britain to the West Indies between 1793 and 1801 died from yellow fever.

4. A dramatic way of saying he is nearing the end of his life. A *hulk* was an old vessel without masts waiting to be demolished or altered to perform a new role. Hulks were used as places to house new navy recruits, as prisons or training facilities. *Lee shore* was a synonym for danger in the days of sail. It is a coastline onto which the wind is blowing in from the sea. A vessel would be destroyed if it was unable to maneuver away from the coast and was blown ashore. A hulk without sails would be unable to maneuver.

5. When you *raise Cain* you are making a serious and probably loud fuss about something. Cain, of course, is the biblical figure who killed his brother Abel. The origin of the phrase is obscure, but the *Guinness Book of Words* suggests that "raise Cain" is a way of saying "raise the devil" without using the word *devil*.

6. See the introduction, p. x.

7. *Lubber* is an old word for, in the 1400s, a lout or a clumsy person. By the 1600s it meant a land-lubber, or clumsy seaman, and that meaning is still current, with additional connotations of lack of skill and laziness.

to me; and if I'm not to have my rum now I'm a poor old hulk on a lee shore,[4] my blood'll be on you, Jim, and that doctor swab"; and he ran on again for a while with curses. "Look, Jim, how my fingers fidges," he continued in the pleading tone. "I can't keep 'em still, not I. I haven't had a drop this blessed day. That doctor's a fool, I tell you. If I don't have a drain o' rum, Jim, I'll have the horrors; I seen some on 'em already. I seen old Flint in the corner there, behind you; as plain as print, I seen him; and if I get the horrors, I'm a man that has lived rough, and I'll raise Cain.[5] Your doctor hisself said one glass wouldn't hurt me. I'll give you a golden guinea[6] for a noggin, Jim."

He was growing more and more excited, and this alarmed me for my father, who was very low that day and needed quiet; besides, I was reassured by the doctor's words, now quoted to me, and rather offended by the offer of a bribe.

"I want none of your money," said I, "but what you owe my father. I'll get you one glass, and no more."

When I brought it to him, he seized it greedily and drank it out.

"Aye, aye," said he, "that's some better, sure enough. And now, matey, did that doctor say how long I was to lie here in this old berth?"

"A week at least," said I.

"Thunder!" he cried. "A week! I can't do that; they'd have the black spot on me by then. The lubbers[7] is going about to get the wind of me this blessed moment; lubbers as couldn't keep what they got, and want to nail what is another's. Is that seamanly behaviour, now, I want to know? But I'm a saving soul. I never wasted good money of mine, nor lost it neither; and

I'll trick 'em again. I'm not afraid on 'em. I'll shake out another reef,[8] matey, and daddle 'em again."

As he was thus speaking, he had risen from bed with great difficulty, holding to my shoulder with a grip that almost made me cry out, and moving his legs like so much dead weight. His words, spirited as they were in meaning, contrasted sadly with the weakness of the voice in which they were uttered. He paused when he had got into a sitting position on the edge.

"That doctor's done me," he murmured. "My ears is singing. Lay me back."

Before I could do much to help him he had fallen back again to his former place, where he lay for a while silent.

"Jim," he said at length, "you saw that seafaring man today?"

"Black Dog?" I asked.

"Ah! Black Dog," says he. "*He's* a bad un; but there's worse that put him on. Now, if I can't get away nohow, and they tip me the black spot, mind you, it's my old sea-chest they're after; you get on a horse—you can, can't you? Well, then, you get on a horse, and go to— well, yes, I will!—to that eternal doctor swab, and tell him to pipe all hands[9]—magistrates and sich—and he'll lay 'em aboard at the Admiral Benbow—all old Flint's[10] crew, man and boy, all on 'em that's left. I was first mate, I was, old Flint's first mate,[11] and I'm the on'y one as knows the place. He gave it me at Savannah,[12] when he lay a-dying, like as if I was to now, you see. But you won't peach[13] unless they get the black spot on me, or unless you see that Black Dog again or a seafaring man with one leg, Jim—him above all."

"But what is the black spot, captain?" I asked.

8. Bones is going to get going and get away. A sailing ship can speed up or slow down its speed by controlling how much sail area it exposes to the wind. One way for a sailing ship to reduce speed is to reduce the sail area that is exposed to the wind. To do that, sailors bunch up a portion of the sail and tie it to its yard—a wooden pole attached to the mast—using short pieces of line sewn onto the sail called reef points. The action is called reefing, or taking in a reef. A sail typically is equipped with several parallel rows of reef points. When more speed is needed and wind conditions permit, sail area is expanded by "shaking out another reef."

Seamen taking in a reef to shorten a sail. The same number of men "shake out a reef"–that is, untie the knots they are tying in this image.

9. To pipe all hands was to use a special whistle to produce a set of sounds that the crew of a vessel would understand as an order to do something or to pay attention because they were going to get a spoken order. Making sounds on the whistle is called "piping."

The special whistle is usually known as a *boatswain's call* or *boatswain's whistle*. A combination of sounds can be produced by the whistle to communicate different orders. Different combinations of sounds were used for such commands as *hoist, heave, belay* (meaning "stop"), *hands to dinner,* and others.

The design of the whistle itself dates back to

medieval times and remains virtually unchanged. In the 1500s in England a boatswain's call, made of gold and hanging from a long gold chain, was a symbol of office of the Lord High Admiral and can be seen in portraits from that period.

Boatswains' calls continue to be used by many navies, in conjunction with a ship's public address system and for ceremonial purposes. Boatswain's calls are available commercially.

A boatswain's (bosun's) call or whistle.

10. The pirate Flint managed to avoid entering the public records that survive. All we know of him and his misdeeds are from the vivid descriptions by Billy Bones and the others who served with him that were recorded by Jim Hawkins.

11. On a merchant ship, the *first mate* is the officer who is in command when the master of the vessel is absent; today the position is known formally as the *first officer*. Larger vessels might have more than one mate.

On Royal Navy ships in the days of sail, an officer might also be mate of the lower deck, meaning he was responsible for the condition of that area and the people there. The mate of the main deck was responsible for supervising activities on that deck.

12. Surely Savannah was an inconvenient haven for pirates, who needed towns where they could discreetly find supplies, recruits, buyers for their loot, and investors, and encounter only erratic law enforcement. Savannah was founded in 1733 as the capital of Georgia, a private philanthropic venture with government support, by a group of altruists in Britain led by a reform-minded army general and member of Parliament, James Edward Oglethorpe. Initially slavery was forbidden, as were rum and lawyers. The Wesley brothers, founders of Methodism, came to help. Admittedly, the town had loosened up by the 1740s, but a tough Royal Navy captain, John Reynolds, was governor in 1754,

"That's a summons, mate. I'll tell you if they get that. But you keep your weather-eye open, Jim, and I'll share with you equals, upon my honour."

He wandered a little longer, his voice growing weaker; but soon after I had given him his medicine, which he took like a child, with the remark, "If ever a seaman wanted drugs, it's me," he fell at last into a heavy, swoonlike sleep, in which I left him. What I should have done had all gone well I do not know. Probably I should have told the whole story to the doctor, for I was in mortal fear lest the captain should repent of his confessions and make an end of me. But as things fell out, my poor father died quite suddenly that evening, which put all other matters on one side. Our natural distress, the visits of the neighbours, the arranging of the funeral, and all the work of the inn to be carried on in the meanwhile kept me so busy that I had scarcely time to think of the captain, far less to be afraid of him.

He got downstairs next morning, to be sure, and had his meals as usual, though he ate little and had more, I am afraid, than his usual supply of rum, for he helped himself out of the bar, scowling and blowing through his nose, and no one dared to cross him. On the night before the funeral he was as drunk as ever; and it was shocking, in that house of mourning, to hear him singing away at his ugly old sea-song; but weak as he was, we were all in the fear of death for him, and the doctor was suddenly taken up with a case many miles away and was never near the house after my father's death. I have said the captain was weak, and indeed he seemed rather to grow weaker than regain his strength. He clambered up and down stairs, and went from the parlour to the bar and back again, and sometimes put his nose out of doors to smell the sea, holding on to the walls as he went for support and breathing hard and fast like a man on a steep mountain. He never particularly addressed me, and it is my belief he had as good as forgotten his confidences; but his temper was more flighty, and allowing for his bodily weakness, more violent than ever. He had an alarming way now when he was drunk of drawing his cutlass and laying it bare before him on the table. But with all that, he minded people less and seemed shut up in his own thoughts and rather wandering. Once, for instance, to our extreme wonder, he piped up to a different air, a kind of country love-song that he must have learned in his youth before he had begun to follow the sea.

So things passed until, the day after the funeral, and about three o'clock of a bitter, foggy, frosty afternoon, I was standing at the door for a moment, full of sad thoughts about my father, when I saw someone drawing slowly near along the road. He was plainly blind, for he tapped before him with a stick and wore a great green shade over his eyes and nose; and he was hunched, as if with age or weakness, and wore a huge old tattered seacloak with a hood that made him appear positively deformed. I never saw in my life a more dreadful-looking figure. He stopped a little from the inn, and raising his voice in an odd sing-song, addressed the air in front of him. "Will any kind friend inform a poor blind man, who has lost the precious sight of his eyes in the gracious defence of his native country, England—and God bless King George![14]— where or in what part of this country he may now be?"

the year Flint died in Savannah. But maybe Flint was discreet and kept out of sight. And who would think of looking for him in Savannah when Charleston, New York, Newport, Rhode Island, and Boston had so much more to offer him?

13. That is, "You won't inform on me." Captain Francis Grose, in the 1796 edition of his 1785 *Classical Dictionary of the Vulgar Tongue*, tells us that *peach* is a shortened version of *to impeach* ("to accuse"). In the 1700s *peach* also meant *to blow the gab, squeak,* or *turn stag,* all variations of the modern *snitch.*

The word has survived, according to Eric Partridge, Grose's most recent editor, since the 1500s, when it was used by Shakespeare. It was a colloquialism in the 18th and 19th centuries and slang in the early 20th.

14. To describe George II of Great Britain and Ireland historians have used language like conceited, hot-tempered, no intellectual interests; also touchy, comic, obstinate; stupid but complicated, not indolent, lacked confidence, could be bullied, and exceedingly impatient. He also had a photographic memory.

George ascended the throne in 1727 and reigned until early in the morning of October 25, 1760, when, as one historian put it, he combined "farce with tragedy" by dying of a stroke after he strained too hard while on the commode. For all his faults, George was also brave, staying by his wife's side when she had smallpox, knowing the disease was often lethal and that he might catch it, which he did. He survived.

His temper was demonstrated the year before the *Hispaniola* sailed when Vice-Admiral John Byng was convicted of not doing his best to win a battle, a verdict that came with an automatic death penalty. The First Lord of the Admiralty, the Earl Temple, described by historian N.A.M. Rodger as "tactless and arrogant," presented George with a petition for clemency that was supported by George's own government. Temple, reports Rodger, "implied that the king, as a coward himself, ought to have compassion on the admiral. That sealed Byng's fate and he was shot on his own quarterdeck." His execution prompted the quip that the British shoot an admiral from time to time "to encourage the others."

In addition to the crown of England, George wore another as Hereditary Prince of Hanover, a state in modern northern Germany where he was born in 1683, the last king of England born abroad and the last to lead his troops in battle.

George II preferred Hanover to England, where, he once said, "he was obliged to enrich people for being rascals and buy them not to cut his throat." The House of Commons of Parliament, he said, was "full of king killers or republicans."

George II at least learned English. His father, George I, who was also born in Hanover, never did. He had been invited to be become king of England because he was descended from King James I of England, who died in 1625, but more important, because he was a Protestant and politically acceptable to the king killers and republicans, unlike the other claimant to the throne, James Edward Stuart.

George II wearing a "campaign" wig at age 70 in 1753, five years before the *Hispaniola* sailed.

"You are at the Admiral Benbow, Black Hill Cove, my good man," said I.

"I hear a voice," said he, "a young voice. Will you give me your hand, my kind young friend, and lead me in?"

I held out my hand, and the horrible, soft-spoken, eyeless creature gripped it in a moment like a vise. I was so much startled that I struggled to withdraw, but the blind man pulled me close up to him with a single action of his arm.

"Now, boy," he said, "take me in to the captain."

"Sir," said I, "upon my word I dare not."

"Oh," he sneered, "that's it! Take me in straight or I'll break your arm."

And he gave it, as he spoke, a wrench that made me cry out.

"Sir," said I, "it is for yourself I mean. The captain is not what he used to be. He sits with a drawn cutlass. Another gentleman——"

"Come, now, march," interrupted he; and I never heard a voice so cruel, and cold, and ugly as that blind man's. It cowed me more than the pain, and I began to obey him at once, walking straight in at the door and towards the parlour, where our sick old buccaneer was sitting, dazed with rum. The blind man clung close to me, holding me in one iron fist and leaning almost more of his weight on me than I could carry. "Lead me straight up to him, and when I'm in view, cry out, 'Here's a friend for you, Bill.' If you don't, I'll do this," and with that he gave me a twitch that I thought would have made me faint. Between this and that, I was so utterly terrified of the blind beggar that I forgot my terror of the captain, and as I opened the

At one look the rum went out of him and left him staring sober.

parlour door, cried out the words he had ordered in a trembling voice.

The poor captain raised his eyes, and at one look the rum went out of him and left him staring sober. The expression of his face was not so much of terror as of mortal sickness. He made a movement to rise, but I do not believe he had enough force left in his body.

"Now, Bill, sit where you are," said the beggar. "If I can't see, I can hear a finger stirring. Business is business. Hold out your left hand. Boy, take his left hand by the wrist and bring it near to my right."

We both obeyed him to the letter, and I saw him pass something from the hollow of the hand that held his stick into the palm of the captain's, which closed upon it instantly.

"And now that's done," said the blind man; and at the words he suddenly left hold of me, and with incredible accuracy and nimbleness, skipped out of the parlour and into the road, where, as I still stood motionless, I could hear his stick go tap-tap-tapping into the distance.

It was some time before either I or the captain seemed to gather our senses, but at length, and about at the same moment, I released his wrist, which I was still holding,

15. Bleeding within an internal organ. The term is often used to describe bleeding into the brain, otherwise known as a stroke.

and he drew in his hand and looked sharply into the palm.

"Ten o'clock!" he cried. "Six hours. We'll do them yet," and he sprang to his feet.

Even as he did so, he reeled, put his hand to his throat, stood swaying for a moment, and then, with a peculiar sound, fell from his whole height face foremost to the floor.

I ran to him at once, calling to my mother. But haste was all in vain. The captain had been struck dead by thundering apoplexy.[15] It is a curious thing to understand, for I had certainly never liked the man, though of late I had begun to pity him, but as soon as I saw that he was dead, I burst into a flood of tears. It was the second death I had known, and the sorrow of the first was still fresh in my heart.

Chapter Four

The Sea-chest

I LOST NO TIME, of course, in telling my mother all that I knew, and perhaps should have told her long before, and we saw ourselves at once in a difficult and dangerous position. Some of the man's money—if he had any—was certainly due to us, but it was not likely that our captain's shipmates, above all the two specimens seen by me, Black Dog and the blind beggar, would be inclined to give up their booty in payment of the dead man's debts. The captain's order to mount at once and ride for Doctor Livesey would have left my mother alone and unprotected, which was not to be thought of. Indeed, it seemed impossible for either of us to remain much longer in the house; the fall of coals in the kitchen grate, the very ticking of the clock, filled us with alarms. The neighbourhood, to our ears, seemed haunted by approaching footsteps; and what between the dead body of the captain on the parlour floor and the thought of that detestable blind beggar hovering near at hand and ready to return, there were moments when, as the saying goes, I jumped in my skin for terror. Something must speedily be resolved upon, and it occurred to us at last to go forth together and seek help in the neighbouring hamlet. No sooner said than done. Bareheaded as we were, we ran out at once in the gathering evening and the frosty fog.

The hamlet lay not many hundred yards away, though out of view, on the other side of the next cove; and what greatly encouraged me, it was in an opposite direction from that whence the blind man had made his appearance and whither he had presumably returned. We were not many minutes on the

1. A lugger is a vessel used for fishing and coastal trading. In the 1750s it typically had a foremast and a mainmast, rigged with irregular four-sided sails set on spars called lugs. Its ability to sail more directly into the wind than many other vessels was helpful when it had to deal with tricky tidal waters. Large luggers fitted with an extra mast were used as smuggling vessels or privateers.

The lugger, used for fishing and coastal trading, was designed to navigate tricky tidal waters.

road, though we sometimes stopped to lay hold of each other and hearken. But there was no unusual sound—nothing but the low wash of the ripple and the croaking of the inmates of the wood.

It was already candle-light when we reached the hamlet, and I shall never forget how much I was cheered to see the yellow shine in doors and windows; but that, as it proved, was the best of the help we were likely to get in that quarter. For—you would have thought men would have been ashamed of themselves—no soul would consent to return with us to the Admiral Benbow. The more we told of our troubles, the more—man, woman, and child—they clung to the shelter of their houses. The name of Captain Flint, though it was strange to me, was well enough known to some there and carried a great weight of terror. Some of the men who had been to field-work on the far side of the Admiral Benbow remembered, besides, to have seen several strangers on the road, and taking them to be smugglers, to have bolted away; and one at least had seen a little lugger[1] in what we called Kitt's Hole. For that matter, anyone who was a comrade of the captain's was enough to frighten them to death. And the short and the long of the matter was, that while we could get several who were willing enough to ride to Dr. Livesey's, which lay in another direction, not one would help us to defend the inn.

They say cowardice is infectious; but then argument is, on the other hand, a great emboldener; and so when each had said his say, my mother made them a speech. She would not, she declared, lose money that belonged to her fatherless boy; "If none of the rest of you dare," she said, "Jim and I dare. Back we will go, the way we came, and small thanks to you big, hulking, chicken-hearted men. We'll have that chest open, if we die for it. And I'll thank you for that bag, Mrs. Crossley, to bring back our lawful money in."

Of course I said I would go with my mother, and of course they all cried out at our foolhardiness, but even then not a man would go along with us. All they would do was to give me a loaded pistol lest we were attacked, and to promise to have horses ready saddled in case we were pursued on our return, while one lad was to ride forward to the doctor's in search of armed assistance.

My heart was beating finely when we two set forth in the cold night upon this dangerous venture. A full moon was beginning to rise and peered redly through the upper edges of the fog, and this increased our haste, for it was plain, before we came forth again, that all would be as bright as day, and our departure exposed to the eyes of any watchers. We slipped along the hedges, noiseless and swift, nor did we see or hear anything to increase our terrors, till, to our relief, the door of the Admiral Benbow had closed behind us.

I slipped the bolt at once, and we stood and panted for a moment in the dark, alone in the house with the dead captain's body. Then my mother got a candle in the bar, and holding each other's hands, we advanced into the parlour. He lay as we had left him, on his back, with his eyes open and one arm stretched out.

And she began to count the captain's score from the sailor's bag.

33

2. *Gully* is an old name for a large knife.

3. Until recognizably modern matches became available in the 1820s, people used to strike flint and steel together to create a spark that could be nursed into a flame to light a fire or a lamp. That could take half an hour or longer if it was wet or windy. For convenience, people carried a little kit consisting of a piece of flint, a piece of steel, and tinder, material that would eventually catch fire when exposed to sparks. Tinder could be anything from fine wood shavings to dried tree fungus mixed with saltpeter, an ingredient used in making gunpowder. The little kit could be carried around in a small box called a tinder box.

The University of Oxford's Pitt Rivers Museum has a collection of tinder boxes from different parts of the world, ranging from enameled boxes that keep out the damp of the Baltic Sea to soft leather pouches from dry, hot African climates.

"Draw down the blind, Jim," whispered my mother; "they might come and watch outside. And now," said she when I had done so, "we have to get the key off *that*; and who's to touch it, I should like to know!" and she gave a kind of sob as she said the words.

I went down on my knees at once. On the floor close to his hand there was a little round of paper, blackened on the one side. I could not doubt that this was the *black spot*; and taking it up, I found written on the other side, in a very good, clear hand, this short message: "You have till ten tonight."

"He had till ten, Mother," said I; and just as I said it, our old clock began striking. This sudden noise startled us shockingly; but the news was good, for it was only six.

"Now, Jim," she said, "that key."

I felt in his pockets, one after another. A few small coins, a thimble, and some thread and big needles, a piece of pigtail tobacco bitten away at the end, his gully[2] with the crooked handle, a pocket compass, and a tinder box[3] were all that they contained, and I began to despair.

"Perhaps it's round his neck," suggested my mother.

Overcoming a strong repugnance, I tore open his shirt at the neck, and there, sure enough, hanging to a bit of tarry string, which I cut with his own gully, we found the key. At this triumph we were filled with hope and hurried upstairs without delay to the little room where he had slept so long and where his box had stood since the day of his arrival.

It was like any other seaman's chest on the outside, the initial "B" burned on the top of it with a hot iron and the corners somewhat smashed and broken as by long, rough usage.

"Give me the key," said my mother; and though the lock was very stiff, she had turned it and thrown back the lid in a twinkling.

A strong smell of tobacco and tar rose from the interior, but nothing was to be seen on the top except a suit of very good clothes, carefully brushed and folded. They had never been worn, my mother said. Under that, the miscellany began—a quadrant,[4] a tin canikin, several sticks of tobacco, two brace of very handsome pistols, a piece of bar silver,[5] an old Spanish watch and some other trinkets of little value and mostly of foreign make, a pair of compasses mounted with brass, and five or six curious West Indian shells. I have often wondered since why he should have carried about these shells with him in his wandering, guilty, and hunted life.

In the meantime, we had found nothing of any value but the silver and the trinkets, and neither of these were in our way. Underneath there was an old boat-cloak, whitened with sea-salt on many a harbour-bar. My mother pulled it up with impatience, and there lay before us, the last things in the chest, a bundle tied up in oilcloth, and looking like papers, and a canvas bag that gave forth, at a touch, the jingle of gold.

"I'll show these rogues that I'm an honest woman," said my mother. "I'll have my dues, and not a farthing over. Hold Mrs. Crossley's bag." And she began to count over the amount of the captain's score from the sailor's bag into the one that I was holding.

It was a long, difficult business, for the coins were of all countries and sizes—doubloons, and louis d'ors, and guineas, and pieces of eight,[6] and I know not what besides, all shaken together at random. The guineas,

4. A handheld navigational instrument used for determining a ship's location on a map by measuring the position of the sun relative to the horizon. Given that Billy Bones was an old seafarer, he might have used an old-fashioned quadrant known as a *backstaff* or *sea quadrant* or *English quadrant*, first used in the late 1500s and still in use into the 1770s.

More likely, since it is clear that he had roamed around the world and his notes show positions recorded with great precision, he would have used a *Hadley reflecting quadrant*, also called an *octant*, invented in 1731, which was in common use by the 1750s. It allowed a navigator to measure the position of the sun or a star relative to the horizon, and also their positions relative to each other. An octant was also easier to use than a backstaff, and mariners continued to use it well into the 1800s. It was accurate to within three miles. A Hadley's quadrant was made mostly of wood, with brass fittings, and was typically about 18 to 20 inches tall. An improved version, called a *sextant*, was also in use in Billy Bones's day. (See illustration, below.)

Sextant.

5. A typical example of Spanish bar silver of the 1700s is about 14 inches long, 5 inches wide, and 2.5 inches thick and weighs more than 60 pounds. Smaller bars have been found.

6. Spanish gold coins came in denominations of half, one, two, four and eight escudos. The eight-escudo coin was called a *doblon*, which in English became *doubloon*.

The gold Louis d'or came denominated as one or two *Louis d'or*, which were the most valuable French coins.

(For information on *guineas*, see the introduction, p. x.)

Pieces of eight was the term in English for the

milled Spanish silver coins worth eight *reales* and known as Spanish dollars. They weighed almost exactly one ounce of silver.

Thanks to the popularity of Spanish silver coins in colonial and newly independent America, U.S. stock exchanges still report changes in the trading price of shares in one-eighth increments. The reason is that when the New York Stock Exchange opened in 1792, changes in price were reported in shillings, which were valued at eight to the Spanish dollar, so changes in value were reported in eighths. The habit stuck. But the decimal system is making headway.

7. Oilskin could be made from linen, cotton, or silk that had been treated with water-repelling linseed oil to waterproof it.

too, were about the scarcest, and it was with these only that my mother knew how to make her count.

When we were about half-way through, I suddenly put my hand upon her arm, for I had heard in the silent frosty air a sound that brought my heart into my mouth—the tap-tapping of the blind man's stick upon the frozen road. It drew nearer and nearer, while we sat holding our breath. Then it struck sharp on the inn door, and then we could hear the handle being turned and the bolt rattling as the wretched being tried to enter; and then there was a long time of silence both within and without. At last the tapping recommenced, and, to our indescribable joy and gratitude, died slowly away again until it ceased to be heard.

"Mother," said I, "take the whole and let's be going," for I was sure the bolted door must have seemed suspicious and would bring the whole hornet's nest about our ears, though how thankful I was that I had bolted it, none could tell who had never met that terrible blind man.

But my mother, frightened as she was, would not consent to take a fraction more than was due to her and was obstinately unwilling to be content with less. It was not yet seven, she said, by a long way; she knew her rights and she would have them; and she was still arguing with me when a little low whistle sounded a good way off upon the hill. That was enough, and more than enough, for both of us.

"I'll take what I have," she said, jumping to her feet.

"And I'll take this to square the count," said I, picking up the oilskin packet.[7]

Next moment we were both groping downstairs, leaving the candle by the empty chest; and the next we had opened the door and were in full retreat. We had not started a moment too soon. The fog was rapidly dispersing, already the moon shone quite clear on the high ground on either side; and it was only in the exact bottom of the dell and round the tavern door that a thin veil still hung unbroken to conceal the first steps of our escape. Far less than halfway to the hamlet, very little beyond the bottom of the hill, we must come forth into the moonlight. Nor was this all, for the sound of several footsteps running came already to our ears, and as we looked back in their direction, a light tossing to and fro and still rapidly advancing showed that one of the newcomers carried a lantern.

"My dear," said my mother suddenly, "take the money and run on. I am going to faint."

This was certainly the end for both of us, I thought. How I cursed the cowardice of the neighbours; how I blamed my poor mother for her honesty and her greed, for her past foolhardiness and present weakness! We were just at the little bridge, by good fortune; and I helped her, tottering as she was, to the edge of the bank, where, sure enough, she gave a sigh and fell on my shoulder. I do not know how I found the strength to do it at all, and I am afraid it was roughly done, but I managed to drag her down the bank and a little way under the arch. Farther I could not move her, for the bridge was too low to let me do more than crawl below it. So there we had to stay—my mother almost entirely exposed and both of us within earshot of the inn.

Chapter Five

The Last of the Blind Man

MY CURIOSITY, IN A SENSE, was stronger than my fear, for I could not remain where I was, but crept back to the bank again, whence, sheltering my head behind a bush of broom, I might command the road before our door. I was scarcely in position ere my enemies began to arrive, seven or eight of them, running hard, their feet beating out of time along the road and the man with the lantern some paces in front. Three men ran together, hand in hand; and I made out, even through the mist, that the middle man of this trio was the blind beggar. The next moment his voice showed me that I was right.

"Down with the door!" he cried.

"Aye, aye, sir!" answered two or three; and a rush was made upon the Admiral Benbow, the lantern-bearer following; and then I could see them pause, and hear speeches passed in a lower key, as if they were surprised to find the door open. But the pause was brief, for the blind man again issued his commands. His voice sounded louder and higher, as if he were afire with eagerness and rage.

"In, in, in!" he shouted, and cursed them for their delay.

Four or five of them obeyed at once, two remaining on the road with the formidable beggar. There was a pause, then a cry of surprise, and then a voice shouting from the house, "Bill's dead."

But the blind man swore at them again for their delay.

"Search him, some of you shirking lubbers, and the rest of you aloft and get the chest," he cried.

I could hear their feet rattling up our old

stairs, so that the house must have shook with it. Promptly afterwards, fresh sounds of astonishment arose; the window of the captain's room was thrown open with a slam and a jingle of broken glass, and a man leaned out into the moonlight, head and shoulders, and addressed the blind beggar on the road below him.

"Pew," he cried, "they've been before us. Someone's turned the chest out alow and aloft."[1]

"Is it there?" roared Pew.

"The money's there."

The blind man cursed the money.

"Flint's fist, I mean," he cried.

"We don't see it here nohow," returned the man.

"Here, you below there, is it on Bill?" cried the blind man again.

At that another fellow, probably him who had remained below to search the captain's body, came to the door of the inn. "Bill's been overhauled a'ready," said he; "nothin' left."

"It's these people of the inn—it's that boy. I wish I had put his eyes out!" cried the blind man, Pew. "They were here no time ago—they had the door bolted when I tried it. Scatter, lads, and find 'em."

"Sure enough, they left their glim[2] here," said the fellow from the window.

"Scatter and find 'em! Rout the house out!" reiterated Pew, striking with his stick upon the road.

Then there followed a great to-do through all our old inn, heavy feet pounding to and fro, furniture thrown over, doors kicked in, until the very rocks re-echoed and the men came out again, one after another, on the road and declared that we were nowhere to be

1. The pirate is telling Pew that the chest has been searched from bottom to top. *Alow* is a nautical word used in the sense of "below," while *aloft* is its opposite and means "above" or "overhead." In his *Sailor's Word-Book* of 1867, Admiral William Henry Smyth notes that the proper usage of *alow and aloft* is *"low"* and *aloft*. Ashore we have the words *low* and *lofty*.

Technical uses of the term include *carrying all sail alow and aloft*, which means using every available sail including studding sails–sails set on light supplementary booms extending out from the main stack of square sails.

2. The man means "their candle"; *glim* is also a term used by burglars in the 1700s for a *dark lantern*, a lamp in which the light source can be masked so that it won't be easily spotted.

3. The biscuit weevil (*Stegobium paniceum*) is better known today as the drugstore beetle in the United States and the biscuit beetle in the United Kingdom. These brown insects are 1/10 inch to 1/7 inch long (2.25 mm to 3.5mm) and fond of stored food products. The beetle gets its modern U.S. name from its taste for prescription drugs; it also enjoys breads, cookies, books, aluminum foil, sheets of lead, and leather, horn, and wooden objects. The feeding habits of the beetle's larvae are the principal cause of damage from *Stegobium* infestation.

In the 1700s ship's biscuit was made from flour mixed with a little–very little–water and slowly baked to create a rock-hard, flat, round object. The baker's objective was to create a source of calories that would last a long time rather than something that tasted good. Care was taken to store a vessel's supply of biscuit safely and away from damp, but even so, biscuits were notorious for attracting weevils, which sailors removed by tapping the biscuit against a hard surface.

There is no reason to suspect that on the *Hispaniola* the daily food allowance of biscuit differed greatly from the Royal Navy's requirement that each member of a crew receive a pound of "well-baked, well-conditioned wheaten biscuit" per man per day. Given that Squire Trelawney was expecting to be away no longer than six months, we can assume that the *Hispaniola* carried more than two tons of biscuit to provide each of the 26 people on board with a pound of biscuit per day.

4. A yellow George was a gold guinea coin. A George could also be a half-crown coin, representing two shillings and six pennies. (For more on British currency, see the introduction, p. x.)

found. And just then the same whistle that had alarmed my mother and myself over the dead captain's money was once more clearly audible through the night, but this time twice repeated. I had thought it to be the blind man's trumpet, so to speak, summoning his crew to the assault, but I now found that it was a signal from the hillside towards the hamlet, and from its effect upon the buccaneers, a signal to warn them of approaching danger.

"There's Dirk again," said one. "Twice! We'll have to budge, mates."

"Budge, you skulk!" cried Pew. "Dirk was a fool and a coward from the first—you wouldn't mind him. They must be close by; they can't be far; you have your hands on it. Scatter and look for them, dogs! Oh, shiver my soul," he cried, "if I had eyes!"

This appeal seemed to produce some effect, for two of the fellows began to look here and there among the lumber, but half-heartedly, I thought, and with half an eye to their own danger all the time, while the rest stood irresolute on the road.

"You have your hands on thousands, you fools, and you hang a leg! You'd be as rich as kings if you could find it, and you know it's here, and you stand there skulking. There wasn't one of you dared face Bill, and I did it—a blind man! And I'm to lose my chance for you! I'm to be a poor, crawling beggar, sponging for rum, when I might be rolling in a coach! If you had the pluck of a weevil[3] in a biscuit you would catch them still."

"Hang it, Pew, we've got the doubloons!" grumbled one.

"They might have hid the blessed thing," said another. "Take the Georges,[4] Pew, and don't stand here squalling."

He struck at them right and left in his blindness.

Squalling was the word for it; Pew's anger rose so high at these objections till at last, his passion completely taking the upper hand, he struck at them right and left in his blindness and his stick sounded heavily on more than one.

These, in their turn, cursed back at the blind miscreant, threatened him in horrid terms, and tried in vain to catch the stick and wrest it from his grasp.

This quarrel was the saving of us, for while it was still raging, another sound came from the top of the hill on the side of the hamlet—the tramp of horses galloping. Almost at the same time a pistol-shot, flash and report, came from the hedge side. And that was plainly the last signal of danger, for the buccaneers turned at once and ran, separating in every direction, one seaward along the cove, one slant across the hill, and so on, so that in half a minute not a sign of them remained but Pew. Him they had deserted, whether in sheer panic or out of revenge for his ill words and blows I know not; but there he remained behind, tapping up and down the road in a frenzy, and groping and calling

41

for his comrades. Finally he took the wrong turn and ran a few steps past me, towards the hamlet, crying, "Johnny, Black Dog, Dirk," and other names, "you won't leave old Pew, mates—not old Pew!"

Just then the noise of horses topped the rise, and four or five riders came in sight in the moonlight and swept at full gallop down the slope.

At this Pew saw his error, turned with a scream, and ran straight for the ditch, into which he rolled. But he was on his feet again in a second and made another dash, now utterly bewildered, right under the nearest of the coming horses.

The rider tried to save him, but in vain. Down went Pew with a cry that rang high into the night; and the four hoofs trampled and spurned him and passed by. He fell on his side, then gently collapsed upon his face and moved no more.

I leaped to my feet and hailed the riders. They were pulling up, at any rate, horrified at the accident; and I soon saw what they were. One, tailing out behind the rest, was a lad that had gone from the hamlet to Dr. Livesey's; the rest were revenue officers,[5] whom he had met by the way, and with whom he had had the intelligence to return at once. Some news of the lugger in Kitt's Hole had found its way to Supervisor Dance and set him forth that night in our direction, and to that circumstance my mother and I owed our preservation from death.

Pew was dead, stone dead. As for my mother, when we had carried her up to the hamlet, a little cold water and salts and that soon brought her back again, and she was none the worse for her terror, though she still continued to deplore the balance of the money. In the meantime the supervisor rode on, as fast as he could, to Kitt's Hole; but his men had to dismount and grope down the dingle,[6] leading, and sometimes supporting, their horses, and in continual fear of ambushes; so it was no great matter for surprise that when they got down to the Hole the lugger was already under way, though still close in. He hailed her. A voice replied, telling him to keep out of the moonlight or he would get some lead in him, and at the same time a bullet whistled close by his arm. Soon after, the lugger doubled the point and disappeared. Mr. Dance stood there, as he said, "like a fish out of water," and all he could do was to dispatch a man to B—— to warn the cutter.[7] "And that," said he, "is just about as good as nothing. They've got off clean, and there's an end. Only," he added, "I'm glad I trod on Master Pew's corns," for by this time he had heard my story.

I went back with him to the Admiral Benbow, and you cannot imagine a house in such a state of smash; the very clock had been thrown down by these fellows in their furious hunt after my mother and myself; and though nothing had actually been taken away except the captain's money-bag and a little silver from the till, I could see at once that we were ruined. Mr. Dance could make nothing of the scene.

"They got the money, you say? Well, then, Hawkins, what in fortune were they after? More money, I suppose?"

"No, sir; not money, I think," replied I. "In fact, sir, I believe I have the thing in my breast pocket; and to tell you the truth, I should like to get it put in safety."

"To be sure, boy; quite right," said he. "I'll take it, if you like."

"I thought perhaps Dr. Livesey——" I began.

6. A deep hollow.

7. This might have been the revenue cutter requested in September 1751 by the collector of customs at Cardiff on the Bristol Channel. He wanted a vessel armed with cannon and heavily manned to patrol the Channel from Bristol to Lundy Island, owned by a Mr. Benson and notorious as a smugglers' base.

Having a cutter on patrol was not a guarantee of success. The previous year the *Sincerity* intercepted a smuggler's vessel and was then attacked by armed residents of the Isle of Man, who seized the government vessel, its firearms, and four of its crew, who then were held prisoner for six months. The *Sincerity* was set adrift.

Between 1763 and 1783, the number of Customs' cruisers was increased from 22 to 42 vessels. However, they were outnumbered by local fleets of specially built small vessels–wherries, pinnaces, barges, and galleys–that could work the shallows and the creeks, and were both outnumbered and out-gunned by larger smuggler-owned vessels carrying 16 to 18 guns. In the county of Devon alone, the smuggling fleet included 25 armed vessels of up to 100 tons each.

Cutter.

43

"Perfectly right," he interrupted very cheerily, "perfectly right—a gentleman and a magistrate. And, now I come to think of it, I might as well ride round there myself and report to him or squire. Master Pew's dead, when all's done; not that I regret it, but he's dead, you see, and people will make it out against an officer of his Majesty's revenue, if make it out they can. Now, I'll tell you, Hawkins, if you like, I'll take you along."

I thanked him heartily for the offer, and we walked back to the hamlet where the horses were. By the time I had told mother of my purpose they were all in the saddle.

"Dogger," said Mr. Dance, "you have a good horse; take up this lad behind you."

As soon as I was mounted, holding on to Dogger's belt, the supervisor gave the word, and the party struck out at a bouncing trot on the road to Dr. Livesey's house.

Chapter Six

The Captain's Papers

WE RODE HARD ALL the way till we drew up before Dr. Livesey's door. The house was all dark to the front.

Mr. Dance told me to jump down and knock, and Dogger gave me a stirrup to descend by. The door was opened almost at once by the maid.

"Is Dr. Livesey in?" I asked.

No, she said, he had come home in the afternoon but had gone up to the hall to dine and pass the evening with the squire.

"So there we go, boys," said Mr. Dance.

This time, as the distance was short, I did not mount, but ran with Dogger's stirrup-leather to the lodge gates[1] and up the long, leafless, moonlit avenue to where the white line of the hall buildings looked on either hand on great old gardens. Here Mr. Dance dismounted, and taking me along with him, was admitted at a word into the house.

The servant led us down a matted passage and showed us at the end into a great library, all lined with

1. In the sense intended here, a lodge is a small house that stands at the entrance gate to a usually long private road leading to a large house set in a park. Its purpose was not so much to serve as a guard post but rather to prepare the visitor for the look-at-me splendor that lay ahead.

"The pretentious rather than the practical was of its essence: it was by nature a frontispiece before it was a dwelling," wrote Timothy Mowl in *The Evolution of the Park Gate Lodge as a Building Type*.

Squire Trelawney was rich but not ducally rich, so he probably had a modest house guarding the entrance to the hall.

bookcases and busts upon the top of them, where the squire and Dr. Livesey sat, pipe in hand, on either side of a bright fire.

I had never seen the squire so near at hand. He was a tall man, over six feet high, and broad in proportion, and he had a bluff, rough-and-ready face, all roughened and reddened and lined in his long travels. His eyebrows were very black, and moved readily, and this gave him a look of some temper, not bad, you would say, but quick and high.

"Come in, Mr. Dance," says he, very stately and condescending.

"Good evening, Dance," says the doctor with a nod. "And good evening to you, friend Jim. What good wind brings you here?"

The supervisor stood up straight and stiff and told his story like a lesson; and you should have seen how the two gentlemen leaned forward and looked at each other, and forgot to smoke in their surprise and interest. When they heard how my mother went back to the inn, Dr. Livesey fairly slapped his thigh, and the squire cried "Bravo!" and broke his long pipe against the grate. Long before it was done, Mr. Trelawney (that, you will remember, was the squire's name) had got up from his seat and was striding about the room, and the doctor, as if to hear the better, had taken off his powdered wig and sat

The doctor opened the seals with great care, and there fell out the map of an island.

there looking very strange indeed with his own close-cropped black poll.

At last Mr. Dance finished the story.

"Mr. Dance," said the squire, "you are a very noble fellow. And as for riding down that black, atrocious miscreant, I regard it as an act of virtue, sir, like stamping on a cockroach. This lad Hawkins is a trump,[2] I perceive. Hawkins, will you ring that bell? Mr. Dance must have some ale."

"And so, Jim," said the doctor, "you have the thing that they were after, have you?"

"Here it is, sir," said I, and gave him the oilskin packet.

The doctor looked it all over, as if his fingers were itching to open it; but instead of doing that, he put it quietly in the pocket of his coat.

"Squire," said he, "when Dance has had his ale he must, of course, be off on his Majesty's service; but I mean to keep Jim Hawkins here to sleep at my house, and with your permission, I propose we should have up the cold pie and let him sup."

"As you will, Livesey," said the squire; "Hawkins has earned better than cold pie."

So a big pigeon pie was brought in and put on a sidetable, and I made a hearty supper, for I was as hungry as a hawk, while Mr. Dance was further complimented and at last dismissed.

"And now, squire," said the doctor.

"And now, Livesey," said the squire in the same breath.

"One at a time, one at a time," laughed Dr. Livesey. "You have heard of this Flint, I suppose?"

"Heard of him!" cried the squire. "Heard of him, you

2. A word not much used anymore for a person who is helpful beyond the normal call of duty, a person who might even be considered a splendid chap in a later age.

3. Blackbeard was bad enough, but compared to Flint he was relatively harmless. The worst atrocity committed by the pirate Blackbeard seems to have been shooting one of his officers, Israel Hands, through the knee during a drinking bout, and the ships he plundered seem to have had more in common with grocery stores than treasure ships. (We are not told what kin the Israel Hands who served on the *Hispaniola* was to the Israel Hands who served with Blackbeard.)

Blackbeard was not a major figure in terms of plunder taken. His first biographer, Captain Charles Johnson, in his *General History of the Pyrates* (1724), listed ships and cargoes taken by Blackbeard. Other than 1,500 pounds sterling in gold and silver taken in 1717, Blackbeard's most noteworthy plunder seems to have been confined to a cargo of sugar and cocoa, a barrel of indigo dye, a bale of cotton, provisions, ships' stores, and 14 slaves. Angus Konstam, a recent biographer, has identified cargoes of Madeira wine, wheat, and wooden staves as being captured by Blackbeard. He also traded five vessels taken off Charleston for 300 to 400 pounds sterling worth of medical supplies.

What Blackbeard did have was presence: the big beard, of course, the bows on that beard, the burning fuses stuck under the brim of his hat. He was a character.

According to Konstam, Blackbeard was the nickname for Edward Teach, and his origins are obscure. Captain Charles Johnson says Teach was from Bristol. The identity of Johnson himself is a mystery. One school of thought holds that Johnson was Daniel Defoe using court records, letters, and newspaper reports as his sources. Others think Defoe did not have the technical knowledge that Johnson displays of sea and ships.

4. An island off the coast of modern Venezuela. What Squire Trelawney was doing there at all is a puzzle. In his day Trinidad was a poor, isolated, virtually uninhabited and undeveloped backwater of Spanish America. A 1777 census reported that just 1,410 people lived on the island.

Trinidad was so poor that in 1757 members of the city council of the village of San José de Oruña, which had served for many years as the principal settlement on the island, claimed they did not own a single sheet of paper between them on which to write the required government re-

say! He was the bloodthirstiest[3] buccaneer that sailed. Blackbeard was a child to Flint. The Spaniards were so prodigiously afraid of him that, I tell you, sir, I was sometimes proud he was an Englishman. I've seen his top-sails with these eyes, off Trinidad,[4] and the cowardly son of a rum-puncheon[5] that I sailed with put back—put back, sir, into Port of Spain."[6]

"Well, I've heard of him myself, in England," said the doctor. "But the point is, had he money?"

"Money!" cried the squire. "Have you heard the story? What were these villains after but money? What do they care for but money? For what would they risk their rascal carcasses but money?"

"That we shall soon know," replied the doctor. "But you are so confoundedly hot-headed and exclamatory that I cannot get a word in. What I want to know is this: Supposing that I have here in my pocket some clue to where Flint buried his treasure, will that treasure amount to much?"

"Amount, sir!" cried the squire. "It will amount to this: If we have the clue you talk about, I fit out a ship in Bristol dock, and take you and Hawkins here along, and I'll have that treasure if I search a year."

"Very well," said the doctor. "Now, then, if Jim is agreeable, we'll open the packet"; and he laid it before him on the table.

The bundle was sewn together, and the doctor had to get out his instrument case and cut the stitches with his medical scissors. It contained two things—a book and a sealed paper.

"First of all we'll try the book," observed the doctor.

The squire and I were both peering over his shoulder as he opened it, for Dr. Livesey had kindly motioned me to come round from the side-table, where I had been eating, to enjoy the sport of the search. On the first page there were only some scraps of writing, such as a man with a pen in his hand might make for idleness or practice. One was the same as the tattoo mark, "Billy Bones his fancy"; then there was "Mr. W. Bones, mate," "No more rum," "Off Palm Key he got itt," and some other snatches, mostly single words and unintelligible. I could not help wondering who it was that had "got itt," and what "itt" was that he got. A knife in his back as like as not.

"Not much instruction there," said Dr. Livesey as he passed on.

The next ten or twelve pages were filled with a curious series of entries. There was a date at one end of the line and at the other a sum of money, as in common account-books, but instead of explanatory writing, only a varying number of crosses between the two. On the 12th of June, 1745, for instance, a sum of seventy pounds had plainly become due to someone, and there was nothing but six crosses to explain the cause. In a few cases, to be sure, the name of a place would be added, as "Offe Caraccas,"[7] or a mere entry of latitude and longitude,[8] as "62° 17' 20", 19° 2' 40"."

The record lasted over nearly twenty years, the amount of the separate entries growing larger as time went on, and at the end a grand total had been made out after five or six wrong additions, and these words appended, "Bones, his pile."

"I can't make head or tail of this," said Dr. Livesey.

"The thing is as clear as noonday," cried the squire. "This is the black-hearted hound's account-book. These crosses stand for the names of ships or towns

ports. At least that is what they claimed. Today the independent Republic of Trinidad and Tobago is known for its petroleum and natural gas resources.

5. A wooden cask that in the 1750s typically contained between 90 and 120 U.S. gallons of rum, although sometimes 130-gallon versions, requiring a cask almost four feet tall, were used.

The gallon here is the U.S. gallon, which started life as Queen Anne's wine gallon, defined by the British parliament in 1707 and still used in the U.S. at the gas pump and the milk jug at the supermarket. Other countries, including Britain and Canada, now use the larger "imperial gallon" of 1824 informally and the metric system formally.

6. In Squire Trelawney's day, Port of Spain (Puerto de España) was a seaside hamlet on Trinidad's Gulf of Paria that in 1754 replaced nearby San José de Oruña as Trinidad's principal European settlement. It is today the capital of Trinidad and Tobago.

7. Caracas is the capital of modern Venezuela, but "Offe La Guaira" would be more precise, since La Guaira is the port that serves Caracas, which is some miles inland.

La Guaira's two protecting forts and 44 pieces of artillery did not save the port from being overwhelmed by French buccaneers in 1680, although troops from Caracas soon arrived to force them away. The Spanish government added more fortifications to the area, which served to repel a British naval force that attacked La Guaira in 1743.

8. The introduction notes (on p. xxiii) that using the coordinates Billy Bones recorded and assuming Greenwich as the site of longitude 0 leaves us with four possibilities for the location of Treasure Island, too far north and too far south. Why we are faced with four choices is a function of how the latitude and longitude grid system works. *Latitude* refers to horizontal parallel lines that circle the earth starting at the equator. They are spaced apart at regular intervals (called *degrees*) of about 69 miles until they reach both poles. At the equator you are at 0 degrees latitude. At 90 degrees north latitude you are at the North Pole. At 90 degrees south latitude you are at the South Pole.

Longitude refers to the parallel vertical lines, also called meridians, that are divided into degrees that also circle the globe but stretch up and down from pole to pole. They extend for 180 degrees east of longitude 0 and 180 west of longitude 0, also called the Prime Meridian. Longitude 0 can theoretically be anywhere. The British started using Greenwich 0 Longitude in 1767; in 1884 other countries also agreed to use that location.

By convention, each degree of latitude and longitude is subdivided into 60 smaller *minutes*, and each minute is subdivided into 60 even smaller *seconds*.

We are left in the dark about the location of Treasure Island because there is no indication whether the notation *latitude 62 degrees 17 minutes and 20 seconds* refers to a line of latitude north or south of the equator. Nor is there any indication whether the notation *longitude 19 degrees 2 minutes and 40 seconds* refers to a line of longitude east or west of longitude 0, the prime meridian.

There also is a second mystery here, and it has to do with the precision with which the chart location is noted.

A position recorded, as Billy Bones did, in degrees-minutes-seconds of latitude and longitude is precise to about 100 feet. Nevertheless the timekeeping technology needed when determining longitude at sea was still under development when Bones was abroad. The first reliable and highly accurate timekeeper for seagoing use, a three-pound, five-inch-diameter watch designed by John Harrison, was completed in 1759. Given the designation "H-4," it was tested, along with two other copies, only in 1761/62 on a voyage to Jamaica and back.

There is also the possibility that one of Billy Bones's shipmates was familiar with the so-called "lunar distance" method of finding longitude without a clock. The method was being developed in the mid-18th century and was used into the 19th century by ship masters who could not afford accurate chronometers or wanted to check their chronometers.

The lunar method relies on three things: the predictability of the orbit of the moon as a way to measure time; the ability to use a sextant to measure the relationship between the horizon, the moon, and a star or the sun; and the availability of tables of pre-computed calculations called

that they sank or plundered. The sums are the scoundrel's share, and where he feared an ambiguity, you see he added something clearer. 'Offe Caraccas,' now; you see, here was some unhappy vessel boarded off that coast. God help the poor souls that manned her—coral long ago."

"Right!" said the doctor. "See what it is to be a traveller. Right! And the amounts increase, you see, as he rose in rank."

There was little else in the volume but a few bearings of places noted in the blank leaves towards the end and a table for reducing French, English, and Spanish moneys to a common value.

"Thrifty man!" cried the doctor. "He wasn't the one to be cheated."

"And now," said the squire, "for the other."

The paper had been sealed in several places with a thimble by way of seal; the very thimble, perhaps, that I had found in the captain's pocket. The doctor opened the seals with great care, and there fell out the map of an island, with latitude and longitude, soundings,[9] names of hills and bays and inlets, and every particular that would be needed to bring a ship to a safe anchorage upon its shores. It was about nine miles long and five across, shaped, you might say, like a fat dragon standing up, and had two fine land-locked harbours, and a hill in the centre part marked "The Spy-glass." There were several additions of a later date, but above all, three crosses of red ink—two on the north part of the island, one in the southwest—and beside this last, in the same red ink, and in a small, neat hand, very different from the captain's tottery characters, these words: "Bulk of treasure here."

Over on the back the same hand had written this further information:

Tall tree, Spy-glass shoulder, bearing a point[10] to the N. of N.N.E. Skeleton Island E.S.E. and by E. Ten feet.

The bar silver[11] is in the north cache; you can find it by the trend of the east hummock, ten fathoms[12] south of the black crag with the face on it.

The arms are easy found, in the sand-hill, N. point of north inlet cape, bearing E. and a quarter N.

J.F.

That was all; but brief as it was, and to me incomprehensible, it filled the squire and Dr. Livesey with delight.

"Livesey," said the squire, "you will give up this wretched practice at once. Tomorrow I start for Bristol. In three weeks' time—three weeks!—two weeks—ten days—we'll have the best ship, sir, and the choicest crew in England. Hawkins shall come as cabin-boy. You'll make a famous cabin-boy, Hawkins. You, Livesey, are ship's doctor; I am admiral. We'll take Redruth, Joyce, and Hunter. We'll have favourable winds, a quick passage, and not the least difficulty in finding the spot, and money to eat, to roll in, to play duck and drake[13] with ever after."

"Trelawney," said the doctor, "I'll go with you; and I'll go bail for it, so will Jim, and be a credit to the undertaking. There's only one man I'm afraid of."

"And who's that?" cried the squire. "Name the dog, sir!"

"You," replied the doctor; "for you cannot hold your tongue. We are not the only men who know of this

"lunar tables" to translate observations into points on a chart. In the early 1750s, accurate tables were just being developed by the German astronomer Tobias Mayer. They were later expanded on by the British.

Again, it is possible that a member of Flint's crew had both the interest and ability to keep up with developments in the lunar distance method, which at that time took about four hours to compute. There was the occasional pirate, such as William Dampier, who was interested in science. Whether these events are probable is another matter.

9. Measurements showing how deep the water is. In the 1700s the measurements were made by dropping over the side a marked line 25 fathoms– 150 feet–long with a 7- to 10-pound lead weight at the end and waiting for it to hit bottom. The line was marked at intervals of 2, 3, 5, 7, 10, 13, 15, 17 and 20 fathoms. A ship's boat might also be equipped with a slightly different line length, markings, and lead. The system of markings had been essentially the same since 1600.

10. In the era when the *Hispaniola* operated, the compass card was divided into 32 points rather than the 360 degrees we use today. Each point was the equivalent of 11¼ degrees. Orders regarding changes in the ship's course were given to the helmsman in points and, if more precision was needed, half and quarter points. The bearings on the treasure map are *compass bearings*. (For *relative bearings*, see note 13 on p. 82.) The compass card was divided as shown in the illustration below.

Compass card.

11. See note 5 on p. 35. It is reasonable to assume that the bar silver in Billy Bones's account book was silver from Spanish America, which between 1550 and 1800 accounted for more than 80 percent of the world's production. By one count, between 1540 and 1700 Spanish America produced about 50,000 tons of silver, with more than 70 percent coming from Potosi in modern Bolivia.

12. Ten fathoms is 60 feet. *Fathom*–an old word meaning "six feet"–dates back to the Anglo-Saxon period of English history, roughly A.D. 550 to 1066, long before modern English evolved.

Anglo-Saxons used a rough and ready way to define some units of measurement: they would spread their arms wide, and the distance between the two hands translates, in modern English, as the unit they called "fathom measure," from their word *faedum*, meaning "embracing arms." It's about six feet. (Our word "feet" is the Anglo-Saxon *fet*, another rough and ready measure.)

13. Duck and drake is a game in which players find small flat stones near a stretch of water and throw them with a sideways, underarm wrist motion. Thrown correctly, a stone will "skip," barely touching the surface of the water, and bounce several times before sinking. The person whose rock skips the most times wins. Coins, since they are flat, would be perfect for playing the game, although that would be expensive. But Squire Trelawney is expecting to find more treasure than he knows what to do with.

paper. These fellows who attacked the inn tonight—bold, desperate blades, for sure—and the rest who stayed aboard that lugger, and more, I dare say, not far off, are, one and all, through thick and thin, bound that they'll get that money. We must none of us go alone till we get to sea. Jim and I shall stick together in the meanwhile; you'll take Joyce and Hunter when you ride to Bristol, and from first to last, not one of us must breathe a word of what we've found."

"Livesey," returned the squire, "you are always in the right of it. I'll be as silent as the grave."

PART II

The
Sea Cook

Chapter Seven

I Go to Bristol

IT WAS LONGER THAN the squire imagined ere we were ready for the sea, and none of our first plans—not even Dr. Livesey's, of keeping me beside him—could be carried out as we intended. The doctor had to go to London for a physician to take charge of his practice; the squire was hard at work at Bristol; and I lived on at the hall under the charge of old Redruth, the gamekeeper,[1] almost a prisoner, but full of sea-dreams and the most charming anticipations of strange islands and adventures. I brooded by the hour together over the map, all the details of which I well remembered. Sitting by the fire in the housekeeper's room, I approached that island in my fancy from every possible direction; I explored every acre of its surface; I climbed a thousand times to that tall hill they call the Spy-glass, and from the top enjoyed the most wonderful and changing prospects. Sometimes the isle was thick with savages, with whom we fought, sometimes full of dangerous animals that hunted us, but in

1. Redruth served as Squire Trelawney's private gamewarden, protecting his lands from hunters and fishermen, and managing the wildlife. His legal authority in that era was formidable and included powers of arrest, search, and seizure.

2. The year is most likely 1758. Here are the clues: Captain Flint, near death in Savannah, gives the treasure map to Billy Bones on July 20, 1754, according to the date on the map. Three of the years that follow are accounted for by the activities of Blind Pew and Ben Gunn. Going forward three years after July 20, 1754, brings us to July 1757. But Squire Trelawney in Bristol has dated his letter "March 1," not July, so 1757 does not work. We know Blind Pew spent all his money in one year and was a virtual beggar for two. Presumably he needed time to get across the Atlantic, a trip that could be lengthy on a sailing ship as seasonal bad weather sets in during autumn and winter. Ben Gunn also had needed time to both find a ship and enough time to irritate his new shipmates to the point that they marooned him on Treasure Island, where he was found three years later by Jim Hawkins. So add a few months and March 1, 1758, makes sense. Harold Francis Watson makes a similar case for 1758 in his *Coasts of Treasure Island*, a survey of 19th-century sea novels, and also asks the question: How did the pirates find Billy Bones in his remote hideout? (For more on Silver's age, see note 7 on p. 89.)

3. Livesey had a long, slow trip ahead of him. London was a 48-hour stagecoach journey from Bristol in 1750.

4. Squire Trelawney forgot his seafaring days when he called the *Hispaniola* a ship. Mariners of the period made a distinction between "ships" and other sailing vessels, and the distinction was based on the way they were rigged, not their size. A ship was a vessel with three masts rigged for sails square on each mast, with each mast composed of three sections. The *Hispaniola* was a schooner–a vessel with two masts and big fore-and-aft sails and square topsails. It was, therefore, not a ship. (See illustration, p. xiii.)

Incidentally, in this case "square" does not refer to the shape of the sail but rather to the way the sail is hung from a mast via a crosspiece or spar known as a yard. If the spar is attached square on the mast–that is, at right angles–the sail is called a square sail.

All vessels reflect compromises in their design, and 18th-century sailing vessels were no exception. An owner could specify that he wanted a vessel built that was fast, could carry a lot of

all my fancies nothing occurred to me so strange and tragic as our actual adventures.

So the weeks passed on, till one fine day there came a letter addressed to Dr. Livesey, with this addition, "To be opened, in the case of his absence, by Tom Redruth or young Hawkins." Obeying this order, we found, or rather I found—for the gamekeeper was a poor hand at reading anything but print—the following important news:

OLD ANCHOR INN, BRISTOL, MARCH 1, 17—[2]

Dear Livesey—As I do not know whether you are at the hall or still in London,[3] I send this in double to both places.

The ship[4] is bought and fitted. She lies at anchor, ready for sea. You never imagined a sweeter schooner[5]—a child might sail her—two hundred tons;[6] name, *Hispaniola*.[7]

I got her through my old friend, Blandly, who has proved himself throughout the most surprising trump. The admirable fellow literally slaved in my interest, and so, I may say, did everyone in Bristol, as soon as they got wind of the port we sailed for—treasure, I mean.

"Redruth," said I, interrupting the letter, "Dr. Livesey will not like that. The squire has been talking, after all."

"Well, who's a better right?" growled the gamekeeper. "A pretty rum go if squire ain't to talk for Dr. Livesey, I should think."

At that I gave up all attempt at commentary and read straight on:

Blandly himself found the *Hispaniola*, and by the most admirable management got her for the merest trifle. There is a class of men in Bristol monstrously prejudiced against Blandly. They go the length of declaring that this honest creature would do anything for money, that the *Hispaniola* belonged to him, and that he sold it me absurdly high—the most transparent calumnies. None of them dare, however, to deny the merits of the ship.

*I said good–bye to mother and the cove
and to dear old Admiral Benbow.*

cargo, could sail almost into the wind and so avoid a lot of zigzagging–"tacking"–when going from point A to point B, and be handled by a small crew so he could save money on wages. If he was lucky he got two of these attributes in a vessel.

For example, the kind of sails a vessel carried would affect speed, but so would the shape of the hull. A slim, fast hull would help speed, but carry less cargo.

A ship-rigged vessel with three masts and square sails would be faster in the right conditions than a vessel rigged with fore-and-aft sails, but would need a bigger crew and would need to tack more often when sailing into the wind.

A simple sloop with a big fore-and-aft mainsail might get by with a small crew, but there was a limit on how big the mainsail could get before it became too heavy to manage.

Ship definitions could get confusing for landsmen because ship owners and builders tinkered with how many square sails and fore-and-aft sails and triangular sails they mounted on their vessels. A square-rigger might have as many fore-and-aft sails as square sails, although they were smaller. And if the wind was strong a ship might shorten its square sails and just use its fore-and-aft "try sails."

For example, the *Bounty* of mutiny fame, which started life as small cargo vessel of about the same tonnage as the *Hispaniola* (almost 221 tons versus 200), could carry a total of 29 sails on three masts and her bowsprit, which resembles a small mast projecting up at an angle from the bow. The *Bounty* carried eight square sails of varying sizes. She also carried nine fore-and-aft sails, also of varying sizes. Captain Bligh reported *Bounty* was "an excellent sea boat."

5. See "You never imagined a sweeter schooner" on p. xii and the illustration on p. xiii.

6. Two hundred tons. See the introduction, p. xiv.

7. *Hispaniola* is an appropriate name for a vessel sailing with a crew of unreformed pirates, since *Hispaniola* was one of the islands in the Caribbean Sea that gave birth to the buccaneer crews of the 1600s who operated from Tortuga, Petit-Goave, Leogane, and Port-de-Paix.

Today, the Spanish-speaking Dominican

Republic occupies the eastern two-thirds of the island; the French-speaking Republic of Haiti occupies the western third, or an area about the size of Maryland. The island was named Isla Espanola by Christopher Columbus in 1492.

Hispaniola is the site of the oldest Spanish settlement in the Americas.

The western portion was not settled extensively by the Spaniards in the 1600s, and the vacuum attracted French-speaking cattle hunters and others from neighboring islands, many of whom used the area as a base for piracy and privateering raids. Spain recognized France's control over the part now known as Haiti in 1697.

By the time the *Hispaniola* made its voyage to Treasure Island, the French had created one of the largest and richest sugar-producing areas in the world, using the labor of enslaved people. During the French Revolution the largest slave revolts in Caribbean history, involving nearly half a million people, ended the French presence and led to the creation of an independent Haiti in 1804.

8. *Deuce*, a word that dates back to the 1600s, is a synonym for *devil*. And the squire would indeed have a problem finding a crew: Britain was beginning the third year of what would be called the Seven Years' War (1756–1763) in Britain and the French and Indian War in America. Britain fought France, which was later joined by Spain. It was the first truly global war in history, and seamen were in demand. Squire Trelawney was competing for seamen with four groups of employers (see the introduction, p. xx).

9. In the next chapter, Jim Hawkins describes John Silver as "very tall and strong, with a face as big as a ham–plain and pale, but intelligent and smiling." Silver reminded Robert Louis Stevenson of his friend the poet, critic, and editor W. E. Henley. Henley's physical appearance–he was big and also one-legged–and several facets of his character and personality were similar to Silver's, Stevenson told his friend in a letter. In particular, Steven saw Henley's "masterfulness" and "maimed strength" in Silver, as well as his ability to evoke dread.

Henley is perhaps best known today as the author of the 1875 poem "Invictus," with its lines "I am the master of my fate: / I am the captain of

So far there was not a hitch. The workpeople, to be sure—riggers and what not—were most annoyingly slow; but time cured that. It was the crew that troubled me.

I wished a round score of men—in case of natives, buccaneers, or the odious French—and I had the worry of the deuce[8] itself to find so much as half a dozen, till the most remarkable stroke of fortune brought me the very man that I required.

I was standing on the dock, when, by the merest accident, I fell in talk with him. I found he was an old sailor, kept a public-house, knew all the seafaring men in Bristol, had lost his health ashore, and wanted a good berth as cook to get to sea again. He had hobbled down there that morning, he said, to get a smell of the salt.

I was monstrously touched—so would you have been—and, out of pure pity, I engaged him on the spot to be ship's cook. Long John Silver,[9] he is called, and has lost a leg; but that I regarded as a recommendation, since he lost it in his country's service, under the immortal

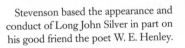

Stevenson based the appearance and conduct of Long John Silver in part on his good friend the poet W. E. Henley.

Hawke.[10] He has no pension, Livesey. Imagine the abominable age we live in!

Well, sir, I thought I had only found a cook, but it was a crew I had discovered. Between Silver and myself we got together in a few days a company of the toughest old salts imaginable—not pretty to look at, but fellows, by their faces, of the most indomitable spirit. I declare we could fight a frigate.[11]

Long John even got rid of two out of the six or seven I had already engaged. He showed me in a moment that they were just the sort of fresh-water swabs we had to fear in an adventure of importance.

I am in the most magnificent health and

Admiral Edward Hawke was known for his good judgment and for being a humane officer.

A Royal Navy frigate had a semi-open upper deck for its guns and a deck below to house the crew. Frigates were used to patrol, scout, escort convoys, and attack enemy merchant ships.

my soul" and also the often-quoted passage "My head is bloody but unbowed."

Henley worked with Stevenson on *Dr. Jekyll and Mr. Hyde*, eventually quarreled with Stevenson, and became a critic of his work.

10. Admiral Edward Hawke (1705–1781) had a reputation for being a humane commander and an officer who led by example.

Hawke was known to his peers for good tactical judgment, especially for his insistence that his captains bring their ships to within less than 50 yards–"pistol shot" distance–from an enemy ship before opening fire.

Hawke would have won Squire Trelawney's admiration for his action at the Battle of Toulon in 1744 against a Franco-Spanish fleet, described by one naval historian as a "fiasco," except for Captain Hawke's capture of the Spanish *Poder* in spite of having a largely inexperienced and sickly crew.

He would also have won the squire's admiration for his 1747 actions against a French fleet. Hawke, now an admiral, led a British force of 14 ships against eight vessels that were protecting a convoy of about 150 ships. Six of the French line-of-battle ships, including three that were larger than any of the British ships, surrendered. About 4,000 hard-to-replace seamen were lost to the French fleet.

The fight made Hawke. He was promoted, made a knight, and elected to Parliament, and he shared in "prize money" payments when the navy bought the captured ships.

Hawke's most enduring fame was earned for his victory in 1759, at the Battle of Quiberon Bay, which was fought in a November gale off a dangerous coast with night coming on, a year after the *Hispaniola* returned from Treasure Island.

11. A frigate could be a ship-rigged merchant ship with a distinctive stern or a small, fast warship. Jobs for navy frigates included relaying orders, an important job in a pre-radio age when specialized flags were used to communicate between ships and a fleet might be spread over several miles of ocean. Other jobs included extending the range of what the fleet could see by scouting ahead with other frigates and relaying back what they saw, escorting convoys, and attacking enemy merchant ships.

12. Mariners who have spent many years at sea. There are four additional meanings for the term *old tarpaulin*. A *tarpaulin* was canvas waterproofed with tar or oil and used, for example, to seal a hatch cover. There was also *paulin*, which was canvas waterproofed with paint. Tarpaulin was also used as material for foul-weather gear by seamen, and became another name for a sailor, abbreviated as *tar*. And in the 17th century an old tarpaulin was an officer who had spent many years learning his business on merchant ships before joining a Royal Navy ship.

13. The phrase is an abbreviation of "Come post-haste"–in other words, "Come quickly."

14. Writing on March 1, Squire Trelawney is allowing six months to travel to Treasure Island and return home. Six months should be plenty of time, based on the schedules established by the first regular mail or "packet" service operated by Edmund Dummer between England and five ports in the Caribbean between 1702 and 1709. Dummer's service in the first year made nine voyages in all seasons, using sloops with fore-and-aft sails. The roundtrips averaged 104 days each.

15. On a merchant vessel the commanding officer was the *master*. On a Royal Navy vessel the *master* was in charge of navigating the vessel, taking it wherever its commander directed.

In the Royal Navy of the 1700s the sailing master was a warrant officer rather than a commissioned officer. The navy made a distinction between sea officers appointed by Admiralty commission and sea officers appointed by warrant from one of the navy's administrative boards. Warrant officers were subordinate to officers of the rank of lieutenant and above. In the U.S. and Britain and a number of other countries today, the distinction between a commissioned officer and a warrant officer is maintained in the armed services.

The term *sea officer* was used to describe what we today would call a naval officer. In those days a *naval officer* was an administrative official of the Navy Board, not a seagoing officer; the term came into its present use in the 1800s.

Clearly, Squire Trelawney plans on being his

spirits, eating like a bull, sleeping like a tree, yet I shall not enjoy a moment till I hear my old tarpaulins[12] tramping round the capstan. Seaward ho! Hang the treasure! It's the glory of the sea that has turned my head. So now, Livesey, come post;[13] do not lose an hour, if you respect me.

Let young Hawkins go at once to see his mother, with Redruth for a guard; and then both come full speed to Bristol.

JOHN TRELAWNEY

POSTSCRIPT—I did not tell you that Blandly, who, by the way, is to send a consort after us if we don't turn up by the end of August,[14] had found an admirable fellow for sailing master[15]—a stiff man, which I regret, but in all other respects a treasure. Long John Silver unearthed a very competent man for a mate, a man named Arrow. I have a boatswain who pipes,[16] Livesey; so things shall go man-o'-war fashion on board the good ship *Hispaniola*.

I forgot to tell you that Silver is a man of substance; I know of my own knowledge that he has a banker's account,[17] which has never been overdrawn. He leaves his wife to manage the inn; and as she is a woman of colour,[18] a pair of old bachelors like you and I may be excused for guessing that it is the wife, quite as much as the health, that sends him back to roving.

J. T.

P.P.S.—Hawkins may stay one night with his mother.

J. T.

You can fancy the excitement into which that letter put me. I was half beside myself with glee; and if ever

I despised a man, it was old Tom Redruth, who could do nothing but grumble and lament. Any of the under-gamekeepers would gladly have changed places with him; but such was not the squire's pleasure, and the squire's pleasure was like law among them all. Nobody but old Redruth would have dared so much as even to grumble.

The next morning he and I set out on foot for the Admiral Benbow, and there I found my mother in good health and spirits. The captain, who had so long been a cause of so much discomfort, was gone where the wicked cease from troubling. The squire had had everything repaired, and the public rooms and the sign repainted, and had added some furniture—above all a beautiful armchair for mother in the bar. He had found her a boy as an apprentice also so that she should not want help while I was gone.

It was on seeing that boy that I understood, for the first time, my situation. I had thought up to that moment of the adventures before me, not at all of the home that I was leaving; and now, at sight of this clumsy stranger, who was to stay here in my place beside my mother, I had my first attack of tears. I am afraid I led that boy a dog's life, for as he was new to the work, I had a hundred opportunities of setting him right and putting him down, and I was not slow to profit by them.

The night passed, and the next day, after dinner, Redruth and I were afoot again and on the road. I said good-bye to mother and the cove where I had lived since I was born, and the dear old Admiral Benbow—since he was repainted, no longer quite so dear. One of my last thoughts was of the captain, who had so

own captain, while his sailing master will take care of the hands-on details of sailing and operating the *Hispaniola*, which require an experienced seaman.

16. See note 9 on p. 25.

17. Bank accounts were not the mass-market consumer products they are today. They were for the well-to-do and for businesses, so it is significant that the Silvers had a bank account. John Silver and his wife would have had an account either at Bristol's first banking company, Tyndall, Lloyd & Co., opened on Broad Street in 1750, or at the second, Goldney, Smith & Co. on Corn Street, opened in 1752. Thomas Goldney II was the biggest single shareholder of the 15 investors who sponsored the 1708 around-the-world privateering voyage by Captain Woodes Rogers.

During the voyage, Rogers stopped at a small island in the Pacific. One of the shore parties returned "and brought an abundance of craw-fish, with a man cloth'd in goat-skins, who looked wilder than the first owners of them. He had been on the island four years and four months." He was Alexander Selkirk, the model for Robinson Crusoe. Later they attacked and looted the city of Guayaquil and captured a Spanish ship en route from Manila to Acapulco that was filled, literally, with treasures.

Later, Rogers was commissioned to close down the pirate community on New Providence Island in the Bahamas. See p. xxiv.

18. Mrs. Silver would not have seemed unusual in the Bristol of the 1750s. The port city had had a few black residents on its streets since about the 1590s, when the Young family employed a black gardener, whose name was not recorded.

Nor was Mrs. Silver the first black woman to work in a Bristol pub. The Horsehead Tavern on Christmas Street (the street still exists, but not the tavern) employed one until her death in 1612. Whether she was a free person or enslaved is not known.

Bristol was one of the principal actors in Britain's share of the trade in enslaved people, which in the 18th century delivered an estimated 2.7 million men, women, and children to the Americas from Africa.

For the most part, Bristol ships picked up their

cargoes from slave-collection points along a 2,000-mile arc of West Africa that started at the Senegal River, continued past Bence Island (a.k.a. Bunce Island), which offered slavers a golf course and slave caddies in kilts, and curved up to Benin and down to Angola. The vessels then headed across the Atlantic to sell their cargoes.

By the time the *Hispaniola* sailed, an average of 21 Bristol ships a year were delivering between them an average of just over 5,000 enslaved Africans each year to the Americas.

Whites were also shipped to North America from Bristol and sold. Some were convicts working off 7- or 14-year sentences. Others were serving out work contracts known as indentures. The contracts could be sold.

Bristol merchants worked at maintaining good relations with the African suppliers of enslaved labor. Gonglass, the son of one such trader–thought to be the West African John Currantee of modern Anomabu in Ghana–was in Bristol in the spring of 1759. On April 4 he visited a local church and chatted in French with the minister.

In the 1750s Mrs. Silver would have known of John Quaco, another free black, who lived in Pipe Lane in central Bristol. He had started out as an enslaved man but had gained his freedom and worked a sailor for more than 20 years. He sometimes shipped out on vessels that transported enslaved people to the West Indies.

19. See note 11 on p. 8.

20. A heath is an open area of countryside with poor soil and drainage; its vegetation tends to be scrub-like, and it is usually regarded as wasteland.

21. Horses became tired pulling a coach filled with passengers and had to be changed at intervals or *stages*, typically 10 miles to 15 miles apart.

22. In the 1750s Bristol's U-shaped harbor wrapped itself around the city center. Facing north, Jim Hawkins would have seen the Quay on his left, about a mile long, with vessels from America, the Caribbean, the Baltic and northern Europe, the Mediterranean, and the Netherlands.

From Virginia came tobacco and iron and from South Carolina came rice, deer hides for making

often strode along the beach with his cocked hat, his sabre-cut cheek, and his old brass telescope. Next moment we had turned the corner and my home was out of sight.

The mail picked us up[19] about dusk at the Royal George on the heath.[20] I was wedged in between Redruth and a stout old gentleman, and in spite of the swift motion and the cold night air, I must have dozed a great deal from the very first, and then slept like a log up hill and down dale through stage after stage,[21] for when I was awakened at last it was by a punch in the ribs, and I opened my eyes to find that we were standing still before a large building in a city street and that the day had already broken a long time.

"Where are we?" I asked.

"Bristol," said Tom. "Get down."

Mr. Trelawney had taken up his residence at an inn far down the docks[22] to superintend the work upon the schooner. Thither we had now to walk, and our way, to my great delight, lay along the quays and beside the great multitude of ships of all sizes and rigs and nations.[23] In one sailors were singing at their work, in another there were men aloft, high over my head, hanging to threads that seemed no thicker than a spider's. Though I had lived by the shore all my life, I seemed never to have been near the sea till then. The smell of tar and salt was something new. I saw the most wonderful figureheads,[24] that had all been far over the ocean. I saw, besides, many old sailors, with rings in their ears, and whiskers curled in ringlets, and tarry pigtails, and their swaggering, clumsy sea-walk; and if I had seen as many kings or archbishops I could not have been more delighted.

A ketch is rigged with a small mast behind a large mast. Facing the viewer in the illustration above is the stern, with its big flag, of a navy "bomb ketch," which carried a mortar in front of its main mast.

Snows had two masts and were square rigged, and were very similar to brigs; both were popular cargo carriers.

Sloops, similar to cutters, were characterized by setting a large mainsail. Variations include vessels with long, protruding bowsprits and big jibs (sails) and setting topsails. The rig is still used in modern yachts.

leather goods, and "naval stores," which included pitch and tar. From the Caribbean came sugar for Bristol's sugar refineries, molasses to be turned into rum, rum already distilled, and dyewoods—wood that contained natural dyes for coloring cloth.

Farther up the Quay, in the section known as the Head of the Quay, smaller coasting vessels unloaded coal, cider, corn, flour, and barley from ports along the River Severn. The vessels included Severn trows, which were sailing barges.

On the western flank of the city was the Back, where coasting vessels, single-masted sloops, and large *trows* unloaded, depending on the season, corn, flour, barley, fish, lumber, firewood, and farm produce from the region and Ireland.

23. Jim Hawkins would have seen three-masted ships and other assorted vessels. Cargo carriers with two masts would have included *snows, ketches, brigs,* and *bilanders.* Single-masted vessels would have included *cutters* and *sloops* with one or two masts, and *schooners.*

24. Examples of ships' figureheads placed at the bows of vessels include carvings of a salmon; a man with a turban; a golden eagle; Friar Tuck from the Robin Hood stories; a man with a sword; a woman; a man with a musket; and a man in Scottish highland dress.

The practice of ornamenting the bows of vessels goes back 5,000 years; eyes painted on each side of the bow has been a constant motif over the years. Vessels in Portugal have painted eyes, as do rowboats in Malta, to this day. The introduction of steel hulls in the 1800s led to the gradual disappearance of the figurehead from warships and merchantmen.

The custom of ornamenting the bows of vessels goes back 5,000 years.

25. See note 9 on p. 25.

26. Along with other comments, the reference to stout blue cloth suggests Squire Trelawney might have served in the Royal Navy. It was only in 1748 that the navy adopted blue with a white facing as the standard colors for a sea officer's uniform coat. Before 1748 there was no requirement that officers dress in a uniform manner in the Royal Navy, unlike the French and Spanish navies.

The push for uniform clothing for officers came from the navy's sea officers themselves as part of an effort to define in a more systematic manner the different ranks of the naval service, their status, and who was senior to whom within given ranks. Under the pre-1748 system the long-serving captain of a big line-of-battle ship could be hard put to assert his senior rank over the commander of a small sloop carrying dispatches and give him orders. In 1748 regulations introduced 11 uniform designs that made clear the distinctions between officers of different ranks and seniority.

Seamen did not get a uniform until 1857, and captains were free to direct how their men dressed.

And I was going to sea myself, to sea in a schooner, with a piping boatswain[25] and pig-tailed singing seamen, to sea, bound for an unknown island, and to seek for buried treasures!

While I was still in this delightful dream, we came suddenly in front of a large inn and met Squire Trelawney, all dressed out like a sea-officer, in stout blue cloth,[26] coming out of the door with a smile on his face and a capital imitation of a sailor's walk.

"Here you are," he cried, "and the doctor came last night from London. Bravo! The ship's company complete!"

"Oh, sir," cried I, "when do we sail?"

"Sail!" says he. "We sail tomorrow!"

Chapter Eight

At the Sign of the Spy-glass

WHEN I HAD DONE breakfasting the squire gave me a note addressed to John Silver, at the sign of the Spy-glass, and told me I should easily find the place by following the line of the docks and keeping a bright lookout for a little tavern with a large brass telescope for sign. I set off, overjoyed at this opportunity to see some more of the ships and seamen, and picked my way among a great crowd of people and carts and bales, for the dock was now at its busiest, until I found the tavern in question.

It was a bright enough little place of entertainment. The sign was newly painted; the windows had neat red curtains; the floor was cleanly sanded. There was a street on each side and an open door on both, which made the large, low room pretty clear to see in, in spite of clouds of tobacco smoke.

The customers were mostly seafaring men, and they talked so loudly that I hung at the door, almost afraid to enter.

As I was waiting, a man came out of a side room, and at a glance I was sure he must be Long John. His left leg was cut off close by the hip, and under the left shoulder he carried a crutch, which he managed with wonderful dexterity, hopping about upon it like a bird. He was very tall and strong, with a face as big as a ham—plain and pale, but intelligent and smiling. Indeed, he seemed in the most cheerful spirits, whistling as he moved about among the tables, with a merry word or a slap on the shoulder for the more favoured of his guests.

Now, to tell you the truth, from the very first mention of Long John in Squire Trelawney's letter I had taken a fear in my mind that he might prove to be the very one-legged sailor whom I had watched for so long at the old Benbow. But one look at the man before me was enough. I had seen the captain, and Black Dog, and the blind man, Pew, and I thought I knew what a buccaneer was like—a very different creature, according to me, from this clean and pleasant-tempered landlord.

I plucked up courage at once, crossed the threshold, and walked right up to the man where he stood, propped on his crutch, talking to a customer.

"Mr. Silver, sir?" I asked, holding out the note.

"Yes, my lad," said he; "such is my name, to be sure. And who may you be?" And then as he saw the squire's letter, he seemed to me to give something almost like a start.

"Oh!" said he, quite loud, and offering his hand. "I see. You are our new cabin-boy; pleased I am to see you."

And he took my hand in his large firm grasp.

Just then one of the customers at the far side rose suddenly and made for the door. It was close by him, and he was out in the street in a moment. But his hurry had attracted my notice, and I recognized him at a glance. It was the tallow-faced man, wanting two fingers, who had come first to the Admiral Benbow.

"Oh," I cried, "stop him! It's Black Dog!"

"I don't care two coppers[1] who he is," cried Silver. "But he hasn't paid his score. Harry, run and catch him."

One of the others who was nearest the door leaped up and started in pursuit.

"If he were Admiral Hawke he shall pay his score," cried Silver; and then, relinquishing my hand, "Who did you say he was?" he asked. "Black what?"

"Dog, sir," said I. "Has Mr. Trelawney not told you of the buccaneers? He was one of them."

"So?" cried Silver. "In my

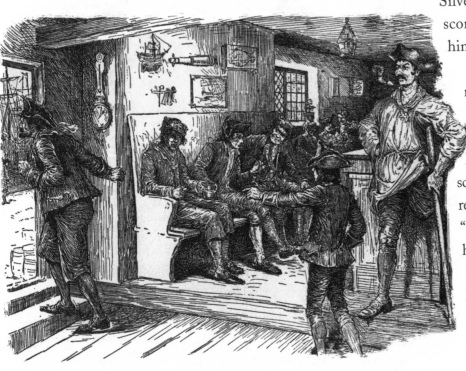

"Oh," I cried, "stop him! It's Black Dog!"

house! Ben, run and help Harry. One of those swabs, was he? Was that you drinking with him, Morgan? Step up here."

The man whom he called Morgan—an old, grey-haired, mahogany-faced sailor—came forward pretty sheepishly, rolling his quid.

"Now, Morgan," said Long John very sternly, "you never clapped your eyes on that Black—Black Dog before, did you, now?"

"Not I, sir," said Morgan with a salute.

"You didn't know his name, did you?"

"No, sir."

"By the powers, Tom Morgan, it's as good for you!" exclaimed the landlord. "If you had been mixed up with the like of that, you would never have put another foot in my house, you may lay to that. And what was he saying to you?"

"I don't rightly know, sir," answered Morgan.

"Do you call that a head on your shoulders, or a blessed dead-eye?"[2] cried Long John. "Don't rightly know, don't you! Perhaps you don't happen to rightly know who you was speaking to, perhaps? Come, now, what was he jawing—v'yages, cap'ns, ships? Pipe up! What was it?"

"We was a-talkin' of keel-hauling,"[3] answered Morgan.

"Keel-hauling, was you? And a mighty suitable thing, too, and you may lay to that. Get back to your place for a lubber, Tom."

And then, as Morgan rolled back to his seat, Silver added to me in a confidential whisper that was very flattering, as I thought, "He's quite an honest man, Tom Morgan, on'y stupid. And now," he ran on again,

1. The coins would have either been *half-pennies* or *farthings*, which were valued at one-quarter of a penny. (For more on the coinage of the 1750s, see the introduction, p. x.)

2. Dead-eyes are non-moving blocks used to attach shrouds (ropes) to different parts of a vessel. Shrouds used to support the lower section of a mast are attached to the hull by dead-eyes. Shrouds used to support upper sections are attached with dead-eyes to crosstrees. (See illustration, p. xiii.)

3. Keel-hauling (or keel-raking) was an exotic and suspiciously over-emphasized punishment described in modern pirate histories: A rope was rigged to pass under the hull of a vessel, and the person being punished was attached to the rope and pulled underwater from one side of the vessel to the other. A weight of iron or lead was attached to the keel-hauled person to keep him clear of the keel, since being scraped against the bottom of a hull encrusted with sharp-edged barnacles was a death sentence. However, actual examples of this punishment being carried out are hard to find.

One recorded example of keel-hauling took place in 1525 when the crew of the *Santa Maria del Parral* mutinied in the Pacific. After seizing the vessel, they killed their captain, Don Jorge Manrique de Najera, by tossing him into the water and throwing lances at him. The mutineers then managed to not only get shipwrecked but also rescued. It was a mixed blessing for one member of the crew. The infuriated commander of the rescuers arrested the leader of the mutiny, keel-hauled him until he died, then cut off his head and left his body for the local wildlife.

Keel-hauling sounds like a lot of trouble to carry out. There were easier ways to punish people, and they show up again and again in the records–hanging, flogging, and so forth, but not keel-hauling.

Keel-hauling is usually referred to as a punishment used on 16th-century and 17th-century Dutch vessels, which, in addition to keel-hauling, administered punishments that included "ducking from the yard-arm and nailing the culprit's hand to the mainmast."

4. Old Bailey Street was the location of the Sessions House, a courthouse that was the site of criminal trials for the city of London and the county of Middlesex. It was also the venue for sessions of the High Court of Admiralty to try crimes "committed on the High Seas." The Sessions House's nickname was the Old Bailey, after the street. Courthouse facilities at the Old Bailey included two iron rings used for holding steady the hands of people sentenced to be branded on the thumb.

The courthouse in the 1750s was next door to Newgate Prison. The "New Gate" started out as one of two entryways through the western side of the Roman and medieval walls of London. The space above the arch of the gate was used as a prison in the 1100s, and modified from time to time, most recently in 1672. Newgate was demolished in the 18th century when the court was enlarged.

The current building we call the Old Bailey dates to 1907 and includes the site of the ancient prison. The complex's official name is the Central Criminal Court.

5. If Jim Hawkins was compiling his memoir in the 1760s or 1770s, he was confused as to what a Bow Street runner did. At that time the term referred to employees of the Bow Street Magistrate's Court who escorted prisoners between Bow Street and London's jails. The first use of the term Bow Street runner to mean a detective or policeman was in a 1785 poem by Henry Bate.

The Bow Street Magistrate's Court continued to be located at No. 4 Bow Street, later expanded to include No. 3, then moved to No. 28 Bow Street, next to a police station, in 1881. The site was sold to a developer and the court closed in 2006.

aloud, "let's see—Black Dog? No, I don't know the name, not I. Yet I kind of think I've—yes, I've seen the swab. He used to come here with a blind beggar, he used."

"That he did, you may be sure," said I. "I knew that blind man too. His name was Pew."

"It was!" cried Silver, now quite excited. "Pew! That were his name for certain. Ah, he looked a shark, he did! If we run down this Black Dog, now, there'll be news for Cap'n Trelawney! Ben's a good runner; few seamen run better than Ben. He should run him down, hand over hand, by the powers! He talked o' keel-hauling, did he? *I'll* keel-haul him!"

All the time he was jerking out these phrases he was stumping up and down the tavern on his crutch, slapping tables with his hand, and giving such a show of excitement as would have convinced an Old Bailey judge[4] or a Bow Street runner.[5] My suspicions had been thoroughly reawakened on finding Black Dog at the Spy-glass, and I watched the cook narrowly. But he was too deep, and too ready, and too clever for me, and by the time the two men had come back out of breath and confessed that they had lost the track in a crowd, and been scolded like thieves, I would have gone bail for the innocence of Long John Silver.

"See here, now, Hawkins," said he, "here's a blessed hard thing on a man like me, now, ain't it? There's Cap'n Trelawney—what's he to think? Here I have this confounded son of a Dutchman sitting in my own house drinking of my own rum! Here you comes and tells me of it plain; and here I let him give us all the slip before my blessed deadlights![6] Now, Hawkins, you do me justice with the cap'n. You're a lad, you are, but you're as smart as paint. I see that when you first came in. Now, here it is: What could I do, with this old timber I hobble on? When I was an AB master[7] mariner I'd have come up alongside of him, hand over hand, and broached him[8] to in a brace of old shakes, I would; but now—"

And then, all of a sudden, he stopped, and his jaw dropped as though he had remembered something.

"The score!" he burst out. "Three goes o' rum! Why shiver my timbers, if I hadn't forgotten my score!"

And falling on a bench, he laughed until the tears ran down his cheeks. I could not help joining, and we laughed together, peal after peal, until the tavern rang again.

"Why, what a precious old sea-calf I am!" he said at last, wiping his cheeks. "You and me should get on well, Hawkins, for I'll take my davy[9] I should be rated ship's boy. But come now, stand by to go about. This won't do. Dooty is dooty, messmates. I'll put on my old cocked hat, and step along of you to Cap'n Trelawney, and report this here affair. For mind you, it's serious, young Hawkins; and neither you nor me's come out of it with what I should make so bold as to call credit. Nor you neither, says you; not smart—none of the pair of us smart. But dash my buttons! That was a good un about my score."

And he began to laugh again, and that so heartily, that though I did not see the joke as he did, I was again obliged to join him in his mirth.

On our little walk along the quays, he made himself the most interesting companion, telling me about the different ships that we passed by, their rig, tonnage, and nationality, explaining the work that was going

6. Strong wooden shutters sized to fit precisely over the outside of a window on a vessel to protect the glass. Silver is referring to his eyes and implying he did not see Black Dog.

7. The 18th-century Royal Navy described crew members with no experience as *landmen*. After a year of service they became *ordinary seamen*. Two years of experience made them *able seamen*, or *AB*; the word *able* is used in the sense of skilled or competent. (The letters *AB* are an abbreviation of the word *able*.) "The able seaman is the seafaring man who knows all the duties of common seamanship, as to rig, steer, reef, furl, take the lead," wrote Admiral William Henry Smyth.

8. Silver is suggesting he would have stopped Black Dog in his tracks. Admiral Smyth tells us that to *broach to* is to "fly up into the wind" and that in extreme cases "the ship might go down stern foremost." The most likely cause is when a following sea lifts a ship's stern out of the water so that the rudder cannot do its job of steering the ship, which then is caught in a trough and loses forward momentum or goes broadside to the direction of the waves at a time when the wind is strong.

9. Davy is an abbreviation of *affidavit*.

forward—how one was discharging, another taking in cargo, and a third making ready for sea—and every now and then telling me some little anecdote of ships or seamen or repeating a nautical phrase till I had learned it perfectly. I began to see that here was one of the best of possible shipmates.

When we got to the inn, the squire and Dr. Livesey were seated together, finishing a quart of ale with a toast in it, before they should go aboard the schooner on a visit of inspection.

Long John told the story from first to last, with a great deal of spirit and the most perfect truth. "That was how it were, now, weren't it, Hawkins?" he would say, now and again, and I could always bear him entirely out.

The two gentlemen regretted that Black Dog had got away, but we all agreed there was nothing to be done, and after he had been complimented, Long John took up his crutch and departed.

"All hands aboard by four this afternoon," shouted the squire after him.

"Aye, aye, sir," cried the cook, in the passage.

"Well, squire," said Dr. Livesey, "I don't put much faith in your discoveries, as a general thing; but I will say this, John Silver suits me."

"The man's a perfect trump," declared the squire.

"And now," added the doctor, "Jim may come on board with us, may he not?"

"To be sure he may," says squire. "Take your hat, Hawkins, and we'll see the ship."

Chapter Nine

Powder and Arms

THE *HISPANIOLA* LAY SOME way out, and we went under the figureheads and round the sterns of many other ships, and their cables sometimes grated underneath our keel, and sometimes swung above us. At last, however, we got alongside, and were met and saluted as we stepped aboard by the mate, Mr. Arrow, a brown old sailor with earrings in his ears and a squint. He and the squire were very thick and friendly, but I soon observed that things were not the same between Mr. Trelawney and the captain.

This last was a sharp-looking man who seemed angry with everything on board

and was soon to tell us why, for we had hardly got down into the cabin when a sailor followed us.

"Captain Smollett, sir, axing to speak with you," said he.

"I am always at the captain's orders. Show him in," said the squire.

The captain, who was close behind his messenger, entered at once and shut the door behind him.

"Well, Captain Smollett, what have you to say? All well, I hope; all shipshape and seaworthy?"

"Well, sir," said the captain, "better speak plain, I believe, even at the risk of offence. I don't like this cruise; I don't like the men; and I don't like my officer. That's short and sweet."

"Perhaps, sir, you don't like the ship?" inquired the squire, very angry, as I could see.

"I can't speak as to that, sir, not having seen her tried," said the captain. "She seems a clever craft; more I can't say."

"Possibly, sir, you may not like your employer, either?" says the squire.

But here Dr. Livesey cut in.

"Stay a bit," said he, "stay a bit. No use of such questions as that but to produce ill feeling. The captain has said too much or he has said too little, and I'm bound to say that I require an explanation of his words. You don't, you say, like this cruise. Now, why?"

"I was engaged, sir, on what we call sealed orders, to sail this ship for that gentleman where he should bid me," said the captain. "So far so good. But now I find that every man before the mast knows more than I do. I don't call that fair, now, do you?"

"No," said Dr. Livesey, "I don't."

"Next," said the captain, "I learn we are going after treasure—hear it from my own hands, mind you. Now, treasure is ticklish work; I don't like treasure voyages on any account, and I don't like them, above all, when they are secret and when (begging your pardon, Mr. Trelawney) the secret has been told to the parrot."

"Silver's parrot?" asked the squire.

"It's a way of speaking," said the captain. "Blabbed, I mean. It's my belief neither of you gentlemen know what you are about, but I'll tell you my way of it—life or death, and a close run."

"That is all clear, and, I dare say, true enough," replied Dr. Livesey. "We take the risk, but we are not so ignorant as you believe us. Next, you say you don't like the crew. Are they not good seamen?"

"I don't like them, sir," returned Captain Smollett. "And I think I should have had the choosing of my own hands, if you go to that."

"Perhaps you should," replied the doctor. "My friend should, perhaps, have taken you along with him; but the slight, if there be one, was unintentional. And you don't like Mr. Arrow?"

"I don't, sir. I believe he's a good seaman, but he's too free with the crew to be a good officer. A mate should keep himself to himself—shouldn't drink with the men before the mast!"

"Do you mean he drinks?" cried the squire.

"No, sir," replied the captain, "only that he's too familiar."

"Well, now, and the short and long of it, captain?" asked the doctor. "Tell us what you want."

"Well, gentlemen, are you determined to go on this cruise?"

"Like iron," answered the squire.

"Very good," said the captain. "Then, as

you've heard me very patiently, saying things that I could not prove, hear me a few words more. They are putting the powder and the arms in the fore hold. Now, you have a good place under the cabin; why not put them there?—first point. Then, you are bringing four of your own people with you, and they tell me some of them are to be berthed forward. Why not give them the berths here beside the cabin?—second point."

"Any more?" asked Mr. Trelawney.

"One more," said the captain. "There's been too much blabbing already."

"Far too much," agreed the doctor.

"I'll tell you what I've heard myself," continued Captain Smollett: "that you have a map of an island, that there's crosses on the map to show where treasure is, and that the island lies—" And then he named the latitude and longitude exactly.

"I never told that," cried the squire, "to a soul!"

"The hands know it, sir," returned the captain.

"Livesey, that must have been you or Hawkins," cried the squire.

"It doesn't much matter who it was," replied the doctor. And I could see that neither he nor the captain paid much regard to Mr. Trelawney's protestations. Neither did I, to be sure, he was so loose a talker; yet in this case I believe he was really right and

that nobody had told the situation of the island.

"Well, gentlemen," continued the captain, "I don't know who has this map; but I make it a point, it shall be kept secret even from me and Mr. Arrow. Otherwise I would ask you to let me resign."

"I see," said the doctor. "You wish us to keep this matter dark and to make a garrison of the stern part of the ship, manned with my friend's own people, and provided with all the arms and powder on board. In other words, you fear a mutiny."

"Sir," said Captain Smollett, "with no intention to take offence, I deny your right to put words into my mouth. No captain, sir, would be justified in going to sea at all if he had ground enough to say that. As for Mr. Arrow, I believe him thoroughly honest; some of the men are the same; all may be for what I know. But I am responsible for the ship's safety and the life of every man Jack aboard of her. I see things going, as I think, not quite right. And I ask you to take certain precautions or let me resign my berth. And that's all."

"Captain Smollett," began the doctor with a smile, "did ever you hear the fable of the mountain and the mouse? You'll excuse me, I dare say, but you remind me of that fable. When you came in here, I'll stake my wig, you meant more than this."

"Doctor," said the captain, "you are smart.

1. The cargo area below deck and forward of the main mast or that part of the hold located nearest to the main hatch.

2. A ship's kitchen. The *Hispaniola*'s galley or its stove, which would likely have been a structure of brick and iron, as can be seen on the 1768 replica schooner HMS *Sultana*. By 1757, according to the historian Brian Lavery, weight-saving iron fire hearths "had become fairly general." The iron stoves had built-in kettles for boiling food, ovens, and a chimney leading to the deck above. Regardless of what kind of stove was installed in the *Hispaniola*, cooking in a cramped space that rolled, heaved and pitched along must have been a challenge for the one-legged Silver, as Jim notes.

3. Pronounced *foh'k'sill* and sometimes spelled *fo'c'sle*, this is a term from ship design of the early Middle Ages that today mostly refers to the space underneath the raised foredeck still found at the bow of some older modern merchant ships.

The term comes from the short raised deck with protecting breastwork that in the period 1100–1400 was added to the bow area of merchant ships to create a fighting platform. It looked a little like a castle, so it came to be known as the *forecastle*. In time the forecastle became an integral part of the hull, and the space underneath the forecastle deck provided living quarters for crew. *Fo'c'sle hands* was a short-hand term for crew members who were not officers or in any position of responsibility. (See also note 9 on p. 8.)

4. A rectangular structure on deck with windows designed to let light into the deck below. The companion has been enlarged to the point that it is almost as big as a *deck house*, which is a cabin built on deck. The deck house was sometimes called a *round house* not because it was round but because, according to Admiral Smyth, you could walk around it.

When I came in here I meant to get discharged. I had no thought that Mr. Trelawney would hear a word."

"No more I would," cried the squire. "Had Livesey not been here I should have seen you to the deuce. As it is, I have heard you. I will do as you desire, but I think the worse of you."

"That's as you please, sir," said the captain. "You'll find I do my duty."

And with that he took his leave.

"Trelawney," said the doctor, "contrary to all my notions, I believe you have managed to get two honest men on board with you—that man and John Silver."

"Silver, if you like," cried the squire; "but as for that intolerable humbug, I declare I think his conduct unmanly, unsailorly, and downright un-English."

"Well," says the doctor, "we shall see."

When we came on deck, the men had begun already to take out the arms and powder, yo-ho-ing at their work, while the captain and Mr. Arrow stood by superintending.

The new arrangement was quite to my liking. The whole schooner had been overhauled; six berths had been made astern out of what had been the after-part of the main hold;[1] and this set of cabins was only joined to the galley[2] and forecastle[3] by a sparred passage on the port side. It had been originally meant that the captain, Mr. Arrow, Hunter, Joyce, the doctor, and the squire were to occupy these six berths. Now Redruth and I were to get two of them and Mr. Arrow and the captain were to sleep on deck in the companion,[4] which had been enlarged on each side till you might almost have called it a round-house.

Very low it was still, of course; but there was room to swing two hammocks, and even the mate seemed pleased with the arrangement. Even he, perhaps, had been doubtful as to the crew, but that is only guess, for as you shall hear, we had not long the benefit of his opinion.

We were all hard at work, changing the powder and the berths, when the last man or two, and Long John along with them, came off in a shore-boat.

The cook came up the side like a monkey for cleverness, and as soon as he saw what was doing, "So ho, mates!" says he. "What's this?"

"We're a-changing of the powder, Jack," answers one.

"Why, by the powers," cried Long John, "if we do, we'll miss the morning tide!"

"My orders!" said the captain shortly. "You may go below, my man. Hands will want supper."

"Aye, aye, sir," answered the cook, and touching his forelock, he disappeared at once in the direction of his galley.

"That's a good man, captain," said the doctor.

"Very likely, sir," replied Captain Smollett. "Easy with that, men— easy," he ran on, to the fellows who were shifting the powder; and then

"Out o' that! Off with you to the cook and get some work."

75

5. Jim Hawkins mentions that the nine-pounder was mounted on a *swivel*, but that is the wrong term. *Swivel* was the term used at the time for a forked metal holder that looked a little like an old-fashioned kid's slingshot; it was used to mount a small gun approximately three feet long that fired an 8-ounce or 12-ounce ball. Swivels were mounted on the rail of a vessel or on the platforms called *tops* halfway up a mast. A small swivel could not carry a smoothbore cannon between 7 feet and 9 feet long, weighing up to about 1.6 tons, that fired a 9-pound solid iron projectile.

Jim's cannon was almost certainly mounted on a *pivoting turntable* installed on the centerline of the vessel so the gun's weight would be distributed uniformly.

suddenly observing me examining the swivel we carried amidships, a long brass nine,[5] "Here you, ship's boy," he cried, "out o' that! Off with you to the cook and get some work."

And then as I was hurrying off I heard him say, quite loudly, to the doctor, "I'll have no favourites on my ship."

I assure you I was quite of the squire's way of thinking, and hated the captain deeply.

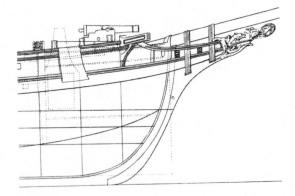

Larger guns were not adequately supported by a swivel and needed to be mounted on a turntable. The image shows a large gun mounted on a turntable.

Chapter Ten

The Voyage

ALL THAT NIGHT we were in a great bustle getting things stowed in their place, and boatfuls of the squire's friends, Mr. Blandly and the like, coming off to wish him a good voyage and a safe return. We never had a night at the Admiral Benbow when I had half the work; and I was dog-tired when, a little before dawn, the boatswain sounded his pipe and the crew began to man the capstan bars.[1] I might have been twice as weary, yet I would not have left the deck, all was so new and interesting to me—the brief commands, the shrill note of the whistle, the men bustling to their places in the glimmer of the ship's lanterns.

"Now, Barbecue, tip us a stave,"[2] cried one voice.

"The old one," cried another.

"Aye, aye, mates," said Long John, who was standing by, with his crutch under his arm, and at once broke out in the air and words I knew so well:

"Fifteen men on the dead man's chest—"

[1]. On an 18th-century vessel a capstan is a type of winch, powered by human muscle and used to raise an anchor or do other heavy lifting chores. (See illustration, p. 78.)

A capstan was a vertical cylinder with slots into which capstan bars were fitted. It looked like a wheel with spokes. Both the size of the capstan and the number of bars varied. The armed transport *Bounty*, which had about the same carrying capacity as the *Hispaniola*, had a capstan with six bars. The number of men assigned to each bar depended on the load to be raised.

Men walked around the cylinder pushing the capstan bars, which turned the cylinder to which the anchor's cable was attached directly if the anchor was not too heavy.

In one modern account, students on a replica of the *Bounty* took three hours to bring on board 180 feet of cable with an anchor at the end. Each 360-degree turn of the capstan brought in just six inches of anchor cable. The original *Bounty* carried five anchors of different sizes and six anchor cables, each 600 feet long.

Bristol's sewage, as well as its industrial waste, flowed into the same river used by visiting vessels. So the crew of the *Hispaniola* had to haul in, and store, a rope covered in mud and slime, and then secure the anchor.

If the anchor cable was particularly thick and

too cumbersome to be attached directly to the capstan, Captain Smollett would have ordered that a messenger be used. This was a lighter rope positioned to connect the anchor cable to the capstan. But the crew would still be dealing with mud and slime as they guided the anchor cable below into its storage area. Ships might deploy more than one anchor if conditions were difficult.

Smaller merchant vessels would be equipped with a windlass, which could be operated with fewer men than a capstan, according to John McKay, who has created modern detailed plans for the *Bounty*. However, they were slow and took up scarce deck space. Larger vessels used capstans, as did Royal Navy vessels which carried larger crews than merchant ships who could be put to work on the capstan or capstans, according to McKay. The *Bounty* was outfitted with both a windlass and a capstan. The 1760s schooner *Sultana* replica makes use of a windlass instead of a capstan.

A capstan was a vertical cylinder with slots into which bars were fitted; it looked like a wheel with spokes. Men walked around the cylinder, pushing the capstan bars, which turned the cylinder, to which the anchor's cable was attached directly if the anchor was not too heavy.

And then the whole crew bore chorus:—

"Yo-ho-ho, and a bottle of rum!"

And at the third "Ho!" drove the bars before them with a will.

Even at that exciting moment it carried me back to the old Admiral Benbow in a second, and I seemed to hear the voice of the captain piping in the chorus. But soon the anchor was short up; soon it was hanging dripping at the bows; soon the sails began to draw, and the land and shipping to flit by on either side; and before I could lie down to snatch an hour of slumber the *Hispaniola* had begun her voyage to the Isle of Treasure.

I am not going to relate that voyage in detail. It was fairly prosperous. The ship proved to be a good ship, the crew were capable seamen, and the captain thoroughly understood his business. But before we came the length of Treasure Island, two or three things had happened which require to be known.

Mr. Arrow, first of all, turned out even worse than the captain had feared. He had no command among the men, and people did what they pleased with him. But that was by no means the worst of it, for after a day or two at sea he began to appear on deck with hazy eye, red cheeks, stuttering tongue, and other marks of drunkenness. Time after time he was ordered below in disgrace. Sometimes he fell and cut himself; sometimes he lay all day long in his little bunk at one side of the companion; sometimes for a day or two he would be almost sober and attend to his work at least passably.

In the meantime, we could never make out where

he got the drink. That was the ship's mystery. Watch him as we pleased, we could do nothing to solve it; and when we asked him to his face, he would only laugh if he were drunk, and if he were sober deny solemnly that he ever tasted anything but water.

He was not only useless as an officer and a bad influence amongst the men, but it was plain that at this rate he must soon kill himself outright, so nobody was much surprised, nor very sorry, when one dark night, with a head sea, he disappeared entirely and was seen no more.

"Overboard!" said the captain. "Well, gentlemen, that saves the trouble of putting him in irons."[3]

But there we were, without a mate; and it was necessary, of course, to advance one of the men. The boatswain,[4] Job Anderson, was the likeliest man aboard, and though he kept his old title, he served in a way as mate. Mr. Trelawney had followed the sea, and his knowledge made him very useful, for he often took a watch himself in easy weather. And the coxswain,[5] Israel Hands, was a careful, wily, old, experienced seaman who could be trusted at a pinch with almost anything.

He was a great confidant of Long John Silver, and so the mention of his name leads me on to speak of our ship's cook, Barbecue, as the men called him.

Aboard ship he carried his crutch by a lanyard round his neck, to have both hands as free as possible. It was something to see him wedge the foot of the crutch against a bulkhead,[6] and propped against it, yielding to every movement of the ship, get on with his cooking like someone safe ashore. Still more strange was it to see him in the heaviest of weather

2. Eighteenth-century slang for "Give us a song." Thanks to Nathaniel Bailey, a compiler of best-selling dictionaries in the 1700s, we know that thieves in the 1700s used the word *tip* as a component of the slang phrases they used. *Tip* here is used in the sense of *give* or *lend*, as in "Tip your lour," meaning "Give me your money." *Tip* was still used in underworld parlance toward the end of the 1700s, according to another avid collector of thieves' slang, Captain Francis Grose.

3. Here the meaning of *in irons* is "confined in iron leg-shackles." From the 1600s to the 1800s, many ships carried loop-shaped shackles called *bilboes* that could be combined with long iron bars to fasten a person's legs to the deck or some other convenient place. They were used to punish crew members.

Visitors to HMS *Victory* in Portsmouth, in Great Britain, can see a set of bilboes installed on one of the gun decks.

Bilboes were also used on land as a variation of the wooden stocks used to restrain people being punished. They are still available commercially today for use by re-enactors.

4. Pronounced *bosun*. Responsible for the upkeep of sails, rigging, anchors, cables, and blocks, and for piping orders and calling the crew to duty. Assisted by *boatswain's mate*; the essence of his job was reporting defects, says Admiral Smyth. See note 9 on page 25 for more on piping.

5. Pronounced *cox-sun*, the coxswain was the sailor or petty officer who steers a ship's boat and is in charge of its crew. He reported to the officer who was in command of the boat. The term is still used today as a title for senior petty officers.

6. Bulkheads are partitions that divide the interior of a vessel into separate compartments. In the 1700s bulkheads were made of various materials, depending on the type of compartment needed. Some were made of wood and were strong, for example, and used to create a vessel's cargo hold. Some were made of easily removed canvas and were used to create cabin space on board a warship. If space was needed to work the guns, the canvas partitions could be removed quickly.

7. To judge from the ability of "that bird" to mimic human speech and its longevity, Silver's parrot was either an African gray parrot, *Psittacus erithacus*, which can live 80 years, or a green-feathered member of the equally talkative group called Amazon parrots (genus *Amazona*). It is more likely that "that bird" was an African gray since she sailed with Captain England, and England operated along the coast of West Africa. In one account England and his men spent several weeks ashore in Whydah in modern Benin. African grays are highly intelligent. According to Professor Irene Pepperberg, in some respects grays are as intelligent as chimpanzees and dolphins, and exhibit some reasoning abilities.

8. How great Edward England was as a pirate is open to question. He operated from the Bahamas, then off West Africa–perhaps–and in the Indian Ocean. He is best known for that rarity in the Golden Age of Piracy, a prolonged ship-to-ship gun battle in 1720 that overwhelmed a large, well-armed freighter, the *Cassandra*. But England soon was dismissed from command by his shipmates for lack of judgment and abandoned on an island in the Indian Ocean.

England–whose name at birth may have been Jasper Seager–was one of some 500 pirates at Nassau in the Bahamas in 1718. That was the year Governor Woodes Rogers arrived to close down Nassau as a pirate staging area.

Like many others, England decided it was time to try his luck elsewhere. According to *A General History of the Pyrates* (1724), England chose the west coast of Africa, taking nine prizes before moving on to the Indian Ocean and the west coast of India with another pirate, John Taylor. Taylor had been elected captain of the *Victory*, a 46-gun ship captured during the African leg of the voyage. A merchant ship captain named William Snelgrave, who had met Taylor while a prisoner, described him later as "as brisk and courageous a Man as I ever saw."

In 1720, off the island of Johanna, now known as Anjouan Island, one of the Comoro Islands, England, in the 24-gun, 300-ton *Fancy*, and Taylor in *Victory*, attacked a ship of the powerful and influential East India Company. This was the 380-ton *Cassandra*, commanded by James Macrae. On and off the fight lasted about seven hours.

cross the deck. He had a line or two rigged up to help him across the widest spaces—Long John's earrings, they were called; and he would hand himself from one place to another, now using the crutch, now trailing it alongside by the lanyard, as quickly as another man could walk. Yet some of the men who had sailed with him before expressed their pity to see him so reduced.

"He's no common man, Barbecue," said the coxswain to me. "He had good schooling in his young days and can speak like a book when so minded; and brave—a lion's nothing alongside of Long John! I seen him grapple four and knock their heads together—him unarmed."

All the crew respected and even obeyed him. He had a way of talking to each and doing everybody some particular service. To me he was unweariedly kind, and always glad to see me in the galley, which he kept as clean as a new pin, the dishes hanging up burnished and his parrot in a cage in one corner.

"Come away, Hawkins," he would say; "come and have a yarn with John. Nobody more welcome than yourself, my son. Sit you down and hear the news. Here's Cap'n Flint—I calls my parrot Cap'n Flint, after the famous buccaneer—here's Cap'n Flint predicting success to our v'yage. Wasn't you, cap'n?"

And the parrot would say, with great rapidity, "Pieces of eight! Pieces of eight! Pieces of eight!" till you wondered that it was not out of breath, or till John threw his handkerchief over the cage.

"Now, that bird," he would say, "is, maybe, two hundred years old,[7] Hawkins—they lives forever mostly; and if anybody's seen more wickedness, it must be the devil himself. She's sailed with England, the great Cap'n England, the pirate.[8] She's been at Madagascar, and at Malabar, and Surinam, and Providence, and Portobello.[9] She was at the fishing up of the wrecked plate ships.[10] It's there she learned 'Pieces of eight,' and little wonder; three hundred and fifty thousand of 'em, Hawkins! She was at the boarding of the viceroy of the Indies out of Goa,[11] she was; and to look at her you would think she was a babby. But you smelt powder—didn't you, cap'n?"

"Stand by to go about,"[12] the parrot would scream.

"Ah, she's a handsome craft, she is," the cook would say, and give her sugar from his pocket, and then the bird would peck at the bars and swear straight on, passing belief for wickedness. "There," John would add, "you can't touch pitch and not be mucked, lad. Here's this poor old innocent bird o' mine swearing blue fire, and none the wiser, you may lay to that. She would swear the same, in a manner of speaking, before chaplain." And John would touch his forelock with a solemn way he had that made me think he was the best of men.

In the meantime, the squire and Captain Smollett were still on pretty distant terms with one another. The squire made no bones about the matter; he despised the captain. The captain, on his part, never spoke but when he was spoken to, and then sharp and short and dry, and not a word wasted. He owned, when driven into a corner, that he seemed to have been wrong about the crew, that some of them were as brisk as he wanted to see and all had behaved fairly well. As for the ship, he had taken a downright fancy to her. "She'll lie a point nearer the wind[13] than a man has a right to expect of his own married wife, sir. But," he would add, "all I say is, we're not home again, and I don't like the cruise."

Macrae, wounded in the head, escaped with most of his men and after 10 days made contact with England, who agreed to let Macrea take the much-damaged *Fancy*, while the pirates kept the abandoned *Cassandra*. This was not a prudent decision, as England's fellow-pirates made clear later.

Macrea managed to reach India in the patched-up *Fancy* and launch a search for England. When England's men learned of the search, they deposed England and left him and three others on the island of Mauritius, where they cobbled together some sort of craft and reached Madagascar.

Another account has England and the others deposited on the northwestern tip of Madagascar, where the author of the 1724 *General History* reported "they subsist at present on the Charity of their Brethren, who had made better Provision for themselves than they had done." Much of what we know or think we know about Edward England comes from the *General History* written by a Captain Charles Johnson or, according to some, by Daniel Defoe. The book is a mixture of fact and fiction. One critic, Jan Rogozinski, who has closely researched England's life and times, dismisses the first part of the chapter "Captain Edward England and his Crew" and its information about England on the west coast of Africa as a fiction by Defoe.

The chapter does contain Macrea's report on the *Cassandra* fight obtained by the author of the *General History* from the East India Company. Information about England also surfaces in various depositions and three memoirs: by one of *Cassandra*'s mates, Richard Lazenby; by the map maker Jacob de Bucquoy; and by John Snelgrave, captain of a London merchantman.

9. For information on Madagascar, Malabar, Surinam, Providence, and Portobello, see the introduction, p. xxii.

10. A Spanish convoy wrecked off Fort Pierce, Florida, in 1715. (For more, see the introduction, p. xxv.)

11. "Probably the richest prize that ever fell into pirate hands," according to John Biddulph, a historian of piracy in the Indian Ocean. Goa, on the west coast of India, was controlled by the Portuguese in 1721. The ex-viceroy, or governor-general, of Goa, the Count of Ericeira, was on his way home after three lucrative years in office. His ship, the *Nostra Senhora de Cabo*, was damaged in a storm, and it put in to modern Reunion Island for repairs. There John Taylor, who had taken command of the *Cassandra* from Edward England, and Oliver La Buse (or La Bouche) in the *Victory*, overwhelmed the Portuguese ship. The value of just the diamonds taken was the equivalent of 90 tons of silver at the very least. There were also 500,000 crowns cash money, plus other valuable cargo. The pirates also kept the *Cabo*. (See also note 8 on p. 80.)

12. "Stand by" is the order to be prepared. "To go about" is to direct the ship on another tack by bringing her bow into the wind. Tacking is the zigzag course made by a ship going forward into the wind.

13. Captain Smollet is being complimentary when he says the *Hispaniola* will sail more directly into the wind than he expected. In Smollett's day the compass's circular card was divided into 32 *points*, each equivalent to 11¼ degrees of a 360-degree circle. Orders to the helmsman were given in *points, half points,* and *quarter points,* rather than in degrees as is done today.

There is a difference between a *compass bearing* used for navigation and plotting a course on a map, and a *relative bearing* used for immediate course corrections and directions. Captain Smollett is here referring to relative bearing.

Nearer the wind refers to the fact that a sailing ship cannot sail head-on into the wind, only at an angle to it. A modern racing yacht can sail as close as 3½ points, or 39 degrees, "off the wind"– that is, at an angle of 39 degrees from the direction the wind is coming from. A square-rigged ship might sail as close as 6 points off the wind, or 70 degrees. The closer a vessel can sail to the wind, the fewer times it will have to tack (zigzag back and forth) to make forward progress (headway) against the wind.

14. In the 1750s, a mixture of one part rum to four parts water. The first order to dilute the daily ration of spirits was given by the Royal Navy's Admiral Edward Vernon in 1740 while at Jamaica.

The order was as follows: "Their half pint of rum to be daily mixed with a quart of water . . . and when so mixed it is to be served to them in

The squire, at this, would turn away and march up and down the deck, chin in air.

"A trifle more of that man," he would say, "and I shall explode."

We had some heavy weather, which only proved the qualities of the *Hispaniola*. Every man on board seemed well content, and they must have been hard to please if they had been otherwise, for it is my belief there was never a ship's company so spoiled since Noah put to sea. Double grog[14] was going on the least excuse; there was duff[15] on odd days, as, for instance, if the squire heard it was any man's birthday, and always a barrel of apples standing broached in the waist[16] for anyone to help himself that had a fancy.

"Never knew good come of it yet," the captain said to Dr. Livesey. "Spoil forecastle hands, make devils. That's my belief."

But good did come of the apple barrel, as you shall hear, for if it had not been for that, we should have had no note of warning and might all have perished by the hand of treachery.

This was how it came about.

We had run up the trades[17] to get the wind of the island we were after—I am not allowed to be more plain—and now we were running down for it with a bright lookout day and night. It was about the last day of our outward voyage by the largest computation; some time that night, or at latest before noon of the morrow, we should sight the Treasure Island. We were heading S.S.W.[18] and had a steady breeze abeam[19] and a quiet sea. The *Hispaniola* rolled steadily, dipping her bowsprit[20] now and then with a whiff of spray. All was drawing alow and aloft; everyone was in the bravest two servings in the day, the one between the hours of 10 and 12 in the morning, and the other between 4 and 6 in the afternoon."

Vernon, as has often been recounted, was called Old Grog because of his habit of wearing a waterproof cloak made out of a fabric called grogram. (For more on rum, see the introduction, p. xv.)

15. "A pudding, or as it is called, a 'duff.' This is nothing more than flour boiled in water and eaten with molasses," Richard Henry Dana tells us in his memoir of life at sea in the 1830s, *Two Years Before the Mast*. "It is very heavy, dark and clammy, yet it is looked upon as a luxury, and really forms an agreeable variety with salt beef and pork."

Dana is talking about an old-fashioned boiled "bag pudding," which has a flour base and can be delicious. The flour and ingredients of choice—meat, mushrooms, beans, chopped apples, raisins, or whatever the cook decides—are placed in a bag that is hung in boiling water or a broth. Plum duff combines flour, suet, and raisins. Variations of a "bag pudding" include steak and kidney pie and traditional Christmas pudding.

16. On the *Hispaniola* the waist was the section of the weather or top deck between the two masts.

17. The *Hispaniola*, like other vessels of the day, sailed part of the way down the west coast of Africa, then turned right and let the northeast trade winds deliver her to the edge of the

Caribbean. This was called *running down the trades*. Since the *Hispaniola* also spent part of the voyage *running up the trades*, she at some point needed to move more to the north to make her approach to Treasure Island, which provides a tiny clue as to the island's location.

The trade winds are a steady, predictable gift of the sun's heat along the earth's equator that makes the air there rise, creating a low-pressure zone that then sucks in air from high-pressure zones to the north and south, resulting in the winds called trade winds.

The spinning of the earth steers the trades to some extent, so that the ones in the Northern Hemisphere blow from the northeast, while the ones in the Southern Hemisphere blow from the southeast.

18. South south west on the compass card used in the 1700s is equivalent to a bearing of 202.5 degrees on the modern compass card, based on a 360-degree circle. (See also note 10 on p. 51 and note 13 on p. 82.)

19. Jim means the breeze was coming in at right angles to the side of the *Hispaniola*.

20. A spar projecting forward and over the bow, used to extend a *jib* above and beyond the bow. The jib is smaller triangular sail useful for maneuvering a vessel. (See illustration, p. xiii.)

Detail of the bowsprit from the schooner diagram on p. xiii.

21. Also called the tiller, the helm is a component of the steering gear of a vessel. On the schooner *Sultana* of 1768 the helm was a slightly curved wooden bar that was attached to the rudder at the rear or stern of the vessel. Pushing or pulling on the helm changed the direction of the rudder, which in turn changed the direction of the vessel. (See illustration, p. xiii, note 3 on p. 103, and note 4 on p. 104.)

22. He is watching the luff, or leading edge, of the mainsail—that is, the edge nearest the mast—to make sure it does not shake, which would signify an inefficient use of the wind. He had probably been given the order to "steer full and by"—that is, to steer comfortably in such a way that the vessel is not sailing into the wind as closely as possible but at the same is not so off the wind that the luff of the sail is rattling and shaking.

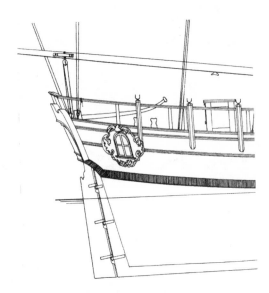

The schooner helm shown here was a curved wooden handle connected to the rudder.

spirits because we were now so near an end of the first part of our adventure.

Now, just after sundown, when all my work was over and I was on my way to my berth, it occurred to me that I should like an apple. I ran on deck. The watch was all forward looking out for the island. The man at the helm[21] was watching the luff of the sail[22] and whistling away gently to himself, and that was the

The man at the helm was watching the luff of the sail.

only sound excepting the swish of the sea against the bows and around the sides of the ship.[23]

In I got bodily into the apple barrel, and found there was scarce an apple left; but sitting down there in the dark, what with the sound of the waters and the rocking movement of the ship, I had either fallen asleep or was on the point of doing so when a heavy man sat down with rather a clash close by. The barrel shook as he leaned his shoulders against it, and I was just about to jump up when the man began to speak. It was Silver's voice, and before I had heard a dozen words, I would not have shown myself for all the world, but lay there, trembling and listening, in the extreme of fear and curiosity, for from these dozen words I understood that the lives of all the honest men aboard depended upon me alone.

23. Robert Louis Stevenson, to whom we owe the publication of Jim Hawkins's memoir, wrote of a similar experience that his father, Thomas Stevenson, had as a boy when he climbed into an apple barrel carried on the deck of another vessel. Like Jim, the conversation he overheard revealed the speaker as a very different person than the straightforward mariner he thought he knew.

The vessel was the lighthouse tender *Regent*, which RLS's engineer grandfather Robert used when inspecting lighthouses around the Scottish coast for the Northern Light House Board in the 1830s, accompanied by his sons. A Captain Soutar was its skipper.

RLS, in his family history, *Records of a Family of Engineers*, described Soutar: "He was active, admirably skilled in his trade, and a man incapable of fear."

Here, from the same book, is Stevenson's account of the incident in question: "So many perils shared and the partial familiarity of so many voyages had given this man a stronghold in my grandfather's estimation; and there is no doubt but he had the art to court and please him with much hypocritical skill. He usually dined on Sundays in the cabin. He used to come down daily after dinner for a glass of port or whisky, often in full in his full rig of sou'-wester, oilskins, and long boots; and I have often heard it described how insinuatingly he carried himself on these appearances, artfully combining the extreme of deference with a blunt and seamanlike demeanour. My father and uncles, with the devilish penetration of the boy, were far from being deceived; and my father, indeed, was favoured with an object-lesson not to be mistaken. He had crept one rainy night into an apple-barrel on deck, and from this place of ambush overheard Soutar and a comrade conversing in their oilskins. The smooth sycophant of the cabin had wholly disappeared, and the boy listened with wonder to a vulgar and truculent ruffian."

Chapter Eleven

What I Heard in the Apple Barrel

1. During the heyday of Anglo-American piracy in the late 1600s and 1700s, the quartermaster on a pirate vessel was elected; his function was to serve as a counterweight to the authority of the captain, also elected. During the years when Flint, England, and the others were active in the Indian Ocean, the quartermaster was the equal of the captain.

As William Snelgrave, a merchant ship captain who had plenty of time to observe the organizational habits of his pirate captors, noted in 1719: "The Captain of a Pirate Ship is chiefly chosen to fight the vessels they meet with. Besides him, they chuse another principal Officer, whom they call Quarter-master, who has the general inspection of all affairs, and often controls the Captain's Orders: This person is also the First Man in boarding any ship they shall attack; or go in the Boat on any desperate Enterprize."

2. A broadside was the simultaneous firing of the big guns located on one side of a vessel. See also note on p. 161.

3. Corso Castle is Cape Coast Castle in present-day Ghana in West Africa. Over a period of six days in April 1722, Cape Coast Castle was the site of a mass hanging by British authorities of 52 pirates who had served with Bartholomew Roberts

"No, not I," said Silver. "Flint was cap'n; I was quartermaster,[1] along of my timber leg. The same broadside[2] I lost my leg, old Pew lost his deadlights. It was a master surgeon, him that ampytated me—out of college and all—Latin by the bucket, and what not; but he was hanged like a dog, and sun-dried like the rest, at Corso Castle.[3] That was Roberts' men, that was, and comed of changing names to their ships— *Royal Fortune* and so on. Now, what a ship was christened, so let her stay, I says. So it was with the *Cassandra*,[4] as brought us all safe home from Malabar, after England took the viceroy of the Indies;[5] so it was with the old *Walrus*, Flint's old ship, as I've seen amuck with the red blood and fit to sink with gold."

"Ah," cried another voice, that of the youngest hand on board, and evidently full of admiration. "He was the flower of the flock, was Flint!"

"Davis[6] was a man too, by all accounts," said Silver. "I never sailed along of him; first with England, then

Corso Castle is Cape Coast Castle in present-day Ghana.

and James Skyrme. Another 20 were sentenced to seven years hard labor in the local mines, where they all died. Seventeen others were shipped back to prison in London, but only four survived the voyage. The court acquitted 74 and reprieved two from hanging. Among those taken were 69 blacks, who were sold. They all had been captured by HMS *Swallow* and tried by a Vice-Admiralty court that had assembled at the Castle. Roberts died in the final fight with the *Swallow*.

Cape Coast Castle served as a fortified warehouse for outgoing cargoes of enslaved Africans and incoming cargoes of goods destined for the sellers of the slaves. The people who had been sold were kept underground in an area called the "slave hole" while waiting to be ferried out by canoe through the surf to waiting ships. Canoes also brought to shore the cargoes from Europe.

The castle itself was a commercial building; subsidized by the British taxpayer, it paid rent to the ruler of the kingdom of Efutu–also spelled Fetu–in what is today the Central Region of Ghana. His capital was about 12 miles from the castle and exists today as a municipality, Effetu. The fort dates back to 1653 and still exists as a museum.

Cape Coast Castle is located on what Portuguese sailors called Cabo Corco, pronounced *Cor-so* and meaning "Short Cape." The English mispronounced the words and turned them into

Cape Coast. They also took over the former Swedish, then Ghanaian, and finally Dutch fort that had been built there and renamed it Cape Coast Castle. The castle, with its shining white walls, was known for the poor construction of its mud-brick bastions, which sometimes collapsed, and its leaky roofs.

The coastline of Ghana is less than 300 miles long, but on this short stretch of West Africa alone an astonishing 40 forts and "castles" plus 28 "lodges," or trading posts, and 8 other assorted fortifications were built on land rented from African rulers over a 300-year period by Portuguese, French, Dutch, British, Swedish, Danish, and German traders. The biggest fortress complexes were called *castles*: they included Elmina Castle, Cape Coast Castle, and Christiansborg Castle.

Some of the forts–for example, at Accra, Komenda, and Sekondi–were so close together that they were within range of each other's artillery. Other regions of West Africa also had fortified trading posts.

The walls and artillery existed mostly to protect competing traders from each other and from the local allies of the traders. Most of the forts had been built by 1700.

The owners of the forts had no jurisdiction beyond the walls. The small staff at Cape Coast Castle was not even allowed to hunt game for sport or food in the nearby forest. However, they could go outside the walls for bowling and picnics.

Many of the old structures survive. Some now serve as prisons, post offices, and government offices. One even serves as the official residence of the chief of state of the Republic of Ghana.

The land-based slaving organizations were only one part of the two-pronged structure that delivered enslaved people to work in the Americas.

The second part was made up of the stream of vessels that arrived with trade goods, worked their way along the coast making their deals with suppliers, and then headed across the Atlantic with their human cargoes. This makes it sound as if the process was a speedy one. It was not. A crew could expect to stay three or four months on the coast as the human cargo was assembled piecemeal. More people died during the months they waited on board ship while a cargo was assembled than on the notorious "middle passage" across the Atlantic.

Death was ecumenical in its reach. By one estimate, one in three Europeans could expect to die of disease in their first four months in Africa. There are many estimates of the death rates among the human cargoes. During a debate in Parliament in 1788, British abolitionist leader William Wilberforce estimated that on British ships 12.5 percent of the Africans died.

In 1821, following its outlawing of the slave trade in 1807, but decades before slavery was abolished, the British government began assuming control of the former slave-trading establishments and eventually declared the establishment of the Gold Coast Colony in 1874, with more territory added in the years that followed. The colony became independent in 1957.

4. The *Cassandra*'s crew, rich from the plunder taken from the former viceroy and his ship (see note 11 on p. 81) voted in September 1722, after further cruising in the Indian Ocean, to return to the Caribbean, which they reached in May 1723. Taylor, the captain who had replaced England, tried to negotiate pardons with the governor of Jamaica without success. He was more successful at Portobello, where the governor issued pardons in return for 121 barrels of gold and silver coins; the *Cassandra*; and a promise not to attack the town. In return the crew kept their diamonds.

with Flint, that's my story; and now here on my own account, in a manner of speaking. I laid by nine hundred safe, from England, and two thousand after Flint. That ain't bad for a man before the mast—all safe in bank. 'Tain't earning now, it's saving does it, you may lay to that. Where's all England's men now? I dunno. Where's Flint's? Why, most on 'em aboard here, and glad to get the duff—been begging before that, some on 'em. Old Pew, as had lost his sight, and might have thought shame, spends twelve hundred pound in a year, like a lord in Parliament. Where is he now? Well, he's dead now and under hatches; but for two year before that, shiver my timbers, the man was starving! He begged, and he stole, and he cut throats, and starved at that, by the powers!"

"Well, it ain't much use, after all," said the young seaman.

"'Tain't much use for fools, you may lay to it—that, nor nothing," cried Silver. "But now, you look here: you're young, you are, but you're as smart as paint. I see that when I set my eyes on you, and I'll talk to you like a man."

You may imagine how I felt when I heard this abominable old rogue addressing another in the very same words of flattery as he had used to myself. I think, if I had been able, that I would have killed him through the barrel. Meantime, he ran on, little supposing he was overheard.

"Here it is about gentlemen of fortune. They lives rough, and they risk swinging, but they eat and drink like fighting-cocks, and when a cruise is done, why, it's hundreds of pounds instead of hundreds of farthings in their pockets. Now, the most goes for rum and a good fling, and to sea again in their shirts. But that's not the course I lay. I puts it all away, some here, some there, and none too much anywheres, by reason of suspicion. I'm fifty,[7] mark you; once back from this cruise, I set up gentleman in earnest. Time enough too, says you. Ah, but I've lived easy in the meantime, never denied myself o' nothing heart desires, and slep' soft and ate dainty all my days but when at sea. And how did I begin? Before the mast, like you!"

"Well," said the other, "but all the other money's

"Here's to ourselves, and plenty of prizes and plenty of duff."

5. Jim Hawkins must have misheard Silver. England had been marooned by his men by the time the viceroy was captured by Taylor, Silver, and the others. (See note 11 on p. 81.)

6. Howel Davis was a pirate captain on the West Coast of Africa before being killed in 1719 by Portuguese troops on the island of Principe. Davis was "a brave and generous man," who "kept his Ship's Company in good order," according to William Snelgrave. Snelgrave, captain of a merchant ship, had met Davis after being captured by Thomas Cocklyn at the mouth of the Sierra Leon River in early 1719.

A Welshman by birth, Davis went to sea at an early age and became familiar with the West Coast of Africa. After an abortive attempt to turn pirate, Davis made his way to New Providence Island in the Bahamas, then back to West Africa, where he captured, looted, and destroyed the Castle of Gambia, a slave depot and trading station operated by a British company.

Davis joined forces with Cocklyn and Oliver La Buse (or La Bouche) until he found that that one of his officers, John Taylor, was being encouraged by Cocklyn to depose Davis from his command. Davis left the pirate squadron and made his way to Principe, off the coast of modern Equatorial Guinea. Here the Portuguese governor allowed himself to be persuaded for a time that his visitor, who was only too happy to trade goods for supplies, was a Royal Navy captain hunting pirates. But the governor's visitor was also a potential embarrassment and problem if his superiors found out about him. The governor solved the problem by having his troops ambush Davis. Davis fell with five bullets in his body. His throat was then cut to make sure he was properly dead.

Taylor went on to depose Captain England after England had taken the *Cassandra*, the ship fondly remembered by John Silver for bringing him back safe and sound from the Indian Ocean. (See also note 8 on p. 80 and note 11 on p. 81.)

7. No, he is not, and his statement is a surprising example of vanity in such a calculating pragmatist. Silver in 1758 is referring to events in 1722 that would have made him a very young teenager at the time if he was 50 in 1758. He also mentions a job—quartermaster on a pirate ship—that would have required him at age 13 or younger to be co-equal to Flint, able to speak up for the interests of the crew and overrule Flint if need be. Silver says later that "Flint his own self was afeard of me."

He would also have been judging minor disputes between the crew, and "*lambs* wasn't the word for Flint's old buccaneers." In addition, he would have been in charge of sharing out food and money. In other words, quartermaster was a difficult and unlikely job for a young person barely a teenager, even a remarkable one like Silver. However, it is possible that a strong, fully grown older teenager or someone in their early 20s might have the confidence of the other crew members and be elected to the position, which would still make Silver older than 50 in 1758.

Silver served with Flint on two different occasions, before 1722 and after, in the 1750s.

When Silver in 1758 gives his age as 50 he also mentions that his leg was amputated by a surgeon who was later hanged with the pirate Roberts at Corso Castle. The hangings took place in 1722, which would have made Silver 14 if he was operated on as late as 1722, which he was not. We know where Silver was in 1722: He was on board the *Cassandra*, and would be until 1723 when the ship reached the Caribbean, as reported in note 4 on p. 88. So he must have been younger when his leg was amputated.

Silver's known whereabouts in 1722 and 1723 in turn raises another question: When did he sail with Flint and with England, because Silver tells us he was with Flint when his leg was amputated prior to 1722 and also was with Flint in the 1750s.

Silver sailed first with Flint, then with England until England was deposed by Taylor, who returned with Silver on the *Cassandra* to the Caribbean, where the crew dispersed. Silver then re-joined Flint. Silver's moving from crew to crew would reflect the shifting allegiances that marked the groupings and regroupings of pirate crews of the period.

8. Slang for "to die," based on the term *slip the cable*, meaning to release a vessel's anchor without first raising the anchor in order to make a fast departure in an emergency.

9. An uncomplimentary name for a small rowboat of undetermined condition (as opposed to a

gone now, ain't it? You daren't show face in Bristol after this."

"Why, where might you suppose it was?" asked Silver derisively.

"At Bristol, in banks and places," answered his companion.

"It were," said the cook; "it were when we weighed anchor. But my old missis has it all by now. And the Spy-glass is sold, lease and goodwill and rigging; and the old girl's off to meet me. I would tell you where, for I trust you, but it'd make jealousy among the mates."

"And can you trust your missus?" asked the other.

"Gentlemen of fortune," returned the cook, "usually trusts little among themselves, and right they are, you may lay to it. But I have a way with me, I have. When a mate brings a slip on his cable[8]—one as knows me, I mean—it won't be in the same world with old John. There was some that was feared of Pew, and some that was feared of Flint; but Flint his own self was feared of me. Feared he was, and proud. They was the roughest crew afloat, was Flint's; the devil himself would have been feared to go to sea with them. Well now, I tell you, I'm not a boasting man, and you seen yourself how easy I keep company; but when I was quartermaster, *lambs* wasn't the word for Flint's old buccaneers. Ah, you may be sure of yourself in old John's ship."

"Well, I tell you now," replied the lad, "I didn't half a quarter like the job till I had this talk with you, John; but there's my hand on it now."

"And a brave lad you were, and smart too," answered Silver, shaking hands so heartily that all the barrel shook, "and a finer figurehead for a gentleman of for-tune I never clapped my eyes on."

By this time I had begun to understand the mean-ing of their terms. By a "gentleman of fortune" they plainly meant neither more nor less than a common pirate, and the little scene that I had overheard was the last act in the corruption of one of the honest hands—perhaps of the last one left aboard. But on this point I was soon to be relieved, for Silver giving a little whis-tle, a third man strolled up and sat down by the party.

"Dick's square," said Silver.

"Oh, I know'd Dick was square," returned the voice of the coxswain, Israel Hands. "He's no fool, is Dick." And he turned his quid and spat. "But look here," he went on, "here's what I want to know, Barbecue: how long are we a-going to stand off and on like a blessed bumboat?[9] I've had a'most enough o' Cap'n Smollett; he's hazed me long enough, by thunder! I want to go into that cabin, I do. I want their pickles and wines, and that."

"Israel," said Silver, "your head ain't much account, nor ever was. But you're able to hear, I reckon; least-ways, your ears is big enough. Now, here's what I say: you'll berth forward, and you'll live hard, and you'll speak soft, and you'll keep sober till I give the word; and you may lay to that, my son."

"Well, I don't say no, do I?" growled the coxswain. "What I say is, when? That's what I say."

"When! By the powers!" cried Silver. "Well now, if you want to know, I'll tell you when. The last moment I can manage, and that's when. Here's a first-rate sea-man, Cap'n Smollett, sails the blessed ship for us. Here's this squire and doctor with a map and such—I

properly maintained ship's boat) that typically was used by residents of a port to reach a ship at anchor in order to sell food, drink, or souvenirs to the mariners.

Admiral Smyth in his 1867 dictionary said the term came from *bombard*, the name given to boats bringing beer supplies, and also to a vessel found in the Mediterranean rigged with two sails like an English ketch.

10. An informal term for members of the crew who were not officers; it comes from the days when crew berthed in the forecastle. (See note 9 on p. 8 and note 3 on p. 74.)

11. The phrase means "as soon as the money's on board."

12. One of several sites on the River Thames where pirates were hanged in public. It was on the foreshore, or tidal riverside beach, in the Wapping area of the East End of London near the low-tide mark, and near today's King Henry's Stairs, the former location of the Execution Dock Stairs. The stairs are next to the modern apartments in the converted King Henry's Wharves, 118–120 Wapping High Street in the modern street numbering system established in 1893. Bodies in the days of *Treasure Island* were left until three tides had washed over them.

Various sites have been offered as the precise location of the gallows, but the distances at issue are measured in terms of a few yards. King Henry's Stairs, overlooked by today's Waterside Gardens, are next to Wapping Pier, where tour boats pick up passengers. This location, just east of the police station and west of Wapping Tube Station, is supported by both the Tower Hamlet Local History Library and Archives and the East London History Society.

Other accounts suggest the gallows were on the little beach near the alleyway with steps that lead down to the Thames, called Wapping Old Stairs, at 62 Wapping High Street.

13. The phrase means "a point more directly into the wind." (See note 13 on p. 82.)

don't know where it is, do I? No more do you, says you. Well then, I mean this squire and doctor shall find the stuff, and help us to get it aboard, by the powers. Then we'll see. If I was sure of you all, sons of double Dutchmen, I'd have Cap'n Smollett navigate us half-way back again before I struck."

"Why, we're all seamen aboard here, I should think," said the lad Dick.

"We're all forecastle hands,[10] you mean," snapped Silver. "We can steer a course, but who's to set one? That's what all you gentlemen split on, first and last. If I had my way, I'd have Cap'n Smollett work us back into the trades at least; then we'd have no blessed miscalculations and a spoonful of water a day. But I know the sort you are. I'll finish with 'em at the island, as soon's the blunt's on board,[11] and a pity it is. But you're never happy till you're drunk. Split my sides, I've a sick heart to sail with the likes of you!"

"Easy all, Long John," cried Israel. "Who's a-crossin' of you?"

"Why, how many tall ships, think ye, now, have I seen laid aboard? And how many brisk lads drying in the sun at Execution Dock?"[12] cried Silver. "And all for this same hurry and hurry and hurry. You hear me? I seen a thing or two at sea, I have. If you would on'y lay your course, and a p'int to windward,[13] you would ride in carriages, you would. But not you! I know you. You'll have your mouthful of rum tomorrow, and go hang."

"Everybody knowed you was a kind of a chapling, John; but there's others as could hand and steer as well as you," said Israel. "They liked a bit o' fun, they did. They wasn't so high and dry, nohow, but took their fling, like jolly companions every one."

"So?" says Silver. "Well, and where are they now? Pew was that sort, and he died a beggar-man. Flint was, and he died of rum at Savannah. Ah, they was a sweet crew, they was! On'y, where are they?"

"But," asked Dick, "when we do lay 'em athwart,[14] what are we to do with 'em, anyhow?"

"There's the man for me!" cried the cook admiringly. "That's what I call business. Well, what would you think? Put 'em ashore like maroons?[15] That would have been England's way. Or cut 'em down like that much pork? That would have been Flint's or Billy Bones's."

"Billy was the man for that," said Israel. "'Dead men don't bite,' says he. Well, he's dead now hisself; he knows the long and short on it now; and if ever a rough hand come to port, it was Billy."

"Right you are," said Silver; "rough and ready. But mark you here, I'm an easy man—I'm quite the gentleman, says you; but this time it's serious. Dooty is dooty, mates. I give my vote—death. When I'm in Parlyment and riding in my coach, I don't want none of these sea-lawyers[16] in the cabin a-coming home, unlooked for, like the devil at prayers. Wait is what I say; but when the time comes, why, let her rip!"

"John," cries the coxswain, "you're a man!"

"You'll say so, Israel, when you see," said Silver. "Only one thing I claim—I claim Trelawney. I'll wring his calf's head off his body with these hands, Dick!" he added, breaking off. "You just jump up, like a sweet lad, and get me an apple, to wet my pipe like."

You may fancy the terror I was in! I should have leaped out and run for it if I had found the strength, but my limbs and heart alike misgave me. I heard Dick

14. "To lay" is used in a number of phrases, including to *lay aloft*, to *lay forward*, and to *lay out*. The basic meaning of the word is "to come" or "to go." Athwart means "across." In navigation it means "across the line of a ship's course." So Dick is asking what will happen when Silver and Co. stop the squire from proceeding on his mission.

15. The word is used here in the sense of people put ashore somewhere and abandoned. Some pirate crews referred to themselves as *marooners* from their habit of using marooning as a punishment for fellow crew members.

16. "Idle, litigious . . . more given to question orders than obey them," was how Admiral Smyth described the kind of sailor called a *sea-lawyer* in his *Sailor's Word-Book* of 1867. He didn't stop there: "One of the pests of the navy as well as of the mercantile marine. Also a name given to the tiger-shark."

17. Hands is referring to "bilge water," the foul-smelling liquid filth found in the lowest areas of a vessel's hull. The meaning here is "Stop talking nonsense." Paradoxically, sailors were happier with foul bilge water below than with clean bilge water, because fresh seawater was a sign of a dangerous leak.

Gravity led the seepage to collect at the bottom of the hull, the area known as "the bilges," where the timbers that made up the sides of a vessel joined the vessel's keel assembly or backbone. "When it stinketh much, it is a sign that it has lain long in the hold of the ship; and on the contrary, when it is clear and sweet, it is a token that it comes freshly in from the sea," wrote Nathanial Boteler, or Butler, a Royal Navy captain, in a 1634 manual. "This stinking water therefore is always a welcome perfume to an old seaman."

18. This is another way of indicating spirits, or a "hard" liquor, such as whiskey, brandy, or rum.

19. A variation of the order to the helmsman to *keep your luff*, which means "keep close to the wind," which in turn means steer a course that aligns the vessel as precisely as possible with the direction from which the wind is coming. *Luff* was sometimes pronounced *loofe*.

20. Jim Hawkins's memory is playing tricks on him again, and he is mixing up schooners and vessels like ketches. He really means the *main mast*, which is the mast nearest the stern on a two-masted schooner.

On a ketch, which has a big foremast, the smaller mast aft of the foremast is called the *mizzen*. See the illustration on p. 63, an image of a big 18th-century ketch, also used for privateering. On ships with three masts, the mast nearest the stern was called the mizzen.

In the late 19th century, schooners with four and more masts were built; the mast farthest to the rear was called the mizzen.

21. The big sail on the foremast. (See illustration, p. xiii.)

begin to rise, and then someone seemingly stopped him, and the voice of Hands exclaimed, "Oh, stow that! Don't you get sucking of that bilge,[17] John. Let's have a go of the rum."

"Dick," said Silver, "I trust you. I've a gauge on the keg, mind. There's the key; you fill a pannikin and bring it up."

Terrified as I was, I could not help thinking to myself that this must have been how Mr. Arrow got the strong waters[18] that destroyed him.

Dick was gone but a little while, and during his absence Israel spoke straight on in the cook's ear. It was but a word or two that I could catch, and yet I gathered some important news, for besides other scraps that tended to the same purpose, this whole clause was audible: "Not another man of them'll jine." Hence there were still faithful men on board.

When Dick returned, one after another of the trio took the pannikin and drank—one "To luck," another with a "Here's to old Flint," and Silver himself saying, in a kind of song, "Here's to ourselves, and hold your luff,[19] plenty of prizes and plenty of duff."

Just then a sort of brightness fell upon me in the barrel, and looking up, I found the moon had risen and was silvering the mizzen-top[20] and shining white on the luff of the fore-sail;[21] and almost at the same time the voice of the lookout shouted, "Land ho!"

Chapter Twelve

Council of War

THERE WAS A GREAT rush of feet across the deck. I could hear people tumbling up from the cabin and the forecastle, and slipping in an instant outside my barrel, I dived behind the fore-sail, made a double towards the stern, and came out upon the open deck in time to join Hunter and Dr. Livesey in the rush for the weather bow.

There all hands were already congregated. A belt of fog had lifted almost simultaneously with the appearance of the moon. Away to the south-west of us we saw two low hills, about a couple of miles apart, and rising behind one of them a third and higher hill, whose peak was still buried in the fog. All three seemed sharp and conical in figure.

So much I saw, almost in a dream, for I had not yet recovered from my horrid fear of a minute or two before. And then I heard the voice of Captain Smollett issuing orders. The *Hispaniola* was laid a couple of points nearer the wind and now sailed a course that would just clear the island on the east.

"And now, men," said the captain, when all was sheeted home,[1] "has any one of you ever seen that land ahead?"

1. Sheeting home is when a sailor hauls on a rope or line (more properly called a *sheet*) connected to a sail until the sail is stiff from the action of the wind on it and he can't pull the rope in any further.

A schooner like the *Hispaniola* had two big fore-and-aft sails, each extended by wooden poles or yards called gaffs at the top and booms at the bottom. To manage them, their *sheets* first would be threaded, or roved, through one or more blocks to create a purchase or tackle. (See note 3 on p. 103.) Managing the *Hispaniola*'s topsails and jib sails would also require sheets and tackles.

2. These names correspond to the three masts on a ship or other three-masted vessel. The foremast, nearest the bow; the main or middle mast; and the smaller mizzen mast aft. (See illustration, p. 59.)

3. William Kidd was a New York-based Scotsman, hanged for piracy and murder at Execution Dock in the Wapping district of London on May 23, 1701, for acts committed while cruising the Indian Ocean.

How Kidd financed his Indian Ocean venture offers a nice window into the habits of public figures at the beginning of the 1700s. Kidd's idea was to make money by hunting pirates and seizing their plunder. He was backed by a group of powerful British politicians who would receive a share of the confiscated plunder in return for their money and the government permits Kidd needed. These included commissions to hunt pirates and attack French shipping, since England was at war with France. Kidd's activities in the Indian Ocean resulted in his arrest after his return to North America. He was brought to London for trial. In the meantime his powerful sponsors were no longer powerful. He had lost whatever political protection he had and had become an embarrassment. At his trial Kidd argued that he had acted legally in the prizes he had taken. Robert C. Ritchie, a professor of history at the University of California at San Diego notes that Kidd crossed the legal boundaries into piracy since only two of six vessels he captured were covered by his commissions.

Captain William Kidd.

4. *Haul your wind* here means "sail closer to the wind." As for *keep the weather of the island*, Silver is saying that Captain Smollett was correct in keeping the *Hispaniola* on a course that kept her in a position where the wind was blowing from the direction of Treasure Island toward the vessel, and not the other way around. The *weather* of an island is the opposite of the *lee* of an island. (For the dangers of a lee shore, see note 4 on p. 24.)

"I have, sir," said Silver. "I've watered there with a trader I was cook in."

"The anchorage is on the south, behind an islet, I fancy?" asked the captain.

"Yes, sir; Skeleton Island they calls it. It were a main place for pirates once, and a hand we had on board knowed all their names for it. That hill to the nor'ard they calls the Fore-mast Hill; there are three hills in a row running south'ard—fore, main, and mizzen,[2] sir. But the main—that's the big un, with the cloud on it—they usually calls the Spy-glass, by reason of a lookout they kept when they was in the anchorage cleaning, for it's there they cleaned their ships, sir, asking your pardon."

"I have a chart here," says Captain Smollett. "See if that's the place."

Long John's eyes burned in his head as he took the chart, but by the fresh look of the paper I knew he was doomed to disappointment. This was not the map we found in Billy Bones's chest, but an accurate copy, complete in all things—names and heights and soundings—with the single exception of the red crosses and the written notes. Sharp as must have been his annoyance, Silver had the strength of mind to hide it.

"Yes, sir," said he, "this is the spot, to be sure, and very prettily drawn out. Who might have done that, I wonder? The pirates were too ignorant, I reckon. Aye, here it is: 'Capt. Kidd's[3] Anchorage'—just the name my shipmate called it. There's a strong current runs along the south, and then away nor'ard up the west coast. Right you was, sir," says he, "to haul your wind and keep the weather of the island.[4] Leastways, if such was your intention as to enter and careen,[5] and there ain't no better place for that in these waters."

"Thank you, my man," says Captain Smollett. "I'll ask you later on to give us a help. You may go."

I was surprised at the coolness with which John avowed his knowledge of the island, and I own I was half-frightened when I saw him drawing nearer to myself. He did not know, to be sure, that I had overheard his council from the apple barrel, and yet I had by this time taken such a horror of his cruelty, duplicity, and power that I could scarce conceal a shudder when he laid his hand upon my arm.

"Ah," says he, "this here is a sweet spot, this island— a sweet spot for a lad to get ashore on. You'll bathe, and you'll climb trees, and you'll hunt goats, you will; and you'll get aloft on them hills like a goat yourself. Why, it makes me young again. I was going to forget my timber leg, I was. It's a pleasant thing to be young and have ten toes, and you may lay to that. When you want to go a bit of exploring, you just ask old John, and he'll put up a snack for you to take along."

And clapping me in the friendliest way upon the shoulder, he hobbled off forward and went below.

Captain Smollett, the squire, and Dr. Livesey were talking together on the quarter-deck,[6] and anxious as I was to tell them my story, I durst not interrupt them openly. While I was still casting about in my thoughts to find some probable excuse, Dr. Livesey called me to his side. He had left his pipe below, and being a slave to tobacco, had meant that I should fetch it; but as soon as I was near enough to speak and not to be overheard, I broke out immediately, "Doctor, let me speak. Get the captain and squire down to the cabin,

5. To careen a vessel in the 1750s was to bring her to a suitable sloping shore, rearrange or unload her ballast and heavy objects, attach cables to her masts, and heave her over to expose one side of the hull. Putting the vessel in this position allowed the crew to make repairs, insert new caulking to seal the ship's seams, and remove the barnacles, worms, seaweed, and other assorted marine growth that inevitably accumulated on a ship's hull over time and seriously reduced a ship's speed or damaged the hull.

The removal process included *breaming*, in which fire was used to burn off the growths, and scraping.

When possible, a mixture of sulphur and tallow was applied to the hull to poison *Teredo navalis* worms, destructive creatures an inch or so wide that can grow to three feet or longer. They eat their way through the timbers of a hull and can destroy a vessel. The mixture also made the vessel more slippery in the water when under sail, and therefore faster. (See also note 3 on p. 16.)

When one side of the hull was clean, the careening process was repeated for the other side.

A shipyard and its dry dock was the best place for careening, but a beach would do if need be, although the process put great strain on a hull.

Port Royal, the great buccaneer outfitting center in Jamaica, initially attracted attention as a convenient place for careening, and its first name, given by the Spaniards who owned it before the English conquest, was Cayo de Carena.

The practice, starting in 1761, of sheathing hulls with thin copper plates reduced the danger from *Teredo navalis*, but seaweed and barnacles remained problems. Today firms offer what they call careening services, using modern technology.

6. The *Hispaniola*'s quarter-deck was a modest affair: a portion of the deck located toward the stern of the vessel and raised a few inches or a foot higher than the rest of the deck. Nevertheless, it was the portion of the deck from which officers commanded the vessel. The *Hispaniola*'s quarter-deck was also the area where the schooner's tiller was located. On a big ship the quarter-deck was a more pronounced area.

"One more cheer for Cap'n Smollett," cried Long John.

7. A boatswain's whistle or pipe was used to sound notes that the crew recognized as the order to assemble on deck. (See note 9 on p. 25.)

8. The *Hispaniola* was a "topsail" schooner—that is, it had small square sails above two big fore-and-aft sails. Each square sail hung from a crosspiece called a *yard*. The name for each end of a yard is the *yard arm*. (See illustration, p. xiii.)

and then make some pretence to send for me. I have terrible news."

The doctor changed countenance a little, but next moment he was master of himself.

"Thank you, Jim," said he quite loudly, "that was all I wanted to know," as if he had asked me a question.

And with that he turned on his heel and rejoined the other two. They spoke together for a little, and though none of them started, or raised his voice, or so much as whistled, it was plain enough that Dr. Livesey had communicated my request, for the next thing that I heard was the captain giving an order to Job Anderson, and all hands were piped on deck.[7]

"My lads," said Captain Smollett, "I've a word to say to you. This land that we have sighted is the place we have been sailing for. Mr. Trelawney, being a very openhanded gentleman, as we all know, has just asked me a word or two, and as I was able to tell him that every man on board had done his duty, alow and aloft, as I never ask to see it done better, why, he and I and the doctor are going below to the cabin to drink your health and luck, and you'll have grog served out for you to drink our health and luck. I'll tell you what I think of this: I think it handsome. And if you think as I do, you'll give a good sea-cheer for the gentleman that does it."

The cheer followed—that was a matter of course; but it rang out so full and hearty that I confess I could hardly believe these same men were plotting for our blood.

"One more cheer for Cap'n Smollett," cried Long John when the first had subsided.

And this also was given with a will.

On the top of that the three gentlemen went below, and not long after, word was sent forward that Jim Hawkins was wanted in the cabin.

I found them all three seated round the table, a bottle of Spanish wine and some raisins before them, and the doctor smoking away, with his wig on his lap, and that, I knew, was a sign that he was agitated. The stern window was open, for it was a warm night, and you could see the moon shining behind on the ship's wake.

"Now, Hawkins," said the squire, "you have something to say. Speak up."

I did as I was bid, and as short as I could make it, told the whole details of Silver's conversation. Nobody interrupted me till I was done, nor did any one of the three of them make so much as a movement, but they kept their eyes upon my face from first to last.

"Jim," said Dr. Livesey, "take a seat."

And they made me sit down at table beside them, poured me out a glass of wine, filled my hands with raisins, and all three, one after the other, and each with a bow, drank my good health, and their service to me, for my luck and courage.

"Now, captain," said the squire, "you were right, and I was wrong. I own myself an ass, and I await your orders."

"No more an ass than I, sir," returned the captain. "I never heard of a crew that meant to mutiny but what showed signs before, for any man that had an eye in his head to see the mischief and take steps according. But this crew," he added, "beats me."

"Captain," said the doctor, "with your permission, that's Silver. A very remarkable man."

"He'd look remarkably well from a yard-arm,[8] sir," returned the captain. "But this is talk; this don't lead to anything. I see three or four points, and with Mr. Trelawney's permission, I'll name them."

"You, sir, are the captain. It is for you to speak," says Mr. Trelawney grandly.

"First point," began Mr. Smollett. "We

must go on, because we can't turn back. If I gave the word to go about, they would rise at once. Second point, we have time before us—at least until this treasure's found. Third point, there are faithful hands. Now, sir, it's got to come to blows sooner or later, and what I propose is to take time by the forelock, as the saying is, and come to blows some fine day when they least expect it. We can count, I take it, on your own home servants, Mr. Trelawney?"

"As upon myself," declared the squire.

"Three," reckoned the captain; "ourselves make seven, counting Hawkins here. Now, about the honest hands?"

"Most likely Trelawney's own men," said the doctor; "those he had picked up for himself before he lit on Silver."

"Nay," replied the squire. "Hands was one of mine."

"I did think I could have trusted Hands," added the captain.

"And to think that they're all English-men!" broke out the squire. "Sir, I could find it in my heart to blow the ship up."

"Well, gentlemen," said the captain, "the best that I can say is not much. We must lay to, if you please, and keep a bright lookout. It's trying on a man, I know. It would be pleasanter to come to blows. But there's no help for it till we know our men. Lay to, and whistle for a wind, that's my view."

"Jim here," said the doctor, "can help us more than anyone. The men are not shy with him, and Jim is a noticing lad."

"Hawkins, I put prodigious faith in you," added the squire.

I began to feel pretty desperate at this, for I felt altogether helpless; and yet, by an odd train of circumstances, it was indeed through me that safety came. In the meantime, talk as we pleased, there were only seven out of the twenty-six on whom we knew we could rely; and out of these seven one was a boy, so that the grown men on our side were six to their nineteen.

PART III

My
Shore Adventure

Chapter Thirteen

How My Shore Adventure Began

THE APPEARANCE OF THE island when I came on deck next morning was altogether changed. Although the breeze had now utterly ceased, we had made a great deal of way during the night and were now lying becalmed about half a mile to the south-east of the low eastern coast. Grey-coloured woods covered a large part of the surface. This even tint was indeed broken up by streaks of yellow sandbreak in the lower lands, and by many tall trees of the pine family, out-topping the others—some singly, some in clumps; but the general colouring was uniform and sad. The hills ran up clear above the vegetation in spires of naked rock. All were strangely shaped, and the Spy-glass, which was by three or four hundred feet the tallest on the island, was likewise the strangest in configuration, running up sheer from almost every side and then suddenly cut off at the top like a pedestal to put a statue on.

The *Hispaniola* was rolling scuppers[1] under in the ocean swell. The booms[2] were tearing at the blocks,[3]

[1]. Regularly spaced openings on the sides of vessels, located where a bulwark meets the upper deck; they provide openings so that water that collects on the upper deck can drain off into the sea. A bulwark looks like a wall and is made of planks attached to a vessel's upper deck.

[2]. A long spar used to extend or *boom out* the foot of a sail. (See illustration, p. xiii.)

[3]. Pulleys that, when combined with rope and attached to something that needs moving, amplify human muscle power. Using one version of a block, a 300-pound object feels as if it weighs 100 pounds. In the 18th century, a vessel similar to the *Hispaniola* could have nearly 200 blocks installed. They were used to manage about three miles of assorted rigging. Blocks were essential for such routine jobs as raising and lowering sails, aligning sails to the wind, controlling booms and yards. Shifting cannon or cargo required blocks, as did managing an anchor before or after it was raised.

Blocks also allowed muscle power to be applied remotely—say, when crew members at deck level needed to change the angle of a spar 80 feet above them.

Many blocks might be needed for some jobs. For example, lifting a ship's boat from its storage position on board, swinging it outward, and then lowering it into the water might require 22 blocks and associated tackle.

Physically, 18th-century blocks were wooden objects, typically 4 inches to 17 inches long, with one or more grooved wheels–called *sheaves*–installed inside them. The groves steadied the rope lines threaded through them. Blocks could contain single sheaves, and blocks containing four parallel sheaves were common. The more sheaves, the more power.

Blocks were made in different sizes. The crew of a vessel would know the difference between a bee-block, cheek-block, d-block, main-sheet-block, monkey-block, nine-pin-block, rack-block, shoe-block, shoulder-block, sister-block, snatch-block, and others. (See illustration, this page.)

4. A narrow, flat slab with a slightly triangular shape that hangs vertically in the water below the stern. Pushing the helm or tiller attached to the rudder to the left or right changes the angle of the rudder in the water, which in turn changes the direction of the vessel. In the 1700s a rudder was assembled using several flat pieces of wood; it was hung from specially designed hinges called pintles.(See illustration, below; also see note 21 on p. 84 and note 7 on p. 105.)

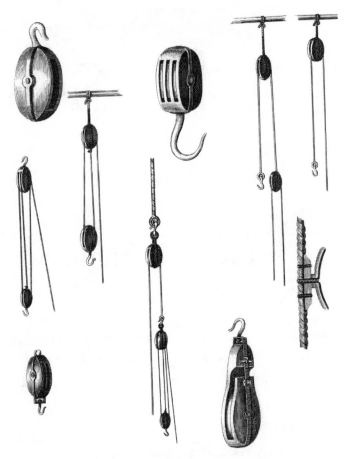

Blocks are pulleys that, when combined with rope, amplify human muscle power. Capt. George Biddlecombe, in his 1848 manual *The Art of Rigging*, estimated that a 200-ton schooner needed about 200 blocks and some three miles of standing and running rigging used to stabilize masts and operate the vessel.

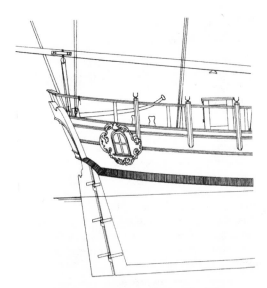

This image shows a rudder hanging below a vessel's stern. It is connected to the hull with hinges, called pintles, that allow the rudder to be turned in different directions.

the rudder[4] was banging to and fro, and the whole ship creaking, groaning, and jumping like a manufactory.[5] I had to cling tight to the backstay,[6] and the world turned giddily before my eyes, for though I was a good enough sailor when there was way on,[7] this standing still and being rolled about like a bottle was a thing I never learned to stand without a qualm or so, above all in the morning, on an empty stomach.

Perhaps it was this—perhaps it was the look of the island, with its grey, melancholy woods, and wild stone spires, and the surf that we could both see and hear foaming and thundering on the steep beach—at least, although the sun shone bright and hot, and the shore birds were fishing and crying all around us, and you would have thought anyone would have been glad to get to land after being so long at sea, my heart sank, as the saying is, into my boots; and from the first look onward, I hated the very thought of Treasure Island.

We had a dreary morning's work before us, for there was no sign of any wind, and the boats had to be got out and manned, and the ship warped[8] three or four miles round the corner of the island and up the narrow passage to the haven behind Skeleton Island. I volunteered for one of the boats, where I had, of course, no business. The heat was sweltering, and the men grumbled fiercely over their work. Anderson was in command of my boat, and instead of keeping the crew in order, he grumbled as loud as the worst.

"Well," he said with an oath, "it's not forever."

I thought this was a very bad sign, for up to that day the men had gone briskly and willingly about their business; but the very sight of the island had relaxed the cords of discipline.

All the way in, Long John stood by the steersman

5. A place where things are made or manufactured. We use the shortened word *factory* today. In the 18th century a *factory* was a trading post, and a *factor* was a business agent.

6. A thick rope that provides front-to-back stability for a mast. Forestays have the same function, but face forward. (See illustration, p. xiii.)

7. This phrase means that the *Hispaniola* was moving fast enough through the water that her rudder could grip the water and direct the course of the vessel, which meant in turn that the helmsman could control the direction of the vessel. (See note 4 on p. 104 and note 21 on p. 84.)

8. Warping a ship was a tedious process by which a vessel uses its anchor to haul itself forward. The equipment needed is a hawser (a thick rope), the onboard capstan or windlass, an anchor, and a ship's boat.

The ship's boat carries the hawser, attached on one end to the vessel and the other to the anchor, ahead of the ship, then drops the anchor over the side. Crew members still on board use the capstan to haul in the hawser. As the hawser comes in, the vessel moves forward. The process is repeated as often as needed until the vessel arrives at its destination.

Variations on using an anchor to move a ship forward include attaching the hawser to a point on shore or to a buoy.

9. That is, Silver gave directions to the seaman steering the vessel. Conning a ship usually took place in circumstances when a compass course was not enough–for example, when coming into an anchorage or passing through an area near land where conditions were difficult. The person conning the vessel would give the helmsman local landmarks and relative compass bearings to steer by, rather than a compass course. Silver would give orders like "steer three points to starboard" rather than "steer south by southwest." (See also note 13 on p. 82.)

10. The man in the chains is taking soundings to determine the depth of the water. The *Hispaniola* had four small, narrow platforms called chains projecting out from her hull to which the four sets of shrouds (ropes) were fastened, two for each mast. (See illustration, p. xiii.)

The two forward chains provided a convenient perch for a crew member to stand and cast a light and measured rope with a weight at the end into the water to check the depth, a process called *taking soundings*. The officers needed to know how much water there was under the hull in order to

Chains on the reproduction schooner *Sultana* are attached to a ledge that projects from the hull. The "man in the chains" stood on the ledge.

and conned[9] the ship. He knew the passage like the palm of his hand, and though the man in the chains[10] got everywhere more water than was down in the chart, John never hesitated once.

"There's a strong scour with the ebb," he said, "and this here passage has been dug out, in a manner of speaking, with a spade."

We brought up just where the anchor was in the chart, about a third of a mile from each shore, the mainland on one side and Skeleton Island on the other. The bottom was clean sand. The plunge of our anchor sent up clouds of birds wheeling and crying over the woods, but in less than a minute they were down again and all was once more silent.

The place was entirely land-locked, buried in woods, the trees coming right down to high-water mark, the shores mostly flat, and the hilltops standing round at a distance in a sort of amphitheatre, one here, one there. Two little rivers, or rather two swamps, emptied out into this pond, as you might call it; and the foliage round that part of the shore had a kind of poisonous brightness. From the ship we could see nothing of the house or stockade, for they were quite buried among trees; and if it had not been for the chart on the companion, we might have been the first that had ever anchored there since the island arose out of the seas.

There was not a breath of air moving, nor a sound but that of the surf booming half a mile away along the beaches and against the rocks outside. A peculiar stagnant smell hung over the anchorage—a smell of sodden leaves and rotting tree trunks. I observed the doctor sniffing and sniffing, like someone tasting a bad egg.

"I don't know about treasure," he said, "but I'll stake my wig there's fever here."

If the conduct of the men had been alarming in the boat, it became truly threatening when they had come aboard. They lay about the deck growling together in talk. The slightest order was received with a black look and grudgingly and carelessly obeyed. Even the honest hands must have caught the infection, for there was not one man aboard to mend another. Mutiny, it was plain, hung over us like a thunder-cloud.

And it was not only we of the cabin party who perceived the danger. Long John was hard at work going from group to group, spending himself in good advice, and as for example no man could have shown a better. He fairly outstripped himself in willingness and civility; he was all smiles to everyone. If an order were given, John would be on his crutch in an instant, with the cheeriest "Aye, aye, sir!" in the world; and when there was nothing else to do, he kept up one song after another, as if to conceal the discontent of the rest.

Of all the gloomy features of that gloomy afternoon, this obvious anxiety on the part of Long John appeared the worst.

We held a council in the cabin.

"Sir," said the captain, "if I risk another order, the whole ship'll come about our ears by the run. You see, sir, here it is. I get a rough answer, do I not? Well, if I speak back, pikes will be going in two shakes;[11] if I don't, Silver will see there's something under that, and the game's up. Now, we've only one man to rely on."

"And who is that?" asked the squire.

"Silver, sir," returned the captain; "he's as anxious as you and I to smother things up. This is a tiff; he'd soon

avoid running aground. The weight, called a plummet, sometimes had sticky tallow inserted into its end so that material on the sea bottom—sand, shell, clay, for example—would stick to it. Experienced seamen could often place their location by seeing what kind of bottom they were over.

11. Boarding-pikes were spears carried to defend against attackers trying to board a vessel.

12. Long, light, and narrow ship's boats, powered by four or six oars, built for speed. They could also be sailed. Originally used by the Royal Navy to chase smugglers, gigs became popular with navy captains in the mid-1700s as useful all-purpose boats to have on board. The *Hispaniola* carried two gigs.

A gig is a long, narrow boat built for speed.

talk 'em out of it if he had the chance, and what I propose to do is to give him the chance. Let's allow the men an afternoon ashore. If they all go, why we'll fight the ship. If they none of them go, well then, we hold the cabin, and God defend the right. If some go, you mark my words, sir, Silver'll bring 'em aboard again as mild as lambs."

It was so decided; loaded pistols were served out to all the sure men; Hunter, Joyce, and Redruth were taken into our confidence and received the news with less surprise and a better spirit than we had looked for, and then the captain went on deck and addressed the crew.

"My lads," said he, "we've had a hot day and are all tired and out of sorts. A turn ashore'll hurt nobody—the boats are still in the water; you can take the gigs,[12] and as many as please may go ashore for the afternoon. I'll fire a gun half an hour before sundown."

I believe the silly fellows must have thought they would break their shins over treasure as soon as they were landed, for they all came out of their sulks in a moment and gave a cheer that started the echo in a faraway hill and sent the birds once more flying and squalling round the anchorage.

The captain was too bright to be in the way. He whipped out of sight in a moment, leaving Silver to arrange the party, and I fancy it was as well he did so. Had he been on deck, he could no longer so much as have pretended not to understand the situation. It was as plain as day. Silver was the captain, and a mighty rebellious crew he had of it. The honest hands—and I was soon to see it proved that there were such on board—must have been very stupid fellows. Or rather, I suppose the truth was this, that all hands were disaffected by the example of the ringleaders—only some more, some less; and a few, being good fellows in the main, could neither be led nor driven any further. It is one thing to be idle and skulk and quite another to take a ship and murder a number of innocent men.

At last, however, the party was made up. Six fellows were to stay on board, and the remaining thirteen, including Silver, began to embark.

Then it was that there came into my head the first of the mad notions that contributed so much to save our lives. If six men were left by Silver, it was plain our party could not take and fight the ship; and since only six were left, it was equally plain that the cabin party had no present need of my assistance. It occurred to me at once to go ashore. In a jiffy I had slipped over the side and curled up in the fore-sheets of the nearest boat, and almost at the same moment she shoved off.

No one took notice of me, only the bow oar saying, "Is that you, Jim? Keep your head

I caught a branch and swung myself out, and plunged into the nearest thicket.

down." But Silver, from the other boat, looked sharply over and called out to know if that were me; and from that moment I began to regret what I had done.

The crews raced for the beach, but the boat I was in, having some start and being at once the lighter and the better manned, shot far ahead of her consort, and the bow had struck among the shore-side trees and I had caught a branch and swung myself out and plunged into the nearest thicket while Silver and the rest were still a hundred yards behind.

"Jim, Jim!" I heard him shouting.

But you may suppose I paid no heed; jumping, ducking, and breaking through, I ran straight before my nose till I could run no longer.

Chapter Fourteen

The First Blow

I WAS SO PLEASED at having given the slip to Long John that I began to enjoy myself and look around me with some interest on the strange land that I was in.

I had crossed a marshy tract full of willows, bulrushes, and odd, outlandish, swampy trees; and I had now come out upon the skirts of an open piece of undulating, sandy country, about a mile long, dotted with a few pines and a great number of contorted trees, not unlike the oak in growth, but pale in the foliage, like willows. On the far side of the open stood one of the hills, with two quaint, craggy peaks shining vividly in the sun.

I now felt for the first time the joy of exploration. The isle was uninhabited; my shipmates I had left behind, and nothing lived in front of me but dumb brutes and fowls. I turned hither and thither among the trees. Here and there were flowering plants, unknown to me; here and there I saw snakes, and one raised his head from a ledge of rock and hissed at me with a noise not unlike the spinning of a top. Little did I suppose that

1. In theory, the presence of live, or evergreen, oaks should help us locate the general area of Treasure Island, but many areas of the world are home to evergreen varieties of oak. *Quercus virginiana*, the live oak found from Virginia to Texas, is also found in Mexico and Cuba, both of which have coastal islands.

he was a deadly enemy and that the noise was the famous rattle.

Then I came to a long thicket of these oaklike trees—live, or evergreen, oaks,[1] I heard afterwards they should be called—which grew low along the sand like brambles, the boughs curiously twisted, the foliage compact, like thatch. The thicket stretched down from the top of one of the sandy knolls, spreading and growing taller as it went, until it reached the margin of the broad, reedy fen, through which the nearest of the little rivers soaked its way into the anchorage. The marsh was steaming in the strong sun, and the outline of the Spy-glass trembled through the haze.

All at once there began to go a sort of bustle among the bulrushes; a wild duck flew up with a quack, another followed, and soon over the whole surface of the marsh a great cloud of birds hung screaming and circling in the air. I judged at once that some of my shipmates must be drawing near along the borders of the fen. Nor was I deceived, for soon I heard the very distant and low tones of a human voice, which, as I continued to give ear, grew steadily louder and nearer.

This put me in a great fear, and I crawled under cover of the nearest live-oak and squatted there, hearkening, as silent as a mouse.

Another voice answered, and then the first voice, which I now recognized to be Silver's, once more took up the story and ran on for a long while in a stream, only now and again interrupted by the other. By the sound they must have been talking earnestly, and almost fiercely; but no distinct word came to my hearing.

At last the speakers seemed to have paused and perhaps to have sat down, for not only did they cease to draw any nearer, but the birds themselves began to grow more quiet and to settle again to their places in the swamp.

And now I began to feel that I was neglecting my business, that since I had been so foolhardy as to come ashore with these desperadoes, the least I could do was to overhear them at their councils, and that my plain and obvious duty was to draw as close as I could manage, under the favourable ambush of the crouching trees.

I could tell the direction of the speakers pretty exactly, not only by the sound of their voices but by the behaviour of the few birds that still hung in alarm above the heads of the intruders.

Crawling on all fours, I made steadily but slowly towards them, till at last, raising my head to an aperture among the leaves, I could see clear down into a little green dell beside the marsh, and closely set about with trees, where Long John Silver and another of the crew stood face to face in conversation.

The sun beat full upon them. Silver had thrown his hat beside him on the ground, and his great, smooth, blond face, all shining with heat, was lifted to the other man's in a kind of appeal.

"Mate," he was saying, "it's because I thinks gold dust of you—gold dust, and you may lay to that! If I hadn't took to you like pitch, do you think I'd have been here a-warning of you? All's up—you can't make nor mend;[2] it's to save your neck that I'm a-speaking, and if one of the wild uns knew it, where'd I be, Tom—now, tell me, where'd I be?"

"Silver," said the other man—and I observed he was not only red in the face, but spoke as hoarse as a crow, and his voice shook too, like a taut rope—"Silver," says

2. There was, according to Commander A. Covey-Crump, of the Royal Navy, an old pipe "Hands to Make and Mend Clothes," which was the traditional chore that sailors on a Royal Navy vessel were set to doing when there was no regular work to be done. *Make and mend* became a term for time off, and today is the official Royal Navy term for a half-day holiday. Silver is telling the crew that they are out of time and in danger.

he, "you're old, and you're honest, or has the name for it; and you've money too, which lots of poor sailors hasn't; and you're brave, or I'm mistook. And will you tell me you'll let yourself be led away with that kind of a mess of swabs? Not you! As sure as God sees me, I'd sooner lose my hand. If I turn agin my dooty—"

And then all of a sudden he was interrupted by a noise. I had found one of the honest hands—well, here, at that same moment, came news of another. Far away out in the marsh there arose, all of a sudden, a sound like the cry of anger, then another on the back of it; and then one horrid, long-drawn scream. The rocks of the Spy-glass re-echoed it a score of times; the whole troop of marshbirds rose again, darkening heaven, with a simultaneous whirr; and long after that death yell was still ringing in my brain, silence had re-established its empire, and only the rustle of the redescending birds and the boom of the distant surges disturbed the languor of the afternoon.

Tom had leaped at the sound, like a horse at the

Just before him Tom lay motionless upon the sward.

spur, but Silver had not winked an eye. He stood where he was, resting lightly on his crutch, watching his companion like a snake about to spring.

"John!" said the sailor, stretching out his hand.

"Hands off!" cried Silver, leaping back a yard, as it seemed to me, with the speed and security of a trained gymnast.

"Hands off, if you like, John Silver," said the other. "It's a black conscience that can make you feared of me. But in heaven's name, tell me, what was that?"

"That?" returned Silver, smiling away, but warier than ever, his eye a mere pin-point in his big face, but gleaming like a crumb of glass. "That? Oh, I reckon that'll be Alan."

And at this point Tom flashed out like a hero.

"Alan!" he cried. "Then rest his soul for a true seaman! And as for you, John Silver, long you've been a mate of mine, but you're mate of mine no more. If I die like a dog, I'll die in my dooty. You've killed Alan, have you? Kill me too, if you can. But I defies you."

And with that, this brave fellow turned his back directly on the cook and set off walking for the beach. But he was not destined to go far. With a cry John seized the branch of a tree, whipped the crutch out of his armpit, and sent that uncouth missile hurtling through the air. It struck poor Tom, point foremost, and with stunning violence,

right between the shoulders in the middle of his back. His hands flew up, he gave a sort of gasp, and fell.

Whether he were injured much or little, none could ever tell. Like enough, to judge from the sound, his back was broken on the spot. But he had no time given him to recover. Silver, agile as a monkey even without leg or crutch, was on the top of him next moment and had twice buried his knife up to the hilt in that defenceless body. From my place of ambush, I could hear him pant aloud as he struck the blows.

I do not know what it rightly is to faint, but I do know that for the next little while the whole world swam away from before me in a whirling mist; Silver and the birds, and the tall Spy-glass hilltop, going round and round and topsy-turvy before my eyes, and all manner of bells ringing and distant voices shouting in my ear.

When I came again to myself the monster had pulled himself together, his crutch under his arm, his hat upon his head. Just before him Tom lay motionless upon the sward; but the murderer minded him not a whit, cleansing his blood-stained knife the while upon a wisp of grass. Everything else was unchanged, the sun still shining mercilessly on the steaming marsh and the tall pinnacle of the mountain, and I could scarce persuade myself that murder had been actually done and a human life cruelly cut short a moment since before my eyes.

But now John put his hand into his pocket, brought out a whistle, and blew upon it several modulated blasts that rang far across the heated air. I could not tell, of course, the meaning of the signal, but it instantly awoke my fears. More men would be coming. I might be discovered. They had already slain two of the honest people; after Tom and Alan, might not I come next?

Instantly I began to extricate myself and crawl back again, with what speed and silence I could manage, to the more open portion of the wood. As I did so, I could hear hails coming and going between the old buccaneer and his comrades, and this sound of danger lent me wings. As soon as I was clear of the thicket, I ran as I never ran before, scarce minding the direction of my flight, so long as it led me from the murderers; and as I ran, fear grew and grew upon me until it turned into a kind of frenzy.

Indeed, could anyone be more entirely lost than I? When the gun fired, how should I dare to go down to the boats among those fiends, still smoking from their crime? Would not the first of them who saw me wring my neck like a snipe's? Would not my absence itself be an evidence to them of my alarm, and therefore of my fatal knowledge? It was all over, I thought. Good-bye to the *Hispaniola*; good-bye to the squire, the doctor, and the captain! There was nothing left for me but death by starvation or death by the hands of the mutineers.

All this while, as I say, I was still running, and without taking any notice, I had drawn near to the foot of the little hill with the two peaks and had got into a part of the island where the live-oaks grew more widely apart and seemed more like forest trees in their bearing and dimensions. Mingled with these were a few scattered pines, some fifty, some nearer seventy, feet high. The air too smelt more freshly than down beside the marsh.

And here a fresh alarm brought me to a standstill with a thumping heart.

Chapter Fifteen

The Man of the Island

FROM THE SIDE OF the hill, which was here steep and stony, a spout of gravel was dislodged and fell rattling and bounding through the trees. My eyes turned instinctively in that direction, and I saw a figure leap with great rapidity behind the trunk of a pine. What it was, whether bear or man or monkey, I could in no wise tell. It seemed dark and shaggy; more I knew not. But the terror of this new apparition brought me to a stand.

I was now, it seemed, cut off upon both sides; behind me the murderers, before me this lurking nondescript. And immediately I began to prefer the dangers that I knew to those I knew not. Silver himself appeared less terrible in contrast with this creature of the woods, and I turned on my heel, and looking sharply behind me over my shoulder, began to retrace my steps in the direction of the boats.

Instantly the figure reappeared, and making a wide circuit, began to head me off. I was tired, at any rate; but had I been as fresh as when I rose, I could see it was in vain for me to contend in speed with such an adversary. From trunk to trunk the creature flitted like a deer, running manlike on two legs, but unlike any man that I had ever seen, stooping almost double as it ran. Yet a man it was, I could no longer be in doubt about that.

I began to recall what I had heard of cannibals. I was within an ace of calling for help. But the mere fact that he was a man, however wild, had somewhat reassured me, and my fear of Silver began to revive in proportion. I stood still, therefore, and cast about for some method of escape; and as I was so

1. This garment is probably a pair of tarred, extra-wide, kilt-like seamen's pants, but could also possibly be leggings or some sort of gaiter.

Captain Grose, the 18th-century recorder of contemporary slang, reported that *gaskin* means breeches or pants. *Galligaskins* were the wide pants used by mariners from at least the 1500s to the early 1800s; the pants were also called *petticoat trousers* and *tarry breeks*, which were the same kind of pants but water-proofed with tar. *Tarry-breek* was also a slang name for a sailor in the north of England.

However, Eric Partridge, the great 20th-century specialist in word usage and history, noted in the reissue of Grose's book, which he edited, that in the dialect of the county of Somerset in the west of England, *gaskins* also referred to *leggings* or *gaiters*. Jim Hawkins is of course from the West Country, so he may have been using a local word for "leggings."

thinking, the recollection of my pistol flashed into my mind. As soon as I remembered I was not defenceless, courage glowed again in my heart and I set my face resolutely for this man of the island and walked briskly towards him.

He was concealed by this time behind another tree trunk; but he must have been watching me closely, for as soon as I began to move in his direction he reappeared and took a step to meet me. Then he hesitated, drew back, came forward again, and at last, to my wonder and confusion, threw himself on his knees and held out his clasped hands in supplication.

At that I once more stopped.

"Who are you?" I asked.

"Ben Gunn," he answered, and his voice sounded hoarse and awkward, like a rusty lock. "I'm poor Ben Gunn, I am; and I haven't spoke with a Christian these three years."

I could now see that he was a white man like myself and that his features were even pleasing. His skin, wherever it was exposed, was burnt by the sun; even his lips were black, and his fair eyes looked quite startling in so dark a face. Of all the beggar-men that I had seen or fancied, he was the chief for raggedness. He was clothed with tatters of old ship's canvas and old seacloth, and this extraordinary patchwork was all held together by a system of the most various and incongruous fastenings, brass buttons, bits of stick, and loops of tarry gaskin.[1] About his waist he wore an old brass-buckled leather belt, which was the one thing solid in his whole accoutrement.

"Three years!" I cried. "Were you shipwrecked?"

"Nay, mate," said he; "marooned."

I had heard the word, and I knew it stood for a horrible kind of punishment common enough among the buccaneers, in which the offender is put ashore with a little powder and shot and left behind on some desolate and distant island.

"Marooned three years agone," he continued, "and lived on goats since then, and berries, and oysters. Wherever a man is, says I, a man can do for himself. But, mate, my heart is sore for Christian diet. You mightn't happen to have a piece of cheese about you, now? No? Well, many's the long night I've dreamed of cheese—toasted, mostly—and woke up again, and here I were."

"If ever I can get aboard again," said I, "you shall have cheese by the stone."[2]

All this time he had been feeling the stuff of my jacket, smoothing my hands, looking at my boots, and generally, in the intervals of his speech, showing a childish pleasure in the presence of a fellow creature. But at my last words he perked up into a kind of startled slyness.

"If ever you can get aboard again, says you?" he repeated. "Why, now, who's to hinder you?"

"Not you, I know," was my reply.

"And right you was," he cried. "Now you—what do you call yourself, mate?"

"Jim," I told him.

"Jim, Jim," says he, quite pleased apparently. "Well, now, Jim, I've lived that rough as you'd be ashamed to hear of. Now, for instance, you wouldn't think I had had a pious mother—to look at me?" he asked.

"Why, no, not in particular," I answered.

"Ah, well," said he, "but I had—remarkable pious.

2. A stone is a medieval measure of weight and is equivalent to 14 pounds. It is still used in Britain, which officially has adopted the metric system.

3. This is Ben Gunn's way of saying *chuck farthing*, a game which in the 1700s, according to Joseph Strutt (1749–1802), required players to toss coins at a spot in the ground they have hollowed out. The players also decide on two marks on the ground at which they can stand and toss coins at the hole they have made. The first mark is some distance from the hole, and all the players toss their coins from this mark. The second mark is closer to the hole. The player whose farthing has landed nearest the hole then is allowed to collect all the coins thrown. He then moves to the second or closer mark and tosses the coins all at the same time at the hole. Some of the coins will fall into the whole, and some will drop nearby. He gets to keep any coins that went into the hole.

And I was a civil, pious boy, and could rattle off my catechism that fast, as you couldn't tell one word from another. And here's what it come to, Jim, and it begun with chuck-farthen[3] on the blessed grave-stones! That's what it begun with, but it went further'n that; and so my mother told me, and predicked the whole, she did, the pious woman! But it were Providence that put me here. I've thought it all out in this here lonely island, and I'm back on piety. You don't catch me tasting rum so much, but just a thimbleful for luck, of course, the first chance I have. I'm bound I'll be good, and I see the way to. And, Jim"—looking all round him and lowering his voice to a whisper—"I'm rich."

I now felt sure that the poor fellow had gone crazy in his solitude, and I suppose I must have shown the feeling in my face, for he repeated the statement hotly: "Rich! Rich! I says. And I'll tell you what: I'll make a man of you, Jim. Ah, Jim, you'll bless your stars, you will, you was the first that found me!"

And at this there came suddenly a lowering shadow over his face, and he tightened his grasp upon my hand and raised a forefinger threateningly before my eyes.

"Now, Jim, you tell me true: that ain't Flint's ship?" he asked.

At this I had a happy inspiration. I began to believe that I had found an ally, and I answered him at once.

"It's not Flint's ship, and Flint is dead; but I'll tell you true, as you ask me—there are some of Flint's hands aboard; worse luck for the rest of us."

"Not a man—with one—leg?" he gasped.

"Silver?" I asked.

"Ah, Silver!" says he. "That were his name."

"He's the cook, and the ringleader too."

He was still holding me by the wrist, and at that he gave it quite a wring.

"If you was sent by Long John," he said, "I'm as good as pork, and I know it. But where was you, do you suppose?"

I had made my mind up in a moment, and by way of answer told him the whole story of our voyage and the predicament in which we found ourselves. He heard me with the keenest interest, and when I had done he patted me on the head.

"You're a good lad, Jim," he said; "and you're all in a clove hitch,[4] ain't you? Well, you just put your trust in Ben Gunn—Ben Gunn's the man to do it. Would you think it likely, now, that your squire would prove a liberal minded one in case of help—him being in a clove hitch, as you remark?"

I told him the squire was the most liberal of men.

"Aye, but you see," returned Ben Gunn, "I didn't mean giving me a gate to keep,[5] and a suit of livery clothes,[6] and such; that's not my mark, Jim. What I mean is, would he be likely to come down to the toon of, say one thousand pounds out of money that's as good as a man's own already?"

"I am sure he would," said I. "As it was, all hands were to share."

"And a passage home?" he added with a look of great shrewdness.

"Why," I cried, "the squire's a gentleman. And besides, if we got rid of the others, we should want you to help work the vessel home."

"Ah," said he, "so you would." And he seemed very much relieved.

"Now, I'll tell you what," he went on. "So much I'll

4. A knot used to fasten a rope to an object, such as a spar, or to standing rigging; it can also be used to tie up a bundle or bale securely. Ben Gunn is telling Jim that he has got himself securely in a fix or jam.

A clove hitch is a knot used to fasten a rope to a spar or to standing rigging.

5. Ben Gunn is saying he doesn't want a modest job like a gatekeeper's. The gate in question might be at the beginning of a drive that leads to a grand house, or one that leads into a city park. The job in the 1700s had overtones of charity, work given to a deserving person, such as a wounded veteran or retired sailor.

6. Livery was clothing worn by servants, a faint echo of the private armies of the 1300s who were identified by their lord's insignia or livery. John MacDonald, a footman who wrote his memoirs after serving 20 employers between 1746 and 1779, described his first livery thus: "I was fitted with a green jacket with a red cape, a red waistcoat, and a leather cap with a forepart lined with red marocco." He was nine years old, and his job was to ride one of the six horses that drew his employer's carriage.

A footman at a lord's grand house, whose job it was to admit visitors through the front door or wait at table, would wear livery, as would that lord's coachman, as would a doorman at the Bank of England and other institutions. Some footmen were literally that; they walked or ran ahead of their employer's carriage.

We still see suits of livery clothes when we see a doorman at a hotel or apartment house in a distinctive costume.

tell you, and no more. I were in Flint's ship when he buried the treasure; he and six along—six strong seamen. They was ashore nigh on a week, and us standing off and on in the old *Walrus*. One fine day up went the signal, and here come Flint by himself in a little boat, and his head done up in a blue scarf. The sun was getting up, and mortal white he looked about the cutwater.[7] But, there he was, you mind, and the six all dead—dead and buried. How he done it, not a man aboard us could make out. It was battle, murder, and sudden death, leastways—him against six. Billy Bones was the mate; Long John, he was quartermaster; and they asked him where the treasure was. 'Ah,' says he, 'you can go ashore, if you like, and stay,' he says; 'but as for the ship, she'll beat up for more, by thunder!' That's what he said.

"Well, I was in another ship three years back, and we sighted this island. 'Boys,' said I, 'here's Flint's treasure; let's land and find it.' The cap'n was displeased at that, but my messmates were all of a mind and landed. Twelve days they looked for it, and every day they had the worse word for me, until one fine morning all hands went aboard. 'As for you, Benjamin Gunn,' says they, 'here's a musket,' they says, 'and a spade, and pick-axe. You can stay here and find Flint's money for yourself,' they says.

"Well, Jim, three years have I been here, and not a bite of Christian diet from that day to this. But now, you look here; look at me. Do I look like a man before the mast?* No, says you. Nor I weren't, neither, I says."

And with that he winked and pinched me hard.

"Just you mention them words to your squire, Jim," he went on. "Nor he weren't, neither—that's the words. Three years he were the man of this island, light and dark, fair and rain; and sometimes he would maybe think upon a prayer (says you), and sometimes he would maybe think of his old mother, so be as she's alive (you'll say); but the most part of Gunn's time (this is what you'll say)—the most part of his time was took up with another matter. And then you'll give him a nip, like I do."

And he pinched me again in the most confidential manner.

"Then," he continued, "then you'll up, and you'll say this: Gunn is a good man (you'll say), and he puts a precious sight more confidence—a precious sight, mind that—in a gen'leman born than in these gen'lemen of fortune, having been one hisself."

"Well," I said, "I don't understand one word that you've been saying. But that's neither here nor there; for how am I to get on board?"

"Ah," said he, "that's the hitch, for sure. Well, there's my boat, that I made with my two hands. I keep her under the white rock. If the worst come to the worst, we might try that after dark. Hi!" he broke out. "What's that?"

For just then, although the sun had still an hour or two to run, all the echoes of the island awoke and bellowed to the thunder of a cannon.

"I'm poor Ben Gunn, I am. Marooned three years agone, and lived on goats since then."

123

8. The masthead is the upper part of a mast above the rigging. *Mastheading* is "a well-known marine punishment said to give midshipmen the best time for reading," according to Admiral Smyth. *Mountings* are Ben Gunn's way of saying *mountains*. He is telling Jim that the goats are hiding from him by going as far up the mountains as possible. (See illustration, p. xiii.)

9. Technically the Union Jack is a small version of the Union Flag, the national flag of the United Kingdom; it is flown on the *jack staff* in the bows of a Royal Navy vessel. Union Jack is often used interchangeably as a term for the Union Flag.

The kingdoms of England and Scotland were united in 1707 to form Great Britain. In 1758 the flag combined the designs of two crosses associated with Christian saints regarded as having a special relationship with the two kingdoms. The red cross on a white background of Saint George is traditionally associated with England, and the white diagonal cross on a blue background of Saint Andrew is traditionally associated with Scotland. The gold cross on a black background of Saint David of Wales, also part of Great Britain since its annexation in 1536, was not included in the Union Flag.

The Union Flag in use in 2014 includes elements of three crosses. The design has been in use since the 1801 legislative union of Ireland with Great Britain when a red diagonal cross on a white background, associated by some with Saint Patrick, the patron saint of Ireland, was added.

Most of Ireland split away from the Union in 1921 and is now the Republic of Eire. In 2014 Scotland has its own legislature again. Wales also has its own National Assembly, as does Northern Ireland.

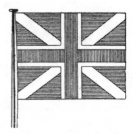

"Union Jack" was originally a Royal Navy term for Britain's Union Flag. This is the version in use before 1801.

"They have begun to fight!" I cried. "Follow me."

And I began to run towards the anchorage, my terrors all forgotten, while close at my side the marooned man in his goatskins trotted easily and lightly.

"Left, left," says he; "keep to your left hand, mate Jim! Under the trees with you! Theer's where I killed my first goat. They don't come down here now; they're all mastheaded on them mountings[8] for the fear of Benjamin Gunn. Ah! And there's the cetemery"—cemetery, he must have meant. "You see the mounds? I come here and prayed, nows and thens, when I thought maybe a Sunday would be about doo. It weren't quite a chapel, but it seemed more solemn like; and then, says you, Ben Gunn was short-handed—no chapling, nor so much as a Bible and a flag, you says."

So he kept talking as I ran, neither expecting nor receiving any answer.

The cannon-shot was followed after a considerable interval by a volley of small arms.

Another pause, and then, not a quarter of a mile in front of me, I beheld the Union Jack[9] flutter in the air above a wood.

PART IV

The
Stockade

Chapter Sixteen

Narrative Continued by the Doctor: How the Ship Was Abandoned

IT WAS ABOUT HALF past one—three bells in sea phrase[1]—that the two boats went ashore from the *Hispaniola*. The captain, the squire, and I were talking matters over in the cabin. Had there been a breath of wind, we should have fallen on the six mutineers who were left aboard with us, slipped our cable, and away to sea. But the wind was wanting; and to complete our helplessness, down came Hunter with the news that Jim Hawkins had slipped into a boat and was gone ashore with the rest.

It never occurred to us to doubt Jim Hawkins, but we were alarmed for his safety. With the men in the temper they were in, it seemed an even chance if we should see the lad again. We ran on deck. The pitch was bubbling in the seams; the nasty stench of the place turned me sick; if ever a man smelt fever and dysentery, it was in that abominable anchorage. The

1. In the days of sail a ship's bell was rung at periodic intervals to mark the passage of time during the seven work periods (watches) into which a vessel's 24-hour day typically was divided. Five of the watches lasted four hours and two of the watches lasted two hours.

The two short or half watches have been called the "first dog watch" and the "last dog watch" since at least the 1600s. The uneven number of watches was designed to let watch members rotate though all the watches.

Until 1805, a ship's day began at noon. The ship's bell was rung at half-hour intervals, with increasing numbers of peals sounded as the watches progressed:

12:30 p.m.	one bell
1:00 p.m.	two bells
1:30 p.m.	three bells
2:00 p.m.	four bells
2:30 p.m.	five bells
3:00 p.m.	six bells
3:30 p.m.	seven bells
4:00 p.m.	eight bells

also the signal for a new watch to begin work

4:30 p.m.	one bell
5:00 p.m.	two bells, etc.

As you can see, three bells is not always one-thirty.

The end of the first dog watch was marked by four bells, the end of the last dog watch by eight bells.

Today a ship's day begins at midnight.

2. A lilting, catchy old tune with various lyrics from the 1600s; it still carries political and religious overtones.

According to a 2005 note by the BBC World Service, the tune began as "a jig with Irish roots, whose first appearance seems to be in a collection published in London 1661 entitled *An Antidote Against Melancholy*, where it is set to the words 'There was an old man of Waltham Cross.'"

In the meantime the tune's most notable lyrics–and there have been several set to the tune–date back to 1687. They were written as a political satire and adopted as a marching song by the troops of the Protestant William III as he fought the Roman Catholic King James II for control of England and Wales, Scotland, and Ireland in the 1680s and 1690s. When James lost, "Lillibullero" was said to "have sung a king out of three kingdoms."

3. A ship's general-purpose utility boat. The *Hispaniola* carried one jolly-boat. (See also note 12 on p. 108.)

4. The walls were loopholed for musket fire, also called *musketry*. The muskets used would have been long-barreled *firelock muskets*, often abbreviated to *firelocks*. Firelocks, which today are usually called *flintlocks*, used flints to create a spark that fired the gunpowder with which the weapon was loaded. By the late 1600s the firelock musket had replaced the *matchlock musket*, which used a burning length of cord, also called *match*, for ignition.

5. Known as William Augustus to his family, Billy to his troops, and "Butcher" Cumberland to the

six scoundrels were sitting grumbling under a sail in the forecastle; ashore we could see the gigs made fast and a man sitting in each, hard by where the river runs in. One of them was whistling "Lillibullero."[2]

Waiting was a strain, and it was decided that Hunter and I should go ashore with the jolly-boat[3] in quest of information.

The gigs had leaned to their right, but Hunter and I pulled straight in, in the direction of the stockade upon the chart. The two who were left guarding their boats seemed in a bustle at our appearance; "Lillibullero" stopped off, and I could see the pair discussing what they ought to do. Had they gone and told Silver, all might have turned out differently; but they had their orders, I suppose, and decided to sit quietly where they were and hark back again to "Lillibullero."

There was a slight bend in the coast, and I steered so as to put it between us; even before we landed we had thus lost sight of the gigs. I jumped out and came as near running as I durst, with a big silk handkerchief under my hat for coolness' sake and a brace of pistols ready primed for safety.

I had not gone a hundred yards when I reached the stockade.

This was how it was: a spring of clear water rose almost at the top of a knoll. Well, on the knoll, and enclosing the spring, they had clapped a stout log-house fit to hold two score of people on a pinch and loopholed for musketry[4] on either side. All round this they had cleared a wide space, and then the thing was completed by a paling six feet high, without door or opening, too strong to pull down without time and labour and too open to shelter the besiegers. The people in the log-house had them in every way; they stood quiet in shelter and shot the others like partridges. All they wanted was a good watch and food, for short of a complete surprise, they might have held the place against a regiment.

What particularly took my fancy was the spring. For though we had a good enough place of it in the cabin of the *Hispaniola*, with plenty of arms and ammunition, and things to eat, and excellent wines, there had been one thing overlooked—we had no water. I was thinking this over when there came ringing over the island the cry of a man at the point of death. I was not new to violent death—I have served his Royal Highness the Duke of Cumberland,[5] and got a wound myself at Fontenoy[6]—but I know my pulse went dot and carry one.[7] "Jim Hawkins is gone," was my first thought.

It is something to have been an old soldier, but more still to have been a doctor. There is no time to dilly-dally in our work. And so now I made up my mind instantly, and with no time lost returned to the shore and jumped on board the jolly-boat.

By good fortune Hunter pulled a good oar. We made the water fly, and the boat was soon alongside and I aboard the schooner.

I found them all shaken, as was natural. The squire was sitting down, as white as a sheet, thinking of the harm he had led us to, the good soul! And one of the six forecastle hands was little better.

"There's a man," says Captain Smollett, nodding towards him, "new to this work. He came nigh-hand fainting, doctor, when he heard the cry. Another touch of the rudder and that man would join us."

The Duke of Cumberland, a son of Britain's King George II, was acclaimed in England and reviled in Scotland.

Scots, the Duke of Cumberland (1721–1765) was the second surviving son of Britain's King George II. Accompanied by 145 tons of personal baggage, Cumberland was the commanding general at the Battle of Fontenoy in 1745, an episode in the War of the Austrian Succession. He also was the commanding general of an Anglo-Scots army at the Battle of Culloden in Scotland in 1746, the last battle to take place on British soil.

After Culloden, Cumberland launched a program of punitive destruction and repression in Scotland that earned him the name "Butcher" Cumberland among the Scots and many of the English.

Back in England, he was acclaimed and received many tributes. The composer Handel wrote the vocal music "See the Conquering Hero Comes" in his honor, and a flower was renamed "Sweet William" for him; according to an often-repeated story, in reply the Scots renamed a weed "Stinking Billy."

Active politically, Cumberland collapsed and died at a meeting at his London house on October 31, 1765. He was 44.

Cumberland has not been forgotten. In 2006 the BBC was criticized for being insensitive by some Scots for choosing an adaptation of "See the Conquering Hero Comes" as theme music for their coverage of the World Cup soccer tournament in Germany.

6. The Battle of Fontenoy in 1745 was an episode in the War of the Austrian Succession, known in North America as King George's War. It took place a few miles from the city of Tournai in Wallonia, a region that is part of modern Belgium.

Dr. Livesey would have been one of the 7,000 to 10,000 Allied casualties, although what he was doing on the battlefield is not known. It was an unlikely place for a doctor. The French suffered an estimated 5,000 to 7,000 dead and wounded

The battle was fought by a British-led force of approximately 46,000, which made a two-column frontal assault against a French force of about 50,000 that had fortified part of the battlefield.

7. Dr. Livesey is saying his heartbeat became irregular. His use of this term is an early variation of the term *dot and go one*, used to describe the gait of a person with one leg shorter than the other who therefore walks in an irregular manner.

8. A square opening with a hinged wooden lid, big enough to accommodate a cannon barrel; it was located between the stern timbers at the rear or stern of a vessel. The fact that the *Hispaniola* had a stern-port is another clue that the schooner had been modified to serve as a privateer.

9. Waterproof metal boxes coated with rustproof tin. These tins contained gunpowder for the firearms.

I told my plan to the captain, and between us we settled on the details of its accomplishment.

We put old Redruth in the gallery between the cabin and the forecastle, with three or four loaded muskets and a mattress for protection. Hunter brought the boat round under the stern-port,[8] and Joyce and I set to work loading her with powder tins,[9] muskets,

"Down, Dog!" cries the captain. And the head popped back again.

bags of biscuits, kegs of pork,[10] a cask of cognac, and my invaluable medicine chest.

In the meantime, the squire and the captain stayed on deck, and the latter hailed the coxswain, who was the principal man aboard.

"Mr. Hands," he said, "here are two of us with a brace of pistols each. If any one of you six make a signal of any description, that man's dead."

They were a good deal taken aback, and after a little consultation one and all tumbled down the fore companion,[11] thinking no doubt to take us on the rear. But when they saw Redruth waiting for them in the sparred gallery, they went about ship at once, and a head popped out again on deck.

"Down, dog!" cries the captain.

And the head popped back again; and we heard no more, for this time, of these six very faint-hearted seamen.

By this time, tumbling things in as they came, we had the jolly-boat loaded as much as we dared. Joyce and I got out through the stern-port, and we made for shore again as fast as oars could take us.

This second trip fairly aroused the watchers along shore. "Lillibullero" was dropped again; and just before we lost sight of them behind the little point, one of them whipped ashore and disappeared. I had half a mind to change my plan and destroy their boats, but I feared that Silver and the others might be close at hand, and all might very well be lost by trying for too much.

We had soon touched land in the same place as before and set to provision the block house.[12] All three made the first journey, heavily laden, and tossed our stores over the palisade.[13] Then, leaving Joyce to guard

10. Kegs are small barrels, and these were filled with pork that had been, according to one Bristol recipe, left in a brine solution for at least four weeks to preserve the meat from spoiling.

Shipboard cuisine during the 1700s generally has not received a good press, often with reason; crews often suffered from scurvy and other diseases of poor nutrition. However, there is evidence that sometimes meals on board a ship could be excellent. For example, the French missionary Père Labat, who has left us useful descriptions of *boucanier* life, took ship to the Caribbean in 1693. He reported being served salads every day that included fresh lettuce, radishes, and chicory, all grown on board. Also regularly on the menu were paté, ham, chicken, roasts, cheese, jams, nuts, stewed fruits, mutton, veal, and wine.

One historian of the Royal Navy of the 1700s, N.A.M. Rodger, notes references to soldiers and passengers on Royal Navy ships in the mid-1700s who "remarked with pleasure on the goodness of navy food."

11. Dr. Livesey would have been clearer if he had said *fore companion-way* to describe the staircase the pirates descended. On p. 74 (see note 4 there), Jim describes a *companion*, a box-like structure designed to let light into the cabin below that had been modified to provide sleeping berths.

12. A simple but effective defensive fortification built of logs that could be built using the same techniques used to build a log cabin. Admiral Smyth tells us that block houses "were primarily constructed in our American colonies because they could be immediately built from the heavy timber felled to clear away the spot, and open lines of fire."

13. A defensive fence made by inserting logs upright and edge to edge until they enclose the stockade; the top of the logs are shaped into a point.

14. A rope that fastens a ship's boat to the ship or to a dock.

15. The sterns of some vessels curve up and out as they emerge from the water, creating an overhang. This area is called a *ship's counter*. (See illustration, p. xiii.)

them—one man, to be sure, but with half a dozen muskets—Hunter and I returned to the jolly-boat and loaded ourselves once more. So we proceeded without pausing to take breath, till the whole cargo was bestowed, when the two servants took up their position in the block house, and I, with all my power, sculled back to the *Hispaniola*.

That we should have risked a second boat load seems more daring than it really was. They had the advantage of numbers, of course, but we had the advantage of arms. Not one of the men ashore had a musket, and before they could get within range for pistol shooting, we flattered ourselves we should be able to give a good account of a half-dozen at least.

The squire was waiting for me at the stern window, all his faintness gone from him. He caught the painter[14] and made it fast, and we fell to loading the boat for our very lives. Pork, powder, and biscuit was the cargo, with only a musket and a cutlass apiece for the squire and me and Redruth and the captain. The rest of the arms and powder we dropped overboard in two fathoms and a half of water, so that we could see the bright steel shining far below us in the sun, on the clean, sandy bottom.

By this time the tide was beginning to ebb, and the ship was swinging round to her anchor. Voices were heard faintly halloaing in the direction of the two gigs; and though this reassured us for Joyce and Hunter, who were well to the eastward, it warned our party to be off.

Redruth retreated from his place in the gallery and dropped into the boat, which we then brought round to the ship's counter,[15] to be handier for Captain Smollett.

"Now, men," said he, "do you hear me?"

There was no answer from the forecastle.

"It's to you, Abraham Gray—it's to you I am speaking."

Still no reply.

"Gray," resumed Mr. Smollett, a little louder, "I am leaving this ship, and I order you to follow your captain. I know you are a good man at bottom, and I dare say not one of the lot of you's as bad as he makes out. I have my watch here in my hand; I give you thirty seconds to join me in."[16]

There was a pause.

"Come, my fine fellow," continued the captain; "don't hang so long in stays.[17] I'm risking my life and the lives of these good gentlemen every second."

There was a sudden scuffle, a sound of blows, and out burst Abraham Gray with a knife cut on the side of the cheek, and came running to the captain like a dog to the whistle.

"I'm with you, sir," said he.

And the next moment he and the captain had dropped aboard of us, and we had shoved off and given way.

We were clear out of the ship, but not yet ashore in our stockade.

16. The question here is, how many of the pirates would understand or have heard the word *seconds* before?

Although pocket watches with seconds hands were used as early as 1675–1680, they were still rare, expensive, and not particularly accurate. Watches didn't become widely available until the next century.

Tall and heavy "longcase" or "grandfather clocks," with their steady ticking, were another matter. They were relatively common, if expensive. Each tick measured one second. The technology of the longcase clock, developed in the late 1600s, relied on the properties of a pendulum for its accuracy. As Samuel L. Macey, a professor at the University of Victoria, put it, "The length of a pendulum controls the time of the swing. Theoretically, a pendulum of 39.14 inches will have a one-second swing in London." *Theoretically* is a careful term here: clockmakers were still working on the problem of friction in the mechanism, and on the effects of heat and cold on metal parts; all three could cause error. The longcase clock was accurate, but it was not portable like a watch.

Dr. Livesey could have bought a watch from one of Bristol's watchmakers: William Bathe was active between 1751 and 1757; James Burr was making both watches and clocks after 1754 and advertised "all sorts of watches made;" Isaac Hewlett was making watches and clocks between 1743 and 1778.

But we need to be careful in thinking that pirates were too ignorant to know about seconds. William Dampier (1651–1715) was an explorer, naturalist, navigator and hydrographer, and also something else. His portrait in Britain's National Portrait Gallery identifies him as "Pirate and Hydrographer."

17. To tack, or zigzag, against the direction of the wind requires that a sailing vessel's direction be altered at intervals. A vessel is said to be *in stays* when it is *going about*–changing from one tack to another–but does not immediately complete the tack and instead remains in a temporary position head-first into the wind. The vessel will either complete the tack or fall back into the course she was on. If she does fall back, she is said to "have missed her stays." If the vessel remains stuck head-first into the wind, she is "in irons." (See note 7 on p. 159.)

Chapter Seventeen

Narrative Continued by the Doctor: The Jolly-boat's Last Trip

1. A gallipot is an inconsequential little boat. In Tobias Smollett's 1748 novel about the seafaring life of Roderick Random, he describes Mr. Morgan scooping butter from "an old gallipot," which the etymologist T. E. Hoad tells us is a word dating back to the 1400s that means "small earthen pot," the kind brought by galley from the Mediterranean. In the 1700s gallipots were used by apothecaries and, so Captain Grose tells us, was also a nickname for apothecary. Another etymologist, Ernest Weekley, offers gallipot as a common name for a vessel from the Mediterranean. Dr. Livesey is using the term here as a dismissive metaphor for *Hispaniola*'s jolly-boat.

2. The gunwale (pronounced *gun'l*) is the top edge of a small boat's hull.

3. To trim the boat is to arrange the distribution of weight within a vessel, whether a small rowboat or a big ship, in order to control how the vessel floats in the water. A vessel can be trimmed so that her bow is higher or lower, her stern is higher or lower, or so she floats on an even keel. How a vessel is trimmed affects how she handles.

THIS FIFTH TRIP WAS quite different from any of the others. In the first place, the little gallipot[1] of a boat that we were in was gravely overloaded. Five grown men, and three of them—Trelawney, Redruth, and the captain—over six feet high, was already more than she was meant to carry. Add to that the powder, pork, and bread-bags. The gunwale[2] was lipping astern. Several times we shipped a little water, and my breeches and the tails of my coat were all soaking wet before we had gone a hundred yards.

The captain made us trim the boat,[3] and we got her to lie a little more evenly. All the same, we were afraid to breathe.

In the second place, the ebb was now making—a strong rippling current running westward through the basin, and then south'ard and seaward down the straits by which we had entered in the morning. Even the ripples were a danger to our overloaded craft, but the worst of it was that we were swept out of our true course and away from our proper landing-place behind the point. If we let the current have its way we should come ashore beside the gigs, where the pirates might appear at any moment.

"I cannot keep her head for the stockade, sir," said I to the captain. I was steering, while he and Redruth, two fresh men, were at the oars. "The tide keeps washing her down. Could you pull a little stronger?"

"Not without swamping the boat," said he. "You must bear up, sir, if you please—bear up until you see you're gaining."

I tried and found by experiment that the tide kept sweeping us westward until I had laid her head due east, or just about right angles to the way we ought to go.

"We'll never get ashore at this rate," said I.

"If it's the only course that we can lie, sir, we must even lie it," returned the captain. "We must keep upstream. You see, sir," he went on, "if once we dropped to leeward[4] of the landing-place, it's hard to say where we should get ashore, besides the chance of being boarded by the gigs; whereas, the way we go the current must slacken, and then we can dodge back along the shore."

"The current's less a'ready, sir," said the man Gray, who was sitting in the fore-sheets;[5] "you can ease her off a bit."

"Thank you, my man," said I, quite as if nothing had happened, for we had all quietly made up our minds to treat him like one of ourselves.

Suddenly the captain spoke up again, and I thought his voice was a little changed.

4. The term leeward (pronounced *loo-ard*) means the downwind side or the side of the landing area sheltered from the wind.

5. The front section of a boat, up in the bows. The term should not be confused with the term for the ropes used to control, or trim, the angle of a sail to the wind.

6. Solid iron cannonballs weighing nine pounds that fit in the *Hispaniola*'s nine-pounder cannon.

7. The jolly-boat is moving just fast enough that the rudder hanging in the water below its stern still can be used to direct the course of the vessel–that is, they can *keep steerage*. The rudder works by deflecting the flow of water. If the boat were to travel any slower, there would not be enough water pressure for the rudder to be able to influence the direction of the little boat and Dr. Livesey would not be able to steer the vessel. Livesey is controlling the rudder by using a tiller, a short wooden bar connected to the top of the rudder. (See note 21 on p. 84.)

8. Squire Trelawney was placing a pinch or so of gunpowder from a small flask into the priming pan of his musket as preparation for firing the gun.

Firing a flintlock musket involved a five-step process for igniting the gunpowder charge that propelled the bullet from the musket's barrel. Ignition was started by pulling on the musket's trigger so that a spring-loaded flint was released to hit a piece of metal on a hinge called a *frizzen* and so create a spark that in turn ignited a small amount of gunpowder placed in a trough or receptacle called a *priming pan*. The priming pan was located over a narrow entry point–called a *touchhole*–that led into the rear end of the musket's barrel where the main charge of gunpowder waited. The ignition of the powder in the priming pan led to the ignition of the main charge.

"The gun!" said he.

"I have thought of that," said I, for I made sure he was thinking of a bombardment of the fort. "They could never get the gun ashore, and if they did, they could never haul it through the woods."

"Look astern, doctor," replied the captain.

We had entirely forgotten the long nine; and there, to our horror, were the five rogues busy about her, getting off her jacket, as they called the stout tarpaulin cover under which she sailed. Not only that, but it flashed into my mind at the same moment that the round-shot[6] and the powder for the gun had been left behind, and a stroke with an axe would put it all into the possession of the evil ones abroad.

"Israel was Flint's gunner," said Gray hoarsely.

At any risk, we put the boat's head direct for the landing-place. By this time we had got so far out of the run of the current that we kept steerage[7] way even at our necessarily gentle rate of rowing, and I could keep her steady for the goal. But the worst of it was that with the course I now held we turned our broadside instead of our stern to the *Hispaniola* and offered a target like a barn door.

I could hear as well as see that brandy-faced rascal Israel Hands plumping down a round-shot on the deck.

"Who's the best shot?" asked the captain.

"Mr. Trelawney, out and away," said I.

"Mr. Trelawney, will you please pick me off one of these men, sir? Hands, if possible," said the captain.

Trelawney was as cool as steel. He looked to the priming of his gun.[8]

"Now," cried the captain, "easy with that gun, sir, or

you'll swamp the boat. All hands stand by to trim her when he aims."

The squire raised his gun, the rowing ceased, and we leaned over to the other side to keep the balance, and all was so nicely contrived that we did not ship a drop.

They had the gun, by this time, slewed round upon the swivel,[9] and Hands, who was at the muzzle with the rammer, was in consequence the most exposed. However, we had no luck, for just as Trelawney fired, down he stooped, the ball whistled over him, and it was one of the other four who fell.

The cry he gave was echoed not only by his companions on board but by a great number of voices from the shore, and looking in that direction I saw the other pirates trooping out from among the trees and tumbling into their places in the boats.

"Here come the gigs, sir," said I.

"Give way, then," cried the captain. "We mustn't mind if we swamp her now. If we can't get ashore, all's up."

"Only one of the gigs is being manned, sir," I added; "the crew of the other most likely going round by shore to cut us off."

"They'll have a hot run, sir," returned the captain. "Jack ashore, you know. It's not them I mind; it's the round-shot. Carpet bowls! My lady's maid couldn't miss. Tell us, squire, when you see the match,[10] and we'll hold water."[11]

In the meanwhile we had been making headway at a good pace for a boat so overloaded, and we had shipped but little water in the process. We were now close in; thirty or forty strokes and we should beach her, for the

9. Livesey, like Jim Hawkins, has called the *pivoting turntable* on which the cannon is mounted a swivel. (See note 5 on p. 76.)

10. The match or match cord was a length of cord soaked in saltpeter and then dried. It could be lit, and the slow-burning end used to ignite the small gunpowder priming charge, which in turn ignited the main charge in a cannon. Captain Smollett is saying that when Trelawney sees the match cord being lit, he and the others should stop the jolly-boat.

11. Holding water is a method to stop the movement of a boat by ceasing to row and then holding the oars steady, blade edge down, so the oars act as a brake.

"Tell us, Squire, when you see the match, and we'll hold water."

ebb had already disclosed a narrow belt of sand below the clustering trees. The gig was no longer to be feared; the little point had already concealed it from our eyes. The ebb-tide, which had so cruelly delayed us, was now making reparation and delaying our assailants. The one source of danger was the gun.

"If I durst," said the captain, "I'd stop and pick off another man."

But it was plain that they meant nothing should delay their shot. They had never so much as looked at their fallen comrade, though he was not dead, and I could see him trying to crawl away.

"Ready!" cried the squire.

"Hold!" cried the captain, quick as an echo.

And he and Redruth backed with a great heave that sent her stern bodily under water. The report fell in at the same instant of time. This was the first that Jim heard, the sound of the squire's shot not having reached him. Where the ball passed, not one of us precisely knew, but I fancy it must have been over our heads and that the wind of it may have contributed to our disaster.

At any rate, the boat sank by the stern, quite gently, in three feet of water, leaving the captain and myself, facing each other, on our feet. The other three took complete headers, and came up again drenched and bubbling.

So far there was no great harm. No lives were lost, and we could wade ashore in safety. But there were all our stores at the bottom, and to make things worse, only two guns out of five remained in a state for service. Mine I had snatched from my knees and held over my head, by a sort of instinct. As for the captain, he had carried his over his shoulder by a bandoleer,[12] and like a wise man, lock uppermost. The other three had gone down with the boat.

To add to our concern, we heard voices already drawing near us in the woods along shore, and we had not only the danger of being cut off from the stockade in our half-crippled state but the fear before us whether, if Hunter and Joyce were attacked by half a dozen, they would have the sense and conduct to stand firm. Hunter was steady, that we knew; Joyce was a doubtful case—a pleasant, polite man for a valet and to brush one's clothes, but not entirely fitted for a man of war.

With all this in our minds, we waded ashore as fast as we could, leaving behind us the poor jolly-boat and a good half of all our powder and provisions.

⟨⟩

12. A wide leather shoulder belt or baldric; the one here has been modified to serve as a sling. His bandoleer could have been a family heirloom from past wars because bandoleers were used in the days of the matchlock musket in the 1600s, not the flintlock musket days of the 1700s. Modern bandoleers have loops to hold metal cartridges that did not exist back then.

One bandoleer that survives in a Swedish museum carried ten small wooden cylinders filled with premeasured charges of gunpowder to speed reloading. The cylinders, suspended from cords, hung in a row from the bandoleer and clinked when one walked, so they were covered in leather to reduce the sound. A bandoleer could easily have been modified by the squire by cutting the cords holding the little powder flasks. Sometimes the wooden cylinders acquired nicknames, like "Corporals," or "The 12 Apostles" (if the bandoleer had 12 flasks).

In Trelawney's day, premeasured, individual charges of gunpowder and one round bullet were wrapped in paper cylinders called cartridges and carried in a leather case. The cartridges were contained in the holes drilled into a wooden block that fitted inside the leather case or pouch. A typical wooden block might hold 18 or more rounds. The Prussian army cartridge case, for example, might hold about 80. The soldier would bite off the top of the pre-packaged paper cartridge where the bullet was located and transfer the bullet to his mouth. After pouring a little powder into the priming pan, he would pour the rest of the gunpowder down the barrel of his musket. Next came the bullet, which he spat down the barrel. He would then wad up the paper and thrust it down the barrel using a ramrod. The wad would keep the powder and bullet in place until he was ready to fire. (See also note 8 on p. 136.)

Chapter Eighteen

Narrative Continued by the Doctor: End of the First Day's Fighting

WE MADE OUR BEST speed across the strip of wood that now divided us from the stockade, and at every step we took the voices of the buccaneers rang nearer. Soon we could hear their footfalls as they ran and the cracking of the branches as they breasted across a bit of thicket.

I began to see we should have a brush for it in earnest and looked to my priming.

"Captain," said I, "Trelawney is the dead shot. Give him your gun; his own is useless."

They exchanged guns, and Trelawney, silent and cool as he had been since the beginning of the bustle, hung a moment on his heel to see that all was fit for service. At the same time, observing Gray to be unarmed, I handed him my cutlass. It did all our hearts good to see him spit in his hand, knit his

brows, and make the blade sing through the air. It was plain from every line of his body that our new hand was worth his salt.

Forty paces farther we came to the edge of the wood and saw the stockade in front of us. We struck the enclosure about the middle of the south side, and almost at the same time, seven mutineers—Job Anderson, the boatswain, at their head—appeared in full cry at the southwestern corner.

They paused as if taken aback, and before they recovered, not only the squire and I, but Hunter and Joyce from the block house, had time to fire. The four shots came in rather a scattering volley, but they did the business: one of the enemy actually fell, and the rest, without hesitation, turned and plunged into the trees.

After reloading, we walked down the outside of the palisade to see to the fallen enemy. He was stone dead—shot through the heart.

We began to rejoice over our good success when just at that moment a pistol cracked in the bush, a ball whistled close past my ear, and poor Tom Redruth stumbled and fell his length on the ground. Both the squire and I returned the shot, but as we had nothing to aim at, it is probable we only wasted powder. Then we reloaded and turned our attention to poor Tom.

The captain and Gray were already examining him, and I saw with half an eye that all was over.

I believe the readiness of our return volley had scattered the mutineers once more, for we were suffered without further molestation to get the poor old gamekeeper hoisted over the stockade and carried, groaning and bleeding, into the log-house.

Poor old fellow, he had not uttered one word of surprise, complaint, fear, or even acquiescence from the very beginning of our troubles till now, when we had laid him down in the log-house to die. He had lain like a Trojan[1] behind his mattress in the gallery; he had followed every order silently, doggedly, and well; he was the oldest of our party by a score of years; and now,

1. Dr. Livesey is demonstrating both his knowledge of Latin and his regard for Redruth's virtues of self-discipline and devotion to duty. These same traits were ascribed some 2,000 years earlier to the Trojan warrior prince Anchises by the Roman poet Virgil in his narrative poem the *Aeneid*.

In some 10,000 lines of verse, the *Aeneid* describes how refugees led by Anchises fled a burning Troy at the end of the Trojan War and found their way to Italy to become the ancestors of the Romans. Roman politicians liked to link their family trees to the mythical Anchises and so associate themselves with his virtues, which were thought to be typically Roman. You could say Redruth was a good Roman.

Livesey would have been familiar with the epic poem, which has been passed through the centuries as one of the great artifacts of European literature. For many centuries, including the first 70 years or so of the 20th, one of the marks of an educated person in Britain and other countries was familiarity with the great writers of Rome, especially Virgil.

sullen, old, serviceable servant, it was he that was to die.

The squire dropped down beside him on his knees and kissed his hand, crying like a child.

"Be I going, doctor?" he asked.

I ran to the door in time to see Jim Hawkins, safe and sound, come climbing over the stockade.

"Tom, my man," said I, "you're going home."

"I wish I had had a lick at them with the gun first," he replied.

"Tom," said the squire, "say you forgive me, won't you?"

"Would that be respectful like, from me to you, squire?" was the answer. "Howsoever, so be it, amen!"

After a little while of silence, he said he thought somebody might read a prayer. "It's the custom, sir," he added apologetically. And not long after, without another word, he passed away.

In the meantime the captain, whom I had observed to be wonderfully swollen about the chest and pockets, had turned out a great many various stores—the British colours, a Bible, a coil of stoutish rope, pen, ink, the logbook, and pounds of tobacco. He had found a longish fir-tree lying felled and trimmed in the enclosure, and with the help of Hunter he had set it up at the corner of the log-house where the trunks crossed and made an angle. Then, climbing on the roof, he had with his own hand bent and run up the colours.

This seemed mightily to relieve him. He

re-entered the log-house and set about counting up the stores as if nothing else existed. But he had an eye on Tom's passage for all that, and as soon as all was over, came forward with another flag and reverently spread it on the body.

"Don't you take on, sir," he said, shaking the squire's hand. "All's well with him; no fear for a hand that's been shot down in his duty to captain and owner. It mayn't be good divinity, but it's a fact."

Then he pulled me aside.

"Dr. Livesey," he said, "in how many weeks do you and squire expect the consort?"

I told him it was a question not of weeks but of months, that if we were not back by the end of August Blandly was to send to find us, but neither sooner nor later. "You can calculate for yourself," I said.

"Why, yes," returned the captain, scratching his head; "and making a large allowance, sir, for all the gifts of Providence, I should say we were pretty close hauled."

"How do you mean?" I asked.

"It's a pity, sir, we lost that second load. That's what I mean," replied the captain. "As for powder and shot, we'll do. But the rations are short, very short—so short, Dr. Livesey, that we're perhaps as well without that extra mouth."

And he pointed to the dead body under the flag.

Just then, with a roar and a whistle, a round-shot passed high above the roof of the log-house and plumped far beyond us in the wood.

"Oho!" said the captain. "Blaze away! You've little enough powder already, my lads."

At the second trial, the aim was better, and the ball descended inside the stockade, scattering a cloud of sand but doing no further damage.

"Captain," said the squire, "the house is quite invisible from the ship. It must be the flag they are aiming at. Would it not be wiser to take it in?"

"Strike my colours!" cried the captain. "No, sir, not I"; and as soon as he had said the words, I think we all agreed with him. For it was not only a piece of stout, seamanly, good feeling; it was good policy besides and showed our enemies that we despised their cannonade.

All through the evening they kept thundering away. Ball after ball flew over or fell short or kicked up the sand in the enclosure, but they had to fire so high that the shot fell dead and buried itself in the soft sand. We had no ricochet to fear, and though one popped in through the roof of the log-house and out again through the floor, we soon got used to that sort of horse-play and minded it no more than cricket.

"There is one thing good about all this," observed the captain; "the wood in front of us is likely clear. The ebb has made a good while; our stores should be uncovered. Volunteers to go and bring in pork."

Gray and Hunter were the first to come forward. Well armed, they stole out of the stockade, but it proved a useless mission. The mutineers were bolder than we fancied or they put more trust in Israel's gunnery. For four or five of them were busy carrying off our stores and wading out with them to one of the gigs that lay close by, pulling an oar or so to hold her steady against the current. Silver was in the stern-sheets in command; and every man of them was now provided with a musket from some secret magazine of their own.

The captain sat down to his log, and here is the beginning of the entry:

> Alexander Smollett, master; David
> Livesey, ship's doctor; Abraham Gray,
> carpenter's mate; John Trelawney, owner;
> John Hunter and Richard Joyce, owner's
> servants, landsmen—being all that is left
> faithful of the ship's company—with stores
> for ten days at short rations, came ashore
> this day and flew British colours on the
> log-house in Treasure Island. Thomas
> Redruth, owner's servant, landsman,
> shot by the mutineers; James Hawkins,
> cabin-boy—

And at the same time, I was wondering over poor Jim Hawkins' fate.

A hail on the land side.

"Somebody hailing us," said Hunter, who was on guard.

"Doctor! Squire! Captain! Hullo, Hunter, is that you?" came the cries.

And I ran to the door in time to see Jim Hawkins, safe and sound, come climbing over the stockade.

Chapter Nineteen

Narrative Resumed by Jim Hawkins: The Garrison in the Stockade

As soon as Ben Gunn saw the colours he came to a halt, stopped me by the arm, and sat down.

"Now," said he, "there's your friends, sure enough."

"Far more likely, it's the mutineers," I answered.

"That!" he cried. "Why, in a place like this, where nobody puts in but gen'lemen of fortune, Silver would fly the Jolly Roger,[1] you don't make no doubt of that. No, that's your friends. There's been blows too, and I reckon your friends has had the best of it; and here they are ashore in the old stockade, as was made years and years ago by Flint. Ah, he was the man to have a headpiece, was Flint! Barring rum, his match were never seen. He were afraid of none, not he; on'y Silver—Silver was that genteel."

"Well," said I, "that may be so, and so be it; all the more reason that I should hurry on and join my friends."

"Nay, mate," returned Ben, "not you. You're a good

Jolly Roger flag.

1. Traditionally, a pirate's flag with a design of a white skull nestled between two white bones on a black or red background was called a Jolly Roger. There were many alternative designs, with motifs that referenced the grave, violence, and the brevity of life.

At least one pirate flag from the 1700s has survived. In 2007 specialists at the Conservation Centre at Southampton University in Britain restored a pirate flag taken in 1780 off North Africa by a Royal Navy sea officer, Lieutenant, later Admiral, Richard Curry. The flag was made from red wool that had started life as a garment (there was a buttonhole); it had a skull and crossbones design cut from painted cotton and was marked with gunpowder residue.

And then there was the Jolly Robin, so called

by the crew of the Bristol privateer *King George*, 500 tons burthen, 29 guns, 180 men, who mutinied on May 5, 1761. At the trial of the seven leaders of the uprising, the court was told they "intended to hoist the Jolly Robin and the Cross Bones at the mast head and go a-pirating in the East Indies." However, somehow *Jolly Robin* does not quite carry the same weight as *Jolly Roger*.

A black flag suggested that an attacker offered to spare lives if there was no resistance. A red flag, a signal that anyone captured carrying a weapon would be killed, was by no means confined to pirate use; armies used it also. For example, the Mexican army hoisted a red flag when it launched its final attack in 1836 on the Alamo and its American and Texan defenders. The term *Jolly Roger* may have come from the French *Joli Rouge* ("Pretty Red"), a sardonic reference, perhaps, to the symbolism of this *red flag of no quarter*. Old Roger was also an 18th-century English nickname for the devil and is mentioned as the name of the flag flown by the pirate John Quelch, executed in Boston in 1702.

According to David Cordingly, the historian who organized the 1992 exhibition *Pirates: Fact and Fiction* at the National Maritime Museum in London, after 1700 pirates started using black flags with designs of skulls, swords, hourglasses, spears, and bleeding hearts on them, with the skull and crossbones popular after 1730. The skull and crossbones design, popular on gravestones for centuries, shows up in a 1717 report of a pirate trial.

2. From about midday to 3:00 p.m. *Noon observation* refers to using a sextant or quadrant at midday to measure the sun's altitude in order to begin calculating a ship's position at sea. (See note 1 on p. 127.)

3. Masts on sailing ships needed permanent, or standing, rigging to provide stability on either side and also from front to back. Stays provided front-to-back stability. The mainstay provided support to the main mast. A ship might have several *stays*—backstays, forestays, topmast stays, topgallant stays, jib stays, and so on. This specialist word survives in our general vocabulary today in the sense of "support," as in "Today tourism, not piracy, is the mainstay of the economy of the Bahamas." (See illustration, p. xiii.)

boy, or I'm mistook; but you're on'y a boy, all told. Now, Ben Gunn is fly. Rum wouldn't bring me there, where you're going—not rum wouldn't, till I see your born gen'leman and gets it on his word of honour. And you won't forget my words: 'A precious sight (that's what you'll say), a precious sight more confidence'—and then nips him."

And he pinched me the third time with the same air of cleverness.

"And when Ben Gunn is wanted, you know where to find him, Jim. Just where you found him today. And him that comes is to have a white thing in his hand, and he's to come alone. Oh! And you'll say this: 'Ben Gunn,' says you, 'has reasons of his own.'"

"Well," said I, "I believe I understand. You have something to propose, and you wish to see the squire or the doctor, and you're to be found where I found you. Is that all?"

"And when? says you," he added. "Why, from about noon observation to about six bells."[2]

"Good," said I, "and now may I go?"

"You won't forget?" he inquired anxiously. "Precious sight, and reasons of his own, says you. Reasons of his own; that's the mainstay;[3] as between man and man. Well, then"—still holding me—"I reckon you can go, Jim. And, Jim, if you was to see Silver, you wouldn't go for to sell Ben Gunn? Wild horses wouldn't draw it from you? No, says you. And if them pirates camp ashore, Jim, what would you say but there'd be widders in the morning?"

Here he was interrupted by a loud report, and a cannonball came tearing through the trees and pitched in the sand not a hundred yards from where we two were talking. The next moment each of us had taken to his heels in a different direction.

For a good hour to come frequent reports shook the island, and balls kept crashing through the woods. I moved from hiding-place to hiding-place, always pursued, or so it seemed to me, by these terrifying missiles. But towards the end of the bombardment, though still I durst not venture in the direction of the stockade, where the balls fell oftenest, I had begun, in a manner, to pluck up my heart again, and after a long detour to the east, crept down among the shore-side trees.

The sun had just set, the sea breeze was rustling and tumbling in the woods and ruffling the grey surface of the anchorage; the tide, too, was far out, and great tracts of sand lay uncovered; the air, after the heat of the day, chilled me through my jacket.

The *Hispaniola* still lay where she had anchored; but, sure enough, there was the Jolly Roger—the black flag of piracy—flying from her peak.[4] Even as I looked, there came another red flash and another report that sent the echoes clattering, and one more round-shot whistled through the air. It was the last of the cannonade.

I lay for some time watching the bustle which succeeded the attack. Men were demolishing something with axes on the beach near the stockade—the poor jolly-boat, I afterwards discovered. Away, near the mouth of the river, a great fire was glowing among the trees, and between that point and the ship one of the gigs kept coming and going, the men, whom I had seen so gloomy, shouting at the oars like children. But there was a sound in their voices which suggested rum.

At length I thought I might return toward the

4. The *Hispaniola* had a big fore-and-aft sail on her tallest or main mast, the one nearest the rear of the vessel. The top edge of the sail was attached to a boom called a gaff. The higher tip of the sail was the *peak*. (See illustration, p. xiii.)

5. The meaning here of bearings is not navigational but instead refers to the waterline, or flotation line, formed around a ship that is fully loaded and properly trimmed. So the kettle is stuck fairly deeply into the sand.

stockade. I was pretty far down on the low, sandy spit that encloses the anchorage to the east, and is joined at half-water to Skeleton Island; and now, as I rose to my feet, I saw, some distance further down the spit and rising from among low bushes, an isolated rock, pretty high, and peculiarly white in colour. It occurred to me that this might be the white rock of which Ben Gunn had spoken and that some day or other a boat might be wanted and I should know where to look for one.

Then I skirted among the woods until I had regained the rear, or shoreward side, of the stockade, and was soon warmly welcomed by the faithful party.

I had soon told my story and began to look about me. The log-house was made of unsquared trunks of pine—roof, walls, and floor. The latter stood in several places as much as a foot or a foot and a half above the surface of the sand. There was a porch at the door, and under this porch the little spring welled up into an artificial basin of a rather odd kind—no other than a great ship's kettle of iron, with the bottom knocked out, and sunk "to her bearings,"[5] as the captain said, among the sand.

Little had been left besides the framework of the house, but in one corner there was a stone slab laid down by way of hearth and an old rusty iron basket to contain the fire.

The slopes of the knoll and all the inside of the stockade had been cleared of timber to build the house, and we could see by the stumps what a fine and lofty grove had been destroyed. Most of the soil had been washed away or buried in drift after the removal of the trees; only where the streamlet ran down from the kettle a thick bed of moss and some ferns and little creeping bushes were still green among the sand. Very close around the stockade—too close for defence, they said—the wood still flourished high and dense, all of fir on the land side, but towards the sea with a large admixture of live-oaks.

The cold evening breeze, of which I have spoken, whistled through every chink of the rude building and sprinkled the floor with a continual rain of fine sand. There was sand in our eyes, sand in our teeth, sand in our suppers, sand dancing in the spring at the bottom of the kettle, for all the world like porridge beginning to boil. Our chimney was a square hole in the roof; it was but a little part of the smoke that found its way out, and the rest eddied about the house and kept us coughing and piping the eye.

Add to this that Gray, the new man, had his face tied up in a bandage for a cut he had got in breaking away from the mutineers and that poor old Tom Redruth, still unburied, lay along the wall, stiff and stark, under the Union Jack.

If we had been allowed to sit idle, we should all have fallen in the blues,[6] but Captain Smollett was never the man for that. All hands were called up before him, and he divided us into watches.[7] The doctor and Gray and I for one; the squire, Hunter, and Joyce upon the other. Tired though we all were, two were sent out for firewood; two more were set to dig a grave for Redruth; the doctor was named cook; I was put sentry at the door; and the captain himself went from one to another, keeping up our spirits and lending a hand wherever it was wanted.

From time to time the doctor came to the door for a little air and to rest his eyes, which were almost

6. According to Captain Grose, in the 1700s *to look blue* meant to seem "confounded, terrified, or disappointed," which is not so far from the modern sense of *the blues* as a word meaning "sadness."

7. The word *watch* has two meanings. In the first meaning, it is an organizational term: A ship's company is divided into two, sometimes three watches. Each watch has enough people to take turns operating the ship on a 24-hour basis. In the 1700s one watch was called the *starboard watch*, the other the *larboard watch* (larboard was the old name for *port*, the left-hand side of a vessel). The names come from the location of the crew members' hammocks on board ship. Today ships have port and starboard watches. Ships with a three-watch system often call the watches *red, white,* and *blue.*

Captain Smollet has divided his little group into two watches. The watch off duty is the "watch below."

The second meaning refers to work periods. (For more, see note 1 on p. 127.)

8. A small, airtight box with a hinged lid, about three inches long and half an inch deep–just big enough to hold a day's supply of snuff and not expose it to air.

Snuff is made from finely ground dry tobacco leaf and flavorings. Users take a small pinch of the powder and sniff it up a nostril. They then also usually sneeze, which expels the snuff. Since snuff is brown, a large colored–not white–handkerchief to collect the expelled powder is an almost essential piece of equipment.

smoked out of his head, and whenever he did so, he had a word for me.

"That man Smollett," he said once, "is a better man than I am. And when I say that it means a deal, Jim."

Another time he came and was silent for a while. Then he put his head on one side, and looked at me.

"Is this Ben Gunn a man?" he asked.

"I do not know, sir," said I. "I am not very sure whether he's sane."

"If there's any doubt about the matter, he is," returned the doctor. "A man who has been three years biting his nails on a desert island, Jim, can't expect to appear as sane as you or me. It doesn't lie in human nature. Was it cheese you said he had a fancy for?"

"Yes, sir, cheese," I answered.

"Well, Jim," says he, "just see the good that comes of being dainty in your food. You've seen my snuff-box,[8] haven't you? And you never saw me take snuff, the reason being that in my snuff-box I carry a piece of Parmesan cheese—a cheese made in Italy, very nutritious. Well, that's for Ben Gunn!"

Before supper was eaten we buried old Tom in the sand and stood round him for a while bare-headed in the breeze. A good deal of firewood had been got in, but not enough for the captain's fancy, and he shook his head over it and told us we "must get back to this tomorrow rather livelier." Then, when we had eaten our pork and each had a good stiff glass of brandy grog, the three chiefs got together in a corner to discuss our prospects.

It appears they were at their wits' end what to do, the stores being so low that we must have been starved into surrender long before help came. But our best hope, it was decided, was to kill off the buccaneers until they either hauled down their flag or ran away with the *Hispaniola*. From nineteen they were already reduced to fifteen, two others were wounded, and one at least—the man shot beside the gun—severely wounded, if he were not dead. Every time we had a crack at them, we were to take it, saving our own lives, with the extremest care. And besides that, we had two able allies—rum and the climate.

As for the first, though we were about half a mile away, we could hear them roaring and singing late into the night; and as for the second, the doctor staked his wig that, camped where they were in the marsh and unprovided with remedies, the half of them would be on their backs before a week.

"So," he added, "if we are not all shot down first they'll be glad to be packing in the schooner. It's always a ship, and they can get to buccaneering again, I suppose."

"First ship that ever I lost," said Captain Smollett.

I was dead tired, as you may fancy; and when I got to sleep, which was not till after a great deal of tossing, I slept like a log of wood.

The rest had long been up and had already break-

We buried old Tom in the sand and stood round him bareheaded in the breeze.

9. In a long-established convention, when two armies face each other, one side may send out a messenger carrying a white flag as a sign that that side wishes to talk to the other without risk of being attacked.

Here are the modern Royal Navy instructions regarding how to treat a flag of truce: "A white flag of truce may be used to signal a wish to talk to the enemy. The side using the white flag must stop fighting and indicate a wish to communicate. Both sides must then stop fighting. Abuse of the white flag is treachery. A flag of truce indicates no more than an intention to enter into negotiations with the enemy. It does not necessarily mean a wish to surrender. A flag party must not be attacked. On completion of its mission it must be allowed to return to its own lines if it wishes to do so. A flag party may be on foot or mobile in a vehicle or aircraft flying the white flag."

fasted and increased the pile of firewood by about half as much again when I was wakened by a bustle and the sound of voices.

"Flag of truce!"[9] I heard someone say; and then, immediately after, with a cry of surprise, "Silver himself!"

And at that, up I jumped, and rubbing my eyes, ran to a loophole in the wall.

Chapter Twenty

Silver's Embassy

SURE ENOUGH, THERE WERE two men just outside the stockade, one of them waving a white cloth, the other, no less a person than Silver himself, standing placidly by.

It was still quite early, and the coldest morning that I think I ever was abroad in—a chill that pierced into the marrow. The sky was bright and cloudless overhead, and the tops of the trees shone rosily in the sun. But where Silver stood with his lieutenant, all was still in shadow, and they waded knee-deep in a low white vapour that had crawled during the night out of the morass. The chill and the vapour taken together told a poor tale of the island. It was plainly a damp, feverish, unhealthy spot.

"Keep indoors, men," said the captain. "Ten to one this is a trick."

Then he hailed the buccaneer.

"Who goes? Stand, or we fire."

"Flag of truce," cried Silver.

The captain was in the porch, keeping himself carefully out of the way of a treacherous shot, should any be intended. He turned and spoke to us, "Doctor's watch on the lookout. Dr. Livesey take the north side, if you please; Jim, the east; Gray, west. The watch below, all hands to load muskets. Lively, men, and careful."

And then he turned again to the mutineers.

"And what do you want with your flag of truce?" he cried.

This time it was the other man who replied.

"Cap'n Silver, sir, to come on board and make terms," he shouted.

"Cap'n Silver! Don't know him. Who's he?"

Come, lasses and lads, take leave of your dads,
  And away to the may-pole hie;
For every he has got him a she,
  And the minstrel's standing by;
For Willie has gotten his Jill,
  And Johnny has got his Joan.

The village of Hayfield in the north of England lays claim to being the place where the song was first heard, at an inn called The George, which still exists. The song's tune is part of the regimental march of the Staffordshire Regiment, one of whose ancestor regiments was established in 1705. The regiment saw service at Lexington, Bunker Hill, and New York during the War for American Independence. In 2007 it was deployed in Iraq as an infantry regiment equipped with armored fighting vehicles.

cried the captain. And we could hear him adding to himself, "Cap'n, is it? My heart, and here's promotion!"

Long John answered for himself. "Me, sir. These poor lads have chosen me cap'n, after your desertion, sir"—laying a particular emphasis upon the word "desertion." "We're willing to submit, if we can come to terms, and no bones about it. All I ask is your word, Cap'n Smollett, to let me safe and sound out of this here stockade, and one minute to get out o' shot before a gun is fired."

"My man," said Captain Smollett, "I have not the slightest desire to talk to you. If you wish to talk to me, you can come, that's all. If there's any treachery, it'll be on your side, and the Lord help you."

"That's enough, cap'n," shouted Long John cheerily. "A word from you's enough. I know a gentleman, and you may lay to that."

We could see the man who carried the flag of truce attempting to hold Silver back. Nor was that wonderful, seeing how cavalier had been the captain's answer. But Silver laughed at him aloud and slapped him on the back as if the idea of alarm had been absurd. Then he advanced to the stockade, threw over his crutch, got a leg up, and with great vigour and skill succeeded in surmounting the fence and dropping safely to the other side.

I will confess that I was far too much taken up with what was going on to be of the slightest use as sentry; indeed, I had already deserted my eastern loophole and crept up behind the captain, who had now seated himself on the threshold, with his elbows on his knees, his head in his hands, and his eyes fixed on the water as it bubbled out of the old iron kettle in the sand. He was whistling to himself, "Come, Lasses and Lads."[1]

Silver had terrible hard work getting up the knoll. What with the steepness of the incline, the thick tree stumps, and the soft sand, he and his crutch were as helpless as a ship in stays.[2] But he stuck to it like a man in silence, and at last arrived before the captain, whom he saluted in the handsomest style. He was tricked out in his best; an immense blue coat, thick with brass buttons, hung as low as to his knees, and a fine laced hat was set on the back of his head.

"Here you are, my man," said the captain, raising his head. "You had better sit down."

"You ain't a-going to let me inside, cap'n?" complained Long John. "It's a main cold morning, to be sure, sir, to sit outside upon the sand."

"Why, Silver," said the captain, "if you had pleased to be an honest man, you might have been sitting in your galley. It's your own doing. You're either my ship's cook—and then you were treated handsome—or Cap'n Silver, a common mutineer and pirate, and then you can go hang!"

2. See note 17 on p. 133.

"Well, well, cap'n," returned the sea-cook, sitting down as he was bidden on the sand, "you'll have to give me a hand up again, that's all. A sweet pretty place you have of it here. Ah, there's Jim! The top of the morning to you, Jim. Doctor, here's my service. Why, there you all are together like a happy family, in a manner of speaking."

"If you have anything to say, my man, better say it," said the captain.

"Right you were, Cap'n Smollett," replied Silver. "Dooty is dooty, to be sure. Well now, you look here, that was a good lay of yours last night. I don't deny it was a good lay. Some of you pretty handy with a handspike-end. And I'll not deny neither but what some of my people was shook—maybe all was shook; maybe I was shook myself; maybe that's why I'm here for terms. But you mark me, cap'n, it won't do twice, by thunder! We'll have to do sentry-go[3] and ease off a point or so on the rum. Maybe you think we were all a sheet in the wind's eye. But I'll tell you I was sober; I was on'y dog tired; and if I'd awoke a second sooner, I'd 'a caught you at the act, I would. He wasn't dead when I got round to him, not he."

"Well?" says Captain Smollett as cool as can be.

All that Silver said was a riddle to him, but you would never have guessed it from his tone. As for me, I began to have an inkling. Ben Gunn's last words came back to my mind. I began to suppose that he had paid the buccaneers a visit while they all lay drunk together round their fire, and I reckoned up with glee that we had only fourteen enemies to deal with.

"Well, here it is," said Silver. "We want that treasure, and we'll have it—that's our point! You would just as soon save your lives, I reckon; and that's yours. You have a chart, haven't you?"

"That's as may be," replied the captain.

"Oh, well, you have, I know that," returned Long John. "You needn't be so husky with a man; there ain't a particle of service in that, and you may lay to it. What I mean is, we want your chart. Now, I never meant you no harm, myself."

"That won't do with me, my man," interrupted the captain. "We know exactly what you meant to do, and we don't care, for now, you see, you can't do it."

And the captain looked at him calmly and proceeded to fill a pipe.

"If Abe Gray—" Silver broke out.

"Avast there!" cried Mr. Smollett. "Gray told me nothing, and I asked him nothing; and what's more, I would see you and him and this whole island blown clean out of the water into blazes first. So there's my mind for you, my man, on that."

This little whiff of temper seemed to cool Silver down. He had been growing nettled before, but now he pulled himself together.

"Like enough," said he. "I would set no limits to what gentlemen might consider shipshape, or might not, as the case were. And seein' as how you are about to take a pipe, cap'n, I'll make so free as do likewise."

"Give me a hand up!" he cried.
"Not I," returned the captain.

4. Silver is referring to a declaration or *affidavit* that is made on oath.

5. At sea, we are told by Admiral Smyth in 1867, *hazing* meant to "punish a man by making him do unnecessary work."

And he filled a pipe and lighted it; and the two men sat silently smoking for quite a while, now looking each other in the face, now stopping their tobacco, now leaning forward to spit. It was as good as the play to see them.

"Now," resumed Silver, "here it is. You give us the chart to get the treasure by, and drop shooting poor seamen and stoving of their heads in while asleep. You do that, and we'll offer you a choice. Either you come aboard along of us, once the treasure shipped, and then I'll give you my affy-davy,[4] upon my word of honour, to clap you somewhere safe ashore. Or if that ain't to your fancy, some of my hands being rough and having old scores on account of hazing,[5] then you can stay here, you can. We'll divide stores with you, man for man; and I'll give my affy-davy, as before, to speak the first ship I sight, and send 'em here to pick you up. Now, you'll own that's talking. Handsomer you couldn't look to get, not you. And I hope"—raising his voice—"that all hands in this here block house will overhaul my words, for what is spoke to one is spoke to all."

Captain Smollett rose from his seat and knocked out the ashes of his pipe in the palm of his left hand.

"Is that all?" he asked.

"Every last word, by thunder!" answered John. "Refuse that, and you've seen the last of me but musket-balls."

"Very good," said the captain. "Now you'll hear me. If you'll come up one by one, unarmed, I'll engage to clap you all in irons and take you home to a fair trial in England. If you won't, my name is Alexander Smollett, I've flown my sovereign's colours, and I'll see you all to Davy Jones.[6] You can't find the treasure. You can't sail the ship—there's not a man among you fit to sail the ship. You can't fight us—Gray, there, got away from five of you. Your ship's in irons,[7] Master Silver; you're on a lee shore,[8] and so you'll find. I stand here and tell you so; and they're the last good words you'll get from me, for in the name of heaven, I'll put a bullet in your back when next I meet you. Tramp, my lad. Bundle out of this, please, hand over hand, and double quick."

Silver's face was a picture; his eyes started in his head with wrath. He shook the fire out of his pipe.

"Give me a hand up!" he cried.

"Not I," returned the captain.

"Who'll give me a hand up?" he roared.

Not a man among us moved. Growling the foulest imprecations, he crawled along the sand till he got hold of the porch and could hoist himself again upon his crutch. Then he spat into the spring.

"There!" he cried. "That's what I think of ye. Before an hour's out, I'll stove in your old block house like a rum puncheon. Laugh, by thunder, laugh! Before an hour's out, ye'll laugh upon the other side. Them that die'll be the lucky ones."

And with a dreadful oath he stumbled off, ploughed down the sand, was helped across the stockade, after four or five failures, by the man with the flag of truce, and disappeared in an instant afterwards among the trees.

6. "This same *Davy Jones*, according to the mythology of sailors, is the fiend that presides over all the evil spirits of the deep, and is often seen in various shapes, perching among the rigging on the eve of hurricanes, ship-wrecks and other disasters to which sea-faring life is exposed, warning the devoted wretch of death and woe," wrote Tobias Smollett in 1751. Smollett was a surgeon's second mate in the Royal Navy, later a writer and author of *Peregrine Pickel*, from which this quotation is taken. Whether he was related to Captain Smollett we do not know.

Captain Francis Grose, in his 1785 dictionary of slang, identifies Davy Jones as "the devil, the spirit of the sea; called *Nekin* in the north countries such as Norway, Denmark, and Sweden." *Davy Jones' locker* is the sea.

Michael Quinion, a contributor to the *Oxford English Dictionary*, has explored six theories about where the idea of Davy Jones, and his locker, originated. They range from a David Jones who kept a pub for sailors to a Davy Jones who was a pirate. None sound convincing to him. "The true source remains unfathomed."

7. A ship is *in irons* when, for whatever reason, including incompetence, she is allowed to face into the wind–*come up to the wind*–and lose her way and can't be steered because the rudder can't grip the water. Not the same as "in stays." (See note 17 on p. 133.)

When a square-rigged ship is in irons her situation can be remedied by *boxhauling*–that is, by manipulating her foresails so she sails backward in a curve until she is in the right position to have her sails working efficiently again and moving the ship forward. The ship can then once more begin the tacking process.

8. See note 4 on p. 24.

Chapter Twenty-One

The Attack

As soon as Silver disappeared, the captain, who had been closely watching him, turned towards the interior of the house and found not a man of us at his post but Gray. It was the first time we had ever seen him angry.

"Quarters!" he roared. And then, as we all slunk back to our places, "Gray," he said, "I'll put your name in the log; you've stood by your duty like a seaman. Mr. Trelawney, I'm surprised at you, sir. Doctor, I thought you had worn the king's coat! If that was how you served at Fontenoy, sir, you'd have been better in your berth."

The doctor's watch were all back at their loopholes, the rest were busy loading the spare muskets, and everyone with a red face, you may be certain, and a flea in his ear, as the saying is.

The captain looked on for a while in silence. Then he spoke.

"My lads," said he, "I've given Silver a broadside.[1] I pitched it in red-hot on purpose; and before the hour's out, as he said, we shall be boarded. We're outnumbered, I needn't tell you that, but we fight in shelter; and a minute ago I should have said we fought with discipline. I've no manner of doubt that we can drub them, if you choose."

Then he went the rounds and saw, as he said, that all was clear.

On the two short sides of the house, east and west, there were only two loopholes; on the south side where the porch was, two again; and on the north side, five. There was a round score of muskets for the seven of us; the firewood had been built into four piles—tables, you might say—one about the middle of each side, and on each of these tables some ammunition and four loaded muskets were laid ready to the hand of the defenders. In the middle, the cutlasses lay ranged.

"Toss out the fire," said the captain; "the chill is past, and we mustn't have smoke in our eyes."

The iron fire-basket was carried bodily out by Mr. Trelawney, and the embers smothered among sand.

"Hawkins hasn't had his breakfast. Hawkins, help yourself, and back to your post to eat it," continued Captain Smollett. "Lively, now, my lad; you'll want it before you've done. Hunter, serve out a round of brandy to all hands."

And while this was going on, the captain completed, in his own mind, the plan of the defence.

"Doctor, you will take the door," he resumed. "See, and don't expose yourself; keep within, and fire through the porch. Hunter, take the east side, there. Joyce, you stand by the west, my man. Mr. Trelawney, you are the best shot—you and Gray will take this long north side, with the five loopholes; it's there the danger is. If they can get up to it and fire in upon us through our own ports, things would begin to look dirty. Hawkins, neither you nor I are much account at the shooting; we'll stand by to load and bear a hand."

As the captain had said, the chill was past. As soon as the sun had climbed above our girdle of trees, it fell with all its force upon the clearing and drank up the vapours at a draught. Soon the sand was baking and the resin melting in the logs of the block house. Jackets

1. Captain Smollett is telling his shipmates that he was very aggressive when talking to Silver. A single broadside, when all the guns on one side of a ship were fired at the same time, was a loud and overwhelming spectacle. An efficient ship could fire a series of broadsides quite rapidly. On June 1, 1794, the 98-gun HMS *Queen* fired 130 broadsides in just under four hours, using 60 tons of shot and 25 tons of gunpowder.

2. Calm caused by periods of low pressure in the gap between the southeast trade winds and the northeast trades. Sailing ships in the doldrums have sometimes been unable to move for hours, days, and even weeks. The doldrums can be found within a band 360 nautical miles to 600 nautical miles wide along the equator (a nautical mile is slightly longer than a land mile), a region that today we call the Intertropical Convergence Zone. Winds blow between high- and low-pressure areas.

Low pressure refers to the pressure of the air on the earth's surface. At sea level, atmospheric pressure on us is about 14.7 pounds per square inch. An area of low pressure is an area where the air is rising and therefore lowering the air pressure below. As the air rises it also cools, so water in the air turns into clouds and rain. That is why we expect rain when low pressure areas are reported in a weather forecast. When air temperature falls, air pressure will increase as cooler air sinks to the surface, creating a *high-pressure* area.

3. Some mariners believed that in a flat calm with not a breath of wind to ripple the surface you could raise a wind by whistling or by sticking a knife into the rear side of a mast. They also believed that whistling when the wind was up would produce a gale. They believed that when the wind veers from right to left it will not continue steady. They also believed that wearing earrings improved their eyesight, which might explain why Mr. Arrow, who had a squint, wore them (see p. 71). Many believed–and continue to believe–as did Silver (see p. 86), that changing a ship's name brought bad luck.

and coats were flung aside, shirts thrown open at the neck and rolled up to the shoulders; and we stood there, each at his post, in a fever of heat and anxiety.

An hour passed away.

"Hang them!" said the captain. "This is as dull as the doldrums.[2] Gray, whistle for a wind."[3]

And just at that moment came the first news of the attack.

"If you please, sir," said Joyce, "if I see anyone, am I to fire?"

"I told you so!" cried the captain.

"Thank you, sir," returned Joyce with the same quiet civility.

Nothing followed for a time, but the remark had set us all on the alert, straining ears and eyes—the musketeers with their pieces balanced in their hands, the captain out in the middle of the blockhouse with his mouth very tight and a frown on his face.

So some seconds passed, till suddenly Joyce whipped up his musket and fired. The report had scarcely died away ere it was repeated and repeated from without in a scattering volley, shot behind shot, like a string of geese, from every side of the enclosure. Several bullets struck the log-house, but not one entered; and as the smoke cleared away and vanished, the stockade and the woods around it looked as quiet and empty as before. Not a bough waved, not the gleam of a musket-barrel betrayed the presence of our foes.

"Did you hit your man?" asked the captain.

"No, sir," replied Joyce. "I believe not, sir."

"Next best thing to tell the truth," muttered Captain Smollett. "Load his gun, Hawkins. How many should you say there were on your side, doctor?"

"I know precisely," said Dr. Livesey. "Three shots were fired on this side. I saw the three flashes—two close together—one farther to the west."

"Three!" repeated the captain. "And how many on yours, Mr. Trelawney?"

But this was not so easily answered. There had come many from the north—seven by the squire's computation, eight or nine according to Gray. From the east and west only a single shot had been fired. It was plain, therefore, that the attack would be developed from the north and that on the other three sides we were only to be annoyed by a show of hostilities. But Captain Smollett made no change in his arrangements. If the mutineers succeeded in crossing the stockade, he argued, they would take possession of any unprotected loophole and shoot us down like rats in our own stronghold.

Nor had we much time left to us for thought. Suddenly, with a loud huzza, a little cloud of pirates leaped from the woods on the north side and ran straight on the stockade. At the same moment, the fire was once more opened from the woods, and a rifle ball[4] sang through the doorway and knocked the doctor's musket into bits.

The boarders swarmed over the fence like monkeys. Squire and Gray fired again and yet again; three men fell, one forwards into the enclosure, two back on the outside. But of these, one was evidently more frightened than hurt, for he was on his feet again in a crack and instantly disappeared among the trees.

Two had bit the dust, one had fled, four had made good their footing inside our defences, while from the shelter of the woods seven or eight men, each evi-

4. A musket with a rifled barrel was a relative rarity on board ship, as well as in the armies of the 1700s. It was reliably accurate at 200 yards and beyond. The rifle's accuracy compared well with the standard and very inaccurate smooth-bore musket, which could hit a generously sized target that measured five feet by six feet only 60 percent of the time at 80 yards. At 250 yards only one out of four bullets from a smoothbore could expect to hit that same big target. Armies compensated for the musket's technical limitations by deploying soldiers in mass formations who fired in unison: at least some bullets were likely to hit their targets. American militia using standard muskets at Concord fired 300 rounds for every British soldier killed.

While the rifle, available since the 1500s, was more accurate, it took more time to reload than a smoothbore. More important, it also was more expensive to manufacture, so in the 1700s its use was restricted to skilled specialist troops. The rifle came into its own as a mass-produced weapon only after the 1850s.

The boarders swarmed over the fence like monkeys.

dently supplied with several muskets, kept up a hot though useless fire on the log-house.

The four who had boarded made straight before them for the building, shouting as they ran, and the men among the trees shouted back to encourage them. Several shots were fired, but such was the hurry of the marksmen that not one appears to have taken effect. In a moment, the four pirates had swarmed up the mound and were upon us.

The head of Job Anderson, the boatswain, appeared at the middle loophole.

"At 'em, all hands—all hands!" he roared in a voice of thunder.

At the same moment, another pirate grasped Hunter's musket by the muzzle, wrenched it from his hands, plucked it through the loophole, and with one stunning blow, laid the poor fellow senseless on the floor. Meanwhile a third, running unharmed all around the house, appeared suddenly in the doorway and fell with his cutlass on the doctor.

Our position was utterly reversed. A moment since we were firing, under cover, at an exposed enemy; now it was we who lay uncovered and could not return a blow.

The log-house was full of smoke, to which we owed our comparative safety. Cries and confusion, the flashes and reports of pistol-shots, and one loud groan rang in my ears.

"Out, lads, out, and fight 'em in the open! Cutlasses!" cried the captain.

I snatched a cutlass from the pile, and someone, at the same time snatching another, gave me a cut across the knuckles which I hardly felt. I dashed out of the door into the clear sunlight. Someone was close behind, I knew not whom. Right in front, the doctor was pursuing his assailant down the hill, and just as my eyes fell upon him, beat down his guard and sent him sprawling on his back with a great slash across his face.

"Round the house, lads! Round the house!" cried the captain; and even in the hurly-burly, I perceived a change in his voice.

Mechanically, I obeyed, turned eastwards, and with my cutlass raised, ran round the corner of the house. Next moment I was face to face with Anderson. He roared aloud, and his hanger[5] went up above his head, flashing in the sunlight. I had not time to be afraid, but as the blow still hung impending, leaped in a trice

5. A hanger is a short, slightly curved sword that was manufactured in large quantities. It was the standard backup weapon of the single-shot, musket-and-bayonet-carrying infantry private in the British and other armies of the period.

Hangers made the soldiers look, as the brave and terrible-tempered General Henry Hawley wrote in 1726, "soldier-like and graceful." But the swords were rarely used in action, noted Hawley, known to his men as Hangman Hawley. Regiments sometimes put all their hangers into storage before going on campaign, since all they did was add to the weight a soldier must carry.

upon one side, and missing my foot in the soft sand, rolled headlong down the slope.

When I had first sallied from the door, the other mutineers had been already swarming up the palisade to make an end of us. One man, in a red night-cap, with his cutlass in his mouth, had even got upon the top and thrown a leg across. Well, so short had been the interval that when I found my feet again all was in the same posture, the fellow with the red night-cap still half-way over, another still just showing his head above the top of the stockade. And yet, in this breath of time, the fight was over and the victory was ours.

Gray, following close behind me, had cut down the big boatswain ere he had time to recover from his lost blow. Another had been shot at a loophole in the very act of firing into the house and now lay in agony, the pistol still smoking in his hand. A third, as I had seen, the doctor had disposed of at a blow. Of the four who had scaled the palisade, one only remained unaccounted for, and he, having left his cutlass on the field, was now clambering out again with the fear of death upon him.

"Fire—fire from the house!" cried the doctor. "And you, lads, back into cover."

But his words were unheeded, no shot was fired, and the last boarder made good his escape and disappeared with the rest into the wood. In three seconds nothing remained of the attacking party but the five who had fallen, four on the inside and one on the outside of the palisade.

The doctor and Gray and I ran full speed for shelter. The survivors would soon be back where they had left their muskets, and at any moment the fire might recommence.

The house was by this time somewhat cleared of smoke, and we saw at a glance the price we had paid for victory. Hunter lay beside his loophole, stunned; Joyce by his, shot through the head, never to move again; while right in the centre, the squire was supporting the captain, one as pale as the other.

"The captain's wounded," said Mr. Trelawney.

"Have they run?" asked Mr. Smollett.

"All that could, you may be bound," returned the doctor; "but there's five of them will never run again."

"Five!" cried the captain. "Come, that's better. Five against three leaves us four to nine. That's better odds than we had at starting. We were seven to nineteen then, or thought we were, and that's as bad to bear."

PART V

My
Sea Adventure

Chapter Twenty-Two

How My Sea Adventure Began

THERE WAS NO RETURN of the mutineers—not so much as another shot out of the woods. They had "got their rations for that day," as the captain put it, and we had the place to ourselves and a quiet time to overhaul the wounded and get dinner. Squire and I cooked outside in spite of the danger, and even outside we could hardly tell what we were at, for horror of the loud groans that reached us from the doctor's patients.

Out of the eight men who had fallen in the action, only three still breathed—that one of the pirates who had been shot at the loophole, Hunter, and Captain Smollett; and of these, the first two were as good as dead; the mutineer indeed died under the doctor's knife, and Hunter, do what we could, never recovered consciousness in this world. He

lingered all day, breathing loudly like the old buccaneer at home in his apoplectic fit, but the bones of his chest had been crushed by the blow and his skull fractured in falling, and some time in the following night, without sign or sound, he went to his Maker.

As for the captain, his wounds were grievous indeed, but not dangerous. No organ was fatally injured. Anderson's ball—for it was Job that shot him first—had broken his shoulder-blade and touched the lung, not badly; the second had only torn and displaced some muscles in the calf. He was sure to recover, the doctor said, but in the meantime, and for weeks to come, he must not walk nor move his arm, nor so much as speak when he could help it.

My own accidental cut across the knuck-

1. "In slight wounds that do not penetrate much deeper than the skin, the best application is a bit of the *common black sticking plaster*," recommended William Buchan, M.D. in his manual *Domestic Medicines* of 1772, which surveyed the medical practices of the day and presented them in understandable terms. It was the reference book used on the *Bounty* of mutiny fame. "This keeps the sides of the wound together, and prevents the air from hurting it, which is all that is necessary," advised the doctor.

One version of black sticking plaster was made by brushing gum water–dissolved gum arabic (gum from several species of the acacia shrub)–on a piece of stretched black silk, and letting it dry. Moistening the surface with the tongue before using it made it sticky again. Gum arabic was made by breaking up dried gum, wrapping the pieces in a linen cloth, and placing them in water until they dissolved, according to a 1735 technical manual by John Barrow.

But mostly when doctors in the 1750s referred to a "plaster" they were talking about some form of medication applied to a flexible material, not about the material itself. The flexible material's job was to keep the medication in place when it was applied to whatever part of a patient's body that needed treatment. The idea was to keep the medication in prolonged contact with the skin, much like a modern medicinal patch.

So Livesey might also have treated Jim's cut with what Buchan called a *common plaster*, made from olive oil boiled with powdered red lead and spread on leather or cloth.

Plasters/patches could be made from cloth or leather treated with powdered lead oxide mixed with olive oil, resin, and wax, to name a few possibilities. Medicinal mixes that might be added included mercury, sulphur compounds, opium, iron oxide, and "Peruvian bark" or quinine.

Ready-made plasters were available from manufacturers like Bowden and Sandwell, who were advertising their products in 1757. Manufacturers made a point of claiming that their plasters "would stick without filleting" and had "an agreeable scent."

Buchan's *Domestic Medicine* was a best seller and went into 142 editions over the next 100 years or so in Britain and America. Lieutenant William Bligh's surgeon, Thomas Huggan, took a

les was a flea-bite. Doctor Livesey patched it up with plaster[1] and pulled my ears for me into the bargain.

After dinner the squire and the doctor sat by the captain's side while in consultation; and when they had talked to their hearts' content, it being then a little past noon, the doctor took up his hat and pistols, girt on a cutlass, put the chart in his pocket, and with a musket over his shoulder crossed the palisade on the north side and set off briskly through the trees.

Gray and I were sitting together at the far end of the block house, to be out of earshot of our officers consulting; and Gray took his pipe out of his mouth and fairly forgot to put it back again, so thunderstruck he was at this occurrence.

"Why, in the name of Davy Jones," said he, "is Dr. Livesey mad?"

"Why no," says I. "He's about the last of this crew for that, I take it."

"Well, shipmate," said Gray, "mad he may not be; but if he's not, you mark my words, I am."

"I take it," replied I, "the doctor has his idea; and if I am right, he's going now to see Ben Gunn."

I was right, as appeared later; but in the meantime, the house being stifling hot and the little patch of sand inside the palisade ablaze with midday sun, I began to get another thought into my head, which was not by any means so right. What I began to do was to envy the doctor walking in the cool shadow of the woods with the birds about him and the pleasant smell of the pines, while I sat grilling, with my clothes stuck to the hot resin, and so much blood about me and so many poor dead bodies lying all around that I took a disgust of the place that was almost as strong as fear.

All the time I was washing out the block house, and then washing up the things from dinner, this disgust and envy kept growing stronger and stronger, till at last, being near a bread-bag, and no one then observing me, I took the first step towards my escapade and filled both pockets of my coat with biscuit.

I was a fool, if you like, and certainly I was going to do a foolish, over-bold act; but I was determined to do it with all the precautions in my power. These biscuits, should anything befall me, would keep me, at least, from starving till far on in the next day.

The next thing I laid hold of was a brace of pistols, and as I already had a powder-horn and bullets, I felt myself well supplied with arms.

As for the scheme I had in my head, it was not a bad one in itself. I was to go down the sandy spit that divides the anchorage on the east from the open sea, find the white rock I had observed last evening, and ascertain whether it was there or not that Ben Gunn had hidden his boat, a thing quite worth doing, as I still believe. But as I was certain I should not be allowed to leave the enclosure, my only plan was to take French leave and slip out when nobody was watching, and that was so bad a way of doing it as made the thing itself wrong. But I was only a boy, and I had made my mind up.

Well, as things at last fell out, I found an admirable opportunity. The squire and Gray were busy helping the captain with his bandages, the coast was clear, I made a bolt for it over the stockade and into the thickest of the trees, and before my absence was observed I was out of cry of my companions.

This was my second folly, far worse than the first,

copy of the sixth edition with him on the *Bounty*. The mutiny's leader, Fletcher Christian, after casting Bligh adrift in the vessel's launch, took the book with him to Pitcairn Island. A Royal Navy midshipman, Charles Blackett, retrieved it in 1837. It is now in the National Maritime Museum in London.

I lifted the side of the tent, and there was Ben Gunn's boat . . .

as I left but two sound men to guard the house; but like the first, it was a help towards saving all of us.

I took my way straight for the east coast of the island, for I was determined to go down the sea side of the spit to avoid all chance of observation from the anchorage. It was already late in the afternoon, although still warm and sunny. As I continued to thread the tall woods, I could hear from far before me not only the continuous thunder of the surf, but a certain tossing of foliage and grinding of boughs which showed me the sea breeze had set in higher than usual. Soon cool draughts of air began to reach me, and a few steps farther I came forth into the open borders of the grove, and saw the sea lying blue and sunny to the horizon and the surf tumbling and tossing its foam along the beach.

I have never seen the sea quiet round Treasure Island. The sun might blaze overhead, the air be without a breath, the surface smooth and blue, but still these great rollers would be running along all the external coast, thundering and thundering by day and night; and I scarce believe there is one spot in the island where a man would be out of earshot of their noise.

I walked along beside the surf with great

enjoyment, till, thinking I was now got far enough to the south, I took the cover of some thick bushes and crept warily up to the ridge of the spit.

Behind me was the sea, in front the anchorage. The sea breeze, as though it had the sooner blown itself out by its unusual violence, was already at an end; it had been succeeded by light, variable airs from the south and south-east, carrying great banks of fog; and the anchorage, under lee of Skeleton Island, lay still and leaden as when first we entered it. The *Hispaniola*, in that unbroken mirror, was exactly portrayed from the truck to the waterline,[2] the Jolly Roger hanging from her peak.

Alongside lay one of the gigs, Silver in the stern-sheets—him I could always recognize—while a couple of men were leaning over the stern bulwarks,[3] one of them with a red cap—the very rogue that I had seen some hours before stride-legs upon the palisade. Apparently they were talking and laughing, though at that distance—upwards of a mile—I could, of course, hear no word of what was said. All at once there began the most horrid, unearthly screaming, which at first startled me badly, though I had soon remembered the voice of Captain Flint and even thought I could make out the bird by her bright plumage as she sat perched upon her master's wrist.

Soon after, the jolly-boat shoved off and pulled for shore, and the man with the red cap and his comrade went below by the cabin companion.

Just about the same time, the sun had gone down behind the Spy-glass, and as the fog was collecting rapidly, it began to grow dark in earnest. I saw I must lose no time if I were to find the boat that evening.

2. This phrase means "from the circular wooden button that tops off a mast down to the waterline." (See illustration, below.)

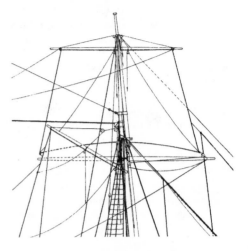

Detail of the truck from the schooner diagram on p. xiii.

3. A sailing ship's bulwarks are a solid barrier made of wood, similar to a railing that rises above the sides of a vessel above its upper deck. The idea is to stop waves washing in and mariners being washed overboard.

4. A seat for a rower that doubles as a cross-piece and helps the coracle keep its shape.

5. An ancient design for a watercraft–more or less round, with a basket-like framework assembled from branches of trees, which can be covered with animal skins or something similar. The result is a light, portable, and serviceable craft. It can still be found in Wales and Ireland. Similar craft have been found in the Arctic, the Middle East, and China. It's antiquity as a design was underlined when in 2014 the British Museum announced that the translation of script from a 4,000-year-old clay tablet from Mesopotamia–today's Iraq–gave details for building a giant coracle with an entry-way so animals could enter "two by two." Noah's ark was a giant oblong, but animals also could enter two by two.

A coracle is a small, roundish boat with a basket-like framework.

The white rock, visible enough above the brush, was still some eighth of a mile further down the spit, and it took me a goodish while to get up with it, crawling, often on all fours, among the scrub. Night had almost come when I laid my hand on its rough sides. Right below it there was an exceedingly small hollow of green turf, hidden by banks and a thick underwood about knee-deep, that grew there very plentifully; and in the centre of the dell, sure enough, a little tent of goatskins, like what the gipsies carry about with them in England.

I dropped into the hollow, lifted the side of the tent, and there was Ben Gunn's boat—home-made if ever anything was home-made: a rude, lop-sided framework of tough wood, and stretched upon that a covering of goatskin, with the hair inside. The thing was extremely small, even for me, and I can hardly imagine that it could have floated with a full-sized man. There was one thwart[4] set as low as possible, a kind of stretcher in the bows, and a double paddle for propulsion.

I had not then seen a coracle,[5] such as the ancient Britons made, but I have seen one since, and I can give you no fairer idea of Ben Gunn's boat than by saying it was like the first and the worst coracle ever made by man. But the great advantage of the coracle it certainly possessed, for it was exceedingly light and portable.

Well, now that I had found the boat, you would have thought I had had enough of truantry for once, but in the meantime I had taken another notion and become so obstinately fond of it that I would have carried it out, I believe, in the teeth of Captain Smollett himself. This was to slip out under cover of the night, cut the *Hispaniola* adrift, and let her go ashore where she fancied. I had quite made up my mind that the mutineers, after their repulse of the morning, had nothing nearer their hearts than to up anchor and away to sea; this, I thought, it would be a fine thing to prevent, and now that I had seen how they left their watchmen unprovided with a boat, I thought it might be done with little risk.

Down I sat to wait for darkness, and made a hearty meal of biscuit. It was a night out of ten thousand for my purpose. The fog had now buried all heaven. As the last rays of daylight dwindled and disappeared, absolute blackness settled down on Treasure Island. And when, at last, I shouldered the coracle and groped my way stumblingly out of the hollow where I had supped, there were but two points visible on the whole anchorage.

One was the great fire on shore, by which the defeated pirates lay carousing in the swamp. The other, a mere blur of light upon the darkness, indicated the position of the anchored ship. She had swung round to the ebb—her bow was now towards me—the only lights on board were in the cabin, and what I saw was merely a reflection on the fog of the strong rays that flowed from the stern window.

The ebb had already run some time, and I had to wade through a long belt of swampy sand, where I sank several times above the ankle, before I came to the edge of the retreating water, and wading a little way in, with some strength and dexterity, set my coracle, keel[6] downwards, on the surface.

6. The spine-like foundation timber assembly that runs along the bottom of a vessel from the bow to the stern.

Chapter Twenty-Three

The Ebb-tide Runs

THE CORACLE—AS I had ample reason to know before I was done with her—was a very safe boat for a person of my height and weight, both buoyant and clever in a seaway; but she was the most cross-grained, lop-sided craft to manage. Do as you pleased, she always made more leeway than anything else, and turning round and round was the manoeuvre she was best at. Even Ben Gunn himself has admitted that she was "queer to handle till you knew her way."

Certainly I did not know her way. She turned in every direction but the one I was bound to go; the most part of the time we were broadside on, and I am very sure I never should have made the ship at all but for the tide. By good fortune, paddle as I pleased, the tide was still sweeping me down;

and there lay the *Hispaniola* right in the fair-way, hardly to be missed.

First she loomed before me like a blot of something yet blacker than darkness, then her spars and hull began to take shape, and the next moment, as it seemed (for, the far-ther I went, the brisker grew the current of the ebb), I was alongside of her hawser[1] and had laid hold.

The hawser was as taut as a bowstring, and the current so strong she pulled upon her anchor. All round the hull, in the black-ness, the rippling current bubbled and chat-tered like a little mountain stream. One cut with my sea-gully and the *Hispaniola* would go humming down the tide.

So far so good, but it next occurred to my recollection that a taut hawser, suddenly cut, is a thing as dangerous as a kicking horse. Ten to one, if I were so foolhardy as to cut the *Hispaniola* from her anchor, I and the coracle would be knocked clean out of the water.

This brought me to a full stop, and if fortune had not again particularly favoured me, I should have had to abandon my design. But the light airs which had begun blowing from the south-east and south had hauled round after nightfall into the south-west. Just while I was meditating, a puff came, caught the *Hispaniola*, and forced her up into the current; and to my great joy, I felt the hawser slacken in my grasp, and the hand by which I held it dip for a second under water.

With that I made my mind up, took out my gully, opened it with my teeth, and cut one strand after another, till the vessel swung only by two. Then I lay quiet, waiting to sever these last when the strain should be once more lightened by a breath of wind.

All this time I had heard the sound of loud voices from the cabin, but to say truth, my mind had been so entirely taken up with other thoughts that I had scarcely given ear. Now, however, when I had nothing else to do, I began to pay more heed.

One I recognized for the coxswain's, Israel Hands, that had been Flint's gunner in former days. The other was, of course, my friend of the red night-cap. Both men were plainly the worse of drink, and they were still drinking, for even while I was listening, one of them, with a drunken cry, opened the stern window and threw out something, which I divined to be an empty bottle. But they were not only tipsy; it was plain that they were furiously angry. Oaths flew like hail-stones, and every now and then there came forth such

1. A thick and heavy rope.

an explosion as I thought was sure to end in blows. But each time the quarrel passed off and the voices grumbled lower for a while, until the next crisis came and in its turn passed away without result.

On shore, I could see the glow of the great camp-fire burning warmly through the shore-side trees. Someone was singing, a dull, old, droning sailor's song, with a droop and a quaver at the end of every verse, and seemingly no end to it at all but the patience of the singer. I had heard it on the voyage more than once and remembered these words:

"But one man of her crew alive,
What put to sea with seventy-five."

And I thought it was a ditty rather too dolefully appropriate for a company that had met such cruel losses in the morning. But, indeed, from what I saw, all these buccaneers were as callous as the sea they sailed on.

At last the breeze came; the schooner sidled and drew nearer in the dark; I felt the hawser slacken once more, and with a good, tough effort, cut the last fibres through.

The breeze had but little action on the coracle, and I was almost instantly swept against the bows of the *Hispaniola*. At the same time, the schooner began to turn upon her heel, spinning slowly, end for end, across the current.

I wrought like a fiend, for I expected every moment to be swamped; and since I found I could not push the coracle directly off, I now shoved straight astern. At length I was clear of my dangerous neighbour, and just as I gave the last impulsion, my hands came across a light cord that was trailing overboard across the stern bulwarks. Instantly I grasped it.

Why I should have done so I can hardly say. It was at first mere instinct, but once I had it in my hands and found it fast, curiosity began to get the upper hand, and I determined I should have one look through the cabin window.

I pulled in hand over hand on the cord, and when I judged myself near enough, rose at infinite risk to about half my height and thus commanded the roof and a slice of the interior of the cabin.

By this time the schooner and her little consort were gliding pretty swiftly through the water; indeed, we had already fetched up level with the camp-fire. The ship was talking, as sailors say, loudly, treading the innumerable ripples with an incessant weltering splash; and until I got my eye above the window-sill I could not comprehend why the watchmen had taken no alarm. One glance, however, was sufficient; and it was only one glance that I durst take from that unsteady skiff. It showed me Hands and his companion locked together in deadly wrestle, each with a hand upon the other's throat.

I dropped upon the thwart again, none too soon, for I was near overboard. I could see nothing for the moment but these two furious, encrimsoned faces swaying together under the smoky lamp, and I shut my eyes to let them grow once more familiar with the darkness.

The endless ballad had come to an end at last, and the whole diminished company about the camp-fire had broken into the chorus I had heard so often:

"Fifteen men on the dead man's chest—

    Yo-ho-ho, and a bottle of rum!

    Drink and the devil had done for the rest—

    Yo-ho-ho, and a bottle of rum!"

I was just thinking how busy drink and the devil were at that very moment in the cabin of the *Hispaniola*, when I was surprised by a sudden lurch of the coracle. At the same moment, she yawed[2] sharply and seemed to change her course. The speed in the meantime had strangely increased.

I opened my eyes at once. All round me were little ripples, combing over with a sharp, bristling sound and slightly phosphorescent. The *Hispaniola* herself, a few yards in whose wake I was still being whirled along, seemed to stagger in her course, and I saw her spars toss a little against the blackness of the night; nay, as I looked longer, I made sure she also was wheeling to the southward.

I glanced over my shoulder, and my heart jumped against my ribs. There, right behind me, was the

It showed me Hands and his companion locked together in deadly wrestle . . .

2. Logically, a sailing vessel would be fortunate to have both wind and sea going in the same direction as the vessel. Unfortunately, there is a side effect: the rudder may not bite into the water as effectively. The result is that the vessel–especially if the helmsman is not paying attention–may *yaw* (deviate) away from its intended course.

glow of the camp-fire. The current had turned at right angles, sweeping round along with it the tall schooner and the little dancing coracle; ever quickening, ever bubbling higher, ever muttering louder, it went spinning through the narrows for the open sea.

Suddenly the schooner in front of me gave a violent yaw, turning, perhaps, through twenty degrees; and almost at the same moment one shout followed another from on board; I could hear feet pounding on the companion ladder and I knew that the two drunkards had at last been interrupted in their quarrel and awakened to a sense of their disaster.

I lay down flat in the bottom of that wretched skiff and devoutly recommended my spirit to its Maker. At the end of the straits, I made sure we must fall into some bar of raging breakers, where all my troubles would be ended speedily; and though I could, perhaps, bear to die, I could not bear to look upon my fate as it approached.

So I must have lain for hours, continually beaten to and fro upon the billows, now and again wetted with flying sprays, and never ceasing to expect death at the next plunge. Gradually weariness grew upon me; a numbness, an occasional stupor, fell upon my mind even in the midst of my terrors, until sleep at last supervened and in my sea-tossed coracle I lay and dreamed of home and the old Admiral Benbow.

Chapter Twenty-Four

The Cruise of the Coracle

IT WAS BROAD DAY when I awoke and found myself tossing at the south-west end of Treasure Island. The sun was up but was still hid from me behind the great bulk of the Spy-glass, which on this side descended almost to the sea in formidable cliffs.

Haulbowline Head[1] and Mizzen-mast Hill were at my elbow, the hill bare and dark, the head bound with cliffs forty or fifty feet high and fringed with great masses of fallen rock. I was scarce a quarter of a mile to seaward, and it was my first thought to paddle in and land.

That notion was soon given over. Among the fallen rocks the breakers spouted and bellowed; loud reverberations, heavy sprays flying and falling, succeeded one another from second to second; and I saw myself, if I ventured nearer, dashed to death upon the rough

1. *Haulbowline* is a variation of *bowlinehaul*, a procedure in which several ship's hands throw all their weight together at the same time to *bowse a bowline*—that is, haul in a rope used to control a sail after the rope has been combined with pulleys or blocks to create a tackle. The procedure also included *veering*: tightening and then easing off the rope—and doing so three times—before making a hard pull.

shore or spending my strength in vain to scale the beetling crags.

Nor was that all, for crawling together on flat tables of rock or letting themselves drop into the sea with loud reports I beheld huge slimy monsters—soft snails, as it were, of incredible bigness—two or three score of them together, making the rocks to echo with their barkings.

I have understood since that they were sea lions,[2] and entirely harmless. But the look of them, added to the difficulty of the shore and the high running of the surf, was more than enough to disgust me of that landing-place. I felt willing rather to starve at sea than to confront such perils.

In the meantime I had a better chance, as I supposed, before me. North of Haulbowline Head, the land runs in a long way, leaving at low tide a long stretch of yellow sand. To the north of that, again, there comes another cape—Cape of the Woods, as it was marked upon the chart—buried in tall green pines, which descended to the margin of the sea.

I remembered what Silver had said about the current that sets northward along the whole west coast of Treasure Island, and seeing from my position that I was already under its influence, I preferred to leave

Haulbowline Head behind me and reserve my strength for an attempt to land upon the kindlier-looking Cape of the Woods.

There was a great, smooth swell upon the sea. The wind blowing steady and gentle from the south, there was no contrariety between that and the current, and the billows rose and fell unbroken.

Had it been otherwise, I must long ago have perished; but as it was, it is surprising how easily and securely my little and light boat could ride. Often, as I still lay at the bottom and kept no more than an eye above the gunwale, I would see a big blue summit heaving close above me; yet the coracle would but bounce a little, dance as if on springs, and subside on the other side into the trough as lightly as a bird.

I began after a little to grow very bold and sat up to try my skill at paddling. But even a small change in the disposition of the weight will produce violent changes in the behaviour of a coracle. And I had hardly moved before the boat, giving up at once her gentle dancing movement, ran straight down a slope of water so steep that it made me giddy, and struck her nose, with a spout of spray, deep into the side of the next wave.

I was drenched and terrified, and fell instantly back into my old position, whereupon the coracle seemed to find her head again and led me as softly as before among the billows. It was plain she was not to be interfered with, and at that rate, since I could in no way influence her course, what hope had I left of reaching land?

I began to be horribly frightened, but I kept my head, for all that. First, moving with all care, I gradually baled out the coracle with my sea-cap; then, getting my eye once more above the gunwale, I set myself to study how it was she managed to slip so quietly through the rollers.

I found each wave, instead of the big, smooth glossy mountain it looks from shore or from a vessel's deck, was for all the world like any range of hills on the dry land, full of peaks and smooth places and valleys. The coracle, left to herself, turning from side to side, threaded, so to speak, her way through these lower parts and avoided the steep slopes and higher, toppling summits of the wave.

"Well, now," thought I to myself, "it is plain I must lie where I am and not disturb the balance; but it is plain also that I can put the paddle over the side and from time to time, in smooth places, give her a shove or two towards land." No sooner thought upon than done. There I lay on my elbows in the most trying attitude, and every now and again gave a weak stroke or two to turn her head to shore.

It was very tiring and slow work, yet I did visibly gain ground; and as we drew near the Cape of the Woods, though I saw I must infallibly miss that point, I had still made some hundred yards of easting. I was, indeed, close in. I could see the cool green tree-tops swaying together in the breeze, and I felt sure I should make the next promontory without fail.

It was high time, for I now began to be tortured with thirst. The glow of the sun from above, its thousandfold reflection from the waves, the sea-water that fell and dried upon me, caking my very lips with salt, combined to make my throat burn and my brain ache. The sight of the trees so near at hand had almost made me sick with longing, but the current had soon carried me past the point, and as the next reach of sea opened out, I beheld a sight that changed the nature of my thoughts.

Right in front of me, not half a mile away, I beheld the *Hispaniola* under sail. I made sure, of course, that I should be taken; but I was so distressed for want of water that I scarce knew whether to be glad or sorry at the thought, and long before I had come to a conclusion, surprise had taken entire possession of my mind and I could do nothing but stare and wonder.

The *Hispaniola* was under her main-sail and two jibs,[3] and the beautiful white canvas shone in the sun like snow or silver. When I first sighted her, all her sails were drawing; she was lying a course about north-west, and I presumed the men on board were going round the island on their way back to the anchorage. Presently she began to fetch more and more to the westward, so that I thought they had sighted me and were going about in chase. At last, however, she fell right into the wind's eye, was taken dead aback, and stood there awhile helpless, with her sails shivering.

"Clumsy fellows," said I; "they must still be drunk as owls." And I thought how Captain Smollett would have set them skipping.

Meanwhile the schooner gradually fell off and filled again upon another tack, sailed swiftly for a minute or so, and brought up once more dead in the wind's eye. Again and again was this repeated. To and fro, up and down, north, south, east, and west, the *Hispaniola* sailed by swoops and dashes, and at each repetition ended as she had begun, with idly flapping canvas. It became plain to me that nobody was steering. And if so, where were the men? Either they were dead drunk or had deserted her, I thought, and perhaps if I could get on board I might return the vessel to her captain.

I felt willing rather to starve at sea than to confront such perils . . .

185

The current was bearing coracle and schooner southward at an equal rate. As for the latter's sailing, it was so wild and intermittent, and she hung each time so long in irons,[4] that she certainly gained nothing, if she did not even lose. If only I dared to sit up and paddle, I made sure that I could overhaul her. The scheme had an air of adventure that inspired me, and the thought of the water-breaker beside the fore companion doubled my growing courage.

Up I got, was welcomed almost instantly by another cloud of spray, but this time stuck to my purpose and set myself, with all my strength and caution, to paddle after the unsteered *Hispaniola*. Once I shipped a sea so heavy that I had to stop and bail, with my heart fluttering like a bird, but gradually I got into the way of the thing and guided my coracle among the waves, with only now and then a blow upon her bows and a dash of foam in my face.

I was now gaining rapidly on the schooner; I could see the brass glisten on the tiller[5] as it banged about, and still no soul appeared upon her decks. I could not choose but suppose she was deserted. If not, the men were lying drunk below, where I might batten them down, perhaps, and do what I chose with the ship.

For some time she had been doing the worst thing possible for me—standing still. She headed nearly due south, yawing, of course, all the time. Each time she fell off, her sails partly filled, and these brought her in a moment right to the wind again. I have said this was the worst thing possible for me, for helpless as she looked in this situation, with the canvas cracking like cannon and the blocks trundling and banging on the deck, she still continued to run away from me, not only with the speed of the current, but by the whole amount of her leeway, which was naturally great.

But now, at last, I had my chance. The breeze fell for some seconds, very low, and the current gradually turning her, the *Hispaniola* revolved slowly round her centre and at last presented me her stern, with the cabin window still gaping open and the lamp over the table still burning on into the day. The main-sail hung drooped like a banner. She was stock-still but for the current.

For the last little while I had even lost, but now, re-doubling my efforts, I began once more to overhaul the chase.

I was not a hundred yards from her when the wind came again in a clap; she filled on the port tack[6] and was off again, stooping and skimming like a swallow.

My first impulse was one of despair, but my second was towards joy. Round she came, till she was broad-side on to me—round still till she had covered a half and then two thirds and then three quarters of the dis-tance that separated us. I could see the waves boiling white under her forefoot. Immensely tall she looked to me from my low station in the coracle.

And then, of a sudden, I began to comprehend. I had scarce time to think—scarce time to act and save myself. I was on the summit of one swell when the schooner came stooping over the next. The bowsprit[7]

6. Since a sailing vessel cannot sail directly into the wind, it must zigzag, or tack, to move ahead into the wind. If the wind is coming toward the left or port side of the vessel, the vessel is on the port tack. If the wind is coming toward the star-board side, the vessel is on the starboard tack.

7. See note 20 on p. 83.

8. An extension boom that projects forward on top of and beyond the bowsprit. The idea is to extend the length of the bowsprit so more jibs can be attached. The boom is attached to the bottom edge of the jib. (See illustration, p. xiii.)

9. Jim caught the spar fastened on top of the bowsprit that projected upward and ahead of the vessel. At the same time, he shoved his foot into one of the *Hispaniola*'s stays, in this case the bobstay that helps keep the bowsprit in position. Jim, writing long after the event, also forgot that while a bowsprit shroud helps brace or stabilize the bowsprit, it is not a brace. On a sailing vessel, braces were used to control a yard to which a sail was fastened. Apparently Jim then lodged his foot in the triangular area where the bobstay and bowsprit shroud came together: a remarkably acrobatic feat. (See illustration, p. xiii.)

was over my head. I sprang to my feet and leaped, stamping the coracle under water. With one hand I caught the jib-boom,[8] while my foot was lodged between the stay and the brace;[9] and as I still clung there panting, a dull blow told me that the schooner had charged down upon and struck the coracle and that I was left without retreat on the *Hispaniola*.

Chapter Twenty-Five

I Strike the Jolly Roger

I HAD SCARCE GAINED a position on the bowsprit when the flying jib[1] flapped and filled upon the other tack, with a report like a gun. The schooner trembled to her keel under the reverse, but next moment, the other sails still drawing, the jib flapped back again and hung idle.

This had nearly tossed me off into the sea; and now I lost no time, crawled back along the bowsprit, and tumbled head foremost on the deck.

I was on the lee side of the forecastle, and the main-sail, which was still drawing, concealed from me a certain portion of the after-deck. Not a soul was to be seen. The planks, which had not been swabbed since the mutiny, bore the print of many feet, and an empty bottle, broken by the neck, tumbled to and fro like a live thing in the scuppers.

Suddenly the *Hispaniola* came right into the wind.[2]

1. A triangular sail set ahead of the foremast and bows. (See illustration, p. xiii.)

2. By their nature, sailing vessels must sail at an angle to the wind; they cannot sail directly into the wind. The *Hispaniola* has changed course and her bows are pointing directly into the wind, which means she is in irons until the action of wind and current nudge her into a new direction.

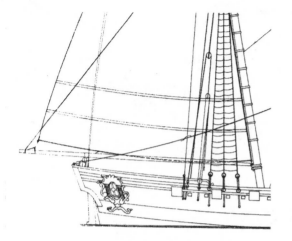

Detail of the main boom from the
schooner diagram on p. xiii.

4. A term for rope used for controlling a sail. Here the sheet making the noise is the main sheet at the rear, or aft, end of the mainsail's boom. (See illustration, p. xiii.) Given the size of the mainsail, the sheet would have been threaded–*roved*–through two blocks to make it easier to manage the sail. (See note 3 on p. 103.)

5. See note 3 on p. 16.

6. An old measure equal to a quarter of a pint. The word in English dates to the 1400s and comes from the Latin *gillo* ("water pot").

The jibs behind me cracked aloud, the rudder slammed to, the whole ship gave a sickening heave and shudder, and at the same moment the main-boom[3] swung inboard, the sheet[4] groaning in the blocks, and showed me the lee after-deck.

There were the two watchmen, sure enough: redcap on his back, as stiff as a handspike, with his arms stretched out like those of a crucifix and his teeth showing through his open lips; Israel Hands propped against the bulwarks, his chin on his chest, his hands lying open before him on the deck, his face as white, under its tan, as a tallow candle.[5]

For a while the ship kept bucking and sidling like a vicious horse, the sails filling, now on one tack, now on another, and the boom swinging to and fro till the mast groaned aloud under the strain. Now and again too there would come a cloud of light sprays over the bulwark and a heavy blow of the ship's bows against the swell; so much heavier weather was made of it by this great rigged ship than by my home-made, lopsided coracle, now gone to the bottom of the sea.

At every jump of the schooner, red-cap slipped to and fro, but—what was ghastly to behold—neither his attitude nor his fixed teeth-disclosing grin was anyway disturbed by this rough usage. At every jump too, Hands appeared still more to sink into himself and settle down upon the deck, his feet sliding ever the farther out, and the whole body canting towards the stern, so that his face became, little by little, hid from me; and at last I could see nothing beyond his ear and the frayed ringlet of one whisker.

At the same time, I observed, around both of them, splashes of dark blood upon the planks and began to feel sure that they had killed each other in their drunken wrath.

While I was thus looking and wondering, in a calm moment, when the ship was still, Israel Hands turned partly round and with a low moan writhed himself back to the position in which I had seen him first. The moan, which told of pain and deadly weakness, and the way in which his jaw hung open went right to my heart. But when I remembered the talk I had overheard from the apple barrel, all pity left me.

I walked aft until I reached the main-mast. "Come aboard, Mr. Hands," I said ironically.

He rolled his eyes round heavily, but he was too far gone to express surprise. All he could do was to utter one word, "Brandy."

It occurred to me there was no time to lose, and dodging the boom as it once more lurched across the deck, I slipped aft and down the companion stairs into the cabin.

It was such a scene of confusion as you can hardly fancy. All the lockfast places had been broken open in quest of the chart. The floor was thick with mud where ruffians had sat down to drink or consult after wading in the marshes round their camp. The bulkheads, all painted in clear white and beaded round with gilt, bore a pattern of dirty hands. Dozens of empty bottles clinked together in corners to the rolling of the ship. One of the doctor's medical books lay open on the table, half of the leaves gutted out, I suppose, for pipelights. In the midst of all this the lamp still cast a smoky glow, obscure and brown as umber.

I went into the cellar; all the barrels were gone, and of the bottles a most surprising number had been drunk out and thrown away. Certainly, since the mutiny began, not a man of them could ever have been sober.

Foraging about, I found a bottle with some brandy left, for Hands; and for myself I routed out some biscuit, some pickled fruits, a great bunch of raisins, and a piece of cheese. With these I came on deck, put down my own stock behind the rudder head and well out of the coxswain's reach, went forward to the water-breaker, and had a good, deep drink of water, and then, and not till then, gave Hands the brandy.

He must have drunk a gill[6] before he took the bottle from his mouth.

"Aye," said he, "by thunder, but I wanted some o' that!"

I had sat down already in my own corner and begun to eat.

"Much hurt?" I asked him.

He grunted, or rather, I might say, he barked.

"If that doctor was aboard," he said, "I'd be right enough in a couple of turns, but I don't have no manner of luck, you see, and that's what's the matter with me. As for that swab, he's good and dead, he is," he added, indicating the man with the red cap. "He warn't no seaman anyhow. And where mought you have come from?"

"Well," said I, "I've come aboard to take possession of this ship, Mr. Hands; and you'll please regard me as your captain until further notice."

He looked at me sourly enough but said nothing. Some of the colour had come back into his cheeks, though he still looked very sick and still continued to slip out and settle down as the ship banged about.

"By the by," I continued, "I can't have these colours, Mr. Hands; and by your leave, I'll strike 'em. Better none than these."

And again dodging the boom, I ran to the colour lines, handed down their cursed black flag, and chucked it overboard.

"God save the king!" said I, waving my cap. "And there's an end to Captain Silver!"

He watched me keenly and slyly, his chin all the while on his breast.

"I reckon," he said at last, "I reckon, Cap'n Hawkins, you'll kind of want to get ashore now. S'pose we talks."

"Why, yes," says I, "with all my heart, Mr. Hands. Say on." And I went back to my meal with a good appetite.

"This man," he began, nodding feebly at the corpse—"O'Brien were his name, a rank Irelander—this man and me got the canvas on her, meaning for to sail her back. Well, *he's* dead now, he is—as dead as bilge; and who's to sail this ship, I don't see. Without I gives you a hint, you ain't that man, as far's I can tell. Now, look here, you gives me food and drink and a old scarf or ankecher to tie my wound up, you do, and I'll tell you how to sail her, and that's about square all round, I take it."

"I'll tell you one thing," says I: "I'm not going back to Captain Kidd's anchorage. I mean to get into North Inlet and beach her quietly there."

"To be sure you did," he cried. "Why, I ain't sich an infernal lubber after all. I can see, can't I? I've tried my fling, I have, and I've lost, and it's you has the wind of me.[7] North Inlet? Why, I haven't no ch'ice, not I! I'd help you sail her up to Execution Dock,[8] by thunder! So I would."

Well, as it seemed to me, there was some sense in this. We struck our bargain on the spot. In three minutes I had the *Hispaniola* sailing easily before the wind along the coast of Treasure Island, with good hopes of turning the northern point ere noon and beating down again as far as North Inlet before high water, when we might beach her safely and wait till the subsiding tide permitted us to land.

Then I lashed the tiller[9] and went below to my own

7. This is a figurative way of saying "It's you who have the advantage of me." The literal sense of what Israel Hands is saying is that Jim Hawkins has the wind behind him. To a sailor attacking another ship, when he has the wind behind him—*the weather gage*—he has an advantage because he has more choices for how to maneuver his vessel than the other ship, which has to maneuver into the wind.

8. See note for Execution Dock on p. 92.

9. Hawkins has taken a length of rope and tied the tiller, or helm, so that it will not swing back and forth aimlessly when he is not holding it and take the *Hispaniola* off its course. He has a nice, easy wind behind him, so he has a good chance of having the *Hispaniola* continue to sail in a straight line. Captain Joshua Slocum, who set out from Boston in 1895 and sailed single-handed around the world in three years in a sloop not quite 37 feet long, would lash the helm at night so he could get some sleep.

"I can't have these colors, Mr. Hands; and by your leave, I'll strike 'em."

chest, where I got a soft silk handkerchief of my mother's. With this, and with my aid, Hands bound up the great bleeding stab he had received in the thigh, and after he had eaten a little and had a swallow or two more of the brandy, he began to pick up visibly, sat straighter up, spoke louder and clearer, and looked in every way another man.

The breeze served us admirably. We skimmed before it like a bird, the coast of the island flashing by and the view changing every minute. Soon we were past the high lands and bowling beside low, sandy country, sparsely dotted with dwarf pines, and soon we were beyond that again and had turned the corner of the rocky hill that ends the island on the north.

I was greatly elated with my new command, and pleased with the bright, sunshiny weather and these different prospects of the coast. I had now plenty of water and good things to eat, and my conscience, which had smitten me hard for my desertion, was quieted by the great conquest I had made. I should, I think, have had nothing left me to desire but for the eyes of the coxswain as they followed me derisively about the deck and the odd smile that appeared continually on his face. It was a smile that had in it something both of pain and weakness—a haggard old man's smile; but there was, besides that, a grain of derision, a shadow of treachery, in his expression as he craftily watched, and watched, and watched me at my work.

Chapter Twenty-Six

Israel Hands

THE WIND, SERVING US to a desire, now hauled into the west. We could run so much the easier from the north-east corner of the island to the mouth of the North Inlet. Only, as we had no power to anchor and dared not beach her till the tide had flowed a good deal farther, time hung on our hands. The coxswain told me how to lay the ship to;[1] after a good many trials I succeeded, and we both sat in silence over another meal.

"Cap'n," said he at length with that same uncomfortable smile, "here's my old shipmate, O'Brien; s'pose you was to heave him overboard. I ain't partic'lar as a rule, and I don't take no blame for settling his hash, but I don't reckon him ornamental now, do you?"

"I'm not strong enough, and I don't like the job; and there he lies, for me," said I.

"This here's an unlucky ship, this *Hispaniola,* Jim," he went on, blinking. "There's a power of men been

1. Jim Hawkins has reduced sail area exposed to the wind, changed how the sails are exposed to the wind, and arranged the tiller in such a way that the *Hispaniola* has stopped, because every time she comes up into the wind, she falls away from the wind. *Lie to* and *heave* to are other phrases that would describe Jim's maneuver. This was hard work for one person.

killed in this *Hispaniola*—a sight o' poor sea-men dead and gone since you and me took ship to Bristol. I never seen sich dirty luck, not I. There was this here O'Brien now—he's dead, ain't he? Well now, I'm no scholar, and you're a lad as can read and figure, and to put it straight, do you take it as a dead man is dead for good, or do he come alive again?"

"You can kill the body, Mr. Hands, but not the spirit; you must know that already," I replied. "O'Brien there is in another world, and may be watching us."

"Ah!" says he. "Well, that's unfort'nate—appears as if killing parties was a waste of time. Howsomever, sperrits don't reckon for much, by what I've seen. I'll chance it with the sperrits, Jim. And now, you've spoke up free, and I'll take it kind if you'd step down into that there cabin and get me a—well, a—shiver my timbers! I can't hit the name on 't; well, you get me a bottle of wine, Jim—this here brandy's too strong for my head."

Now, the coxswain's hesitation seemed to be unnatural, and as for the notion of his preferring wine to brandy, I entirely disbe-lieved it. The whole story was a pretext. He wanted me to leave the deck—so much was plain; but with what purpose I could in no way imagine. His eyes never met mine; they kept wandering to and fro, up and down,

now with a look to the sky, now with a flit-ting glance upon the dead O'Brien. All the time he kept smiling and putting his tongue out in the most guilty, embarrassed manner, so that a child could have told that he was bent on some deception. I was prompt with my answer, however, for I saw where my ad-vantage lay and that with a fellow so densely stupid I could easily conceal my suspicions to the end.

"Some wine?" I said. "Far better. Will you have white or red?"

"Well, I reckon it's about the blessed same to me, shipmate," he replied; "so it's strong, and plenty of it, what's the odds?"

"All right," I answered. "I'll bring you port, Mr. Hands. But I'll have to dig for it."

With that I scuttled down the companion with all the noise I could, slipped off my shoes, ran quietly along the sparred gallery, mounted the forecastle ladder, and popped my head out of the fore companion. I knew he would not expect to see me there, yet I took every precaution possible, and certainly the worst of my suspicions proved too true.

He had risen from his position to his hands and knees, and though his leg obviously hurt him pretty sharply when he moved—for I could hear him stifle a groan—yet it was at a good, rattling rate that he trailed himself across the deck. In half a minute he had reached the port scuppers and picked, out of a coil of rope, a long knife, or rather a short dirk,[2] discoloured to the hilt with blood. He looked upon it for a moment, thrusting forth his under jaw, tried the point upon his hand, and then, hastily concealing it in the bosom of his jacket, trundled back again into his old place against the bulwark.

This was all that I required to know. Israel could move about, he was now armed, and if he had been at so much trouble to get rid of me, it was plain that I was meant to be the victim. What he would do afterwards—whether he would try to crawl right across the island from North Inlet to the camp among the swamps or whether he would fire Long Tom, trusting that his own comrades might come first to help him— was, of course, more than I could say.

Yet I felt sure that I could trust him in one point, since in that our interests jumped together, and that was in the disposition of the schooner. We both desired to have her stranded safe enough, in a sheltered place, and so that, when the time came, she could be got off again with as little labour and danger as might be; and until that was done I considered that my life would certainly be spared.

While I was thus turning the business over in my mind, I had not been idle with my body. I had stolen back to the cabin, slipped once more into my shoes, and laid my hand at random on a bottle of wine, and now, with this for an excuse, I made my reappearance on the deck.

2. *Dirk* is a Scottish word for "dagger" dating back to the 1100s.

Hands lay as I had left him, all fallen together in a bundle and with his eyelids lowered as though he were too weak to bear the light. He looked up, however, at my coming, knocked the neck off the bottle like a man who had done the same thing often, and took a good swig, with his favourite toast of "Here's luck!" Then he lay quiet for a little, and then, pulling out a stick of tobacco, begged me to cut him a quid.

"Cut me a junk o' that," says he, "for I haven't no knife and hardly strength enough, so be as I had. Ah, Jim, Jim, I reckon I've missed stays! Cut me a quid, as'll likely be the last, lad, for I'm for my long home, and no mistake."

"Well," said I, "I'll cut you some tobacco, but if I was you and thought myself so badly, I would go to my prayers like a Christian man."

"Why?" said he. "Now, you tell me why."

"Why?" I cried. "You were asking me just now about the dead. You've broken your trust; you've lived in sin and lies and blood; there's a man you killed lying at your feet this moment, and you ask me why! For God's mercy, Mr. Hands, that's why."

I spoke with a little heat, thinking of the bloody dirk he had hidden in his pocket and designed, in his ill thoughts, to end me with. He, for his part, took a great draught of the wine and spoke with the most unusual solemnity.

"For thirty years," he said, "I've sailed the seas and seen good and bad, better and worse, fair weather and foul, provisions running out, knives going, and what not. Well, now I tell you, I never seen good come o' goodness yet. Him as strikes first is my fancy; dead men don't bite; them's my views—amen, so be it. And now, you look here," he added, suddenly changing his tone, "we've had about enough of this foolery. The tide's made good enough by now. You just take my orders, Cap'n Hawkins, and we'll sail slap in and be done with it."

All told, we had scarce two miles to run; but the navigation was delicate, the entrance to this northern anchorage was not only narrow and shoal, but lay east and west, so that the schooner must be nicely handled to be got in. I think I was a good, prompt subaltern,[3] and I am very sure that Hands was an excellent pilot, for we went about and about and dodged in, shaving the banks, with a certainty and a neatness that were a pleasure to behold.

Scarcely had we passed the heads before the land closed around us. The shores of North Inlet were as thickly wooded as those of the southern anchorage, but the space was longer and narrower and more like, what in truth it was, the estuary of a river. Right before us, at the southern end, we saw the wreck of a ship in the last stages of dilapidation. It had been a great vessel of three masts but had lain so long exposed to the injuries of the weather that it was hung about with great webs of dripping seaweed, and on the deck of it shore bushes had taken root and now flourished thick with flowers. It was a sad sight, but it showed us that the anchorage was calm.

"Now," said Hands, "look there; there's a pet bit for to beach a ship in. Fine flat sand, never a cat's paw, trees all around of it, and flowers a-blowing like a garding on that old ship."

"And once beached," I inquired, "how shall we get her off again?"

"Why, so," he replied: "you take a line ashore there on the other side at low water, take a turn about one o' them big pines; bring it back, take a turn round the capstan, and lie to for the tide. Come high water, all hands take a pull upon the line, and off she comes as sweet as natur'. And now, boy, you stand by. We're near the bit now, and she's too much way on her. Starboard a little—so—steady—starboard—larboard a little—steady—steady!"

So he issued his commands, which I breathlessly obeyed, till, all of a sudden, he cried, "Now, my hearty, luff!"[4] And I put the helm hard up, and the *Hispaniola* swung round rapidly and ran stem on[5] for the low, wooded shore.

3. A general term for a junior army officer that became common in the 1700s. For example, in the British Army today a second lieutenant is often referred to as a subaltern.

4. See note 19 on p. 94.

5. On the *Hispaniola*, the stem post—an upright timber that started at the keel and curved upward—was the farthest forward part of the vessel's wooden frame. In large ships it would be a composite piece. *Bow* and *stem* are commonly used interchangeably. The bow is the fore end of a vessel. The *starboard bow* and *port bow* come together at the stem.

The excitement of these last manoeuvres had somewhat interfered with the watch I had kept hitherto, sharply enough, upon the coxswain. Even then I was still so much interested, waiting for the ship to touch, that I had quite forgot the peril that hung over my head and stood craning over the starboard bulwarks and watching the ripples spreading wide before the bows. I might have fallen without a struggle for my life had not a sudden disquietude seized upon me and made me turn my head. Perhaps I had heard a creak or seen his shadow moving with the tail of my eye; perhaps it was an instinct like a cat's; but, sure enough, when I looked round, there was Hands, already half-way towards me, with the dirk in his right hand.

We must both have cried out aloud when our eyes met, but while mine was the shrill cry of terror, his was a roar of fury like a charging bull's. At the same instant, he threw himself forward and I leapt sideways towards the bows. As I did so, I let go of the tiller, which sprang sharp to leeward, and I think this saved my

The coxswain loosed his grasp upon the shrouds and plunged head first into the water.

life, for it struck Hands across the chest and stopped him, for the moment, dead.

Before he could recover, I was safe out of the corner where he had me trapped, with all the deck to dodge about. Just forward of the main-mast I stopped, drew a pistol from my pocket, took a cool aim, though he had already turned and was once more coming directly after me, and drew the trigger. The hammer fell, but there followed neither flash nor sound; the priming was useless with sea-water. I cursed myself for my neglect. Why had not I, long before, reprimed and reloaded my only weapons? Then I should not have been as now, a mere fleeing sheep before this butcher.

Wounded as he was, it was wonderful how fast he could move, his grizzled hair tumbling over his face, and his face itself as red as a red ensign[6] with his haste and fury. I had no time to try my other pistol, nor indeed much inclination, for I was sure it would be useless. One thing I saw plainly: I must not simply retreat before him, or he would speedily hold me boxed into the bows, as a moment since he had so nearly boxed me in the stern. Once so caught, and nine or ten inches of the blood-stained dirk would be my last experience on this side of eternity. I placed my palms against the main-mast, which was of a goodish bigness, and waited, every nerve upon the stretch.

Seeing that I meant to dodge, he also paused; and a moment or two passed in feints on his part and corresponding movements upon mine. It was such a game as I had often played at home about the rocks of Black

6. Jim Hawkins is comparing the shade of Israel Hands's red face to the Red Ensign, one of the flags used by the Royal Navy until 1864. The flag had the Union Flag of Great Britain in the upper left canton (corner). The rest of the flag was red. In the 1750s the navy also used two other flags, the White Ensign and the Blue Ensign, to identify its ships and the seniority of their commanders. Those two flags also had the Union Flag in the upper left corner.

The practice of using colored flags offers a window into early methods used to command and control the activities of groups of ships at sea by the British. As early 1617, and probably earlier, the fleet of the Royal Navy was divided into three groups or *squadrons*, each with its own flag: one red, one white, one blue. The squadron with the red flag was commanded by an admiral; the squadron with the white flag was commanded by a *vice admiral*; the third had a blue flag and was commanded by a *rear admiral*. Over the years the navy would become much larger and complex, with many more admirals, but the three flag colors remained in use as a way to label seniority of rank. In the terminology of the day, for example, the most junior admiral was the *rear admiral of the blue*. The next step up for him would be rear admiral of the white, then *rear admiral of the red*. The sequence would continue with the next step for him being *vice admiral of the blue* and so on up the red-white-blue ladder.

You could tell which ship carried which grade of admiral by which mast carried the squadronal flag. The ship carrying an admiral flew the squadron's flag on the foremast; a vice admiral's was on the main mast, while the rear admiral's was on the mizzen mast.

To confuse matters, the most senior admiral of the fleet was not called *admiral of the red*; he was called *admiral of the fleet* and he did not fly a Red Ensign from his ship; he flew the Union Flag. To further confuse matters, there were also admirals informally known as *yellow admirals*, who were captains promoted to admiral on retirement; they did not serve as admirals and did not have titles with red, white, or blue in them.

In 1864 the red-white-blue system of ranking senior officers was abolished. The Red Ensign now was designated the national flag to be flown by civilian merchant ships; the White Ensign was to be flown by Royal Navy vessels, and the Blue

Ensign to be flown by non-military government ships, yacht clubs, and others. The Royal Air Force uses a light blue ensign.

A note on modern usage: the term *flag ship* is still used to denote the ship that carries the commander of a group of naval vessels, and when a naval officer in the United States Navy and in the navies of British Commonwealth nations is promoted to admiral he *gets his flag.*

7. Shrouds–part of the nonmoving, or standing, rigging of a vessel–were groups of heavy rope that were fastened to each side of a mast or the bowsprit to provide side-to-side stability. (For more on *shrouds,* see note 2 on p. 67 and note 9 on p. 188; also see illustration, p. xiii.)

Jim Hawkins's memory is a little hazy here; he has confused the big main mast of the *Hispaniola* with a small mizzen mast. Both are in the same location–to the rear of the foremast–but on different kinds of vessels. The *mizzen* is the mast farthest to the rear on a three-masted vessel. It also refers to the second mast on some vessels; for example, on a ketch the second mast is shorter than the main mast in front of it.

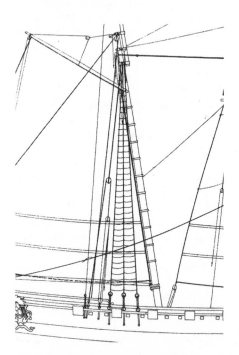

Detail of the mizzen shrouds from the schooner diagram on p. xiii.

Hill Cove, but never before, you may be sure, with such a wildly beating heart as now. Still, as I say, it was a boy's game, and I thought I could hold my own at it against an elderly seaman with a wounded thigh. Indeed my courage had begun to rise so high that I allowed myself a few darting thoughts on what would be the end of the affair, and while I saw certainly that I could spin it out for long, I saw no hope of any ultimate escape.

Well, while things stood thus, suddenly the *Hispaniola* struck, staggered, ground for an instant in the sand, and then, swift as a blow, canted over to the port side till the deck stood at an angle of forty-five degrees and about a puncheon of water splashed into the scupper holes and lay, in a pool, between the deck and bulwark.

We were both of us capsized in a second, and both of us rolled, almost together, into the scuppers, the dead red-cap, with his arms still spread out, tumbling stiffly after us. So near were we, indeed, that my head came against the coxswain's foot with a crack that made my teeth rattle. Blow and all, I was the first afoot again, for Hands had got involved with the dead body. The sudden canting of the ship had made the deck no place for running on; I had to find some new way of escape, and that upon the instant, for my foe was almost touching me. Quick as thought, I sprang into the mizzen shrouds,[7] rattled up hand over hand, and did not draw a breath till I was seated on the cross-trees.[8]

I had been saved by being prompt; the dirk had struck not half a foot below me as I pursued my upward flight; and there stood Israel Hands with his mouth open and his face upturned to mine, a perfect statue of surprise and disappointment.

Now that I had a moment to myself, I lost no time in changing the priming of my pistol, and then, having one ready for service, and to make assurance doubly sure, I proceeded to draw the load of the other and recharge it afresh from the beginning.

My new employment struck Hands all of a heap; he began to see the dice going against him, and after an obvious hesitation, he also hauled himself heavily into the shrouds, and with the dirk in his teeth, began slowly and painfully to mount. It cost him no end of time and groans to haul his wounded leg behind him, and I had quietly finished my arrangements before he was much more than a third of the way up. Then, with a pistol in either hand, I addressed him.

"One more step, Mr. Hands," said I, "and I'll blow your brains out! Dead men don't bite, you know," I added with a chuckle.

He stopped instantly. I could see by the working of his face that he was trying to think, and the process was so slow and laborious that, in my new-found security, I laughed aloud. At last, with a swallow or two, he spoke, his face still wearing the same expression of extreme perplexity. In order to speak he had to take the dagger from his mouth, but in all else he remained unmoved.

"Jim," says he, "I reckon we're fouled, you and me,[9] and we'll have to sign articles.[10] I'd have had you but for that there lurch, but I don't have no luck, not I; and

8. In this instance, Jim is perched on the fittings that fasten the shorter topmast to the longer main mast below it. (See illustration, p. 200.)

9. A figurative way of saying "We are in an impossible situation." In maritime usage, the word *foul* refers to a piece of equipment, like an anchor, that has become tangled up in a rope or something similar—hence the term a *fouled anchor*.

10. The phrase means he'll have to sign a surrender agreement, which contains a list of conditions, or *articles*, under which the surrender will be made.

11. In other words, "I'll have to surrender." A ship when it surrenders "strikes its colors"–that is, lowers the flag that signifies its nationality. The word *strike* can also be used when referring to other objects that need to be lowered, as in, for example, phrases like "strike that yard" and "strike the topmast."

I reckon I'll have to strike,[11] which comes hard, you see, for a master mariner to a ship's younker like you, Jim."

I was drinking in his words and smiling away, as conceited as a cock upon a wall, when, all in a breath, back went his right hand over his shoulder. Something sang like an arrow through the air; I felt a blow and then a sharp pang, and there I was pinned by the shoulder to the mast. In the horrid pain and surprise of the moment—I scarce can say it was by my own volition, and I am sure it was without a conscious aim—both my pistols went off, and both escaped out of my hands. They did not fall alone; with a choked cry, the coxswain loosed his grasp upon the shrouds and plunged head first into the water.

Chapter Twenty-Seven

"Pieces of Eight"

OWING TO THE CANT of the vessel, the masts hung far out over the water, and from my perch on the cross-trees I had nothing below me but the surface of the bay. Hands, who was not so far up, was in consequence nearer to the ship and fell between me and the bulwarks. He rose once to the surface in a lather of foam and blood and then sank again for good. As the water settled, I could see him lying huddled together on the clean, bright sand in the shadow of the vessel's sides. A fish or two whipped past his body. Sometimes, by the quivering of the water, he appeared to move a little, as if he were trying to rise. But he was dead enough, for all that, being both shot and drowned, and was food

for fish in the very place where he had designed my slaughter.

I was no sooner certain of this than I began to feel sick, faint, and terrified. The hot blood was running over my back and chest. The dirk, where it had pinned my shoulder to the mast, seemed to burn like a hot iron; yet it was not so much these real sufferings that distressed me, for these, it seemed to me, I could bear without a murmur; it was the horror I had upon my mind of falling from the cross-trees into that still green water, beside the body of the coxswain.

I clung with both hands till my nails ached, and I shut my eyes as if to cover up the peril. Gradually my mind came back again, my pulses quieted down to a more natural time, and I was once more in possession of myself.

It was my first thought to pluck forth the dirk, but either it stuck too hard or my nerve failed me, and I desisted with a violent shudder. Oddly enough, that very shudder did the business. The knife, in fact, had come the nearest in the world to missing me altogether; it held me by a mere pinch of skin, and this the shudder tore away. The blood ran down the faster, to be sure, but I was my own master again and only tacked to the mast by my coat and shirt.

These last I broke through with a sudden jerk, and then regained the deck by the starboard shrouds. For nothing in the world would I have again ventured, shaken as I was, upon the overhanging port shrouds from which Israel had so lately fallen.

I went below and did what I could for my wound; it pained me a good deal and still bled freely, but it was neither deep nor dangerous, nor did it greatly gall me when I used my arm. Then I looked around me, and as the ship was now, in a sense, my own, I began to think of clearing it from its last passenger—the dead man, O'Brien.

He had pitched, as I have said, against the bulwarks, where he lay like some horrible, ungainly sort of puppet, life-size, indeed, but how different from life's colour or life's comeliness! In that position I

With my arms before me I walked steadily in.

206

could easily have my way with him, and as the habit of tragical adventures had worn off almost all my terror for the dead, I took him by the waist as if he had been a sack of bran and with one good heave tumbled him overboard. He went in with a sounding plunge; the red cap came off and remained floating on the surface; and as soon as the splash subsided, I could see him and Israel lying side by side, both wavering with the tremulous movement of the water. O'Brien, though still quite a young man, was very bald. There he lay, with that bald head across the knees of the man who had killed him and the quick fishes steering to and fro over both.

I was now alone upon the ship; the tide had just turned. The sun was within so few degrees of setting that already the shadow of the pines upon the western shore began to reach right across the anchorage and fall in patterns on the deck. The evening breeze had sprung up, and though it was well warded off by the hill with the two peaks upon the east, the cordage[1] had begun to sing a little softly to itself and the idle sails to rattle to and fro.

I began to see a danger to the ship. The jibs I speedily doused and brought tumbling to the deck, but the mainsail was a harder matter. Of course, when the schooner canted over, the boom had swung out-board, and the cap of it and a foot or two of sail hung even under water. I thought this made it still more dangerous; yet the strain was so heavy that I half feared to meddle. At last I got my knife and cut the halyards.[2]

1. An umbrella term for all the various types of rope employed on a sailing vessel—such as running rigging, as opposed to standing rigging—as well as the raw material for making rope.

2. Ropes used to hoist or lower a sail. The word is also spelled *halliards* and *haulyards*.

207

3. See note 4 on p. 147. (Also see illustration, p. xiii.)

4. When a vessel is on her beam-ends, she has tipped far over on her side.

The peak[3] dropped instantly, a great belly of loose canvas floated broad upon the water, and since, pull as I liked, I could not budge the downhall, that was the extent of what I could accomplish. For the rest, the *Hispaniola* must trust to luck, like myself.

By this time the whole anchorage had fallen into shadow—the last rays, I remember, falling through a glade of the wood and shining bright as jewels on the flowery mantle of the wreck. It began to be chill; the tide was rapidly fleeting seaward, the schooner settling more and more on her beam-ends.[4]

I scrambled forward and looked over. It seemed shallow enough, and holding the cut hawser in both hands for a last security, I let myself drop softly overboard. The water scarcely reached my waist; the sand was firm and covered with ripple marks, and I waded ashore in great spirits, leaving the *Hispaniola* on her side, with her main-sail trailing wide upon the surface of the bay. About the same time, the sun went fairly down and the breeze whistled low in the dusk among the tossing pines.

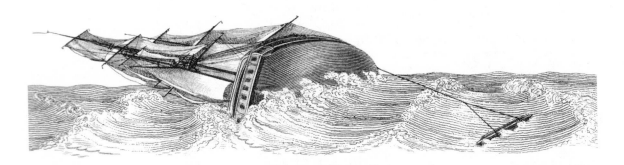

A vessel on her beam-ends.

At least, and at last, I was off the sea, nor had I returned thence empty-handed. There lay the schooner, clear at last from buccaneers and ready for our own men to board and get to sea again. I had nothing nearer my fancy than to get home to the stockade and boast of my achievements. Possibly I might be blamed a bit for my truantry, but the recapture of the *Hispaniola* was a clenching answer, and I hoped that even Captain Smollett would confess I had not lost my time.

So thinking, and in famous spirits, I began to set my face homeward for the block house and my companions. I remembered that the most easterly of the rivers which drain into Captain Kidd's anchorage ran from the two-peaked hill upon my left, and I bent my course in that direction that I might pass the stream while it was small. The wood was pretty open, and keeping along the lower spurs, I had soon turned the corner of that hill, and not long after waded to the mid-calf across the watercourse.

This brought me near to where I had encountered Ben Gunn, the maroon; and I walked more circumspectly, keeping an eye on every side. The dusk had come nigh hand completely, and as I opened out the cleft between the two peaks, I became aware of a wavering glow against the sky, where, as I judged, the man of the island was cooking his supper before a roaring fire. And yet I wondered, in my heart, that he should show himself so careless. For if I could see this radiance, might it not reach the eyes of Silver himself where he camped upon the shore among the marshes?

Gradually the night fell blacker; it was all I could do to guide myself even roughly towards my destination; the double hill behind me and the Spy-glass on my right hand loomed faint and fainter; the stars were few and pale; and in the low ground where I wandered I kept tripping among bushes and rolling into sandy pits.

Suddenly a kind of brightness fell about me. I looked up; a pale glimmer of moonbeams had alighted on the summit of the Spy-glass, and soon after I saw something broad and silvery moving low down behind the trees, and knew the moon had risen.

With this to help me, I passed rapidly over what remained to me of my journey, and sometimes walking, sometimes running, impatiently drew near to the stockade. Yet, as I began to thread the grove that lies before it, I was not so thoughtless but that I slacked my pace and went a trifle warily. It would have been a poor end of my adventures to get shot down by my own party in mistake.

The moon was climbing higher and higher, its light began to fall here and there in masses through the more open districts of the wood, and right in front of me a glow of a different colour appeared among the trees. It was red and hot, and now and again it was a little darkened—as it were, the embers of a bonfire smouldering.

For the life of me I could not think what it might be.

At last I came right down upon the borders of the clearing. The western end was already steeped in moonshine; the rest, and the block house itself, still lay in a black shadow chequered with long silvery streaks of light. On the other side of the house an immense fire had burned itself into clear embers and shed a steady, red reverberation, contrasted strongly with the mellow paleness of the moon. There was not a soul stirring nor a sound beside the noises of the breeze.

I stopped, with much wonder in my heart, and perhaps a little terror also. It had not been our way to build great fires; we were, indeed, by the captain's orders, somewhat niggardly of firewood, and I began to fear that something had gone wrong while I was absent.

I stole round by the eastern end, keeping close in shadow, and at a convenient place, where the darkness was thickest, crossed the palisade.

To make assurance surer, I got upon my hands and knees and crawled, without a sound, towards the corner of the house. As I drew nearer, my heart was suddenly and greatly lightened. It was not a pleasant noise in itself, and I have often complained of it at other times, but just then it was like music to hear my friends snoring together so loud and peaceful in their sleep. The sea-cry of the watch, that beautiful "All's well," never fell more reassuringly on my ear.

In the meantime, there was no doubt of one thing; they kept an infamous bad watch. If it had been Silver and his lads that were now creeping in on them, not a soul would have seen daybreak. That was what it was, thought I, to have the captain wounded; and again I blamed myself sharply for leaving them in that danger with so few to mount guard.

By this time I had got to the door and stood up. All was dark within, so that I could distinguish nothing by the eye. As for sounds, there was the steady drone of the snorers and a small occasional noise, a flickering or pecking that I could in no way account for.

With my arms before me I walked steadily in. I should lie down in my own place (I thought with a silent chuckle) and enjoy their faces when they found me in the morning.

My foot struck something yielding—it was a sleeper's leg; and he turned and groaned, but without awaking.

And then, all of a sudden, a shrill voice broke forth out of the darkness:

"Pieces of eight! Pieces of eight! Pieces of eight! Pieces of eight! Pieces of eight!" and so forth, without pause or change, like the clacking of a tiny mill.

Silver's green parrot, Captain Flint! It was she whom I had heard pecking at a piece of bark; it was she, keeping better watch than any human being, who thus announced my arrival with her wearisome refrain.

I had no time left me to recover. At the sharp, clipping tone of the parrot, the sleepers awoke and sprang up; and with a mighty oath, the voice of Silver cried, "Who goes?"

I turned to run, struck violently against one person, recoiled, and ran full into the arms of a second, who for his part closed upon and held me tight.

"Bring a torch, Dick," said Silver when my capture was thus assured.

And one of the men left the log-house and presently returned with a lighted brand.

PART VI

Captain Silver

Chapter Twenty-Eight

In the Enemy's Camp

THE RED GLARE OF the torch, lighting up the interior of the block house, showed me the worst of my apprehensions realized. The pirates were in possession of the house and stores: there was the cask of cognac, there were the pork and bread, as before, and what tenfold increased my horror, not a sign of any prisoner. I could only judge that all had perished, and my heart smote me sorely that I had not been there to perish with them.

There were six of the buccaneers, all told; not another man was left alive. Five of them were on their feet, flushed and swollen, suddenly called out of the first sleep of drunkenness. The sixth had only risen upon his elbow; he was deadly pale, and the blood-stained bandage round his head told that he had recently been wounded, and still more recently dressed. I remembered the man who had been shot and had run back among the woods in the great attack, and doubted not that this was he.

The parrot sat, preening her plumage, on Long John's shoulder. He himself, I thought, looked somewhat paler and more stern than I was used to. He still wore the fine broadcloth suit in which he had fulfilled his mission, but it was bitterly the worse for wear, daubed with clay and torn with the sharp briers of the wood.

"So," said he, "here's Jim Hawkins, shiver my timbers! Dropped in, like, eh? Well, come, I take that friendly."

And thereupon he sat down across the brandy cask and began to fill a pipe.

"Give me a loan of the link, Dick," said he; and then, when he had a good light, "That'll do, lad," he added; "stick the glim in the wood heap; and you, gentlemen, bring yourselves to! You needn't stand up for Mr. Hawkins; *he'll* excuse you, you may lay to that. And so, Jim"—stopping the tobacco—"here you were, and quite a pleasant surprise for poor old John. I see you were smart when first I set my eyes on you, but this here gets away from me clean, it do."

To all this, as may be well supposed, I made no answer. They had set me with my back against the wall, and I stood there, looking Silver in the face, pluckily enough, I hope, to all outward appearance, but with black despair in my heart.

Silver took a whiff or two of his pipe with great composure and then ran on again.

"Now, you see, Jim, so be as you *are* here," says he, "I'll give you a piece of my mind. I've always liked you, I have, for a lad of spirit, and the picter of my own self when I was young and handsome. I always wanted you to jine and take your share, and die a gentle-man, and now, my cock, you've got to. Cap'n Smollett's a fine seaman, as I'll own up to any day, but stiff on discipline. 'Dooty is dooty,' says he, and right he is. Just you keep clear of the cap'n. The doctor himself is gone dead again you—'ungrateful scamp' was what he said; and the short and the long of the whole story is about here: you can't go back to your own lot, for they won't have you; and without you start a third ship's company all by yourself, which might be lonely, you'll have to jine with Cap'n Silver."

So far so good. My friends, then, were still alive, and though I partly believed the truth of Silver's statement, that the cabin party were incensed at me for my desertion, I was more relieved than distressed by what I heard.

"I don't say nothing as to your being in our hands," continued Silver, "though there you are, and you may lay to it. I'm all for ar-gyment; I never seen good come out o' threatening. If you like the service, well, you'll jine; and if you don't, Jim, why, you're free to answer no—free and welcome, ship-mate; and if fairer can be said by mortal seaman, shiver my sides!"

"Am I to answer, then?" I asked with a very tremulous voice. Through all this sneer-ing talk, I was made to feel the threat of death that overhung me, and my cheeks burned and my heart beat painfully in my breast.

"Lad," said Silver, "no one's a-pressing of you. Take your bearings. None of us won't hurry you, mate; time goes so pleasant in your company, you see."

"Well," says I, growing a bit bolder, "if I'm to choose, I declare I have a right to know what's what, and why you're here, and where my friends are."

"Wot's wot?" repeated one of the buccaneers in a deep growl. "Ah, he'd be a lucky one as knowed that!"

"You'll perhaps batten down your hatches till you're spoke to, my friend," cried Silver truculently to this speaker. And then, in his first gracious tones, he replied to me, "Yesterday morning, Mr. Hawkins," said he, "in the dog-watch,[1] down came Doctor Livesey with a flag of truce. Says he, 'Cap'n Silver, you're sold out. Ship's gone.' Well, maybe we'd been taking a glass, and a song to help it round. I won't say no. Leastways, none of us had looked out. We looked out, and by thunder, the old ship was gone! I never seen a pack o' fools look fishier; and you may lay to that, if I tells you that looked the fishiest. 'Well,' says the doctor, 'let's bargain.' We bargained, him and I, and here we are: stores, brandy, block house, the fire-wood you was thoughtful enough to cut, and in a manner of speaking, the whole blessed boat, from cross-trees to kelson.[2] As for them, they've tramped; I don't know where's they are."

He drew again quietly at his pipe.

"And lest you should take it into that head of

1. Jim Hawkins's memory of what Silver said is hazy again. Both dog-watches–first dog and last dog–are afternoon and early-evening watches, not morning watches. (See note 1 on p. 127.)

2. This is another way of saying "from top to bottom." Cross-trees are high up on a mast; the kelson, or keelson, down below, is an internal keel assembly at the bottom of the hull that strengthens the keel.

yours," he went on, "that you was included in the treaty, here's the last word that was said: 'How many are you,' says I, 'to leave?' 'Four,' says he; 'four, and one of us wounded. As for that boy, I don't know where he is, confound him,' says he, 'nor I don't much care. We're about sick of him.' These was his words."

"Is that all?" I asked.

"Well, it's all that you're to hear, my son," returned Silver.

"And now I am to choose?"

"And now you are to choose, and you may lay to that," said Silver.

"Well," said I, "I am not such a fool but I know pretty well what I have to look for. Let the worst come to the worst, it's little I care. I've seen too many die since I fell in with you. But there's a thing or two I have to tell you," I said, and by this time I was quite excited; "and the first is this: here you are, in a bad way—ship lost, treasure lost, men lost, your whole business gone to wreck; and if you want to know who did it—it was I! I was in the apple barrel the night we sighted land, and I heard you, John, and you, Dick Johnson, and Hands, who is now at the bottom of the sea, and told every word you said before the hour was out. And as for the schooner, it was I

who cut her cable, and it was I that killed the men you had aboard of her, and it was I who brought her where you'll never see her more, not one of you. The laugh's on my side; I've had the top of this business from the first; I no more fear you than I fear a fly. Kill me, if you please, or spare me. But one thing I'll say, and no more; if you spare me, bygones are bygones, and when you fellows are in court for piracy, I'll save you all I can. It is for you to choose. Kill another and do yourselves no good, or spare me and keep a witness to save you from the gallows."

I stopped, for, I tell you, I was out of breath, and to my wonder, not a man of them moved, but all sat staring at me like as many sheep. And while they were still staring, I broke out again, "And now, Mr. Silver," I said, "I believe you're the best man here, and if things go to the worst, I'll take it kind of you to let the doctor know the way I took it."

"I'll bear it in mind," said Silver with an accent so curious that I could not, for the life of me, decide whether he were laughing at my request or had been favourably affected by my courage.

"I'll put one to that," cried the old mahogany-faced seaman—Morgan by name—whom I had seen in Long John's public-house upon the quays of Bristol. "It was him that knowed Black Dog."

"Well, and see here," added the sea-cook. "I'll put another again to that, by thunder! For it was this same boy that faked the chart from Billy Bones. First and last, we've split upon Jim Hawkins!"

"Then here goes!" said Morgan with an oath.

And he sprang up, drawing his knife as if he had been twenty.

"Avast, there!" cried Silver. "Who are you, Tom Morgan? Maybe you thought you was cap'n here, perhaps. By the powers, but I'll teach you better! Cross me, and you'll go where many a good man's gone before you, first and last, these thirty year back—some to the yard-arm, shiver my timbers, and some by the board, and all to feed the fishes. There's never a man looked me between the eyes and seen a good day a'terwards, Tom Morgan, you may lay to that."

"Take a cutlass, him that dares, and I'll see the colour of his inside, crutch and all, before that pipe's empty."

3. Silver here is being sarcastic: no one was in a cheerful good mood. Here is a good example of how the meaning of a word can change over time. *Gay* started out as the Old French word *gai*, and in the 1200s was used in English in the sense of *mirthful*. By the 1400s it conveyed the sense of showiness, and by the 1600s it carried a suggestion of dissipation. In the 1700s, 1800s, and into the 1900s, the word suggested a cheerful good mood. By the end of the 1900s, *gay* had become a synonym for *homosexual*.

4. Pirate crews commonly elected their captains and quartermasters, and also deposed them from time to time, as in the case of Captain England, as discussed in the note on p. 80.

A deposed captain also might leave, with those members of the crew who still supported him, and start over. A more extreme example of the precariousness of the job of pirate captain can be seen in the career of Thomas Anstis, who was "sometimes in the office of captain, sometimes quartermaster and often boatswain and foremast-man," according to a Royal Navy captain who questioned some of his crew, reports the historian Peter Earle. Anstis was terminated in 1723 by some of his men, who shot him while he was asleep in his hammock before going on to kill the quartermaster and other leaders and imprisoning the rest of the crew. They then surrendered their vessel to the authorities, who let them go but hanged the others.

5. A sea-mile in the 1750s was 800 feet longer than a land mile's 5,280 feet. That 18th-century sea-mile was the equivalent of 1/60th, or one minute, of one degree of latitude.

Map makers for centuries have laid an imaginary circular grid on the earth made up of lines of horizontal *latitude* starting at the equator and vertical lines of *longitude* that went from pole to pole. Their objective was to make it possible to create maps of our planet and use them for navigation, among other uses. Each line of latitude that circles the earth is divided into 360 degrees, and each degree is in turn divided into 60 minutes. (For more, see the introduction, p. xxiii.)

Since the earth is not a perfectly round ball, a degree of latitude is 6,046 feet at the equator and 6,108 feet at the poles. For many years the sea-mile was defined as the length of one minute of

Morgan paused, but a hoarse murmur rose from the others.

"Tom's right," said one.

"I stood hazing long enough from one," added another. "I'll be hanged if I'll be hazed by you, John Silver."

"Did any of you gentlemen want to have it out with *me*?" roared Silver, bending far forward from his position on the keg, with his pipe still glowing in his right hand. "Put a name on what you're at; you ain't dumb, I reckon. Him that wants shall get it. Have I lived this many years, and a son of a rum puncheon cock his hat athwart my hawse at the latter end of it? You know the way; you're all gentlemen o' fortune, by your account. Well, I'm ready. Take a cutlass, him that dares, and I'll see the colour of his inside, crutch and all, before that pipe's empty."

Not a man stirred; not a man answered.

"That's your sort, is it?" he added, returning his pipe to his mouth. "Well, you're a gay lot[3] to look at, anyway. Not much worth to fight, you ain't. P'r'aps you can understand King George's English. I'm cap'n here by 'lection.[4] I'm cap'n here because I'm the best man by a long sea-mile.[5] You won't fight, as gentlemen o' fortune should; then, by thunder, you'll obey, and you may lay to it! I like that boy, now; I never seen a better boy than that. He's more a man than any pair of rats of you in this here house, and what I say is this: let me see him that'll lay a hand on him—that's what I say, and you may lay to it."

There was a long pause after this. I stood straight up against the wall, my heart still going like a sledge-hammer, but with a ray of hope now shining in my bosom. Silver leant back against the wall, his arms crossed, his pipe in the corner of his mouth, as calm as though he had been in church; yet his eye kept wandering furtively, and he kept the tail of it on his unruly followers. They, on their part, drew gradually together towards the far end of the block house, and the low hiss of their whispering sounded in my ear continuously, like a stream. One after another, they would look up, and the red light of the torch would fall for a second on their nervous faces; but it was not towards me, it was towards Silver that they turned their eyes.

"You seem to have a lot to say," remarked Silver, spitting far into the air. "Pipe up and let me hear it, or lay to."

"Ax your pardon, sir," returned one of the men; "you're pretty free with some of the rules; maybe you'll kindly keep an eye upon the rest. This crew's dissatisfied; this crew don't vally bullying a marlin-spike;[6] this crew has its rights like other crews, I'll make so free as that; and by your own rules, I take it we can talk together. I ax your pardon, sir, acknowledging you for to be capting at this present; but I claim my right, and steps outside for a council."

And with an elaborate sea-salute, this fellow, a long, ill-looking, yellow-eyed man of five and thirty, stepped coolly towards the door and disappeared out of the house. One after another the rest followed his example,

one degree at latitude 48, or 6,080 feet. In 1929 the International Nautical Mile was defined as 1,852 meters, or about 6,076 feet.

6. A short, round metal spike that tapers to a point. The point is used to pry apart the strands used in manufacturing a length of rope. This prying apart is often done to make room for strands from a second length of rope when two ropes are spliced, or joined, together. A wooden version of a marlin-spike is called a *fid*.

The point of a marlin spike helps pry apart rope strands before two lengths of rope are spliced together.

each making a salute as he passed, each adding some apology. "According to rules," said one. "Forecastle council," said Morgan. And so with one remark or another all marched out and left Silver and me alone with the torch.

The sea-cook instantly removed his pipe.

"Now, look you here, Jim Hawkins," he said in a steady whisper that was no more than audible, "you're within half a plank of death, and what's a long sight worse, of torture. They're going to throw me off. But, you mark, I stand by you through thick and thin. I didn't mean to; no, not till you spoke up. I was about desperate to lose that much blunt, and be hanged into the bargain. But I see you was the right sort. I says to myself, you stand by Hawkins, John, and Hawkins'll stand by you. You're his last card, and by the living thunder, John, he's yours! Back to back, says I. You save your witness, and he'll save your neck!"

I began dimly to understand.

"You mean all's lost?" I asked.

"Aye, by gum, I do!" he answered. "Ship gone, neck gone—that's the size of it. Once I looked into that bay, Jim Hawkins, and seen no schooner—well, I'm tough, but I gave out. As for that lot and their council, mark me, they're outright fools and cow-

ards. I'll save your life—if so be as I can—from them. But, see here, Jim—tit for tat—you save Long John from swinging."

I was bewildered; it seemed a thing so hopeless he was asking—he, the old buccaneer, the ringleader throughout.

"What I can do, that I'll do," I said.

"It's a bargain!" cried Long John. "You speak up plucky, and by thunder, I've a chance!"

He hobbled to the torch, where it stood propped among the firewood, and took a fresh light to his pipe.

"Understand me, Jim," he said, returning. "I've a head on my shoulders, I have. I'm on squire's side now. I know you've got that ship safe somewheres. How you done it, I don't know, but safe it is. I guess Hands and O'Brien turned soft. I never much believed in neither of *them*. Now you mark me. I ask no questions, nor I won't let others. I know when a game's up, I do; and I know a lad that's staunch. Ah, you that's young—you and me might have done a power of good together!"

He drew some cognac from the cask into a tin cannikin.

"Will you taste, messmate?" he asked; and when I had refused: "Well, I'll take a drain myself, Jim," said he. "I need a caulker,[7] for there's trouble on hand. And talking o' trouble, why did that doctor give me the chart, Jim?"

My face expressed a wonder so unaffected that he saw the needlessness of further questions.

"Ah, well, he did, though," said he. "And there's something under that, no doubt—something, surely, under that, Jim—bad or good."

And he took another swallow of the brandy, shaking his great fair head like a man who looks forward to the worst.

7. Slang for "I need a drink."

Chapter Twenty-Nine

The Black Spot Again

THE COUNCIL OF THE buccaneers had lasted some time, when one of them re-entered the house, and with a repetition of the same salute, which had in my eyes an ironical air, begged for a moment's loan of the torch. Silver briefly agreed, and this emissary retired again, leaving us together in the dark.

"There's a breeze coming, Jim," said Silver, who had by this time adopted quite a friendly and familiar tone.

I turned to the loophole nearest me and looked out. The embers of the great fire had so far burned themselves out and now glowed so low and duskily that I understood why these conspirators desired a torch. About half-way down the slope to the stock-ade, they were collected in a group; one held the light, another was on his knees in their midst, and I saw the blade of an open knife shine in his hand with varying colours in the moon and torchlight. The rest were all somewhat stooping, as though watching the manoeuvres of this last. I could just make out that he had a book as well as a knife in his hand, and was still wondering how anything so incongruous had come in their possession when the kneeling figure rose once more to his feet and the whole party began to move together towards the house.

"Here they come," said I; and I returned to my former position, for it seemed beneath my dignity that they should find me watching them.

"Well, let 'em come, lad—let 'em come," said Silver cheerily. "I've still a shot in my locker."

The door opened, and the five men, standing huddled together just inside, pushed one of their number forward. In any other circumstances it would have been comical to see his slow advance, hesitating as he set down each foot, but holding his closed right hand in front of him.

"Step up, lad," cried Silver. "I won't eat you. Hand it over, lubber. I know the rules, I do; I won't hurt a depytation."

Thus encouraged, the buccaneer stepped forth more briskly, and having passed something to Silver, from hand to hand, slipped yet more smartly back again to his companions.

The sea-cook looked at what had been given him.

"The black spot! I thought so," he observed. "Where might you have got the paper? Why, hillo! Look here, now; this ain't lucky! You've gone and cut this out of a Bible. What fool's cut a Bible?"

"Ah, there!" said Morgan. "There! Wot did I say? No good'll come o' that, I said."

"Well, you've about fixed it now, among you," continued Silver. "You'll all swing now, I reckon. What softheaded lubber had a Bible?"

"It was Dick," said one.

"Dick, was it? Then Dick can get to prayers," said Silver. "He's seen his slice of luck, has Dick, and you may lay to that."

But here the long man with the yellow eyes struck in.

"Belay that talk, John Silver," he said. "This crew has tipped you the black spot in full council, as in dooty bound; just you turn it over, as in dooty bound, and see what's wrote there. Then you can talk."

"Thanky, George," replied the sea-cook. "You always was brisk for business, and has the rules by heart, George, as I'm pleased to see. Well, what is it, anyway? Ah! 'Deposed'—that's it, is it? Very pretty wrote, to be sure; like print, I swear. Your hand o' write, George? Why, you was gettin' quite a leadin' man in this here crew. You'll be cap'n next, I shouldn't wonder. Just oblige me with that torch again, will you? This pipe don't draw."

"Come, now," said George, "you don't fool this crew no more. You're a funny man, by your account; but you're over now, and you'll maybe step down off that barrel and help vote."

"I thought you said you knowed the rules," returned Silver contemptuously. "Leastways,

1. George is concerned they will all be hanged by the neck until, as the judges would instruct, they were "dead, dead, dead." Convention and judicial habit then called for the corpses to be left hanging from a wooden frame or gibbet as a warning to others until the bodies had rotted or dried out. Sometimes the corpses were coated with tar to slow down the process of decay and so prolong the warning. George was right to be nervous. According to the historian Marcus Rediker, perhaps 500 to 600 pirates of British and North American origin were hanged between 1716 and 1726. (For more, see note 3 on p. 86.)

The drawing, by Thomas Rowlandson, shows someone who has been hanged and now is being dried out by the sun.

2. Plum-duff is a dessert made out of flour, suet, and raisins. (See note 15 on p. 83.)

if you don't, I do; and I wait here—and I'm still your cap'n, mind—till you outs with your grievances and I reply; in the meantime, your black spot ain't worth a biscuit. After that, we'll see."

"Oh," replied George, "you don't be under no kind of apprehension; *we're* all square, we are. First, you've made a hash of this cruise—you'll be a bold man to say no to that. Second, you let the enemy out o' this here trap for nothing. Why did they want out? I dunno, but it's pretty plain they wanted it. Third, you wouldn't let us go at them upon the march. Oh, we see through you, John Silver; you want to play booty, that's what's wrong with you. And then, fourth, there's this here boy."

"Is that all?" asked Silver quietly.

"Enough, too," retorted George. "We'll all swing and sun-dry[1] for your bungling."

"Well now, look here, I'll answer these four p'ints; one after another I'll answer 'em. I made a hash o' this cruise, did I? Well now, you all know what I wanted, and you all know if that had been done that we'd 'a been aboard the *Hispaniola* this night as ever was, every man of us alive, and fit, and full of good plum-duff,[2] and the treasure in the hold of her, by thunder! Well, who crossed me? Who forced my hand, as was the lawful cap'n? Who tipped me the black spot the day we landed and began this dance? Ah, it's a fine dance—I'm with you there—and looks mighty like a hornpipe in a rope's end at Execution Dock by London town, it does. But who done it? Why, it was Anderson, and Hands, and you, George Merry! And you're the last above board of that same meddling crew; and you have the Davy Jones's insolence to up and stand for cap'n over me—you, that sank the lot of us! By the powers! But this tops the stiffest yarn to nothing."

Silver paused, and I could see by the faces of George and his late comrades that these words had not been said in vain.

"That's for number one," cried the accused, wiping the sweat from his brow, for he had been talking with a vehemence that shook the house. "Why, I give you my word, I'm sick to speak to you. You've neither sense nor memory, and I leave it to fancy where your mothers was that let you come to sea. Sea! Gentlemen o' fortune! I reckon tailors is your trade."

"Go on, John," said Morgan. "Speak up to the others."

"Ah, the others!" returned John. "They're a nice lot, ain't they? You say this cruise is bungled. Ah! By gum, if you could understand how bad it's bungled, you would see! We're that near the gibbet that my neck's stiff with thinking on it. You've seen 'em, maybe, hanged in chains, birds about 'em, seamen p'inting 'em out as they go down with the tide. 'Who's that?' says one. 'That! Why, that's John Silver. I knowed him well,' says another. And you can hear the chains a-jangle as you go about and reach for the other buoy.[3] Now, that's about where we are, every mother's son of us, thanks to him, and Hands, and Anderson, and other ruination fools of you. And if you want to know about number

3. When a ship is under sail and tacking, the distance she sails after making a tack is called a *reach*. A buoy in the 1750s was a marker made from a sealed cask or block of wood and then anchored over a particular spot to mark it for whatever reason.

A *reach*, or *ratch*, was also the name given to a straight stretch of river that could be navigated by a vessel. Mariners on the River Thames have names for the river's reaches as it flows from London to the sea: Limehouse Reach, Woolwich Reach, Gallion's Reach, Barking Reach, Halfway Reach, Erith Reach, Long Reach, Tilbury Reach.

Tilbury Point was often used to display the bodies of pirates and others who had been hanged, including Captain William Kidd. He was hanged twice in 1701 on the tidal river beach at Wapping. The first time the rope broke. His body was later moved downriver to Tilbury Point and placed in a body cage made of chains that was then suspended from a gibbet. (See note 3 on p. 96 and note 12 on p. 92.)

four, and that boy, why, shiver my timbers, isn't he a hostage? Are we a-going to waste a hostage? No, not us; he might be our last chance, and I shouldn't wonder. Kill that boy? Not me, mates! And number three? Ah, well, there's a deal to say to number three. Maybe you don't count it nothing to have a real college doctor come to see you every day—you, John, with your head broke—or you, George Merry, that had the ague shakes[4] upon you not six hours agone, and has your eyes the colour of lemon peel to this same moment on the clock? And maybe, perhaps, you didn't know there was a consort coming either? But there is, and not so long till then; and we'll see who'll be glad to have a hostage when it comes to that. And as for number two, and why I made a bargain—well, you came crawling on your knees to me to make it—on your knees you came, you was that downhearted—and you'd have starved too if I hadn't—but that's a trifle! You look there—that's why!"

And he cast down upon the floor a paper that I instantly recognized—none other than the chart on yellow paper, with the three red crosses, that I had found in the oilcloth at the bottom of the captain's chest. Why the doctor had given it to him was more than I could fancy.

But if it were inexplicable to me, the appearance of the chart was incredible to the surviving mutineers. They leaped upon it like cats upon a mouse. It went from hand to hand, one tearing it from another; and by the oaths and the cries and the childish laughter with which they accompanied their examination, you would have thought, not only they were fingering the very gold, but were at sea with it, besides, in safety.

"Yes," said one, "that's Flint, sure enough. J. F., and a score below, with a clove hitch to it; so he done ever."

"Mighty pretty," said George. "But how are we to get away with it, and us no ship?"

Silver suddenly sprang up, and supporting himself with a hand against the wall: "Now I give you warning, George," he cried. "One more word of your sauce, and I'll call you down and fight you. How? Why, how do I know? You had ought to tell me that—you and the rest, that lost me my schooner, with your interference, burn you! But not you, you can't; you hain't got the invention of a cockroach. But civil you can speak, and shall, George Merry, you may lay to that."

"That's fair enow," said the old man Morgan.

"Fair! I reckon so," said the sea-cook. "You lost the ship; I found the treasure. Who's the better man at that? And now I resign, by thunder! Elect whom you please to be your cap'n now; I'm done with it."

"Silver!" they cried. "Barbecue forever! Barbecue for cap'n!"

"So that's the toon, is it?" cried the cook. "George, I reckon you'll have to wait another turn, friend; and lucky for you as I'm not a revengeful man. But that was never my way. And now, shipmates, this black spot? 'Tain't

I saw the blade of an open knife shine in his hand.

much good now, is it? Dick's crossed his luck and spoiled his Bible, and that's about all."

"It'll do to kiss the book on still, won't it?" growled Dick, who was evidently uneasy at the curse he had brought upon himself.

"A Bible with a bit cut out!" returned Silver derisively. "Not it. It don't bind no more'n a ballad-book."

"Don't it, though?" cried Dick with a sort of joy. "Well, I reckon that's worth having too."

"Here, Jim—here's a cur'osity for you," said Silver, and he tossed me the paper.

It was around about the size of a crown piece. One side was blank, for it had been the last leaf; the other contained a verse or two of Revelation[7]—these words among the rest, which struck sharply home upon my mind: "Without are dogs and murderers." The printed side had been blackened with wood ash, which already began to come off and soil my fingers; on the blank side had been written with the same material the one word "Depposed." I have that curiosity beside me at this moment, but not a trace of writing now remains beyond a single scratch, such as a man might make with his thumbnail.

That was the end of the night's business. Soon after, with a drink all round, we lay down to sleep, and the outside of Silver's vengeance was to put George Merry up for sentinel and threaten him with death if he should prove unfaithful.

It was long ere I could close an eye, and heaven knows I had matter enough for thought in the man whom I had slain that afternoon, in my own most perilous position, and above all, in the remarkable game that I saw Silver now engaged upon—keeping the mutineers together with one hand and grasping with the other after every means, possible and impossible, to make his peace and save his miserable life. He himself slept peacefully and snored aloud, yet my heart was sore for him, wicked as he was, to think on the dark perils that environed and the shameful gibbet that awaited him.

Chapter Thirty

On Parole

I WAS WAKENED—INDEED, we were all wakened, for I could see even the sentinel shake himself together from where he had fallen against the door-post—by a clear, hearty voice hailing us from the margin of the wood:

"Block house, ahoy!" it cried. "Here's the doctor."

And the doctor it was. Although I was glad to hear the sound, yet my gladness was not without admixture. I remembered with confusion my insubordinate and stealthy conduct, and when I saw where it had brought me—among what companions and surrounded by what dangers—I felt ashamed to look him in the face.

He must have risen in the dark, for the day had hardly come; and when I ran to a loophole and looked out, I saw him standing, like Silver once before, up to the midleg in creeping vapour.

"You, doctor! Top o' the morning to you, sir!" cried Silver, broad awake and beaming with good nature in a moment. "Bright and early, to be sure; and it's the early bird, as the saying goes, that gets the rations. George, shake up your timbers, son, and help Dr. Livesey over the ship's side. All a-doin' well, your patients was—all well and merry."

So he pattered on, standing on the hilltop with his crutch under his elbow and one hand upon the side of the log-house—quite the old John in voice, manner, and expression.

"We've quite a surprise for you too, sir,"

he continued. "We've a little stranger here—he! he! A noo boarder and lodger, sir, and looking fit and taut as a fiddle; slep' like a supercargo,[1] he did, right alongside of John—stem to stem we was, all night."

Dr. Livesey was by this time across the stockade and pretty near the cook, and I could hear the alteration in his voice as he said, "Not Jim?"

"The very same Jim as ever was," says Silver.

The doctor stopped outright, although he did not speak, and it was some seconds before he seemed able to move on.

"Well, well," he said at last, "duty first and pleasure afterwards, as you might have said yourself, Silver. Let us overhaul these patients of yours."

A moment afterwards he had entered the block house and with one grim nod to me proceeded with his work among the sick. He seemed under no apprehension, though he must have known that his life, among these treacherous demons, depended on a hair; and he rattled on to his patients as if he were paying an ordinary professional visit in a quiet English family. His manner, I suppose, reacted on the men, for they behaved to him as if nothing had occurred, as if he were still ship's doctor and they still faithful hands before the mast.

"You're doing well, my friend," he said to the fellow with the bandaged head, "and if ever any person had a close shave, it was you; your head must be as hard as iron. Well, George, how goes it? You're a pretty colour, certainly; why, your liver man, is upside down. Did you take that medicine? Did he take that medicine, men?"

"Aye, aye, sir, he took it, sure enough," returned Morgan.

"Because, you see, since I am mutineers' doctor, or prison doctor as I prefer to call it," says Doctor Livesey in his pleasantest way, "I make it a point of honour not to lose a man for King George (God bless him!) and the gallows."

The rogues looked at each other but swallowed the home-thrust in silence.

"Dick don't feel well, sir," said one.

"Don't he?" replied the doctor. "Well, step up here, Dick, and let me see your tongue. No, I should be surprised if he did! The man's tongue is fit to frighten the French. Another fever."

"Ah, there," said Morgan, "that comed of sp'iling Bibles."

"That comed—as you call it—of being arrant asses," retorted the doctor, "and not having sense enough to know honest air from poison, and the dry land from a vile, pestiferous slough. I think it most probable— though of course it's only an opinion—that you'll all have the deuce to pay before you get that malaria[2] out of your systems. Camp in a bog, would you? Silver, I'm surprised at you. You're less of a fool than many, take you all round; but you don't appear to me to have the rudiments of a notion of the rules of health.

"Well," he added after he had dosed them round

2. Malaria is a disease caused by blood parasites that attack human organs. The parasites are carried by the *Anopheles* mosquito, which passes the parasites on to humans when it feeds by extracting their blood. Symptoms include severe chills that cause the body to shake, followed by fever and sweating, headache, muscle aches, and vomiting. The parasites can cause brain disease, anemia from the destruction of blood cells, and kidney failure. According to a 2012 report by the World Health Organization, 660,000 people die of malaria each year, mostly young children.

The word we use for the disease, which has a recorded history going back 4,000 years, comes from the Italian *mala aria* ("bad air"); people in Italy had noticed that the disease seemed to be linked to the marshes and their bad smells.

The observation of a relationship between the disease and swamps and marches was correct, but linking the cause of the disease with smelly air was not. First, malaria was linked to parasites by French and Italian doctors, and in 1897 mosquitoes were linked to the malaria parasite by Ronald Ross.

The linkage allowed campaigns to be mounted against the environments that malaria-carrying mosquitoes enjoy, including the still water found in swamps and marshes, not to mention ditches, old car tires, and ornamental ponds.

According to language researcher Eric Partridge, the earliest appearance in English, of the word *mal'aria* was in a letter of 1740 by Horace Walpole, who was scathing about Bristol in another letter. (See the introduction, p. xvii.)

and they had taken his prescriptions, with really laugh-able humility, more like charity schoolchildren than blood-guilty mutineers and pirates—"well, that's done for today. And now I should wish to have a talk with that boy, please."

And he nodded his head in my direc-tion carelessly.

George Merry was at the door, spitting and spluttering over some bad-tasted medicine; but at the first word of the doctor's proposal he swung round with a deep flush and cried "No!" and swore.

Silver struck the barrel with his open hand.

"Si-lence!" he roared and looked about him positively like a lion. "Doctor," he went on in his usual tones, "I was a-thinking of that, knowing as how you had a fancy for the boy. We're all humbly grateful for your kindness, and as you see, puts faith in you and takes the drugs down like that much grog. And I take it I've found a way as'll suit all. Hawkins, will you give me your word of honour as a young gentleman—for a young gentleman you are, although poor born—your word of honour not to slip your cable?"

I readily gave the pledge required.

"One jump, and you're out, and we'll run for it like antelopes."

"Then, doctor," said Silver, "you just step outside o' that stockade, and once you're there I'll bring the boy down on the inside, and I reckon you can yarn through the spars. Good day to you, sir, and all our dooties to the squire and Cap'n Smollett."

The explosion of disapproval, which nothing but Silver's black looks had restrained, broke out immediately the doctor had left the house. Silver was roundly accused of playing double—of trying to make a separate peace for himself, of sacrificing the interests of his accomplices and victims, and, in one word, of the identical, exact thing that he was doing. It seemed to me so obvious, in this case, that I could not imagine how he was to turn their anger. But he was twice the man the rest were, and his last night's victory had given him a huge preponderance on their minds. He called them all the fools and dolts you can imagine, said it was necessary I should talk to the doctor, fluttered the chart in their faces, asked them if they could afford to break the treaty the very day they were bound a-treasure-hunting.

"No, by thunder!" he cried. "It's us must break the treaty when the time comes; and till then I'll gammon[3] that doctor, if I have to ile his boots with brandy."

And then he bade them get the fire lit, and stalked out upon his crutch, with his hand on my shoulder, leaving them in a disarray, and silenced by his volubility rather than convinced.

"Slow, lad, slow," he said. "They might round upon us in a twinkle of an eye if we was seen to hurry."

3. To gammon is to deceive. The word entered the language in the late 1600s.

Very deliberately, then, did we advance across the sand to where the doctor awaited us on the other side of the stockade, and as soon as we were within easy speaking distance Silver stopped.

"You'll make a note of this here also, doctor," says he, "and the boy'll tell you how I saved his life, and were deposed for it too, and you may lay to that. Doctor, when a man's steering as near the wind as me—playing chuck-farthing with the last breath in his body, like—you wouldn't think it too much, mayhap, to give him one good word? You'll please bear in mind it's not my life only now—it's that boy's into the bargain; and you'll speak me fair, doctor, and give me a bit o' hope to go on, for the sake of mercy."

Silver was a changed man once he was out there and had his back to his friends and the block house; his cheeks seemed to have fallen in, his voice trembled; never was a soul more dead in earnest.

"Why, John, you're not afraid?" asked Dr. Livesey.

"Doctor, I'm no coward; no, not I—not *so* much!" and he snapped his fingers. "If I was I wouldn't say it. But I'll own up fairly, I've the shakes upon me for the gallows. You're a good man and a true; I never seen a better man! And you'll not forget what I done

good, not any more than you'll forget the bad, I know. And I step aside—see here—and leave you and Jim alone. And you'll put that down for me too, for it's a long stretch, is that!"

So saying, he stepped back a little way, till he was out of earshot, and there sat down upon a tree-stump and began to whistle, spinning round now and again upon his seat so as to command a sight, sometimes of me and the doctor and sometimes of his unruly ruffians as they went to and fro in the sand between the fire—which they were busy rekindling—and the house, from which they brought forth pork and bread to make the breakfast.

"So, Jim," said the doctor sadly, "here you are. As you have brewed, so shall you drink, my boy. Heaven knows, I cannot find it in my heart to blame you, but this much I will say, be it kind or unkind: when Captain Smollett was well, you dared not have gone off; and when he was ill and couldn't help it, by George, it was downright cowardly!"

I will own that I here began to weep. "Doctor," I said, "you might spare me. I have blamed myself enough; my life's forfeit anyway, and I should have been dead by now if Silver hadn't stood for me; and doctor, believe this, I can die—and I dare say I deserve it—but what I fear is torture. If they come to torture me—"

"Jim," the doctor interrupted, and his voice was quite changed, "Jim, I can't have this. Whip over, and we'll run for it."

"Doctor," said I, "I passed my word."

"I know, I know," he cried. "We can't help that, Jim, now. I'll take it on my shoulders, holus bolus,[4] blame and shame, my boy; but stay here, I cannot let you. Jump! One jump, and you're out, and we'll run for it like antelopes."

"No," I replied; "you know right well you wouldn't do the thing yourself—neither you nor squire nor captain; and no more will I. Silver trusted me; I passed my word, and back I go. But, doctor, you did not let me finish. If they come to torture me, I might let slip a word of where the ship is, for I got the ship, part by luck and part by risking, and she lies in North Inlet, on the southern beach, and just below high water. At half tide she must be high and dry."

"The ship!" exclaimed the doctor.

Rapidly I described to him my adventures, and he heard me out in silence.

"There is a kind of fate in this," he observed when I had done. "Every step, it's you that saves our lives; and do you suppose by any chance that we are going to let you lose yours? That would be a poor return, my boy. You found out the plot; you found Ben Gunn— the best deed that ever you did, or will do, though you live to ninety. Oh, by Jupiter, and talking of Ben Gunn!

4. The expression, used here in the sense of "all at once," has been traced back to the mid-1800s, and Dr. Livesey's use of it pushes the history of its usage back to the 1750s.

Bolus in the mid-1700s also was a nickname for an apothecary, a professional who in that period not only manufactured medicines but also acted as a "general practitioner" or doctor. The word, which has been in use in Britain since the 1500s, also means a big lump of matter, a big pill, or a big dose of medicine.

Why, this is the mischief in person. Silver!" he cried. "Silver! I'll give you a piece of advice," he continued as the cook drew near again; "don't you be in any great hurry after that treasure."

"Why, sir, I do my possible, which that ain't," said Silver. "I can only, asking your pardon, save my life and the boy's by seeking for that treasure; and you may lay to that."

"Well, Silver," replied the doctor, "if that is so, I'll go one step further: look out for squalls when you find it."

"Sir," said Silver, "as between man and man, that's too much and too little. What you're after, why you left the block house, why you given me that there chart, I don't know, now, do I? And yet I done your bidding with my eyes shut and never a word of hope! But no, this here's too much. If you won't tell me what you mean plain out, just say so and I'll leave the helm."

"No," said the doctor musingly; "I've no right to say more; it's not my secret, you see, Silver, or, I give you my word, I'd tell it you. But I'll go as far with you as I dare go, and a step beyond, for I'll have my wig sorted by the captain or I'm mistaken! And first, I'll give you a bit of hope; Silver, if we both get alive out of this wolf-trap, I'll do my best to save you, short of perjury."

Silver's face was radiant. "You couldn't say more, I'm sure, sir, not if you was my mother," he cried.

"Well, that's my first concession," added the doctor. "My second is a piece of advice: keep the boy close beside you, and when you need help, halloo. I'm off to seek it for you, and that itself will show you if I speak at random. Good-bye, Jim."

And Dr. Livesey shook hands with me through the stockade, nodded to Silver, and set off at a brisk pace into the wood.

Chapter Thirty-One

The Treasure-hunt—Flint's Pointer

"Jim," said Silver when we were alone, "if I saved your life, you saved mine; and I'll not forget it. I seen the doctor waving you to run for it—with the tail of my eye, I did; and I seen you say no, as plain as hearing. Jim, that's one to you. This is the first glint of hope I had since the attack failed, and I owe it you. And now, Jim, we're to go in for this here treasure-hunting, with sealed orders too, and I don't like it; and you and me must stick close, back to back like, and we'll save our necks in spite o' fate and fortune."

Just then a man hailed us from the fire that breakfast was ready, and we were soon seated here and there about the sand over biscuit and fried junk.[1] They had lit a fire fit to roast an ox, and it was now grown so hot that they could only approach it from the windward, and even there not without precaution. In the same wasteful spirit, they had cooked, I suppose, three times

1. Junk, according to the old mariner Admiral Smyth, was old rope or hawser that was good only for making swabs (see note 1 on p. 23), oakum (used in making the seams of hulls and decks watertight), and mats, among other items. The term was also applied to the salt beef that was issued to sailors as rations. The beef was "as tough to the teeth as old rope, hence the epithet," wrote the admiral.

more than we could eat; and one of them, with an empty laugh, threw what was left into the fire, which blazed and roared again over this unusual fuel. I never in my life saw men so careless of the morrow; hand to mouth is the only word that can describe their way of doing; and what with wasted food and sleeping sentries, though they were bold enough for a brush and be done with it, I could see their entire unfitness for anything like a prolonged campaign.

Even Silver, eating away, with Captain Flint upon his shoulder, had not a word of blame for their recklessness. And this the more surprised me, for I thought he had never shown himself so cunning as he did then.

"Aye, mates," said he, "it's lucky you have Barbecue to think for you with this here head. I got what I wanted, I did. Sure enough, they have the ship. Where they have it, I don't know yet; but once we hit the treasure, we'll have to jump about and find out. And then, mates, us that has the boats, I reckon, has the upper hand."

Thus he kept running on, with his mouth full of the hot bacon; thus he restored their hope and confidence, and, I more than suspect, repaired his own at the same time.

"As for hostage," he continued, "that's his last talk, I guess, with them he loves so dear.

I've got my piece o' news, and thanky to him for that; but it's over and done. I'll take him in a line when we go treasure-hunting, for we'll keep him like so much gold, in case of accidents, you mark, and in the meantime. Once we got the ship and treasure both and off to sea like jolly companions, why then we'll talk Mr. Hawkins over, we will, and we'll give him his share, to be sure, for all his kindness."

It was no wonder the men were in a good humour now. For my part, I was horribly cast down. Should the scheme he had now sketched prove feasible, Silver, already doubly a traitor, would not hesitate to adopt it. He had still a foot in either camp, and there was no doubt he would prefer wealth and freedom with the pirates to a bare escape from hanging, which was the best he had to hope on our side.

Nay, and even if things so fell out that he was forced to keep his faith with Dr. Livesey, even then what danger lay before us! What a moment that would be when the suspicions of his followers turned to certainty and he and I should have to fight for dear life— he a cripple and I a boy—against five strong and active seamen!

Add to this double apprehension the mystery that still hung over the behaviour of my friends, their unexplained desertion of the stockade, their inexplicable cession of the chart, or harder still to understand, the doctor's last warning to Silver, "Look out for squalls when you find it," and you will readily believe how little taste I found in my breakfast and with how uneasy a heart I set forth behind my captors on the quest for treasure.

We made a curious figure, had anyone been there to see us—all in soiled sailor clothes and all but me armed to the teeth.

Silver had two guns slung about him—one before and one behind—besides the great cutlass at his waist and a pistol in each pocket of his square-tailed coat. To complete his strange appearance, Captain Flint sat perched upon his shoulder and gabbling odds and ends of purposeless sea-talk. I had a line about my waist and followed obediently after the sea-cook, who held the loose end of the rope, now in his free hand, now between his powerful teeth. For all the world, I was led like a dancing bear.

For all the world, I was led like a dancing bear.

The other men were variously burthened, some carrying picks and shovels—for that had been the very first necessary they brought ashore from the *Hispaniola*—others laden with pork, bread, and brandy for the midday meal. All the stores, I observed, came from our stock, and I could see the truth of Silver's words the night before. Had he not struck a bargain with the doctor, he and his mutineers, deserted by the ship, must have been driven to subsist on clear water and the proceeds of their hunting. Water would have been little to their taste; a sailor is not usually a good shot; and besides all that, when they were so short of eatables, it was not likely they would be very flush of powder.

Well, thus equipped, we all set out—even the fellow with the broken head, who should certainly have kept in shadow—and straggled, one after another, to the beach, where the two gigs awaited us. Even these bore trace of the drunken folly of the pirates, one in a broken thwart, and both in their muddy and unbailed condition. Both were to be carried along with us for the sake of safety; and so, with our numbers divided between them, we set forth upon the bosom of the anchorage.

As we pulled over, there was some discussion on the chart. The red cross was, of course, far too large to be a guide; and the terms of the note on the back, as you will hear, admitted of some ambiguity. They ran, the reader may remember, thus:

Tall tree, Spy-glass shoulder, bearing a point to the N. of N.N.E.

Skeleton Island E.S.E. and by E.

Ten feet.

A tall tree was thus the principal mark. Now, right before us the anchorage was bounded by a plateau from two to three hundred feet high, adjoining on the north the sloping southern shoulder of the Spy-glass and rising again towards the south into the rough, cliffy eminence called the Mizzenmast Hill. The top of the plateau was dotted thickly with pine-trees of varying height. Every here and there, one of a different species rose forty or fifty feet clear above its neighbours, and which of these was the particular "tall tree" of Captain Flint could only be decided on the spot, and by the readings of the compass.

Yet, although that was the case, every man on board the boats had picked a favourite of his own ere we were half-way over, Long John alone shrugging his shoulders and bidding them wait till they were there.

We pulled easily, by Silver's directions, not to weary the hands prematurely, and after quite a long passage, landed at the mouth of the second river—that which runs down a woody cleft of the Spy-glass. Thence, bending to our left, we began to ascend the slope towards the plateau.

At the first outset, heavy, miry ground and a matted, marish[2] vegetation greatly delayed our progress; but by little and little the hill began to steepen and become stony under foot, and the wood to change its character and to grow in a more open order. It was, indeed, a most pleasant portion of the island that we were now approaching. A heavy-scented broom and many flowering shrubs had almost taken the place of grass. Thickets of green nutmeg-trees[3] were dotted here and there with the red columns and the broad shadow of the pines; and the first mingled their spice with the aroma of the others. The air, besides, was fresh and stirring, and this, under the sheer sunbeams, was a wonderful refreshment to our senses.

The party spread itself abroad, in a fan shape, shouting and leaping to and fro. About the centre, and a good way behind the rest, Silver and I followed—I tethered by my rope, he ploughing, with deep pants, among the sliding gravel. From time to time, indeed, I had to lend him a hand, or he must have missed his footing and fallen backward down the hill.

We had thus proceeded for about half a mile and were approaching the brow of the plateau when the man upon the farthest left began to cry aloud, as if in terror. Shout after shout came from him, and the others began to run in his direction.

2. A variation from the 1600s of the word *marshy*.

3. Trees that produce a spice used to add flavor to food; they also offer a clue to the location of Treasure Island. Some of the Windward Islands of the Caribbean—the group that includes Martinique, St. Lucia, Grenada, the Grenadines, and others—had become a refuge of sorts for small planters unable to compete with the big sugar plantations on the other islands, and some of them grew nutmeg. Treasure Island might have been the site of a nutmeg plantation abandoned during one of the many wars of the 1700s.

"He can't 'a found the treasure," said old Morgan, hurrying past us from the right, "for that's clean a-top."

Indeed, as we found when we also reached the spot, it was something very different. At the foot of a pretty big pine and involved in a green creeper, which had even partly lifted some of the smaller bones, a human skeleton lay, with a few shreds of clothing, on the ground. I believe a chill struck for a moment to every heart.

"He was a seaman," said George Merry, who, bolder than the rest, had gone up close and was examining the rags of clothing. "Leastways, this is good sea-cloth."

"Aye, aye," said Silver; "like enough; you wouldn't look to find a bishop here, I reckon. But what sort of a way is that for bones to lie? 'Tain't in natur'."

Indeed, on a second glance, it seemed impossible to fancy that the body was in a natural position. But for some disarray (the work, perhaps, of the birds that had fed upon him or of the slow-growing creeper that had gradually enveloped his remains) the man lay perfectly straight—his feet pointing in one direction, his hands, raised above his head like a diver's, pointing directly in the opposite.

"I've taken a notion into my old numbskull," observed Silver. "Here's the compass; there's the tip-top p'int o' Skeleton Island, stickin' out like a tooth. Just take a bearing, will you, along the lines of them bones."

It was done. The body pointed straight in the direction of the island, and the compass read duly E.S.E. and by E.

"I thought so," cried the cook; "this here is a p'inter. Right up there is our line for the Pole Star and the jolly dollars. But, by thunder! If it don't make me cold inside to think of Flint. This is one of *his* jokes, and no mistake. Him and these six was alone here; he killed 'em, every man; and this one he hauled here and laid down by compass, shiver my timbers! They're long bones, and the hair's been yellow. Aye, that would be Allardyce. You mind Allardyce, Tom Morgan?"

"Aye, aye," returned Morgan; "I mind him; he owed me money, he did, and took my knife ashore with him."

"Speaking of knives," said another, "why don't we find his'n lying round? Flint warn't the man to pick a seaman's pocket; and the birds, I guess, would leave it be."

"By the powers, and that's true!" cried Silver.

"There ain't a thing left here," said Merry, still feeling round among the bones; "not a copper doit[4] nor a baccy box. It don't look nat'ral to me."

"No, by gum, it don't," agreed Silver; "not nat'ral, nor not nice, says you. Great guns! Messmates, but if Flint was living, this would be a hot spot for you and me. Six they were, and six are we; and bones is what they are now."

"I saw him dead with these here deadlights," said Morgan. "Billy took me in. There he laid, with penny-pieces on his eyes."

"Dead—aye, sure enough he's dead and gone below," said the fellow with the bandage; "but if ever sperrit walked, it would be Flint's. Dear heart, but he died bad, did Flint!"

"Aye, that he did," observed another; "now he raged, and now he hollered for the rum, and now he sang. 'Fifteen Men' were his only song, mates; and I tell you true, I never rightly liked to hear it since. It was main hot, and the windy was open, and I hear that old song comin' out as clear as clear—and the death-haul on the man already."

"Come, come," said Silver; "stow this talk. He's dead, and he don't walk, that I know; leastways, he won't walk by day, and you may lay to that. Care killed a cat. Fetch ahead for the doubloons."

We started, certainly; but in spite of the hot sun and the staring daylight, the pirates no longer ran separate and shouting through the wood, but kept side by side and spoke with bated breath. The terror of the dead buccaneer had fallen on their spirits.

4. Doits were first made in 1728 by mints in six provinces of the Netherlands for use by the Dutch United East India Company, which in turn used them in the areas in which it traded across Asia. Large quantities of low-value copper and higher-value silver doits were produced, and a few gold doits as well. The use of the word by Merry suggests he was acquainted with Asian waters.

Chapter Thirty-Two

The Treasure-hunt—
The Voice Among the Trees

PARTLY FROM THE DAMPING influence of this alarm, partly to rest Silver and the sick folk, the whole party sat down as soon as they had gained the brow of the ascent.

The plateau being somewhat tilted towards the west, this spot on which we had paused commanded a wide prospect on either hand. Before us, over the tree-tops, we beheld the Cape of the Woods fringed with surf; behind, we not only looked down upon the anchorage and Skeleton Island, but saw—clear across the spit and the eastern lowlands—a great field of open sea upon the east. Sheer above us rose the Spy-glass, here dotted with single pines, there black with precipices. There was no sound but that of the distant breakers, mounting from all round, and the chirp of countless insects in the brush. Not a man, not a sail, upon the sea; the very largeness of the view increased the sense of solitude.

Silver, as he sat, took certain bearings with his compass.

"There are three 'tall trees,'" said he, "about in the right line from Skeleton Island. 'Spy-glass shoulder,' I take it, means that lower p'int there. It's child's play to find the stuff now. I've half a mind to dine first."

"I don't feel sharp," growled Morgan. "Thinkin' o' Flint—I think it were—as done me."

"Ah, well, my son, you praise your stars he's dead," said Silver.

"He were an ugly devil," cried a third pirate with a shudder; "that blue in the face too!"

"That was how the rum took him," added Merry. "Blue! Well, I reckon he was blue. That's a true word."

Ever since they had found the skeleton and got upon this train of thought, they had spoken lower and lower, and they had almost got to whispering by now, so that the sound of their talk hardly interrupted the silence of the wood. All of a sudden, out of the middle of the trees in front of us, a thin, high, trembling voice struck up the well-known air and words:

"Fifteen men on the dead man's chest—
Yo-ho-ho, and a bottle of rum!"

I never have seen men more dreadfully affected than the pirates. The colour went from their six faces like enchantment; some leaped to their feet, some clawed hold of others; Morgan grovelled on the ground.

"It's Flint, by——!" cried Merry.

The song had stopped as suddenly as it began—broken off, you would have said, in the middle of a note, as though someone had laid his hand upon the singer's mouth. Coming so far through the clear, sunny atmosphere among the green tree-tops, I thought it had sounded airily and sweetly; and the effect on my companions was the stranger.

"Come," said Silver, struggling with his ashen lips to get the word out; "this won't do. Stand by to go about. This is a rum start, and I can't name the voice, but it's someone skylarking—someone that's flesh and blood, and you may lay to that."

His courage had come back as he spoke, and some of the colour to his face along with it. Already the others had begun to lend an ear to this encouragement and were coming a little to themselves, when the same voice broke out again—not this time singing, but in a faint distant hail that echoed yet fainter among the clefts of the Spy-glass.

"Darby M'Graw," it wailed—for that is the word that best describes the sound—"Darby M'Graw! Darby M'Graw!" again and again and again; and then rising a little higher, and with an oath that I leave out: "Fetch aft the rum, Darby!"

The buccaneers remained rooted to the ground, their eyes starting from their heads. Long after the voice had died away they still stared in silence, dreadfully, before them.

"That fixes it!" gasped one. "Let's go."

1. As noted in the introduction, 700,000 pounds sterling in the 1750s was enough to buy a fleet of 11 duplicates of HMS *Victory*, the 104-gun battleship best known as Admiral Horatio Nelson's flagship at the Battle of Trafalgar. It was wages for one year for 49,000 Royal Navy seamen rated able-bodied. According to Bank of England calculations, 700,000 pounds would be worth about 131.4 million pounds sterling today, or about $200 million.

"They was his last words," moaned Morgan, "his last words above board."

Dick had his Bible out and was praying volubly. He had been well brought up, had Dick, before he came to sea and fell among bad companions.

Still Silver was unconquered. I could hear his teeth rattle in his head, but he had not yet surrendered.

"Nobody in this here island ever heard of Darby," he muttered; "not one but us that's here." And then, making a great effort: "Shipmates," he cried, "I'm here to get that stuff, and I'll not be beat by man or devil. I never was feared of Flint in his life, and, by the powers, I'll face him dead. There's seven hundred thousand pound[1] not a quarter of a mile from here. When did ever a gentleman o' fortune show his stern to that much dollars for a boozy old seaman with a blue mug—and him dead too?"

But there was no sign of reawakening courage in his followers, rather, indeed, of growing terror at the irreverence of his words.

"Belay there, John!" said Merry. "Don't you cross a sperrit."

And the rest were all too terrified to reply. They would have run away severally had they dared; but fear kept them together, and kept them close by John, as if his daring helped them. He, on his part, had pretty well fought his weakness down.

"Sperrit? Well, maybe," he said. "But there's one thing not clear to me. There was an echo. Now, no man ever seen a sperrit with a shadow; well then, what's he doing with an echo to him, I should like to know? That ain't in natur', surely?"

This argument seemed weak enough to me. But you can never tell what will affect the superstitious, and to my wonder, George Merry was greatly relieved.

"Well, that's so," he said. "You've a head upon your shoulders, John, and no mistake. 'Bout ship, mates! This here crew is on a wrong tack, I do believe. And come to think on it, it was like Flint's voice, I grant you, but not just so clear-away like it, after all. It was liker somebody else's voice now—it was liker——"

"By the powers, Ben Gunn!" roared Silver.

"Aye, and so it were," cried Morgan, springing on his knees. "Ben Gunn it were!"

"It don't make much odds, do it, now?" asked Dick. "Ben Gunn's not here in the body any more'n Flint."

But the older hands greeted this remark with scorn.

"Why, nobody minds Ben Gunn," cried Merry; "dead or alive, nobody minds him."

It was extraordinary how their spirits had returned and how the natural colour had revived in their faces. Soon they were chatting together, with intervals of listening; and not long after,

"Darby M'Graw!" it wailed. "Darby M'Graw!"

249

hearing no further sound, they shouldered the tools and set forth again, Merry walking first with Silver's compass to keep them on the right line with Skeleton Island. He had said the truth: dead or alive, nobody minded Ben Gunn.

Dick alone still held his Bible, and looked around him as he went, with fearful glances; but he found no sympathy, and Silver even joked him on his precautions.

"I told you," said he—"I told you you had sp'iled your Bible. If it ain't no good to swear by, what do you suppose a sperrit would give for it? Not that!" and he snapped his big fingers, halting a moment on his crutch.

But Dick was not to be comforted; indeed, it was soon plain to me that the lad was falling sick; hastened by heat, exhaustion, and the shock of his alarm, the fever, predicted by Dr. Livesey, was evidently growing swiftly higher.

It was fine open walking here, upon the summit; our way lay a little downhill, for, as I have said, the plateau tilted towards the west. The pines, great and small, grew wide apart; and even between the clumps of nutmeg and azalea, wide open spaces baked in the hot sunshine. Striking, as we did, pretty near north-west across the island, we drew, on the one hand, ever nearer under the shoulders of the Spy-glass, and on the other, looked ever wider over that western bay where I had once tossed and trembled in the coracle.

The first of the tall trees was reached, and by the bearing proved the wrong one. So with the second. The third rose nearly two hundred feet into the air above a clump of underwood—a giant of a vegetable, with a red column as big as a cottage, and a wide shadow around in which a company could have manoeuvred. It was conspicuous far to sea both on the east and west and might have been entered as a sailing mark upon the chart.

But it was not its size that now impressed my companions; it was the knowledge that seven hundred thousand pounds in gold lay somewhere buried below its spreading shadow. The thought of the money, as they drew nearer, swallowed up their previous terrors. Their eyes burned in their heads; their feet grew speedier and lighter; their whole soul was bound up in that fortune, that whole lifetime of extravagance and pleasure, that lay waiting there for each of them.

Silver hobbled, grunting, on his crutch; his nostrils stood out and quivered; he cursed like a madman when the flies settled on his hot and shiny countenance; he plucked furiously at the line that held me to him and from time to time turned his eyes upon me with a deadly look. Certainly he took no pains to hide his thoughts, and certainly I read them like print. In the immediate nearness of the gold, all else had been forgotten: his promise and the doctor's warning were both things of the past, and I could not doubt that he hoped to seize upon the treasure, find and board the *Hispaniola* under cover of night, cut every honest throat about that island, and sail away as he had at first intended, laden with crimes and riches.

Shaken as I was with these alarms, it was hard for me to keep up with the rapid pace of the treasure-hunters. Now and again I stumbled, and it was then that Silver plucked so roughly at the rope and launched at me his murderous glances. Dick, who had dropped behind us and now brought up the rear, was babbling to himself both prayers and curses as his fever kept rising. This also added to my wretchedness, and to crown all, I was haunted by the thought of the tragedy that had once been acted on that plateau, when that ungodly buccaneer with the blue face—he who died at Savannah, singing and shouting for drink—had there, with his own hand, cut down his six accomplices. This grove that was now so peaceful must then have rung with cries, I thought; and even with the thought I could believe I heard it ringing still.

We were now at the margin of the thicket.

"Huzza, mates, all together!" shouted Merry; and the foremost broke into a run.

And suddenly, not ten yards further, we beheld them stop. A low cry arose. Silver

2. *Probation* here means "examination"; it is derived from the Latin medical word *proba*, which has the same meaning.

doubled his pace, digging away with the foot of his crutch like one possessed; and next moment he and I had come also to a dead halt.

Before us was a great excavation, not very recent, for the sides had fallen in and grass had sprouted on the bottom. In this were the shaft of a pick broken in two and the boards of several packing-cases strewn around. On one of these boards I saw, branded with a hot iron, the name *Walrus*—the name of Flint's ship.

All was clear to probation.[2] The *cache* had been found and rifled; the seven hundred thousand pounds were gone!

Chapter Thirty-Three

The Fall of a Chieftain

THERE NEVER WAS SUCH an overturn in this world. Each of these six men was as though he had been struck. But with Silver the blow passed almost instantly. Every thought of his soul had been set full-stretch, like a racer, on that money; well, he was brought up, in a single second, dead; and he kept his head, found his temper, and changed his plan before the others had had time to realize the disappointment.

"Jim," he whispered, "take that, and stand by for trouble."

And he passed me a double-barrelled pistol.

At the same time, he began quietly moving northward, and in a few steps had put the hollow between us two and the other five. Then he looked at me and nodded, as much as to say, "Here is a narrow corner," as, indeed, I thought it was. His looks were not quite friendly, and I was so revolted at these constant changes that I could not forbear whispering, "So you've changed sides again."

There was no time left for him to answer in. The buccaneers, with oaths and cries, began to leap, one after another, into the pit and to dig with their fingers, throwing the boards aside as they did so. Morgan found a piece of gold. He held it up with a perfect spout of oaths. It was a two-guinea piece, and it went from hand to hand among them for a quarter of a minute.

"Two guineas!" roared Merry, shaking it at Silver. "That's your seven hundred thousand pounds, is it? You're the man for bargains, ain't you? You're him that never bungled nothing, you wooden-headed lubber!"

"Dig away, boys," said Silver with the coolest insolence; "you'll find some pig-nuts and I shouldn't wonder."

"Pig-nuts!" repeated Merry, in a scream. "Mates, do you hear that? I tell you now, that man there knew it all along. Look in the face of him and you'll see it wrote there."

"Ah, Merry," remarked Silver, "standing for cap'n again? You're a pushing lad, to be sure."

But this time everyone was entirely in Merry's favour. They began to scramble out of the excavation, darting furious glances behind them. One thing I observed, which looked well for us: they all got out upon the opposite side from Silver.

Well, there we stood, two on one side, five on the other, the pit between us, and nobody screwed up high enough to offer the first blow. Silver never moved; he watched them, very upright on his crutch, and looked as cool as ever I saw him. He was brave, and no mistake.

At last Merry seemed to think a speech might help matters.

"Mates," says he, "there's two of them alone there; one's the old cripple that brought us all here and blundered us down to this; the other's that cub that I mean to have the heart of. Now, mates——"

He was raising his arm and his voice, and plainly meant to lead a charge. But just then—crack! crack! crack!—three musket-shots flashed out of the thicket. Merry tumbled head foremost into the excavation; the man with the bandage spun round like a teetotum[1] and fell all his length upon his side, where he lay dead, but still twitching; and the other three turned and ran for it with all their might.

Before you could wink, Long John had fired two barrels of a pistol into the struggling Merry, and as the man rolled up his eyes at him in the last agony, "George," said he, "I reckon I settled you."

At the same moment, the doctor, Gray, and Ben Gunn joined us, with smoking muskets, from among the nutmeg-trees.

"Forward!" cried the doctor. "Double quick, my lads. We must head 'em off the boats."

And we set off at a great pace, sometimes plunging through the bushes to the chest.

I tell you, but Silver was anxious to keep up with us. The work that man went through, leaping on his crutch till the muscles of his chest were fit to burst, was work no sound man ever equalled; and so thinks the doctor. As it was, he was already thirty yards behind us and on the verge of strangling when we reached the brow of the slope.

"Doctor," he hailed, "see there! No hurry!"

Sure enough there was no hurry. In a more open part of the plateau, we could see the three survivors still running in the same direction as they had started, right for Mizzen-mast Hill. We were already between them and the boats; and so we four sat down to breathe, while Long John, mopping his face, came slowly up with us.

"Thank ye kindly, doctor," says he. "You came in in about the nick, I guess, for me and Hawkins. And so it's you, Ben Gunn!" he added. "Well, you're a nice one, to be sure."

"I'm Ben Gunn, I am," replied the maroon, wriggling like an eel in his embarrassment. "And," he added, after a long pause, "how do, Mr. Silver? Pretty well, I thank ye, says you."

"Ben, Ben," murmured Silver, "to think as you've done me!"

The doctor sent back Gray for one of the pick-axes deserted, in their flight, by the mutineers, and then as we proceeded leisurely downhill to where the boats were lying, related in a few words what had taken place. It was a story that profoundly interested Silver; and Ben Gunn, the half-idiot maroon, was the hero from beginning to end.

Ben, in his long, lonely wanderings about the island,

1. An 8th-century four-sided top spun with the fingers. The spinner wins or loses depending on whether the side with a T (for *totum*, Latin for "all") is the side facing up when it stops spinning.

255

*Merry tumbled head foremost
into the excavation.*

safety since two months before the arrival of the *Hispaniola.*

When the doctor had wormed this secret from him on the afternoon of the attack, and when next morning he saw the anchorage deserted, he had gone to Silver, given him the chart, which was now useless—given him the stores, for Ben Gunn's cave was well supplied with goats' meat salted by himself—given anything and everything to get a chance of moving in safety from the stockade to the two-pointed hill, there to be clear of malaria and keep a guard upon the money.

"As for you, Jim," he said, "it went against my heart, but I did what I thought best for those who had stood by their duty; and if you were not one of these, whose fault was it?"

had found the skeleton—it was he that had rifled it; he had found the treasure; he had dug it up (it was the haft of his pick-axe that lay broken in the excavation); he had carried it on his back, in many weary journeys, from the foot of the tall pine to a cave he had on the two-pointed hill at the north-east angle of the island, and there it had lain stored in

That morning, finding that I was to be involved in the horrid disappointment he had prepared for the mutineers, he had run all the way to the cave, and leaving the squire to guard the captain, had taken Gray and the maroon and started, making the diagonal across the island to be at hand beside the pine. Soon, however, he saw that our party had the start of him; and Ben Gunn, being fleet of foot, had been dispatched in front to do his best alone. Then it had occurred to him to work upon the superstitions of his former shipmates, and he was so far successful that Gray and the doctor had come up and were already ambushed before the arrival of the treasure-hunters.

"Ah," said Silver, "it were fortunate for me that I had Hawkins here. You would have let old John be cut to bits, and never given it a thought, doctor."

"Not a thought," replied Dr. Livesey cheerily.

And by this time we had reached the gigs. The doctor, with the pick-axe, demolished one of them, and then we all got aboard the other and set out to go round by sea for North Inlet.

This was a run of eight or nine miles. Silver, though he was almost killed already with fatigue, was set to an oar, like the rest of us, and we were soon skimming swiftly over a smooth sea. Soon we passed out of the straits and doubled the south-east corner of the island, round which, four days ago, we had towed the *Hispaniola*.

As we passed the two-pointed hill, we could see the black mouth of Ben Gunn's cave and a figure standing by it, leaning on a musket. It was the squire, and we waved a handkerchief and gave him three cheers, in which the voice of Silver joined as heartily as any.

Three miles farther, just inside the mouth of North Inlet, what should we meet but the *Hispaniola*, cruising by herself? The last flood had lifted her, and had there been much wind or a strong tide current, as in the southern anchorage, we should never have found her more, or found her stranded beyond help. As it was, there was little amiss beyond the wreck of the main-sail. Another anchor was got ready and dropped in a fathom and a half of water. We all pulled round again to Rum Cove, the nearest point for Ben Gunn's treasure-house; and then Gray, single-handed, returned with the gig to the *Hispaniola*, where he was to pass the night on guard.

A gentle slope ran up from the beach to the entrance of the cave. At the top, the squire met us. To me he was cordial and kind, saying nothing of my escapade either in the way of blame or praise. At Silver's polite salute he somewhat flushed.

"John Silver," he said, "you're a prodigious villain and impostor—a monstrous impostor, sir. I am told I am not to prosecute you. Well, then, I will not. But the dead men, sir, hang about your neck like mill-stones."

"Thank you kindly, sir," replied Long John, again saluting.

"I dare you to thank me!" cried the squire. "It is a gross dereliction of my duty. Stand back."

And thereupon we all entered the cave. It was a large, airy place, with a little spring and a pool of clear water, overhung with ferns. The floor was sand. Before a big fire lay Captain Smollett; and in a far corner, only duskily flickered over by the blaze, I beheld great heaps of coin and quadrilaterals built of bars of gold. That was Flint's treasure that we had come so far to seek and that had cost already the lives of seventeen men from the *Hispaniola*. How many it had cost in the amassing, what blood and sorrow, what good ships scuttled on the deep, what brave men walking the plank blindfold, what shot of cannon, what shame and lies and cruelty, perhaps no man alive could tell. Yet there were still three upon that island—Silver, and old Morgan, and Ben Gunn—who had each taken his share in these crimes, as each had hoped in vain to share in the reward.

"Come in, Jim," said the captain. "You're a good boy in your line, Jim, but I don't think you and me'll go to sea again. You're too much of the born favourite for me. Is that you, John Silver? What brings you here, man?"

"Come back to my dooty, sir," returned Silver.

"Ah!" said the captain, and that was all he said.

What a supper I had of it that night, with all my friends around me; and what a meal it was, with Ben Gunn's salted goat and some delicacies and a bottle of old wine from the *Hispaniola*. Never, I am sure, were people gayer or happier. And there was Silver, sitting back almost out of the firelight, but eating heartily, prompt to spring forward when anything was wanted, even joining quietly in our laughter—the same bland, polite, obsequious seaman of the voyage out.

Chapter Thirty-Four

And Last

THE NEXT MORNING WE fell early to work, for the transportation of this great mass of gold near a mile by land to the beach, and thence three miles by boat to the *Hispaniola,* was a considerable task for so small a number of workmen. The three fellows still abroad upon the island did not greatly trouble us; a single sentry on the shoulder of the hill was sufficient to ensure us against any sudden onslaught, and we thought, besides, they had had more than enough of fighting.

Therefore the work was pushed on briskly. Gray and Ben Gunn came and went with the boat, while the rest during their absences piled treasure on the beach. Two of the bars, slung in a rope's-end, made a good load for a grown man—one that he was glad to walk slowly with. For my part, as I was not much use at carrying, I was kept busy all day in the cave packing the minted money into bread-bags.

It was a strange collection, like Billy Bones's hoard for the diversity of coinage, but so much larger and so much more varied that I think I never had more pleasure than in sorting them. English, French, Spanish, Portuguese, Georges, and Louises, doubloons

1. The moidore was one of several gold coins minted by Portugal; it was worth about 27 British shillings. Brazil, a Portuguese colony in the 1700s, was not a major gold producer until a gold boom began in 1695, with production reaching 16 tons per year between 1741 and 1760.

2. The word *sequin* entered the English language from the Italian word *zecchino*, a nickname people in Venice gave to their gold ducat coin, which was struck in the Zecca, the Venetians' name for their mint, according to Dr. Michael L. Bates of the American Numismatic Society.

The Italians in turn got their word for mint from *sikka*, the Arabic word for "mint." Mints in Turkey, Egypt, Tunis, and Algiers produced coins similar to the Venetian ducat that were also called sequins in English, which borrowed the name again and gave it to the glittery little costume jewelry disks sewn on clothing. It is the custom in some Mediterranean societies to sew coins onto clothing.

Coin images, from Diderot's *Encyclopédie*, showing Georges, Louises, and Genoese gold sequins.

and double guineas and moidores[1] and sequins,[2] the pictures of all the kings of Europe for the last hundred years, strange Oriental pieces stamped with what looked like wisps of string or bits of spider's web, round pieces and square pieces, and pieces bored through the middle, as if to wear them round your neck—nearly every variety of money in the world must, I think, have found a place in that collection; and for number, I am sure they were like autumn leaves, so that my back ached with stooping and my fingers with sorting them out.

Day after day this work went on; by every evening a fortune had been stowed aboard, but there was another fortune waiting for the morrow; and all this time we heard nothing of the three surviving mutineers.

At last—I think it was on the third night—the doctor and I were strolling on the shoulder of the hill where it overlooks the lowlands of the isle, when, from out the thick darkness below, the wind brought us a noise between shrieking and singing. It was only a snatch that reached our ears, followed by the former silence.

"Heaven forgive them," said the doctor; "'tis the mutineers!"

"All drunk, sir," struck in the voice of Silver from behind us.

Silver, I should say, was allowed his entire liberty, and in spite of daily rebuffs, seemed to regard himself once more as quite a privileged and friendly dependent. Indeed, it was remarkable how well he bore these slights and with what unwearying politeness he kept on trying to ingratiate himself with all. Yet, I think, none treated him better than a dog, unless it was Ben Gunn, who was still terribly afraid of his old quarter-master, or myself, who had really something to thank him for; although for that matter, I suppose, I had reason to think even worse of him than anybody else, for I had seen him meditating a fresh treachery upon the plateau. Accordingly, it was pretty gruffly that the doctor answered him.

"Drunk or raving," said he.

"Right you were, sir," replied Silver; "and precious little odds which, to you and me."

"I suppose you would hardly ask me to call you a humane man," returned the doctor with a sneer, "and so my feelings may surprise you, Master Silver. But if I were sure they were raving—as I am morally certain one, at least, of them is down with fever—I should leave this camp, and at whatever risk to my own carcass, take them the assistance of my skill."

"Ask your pardon, sir, you would be very wrong," quoth Silver. "You would lose your precious life, and you may lay to that. I'm on your side now, hand and glove; and I shouldn't wish for to see the party weakened, let alone yourself, seeing as I know what I owes you. But these men down there, they couldn't keep their word—no, not supposing they wished to; and what's more, they couldn't believe as you could."

"No," said the doctor. "You're the man to keep your word, we know that."

Well, that was about the last news we had of the three pirates. Only once we heard a gunshot a great way off and supposed them to be hunting. A council was held, and it was decided that we must desert them on the island—to the huge glee, I must say, of Ben Gunn, and with the strong approval of Gray. We left a good stock of powder and shot, the bulk of the salt goat, a few medicines, and some other necessaries, tools, clothing, a spare sail, a fathom or two of rope, and by the particular desire of the doctor, a handsome present of tobacco.

That was about our last doing on the island. Before that, we had got the treasure stowed and had shipped enough water and the remainder of the goat meat in case of any distress; and at last, one fine morning, we weighed anchor, which was about all that we could manage, and stood out of North Inlet, the same colours flying that the captain had flown and fought under at the palisade.

The three fellows must have been watching us closer than we thought for, as we soon had proved. For coming through the narrows, we had to lie very near the southern point, and there we saw all three of them kneeling together on a spit of sand, with their arms raised in supplication. It went to all our hearts, I think, to leave them in that wretched state; but we could not risk another

mutiny; and to take them home for the gibbet would have been a cruel sort of kindness. The doctor hailed them and told them of the stores we had left, and where they were to find them. But they continued to call us by name and appeal to us, for God's sake, to be merciful and not leave them to die in such a place.

I was kept busy packing the minted money into bread-bags.

At last, seeing the ship still bore on her course and was now swiftly drawing out of earshot, one of them—I know not which it was—leapt to his feet with a hoarse cry, whipped his musket to his shoulder, and sent a shot whistling over Silver's head and through the main-sail.

After that, we kept under cover of the bulwarks, and when next I looked out they had disappeared from the spit, and the spit itself had almost melted out of sight in the growing distance. That was, at least, the end of that; and before noon, to my inexpressible joy, the highest rock of Treasure Island had sunk into the blue round of sea.

We were so short of men that everyone on board had to bear a hand—only the captain lying on a mattress in the stern and giving his orders, for though greatly recovered he was still in want of quiet. We laid her head for the nearest port in Spanish America,[3] for we could not risk the voyage home without fresh hands; and as it was, what with baffling winds and a couple of fresh gales, we were all worn out before we reached it.

It was just at sundown when we cast anchor in a most beautiful land-locked gulf, and were immediately surrounded by shore boats full of Negroes and Mexican Indians and half-bloods selling fruits and vegetables and offering to dive for bits of money. The sight of so many good-humoured faces (especially the blacks), the taste of the tropical fruits, and above all the lights that began to shine in the town made a most charming contrast to our dark and bloody sojourn on the island; and the doctor and the squire, taking me along with them, went ashore to pass the early part of the night. Here they met the captain of an English man-of-war, fell in talk with him, went on board his ship, and, in short, had so agreeable a time that day was breaking when we came alongside the *Hispaniola*.

Ben Gunn was on deck alone, and as soon as we came on board he began, with wonderful contortions, to make us a confession. Silver was gone. The maroon had connived at his escape in a shore boat some hours ago, and he now assured us he had only done so to preserve our lives, which would certainly have been forfeit if "that man with the one leg had stayed aboard." But this was not all. The sea-cook had not

3. Squire Trelawney had plenty of choices, depending on where Treasure Island is located. The nearest port in Spanish America might have included St. Augustine and Pensacola in modern Florida or Caribbean coastal ports in modern Mexico, Honduras, Nicaragua, Costa Rica, Panama, Colombia, or Venezuela.

St. Augustine would have been a poor choice, unless the squire was looking for a fight. French privateers used the port to refit and replenish supplies. A few months after the *Hispaniola* left Treasure Island, the privateers brought in 11 captured British vessels. France was at war with Britain, and her ally Spain would soon follow. (See map on p. xviii.)

4. In the 1700s, a ship had square-rigged sails on three masts, with each mast having three sections: a lower-mast, topmast, and topgallant-mast. Square-rigged means sails with four corners (not square-shaped) fastened, or bent, onto yards that are horizontal to the hull and extend to the left and right of the mast to which they are attached. (See note 4 on p. 56.)

A full-rigged ship had square-rigged sails on three masts; each mast had three sections: a lower-mast, topmast, and topgallant-mast.

gone empty-handed. He had cut through a bulkhead unobserved and had removed one of the sacks of coin, worth perhaps three or four hundred guineas, to help him on his further wanderings.

I think we were all pleased to be so cheaply quit of him.

Well, to make a long story short, we got a few hands on board, made a good cruise home, and the *Hispaniola* reached Bristol just as Mr. Blandly was beginning to think of fitting out her consort. Five men only of those who had sailed returned with her. "Drink and the devil had done for the rest," with a vengeance, although, to be sure, we were not quite in so bad a case as that other ship they sang about:

> *With one man of her crew alive,*
> *What put to sea with seventy-five.*

All of us had an ample share of the treasure and used it wisely or foolishly, according to our natures. Captain Smollett is now retired from the sea. Gray not only saved his money, but being suddenly smit with the desire to rise, also studied his profession, and he is now mate and part owner of a fine full-rigged ship,[4] married besides, and the father of a family. As for Ben Gunn, he got a thousand pounds, which he spent or lost in three weeks, or to be more exact, in nineteen days, for he was back begging on the twentieth. Then he was given a lodge to keep, exactly as he had feared upon the island; and he still lives, a great favourite, though something of a butt, with the country boys, and a notable singer in church on Sundays and saints' days.

Of Silver we have heard no more. That formidable seafaring man with one leg has at last gone clean out of my life; but I dare say he met his old Negress, and perhaps still lives in comfort with her and Captain Flint. It is to be hoped so, I suppose, for his chances of comfort in another world are very small.

The bar silver and the arms still lie, for all that I know, where Flint buried them; and certainly they shall lie there for me. Oxen and wain-ropes[5] would not bring me back again to that accursed island; and the worst dreams that ever I have are when I hear the surf booming about its coasts or start upright in bed with the sharp voice of Captain Flint still ringing in my ears: "Pieces of eight! Pieces of eight!"

5. *Wain* is an old name for a cart or wagon.

Robert Louis Stevenson

1850–1894

ORIGINALLY—and briefly—titled *The Sea Cook*, *Treasure Island* was begun during the rainy month of August 1881 in Scotland and was published as an 18-part magazine serial in the weeks leading up to Robert Louis Stevenson's 31st birthday that November. A revised version, published as a book in 1883, has been in print ever since.

It was Stevenson's first novel, though not his first published work. But it was the first time he reached a wide audience. Fans included the formidable E. W. Gladstone, four times prime minister of the United Kingdom, who was "apparently unable to put the book down," according to Claire Harman, a recent biographer of Stevenson's.

The Stevensons—grandfather, father, and two uncles—were Scottish civil engineers who built lighthouses in difficult locations, as well as harbors and docks—a career that did not appeal to the future author of *Treasure Island*. He wanted to write. To please his parents he qualified as a lawyer, after dropping his engineering courses, and at that point they agreed to subsidize his writing career.

When he was 23 he met an unhappily married woman, 36-year-old Fanny Van de Grift Osbourne, an American with a daughter and a son. He followed the three to their California home in 1879. After her divorce they married, in May 1880, and he brought her and her children back to Scotland, where his parents welcomed her. A year later he was working on *Treasure Island*, to the delight of his father.

By age 31 Stevenson had written travel books, magazine articles, essays, literary criticism, and poetry. Though he was well regarded by people influential in the literary world, writing did not come close to paying the bills. He continued to rely on an allowance from his supportive, worried parents. Even with the success of *Treasure Island*, it was not until he was 37 that "R.L.S.'s income was derived entirely from his writings," according to George L. McKay in his study of Stevenson's finances.

However, Stevenson's spending also grew, because of his lifelong generosity to family, friends, and strangers, as well as his increased living expenses. These included two extended cruises across the Pacific and a 400-acre estate on the Samoan island of Upolu. Here he built an expensive European-style house and maintained an entourage of family, staff, and guests. To pay for it all Stevenson wrote and wrote. He called himself the Work Horse.

Those who knew him said he had an engaging and attractive personality. He could also be tough and obstinate. Poor health complicated his life. Recurring fevers, chest infections, and ailments ranging from ophthalmia to sciatica weakened his body. He was thin and frail; he often coughed blood and nearly died in 1879 and 1884. He spent much of his life satisfying his appetite for travel and looking for places that eased his lungs, including Switzerland, France, Italy, America, Polynesia, and finally Samoa. Surprisingly for such a productive writer, he was "a slave to writer's block" and left behind hundreds of unfinished works, according to Harman.

Stevenson collapsed on December 3, 1894, while helping his wife make mayonnaise, and died that evening. The cause of death was reported as a cerebral hemorrhage.

Over the course of his 44 years, Stevenson had written enough to fill a 35-volume centenary edition of his works and an 8-volume edition of his letters. The many books he is remembered for include *A Child's Garden of Verses* (1885), *The Strange Case of Dr. Jekyll and Mr. Hyde* (1886), and *Kidnapped* (1886).

Bibliography

Anderson, Fred, and Andrew Clayton, *The Dominion of War: Empire and Liberty in North America 1500–2000*, New York: Viking, 2005.

Armitage, David, and Michael J. Braddick, eds., *The British Atlantic World 1500–1800*, New York: Palgrave Macmillan, 2002.

Arnade, Charles W., "Raids, Sieges, and International Wars," in *The New History of Florida*, Gainesville: University Press of Florida, 1996.

Ashworth, William J., *Customs and Excise: Trade, Production, and Consumption in England, 1640–1845*, Oxford: Oxford University Press, 2003.

Barker, Derek, "The Uniform Dress of 1748," in *The Mariner's Mirror*, vol. 65, no. 3, Aug. 1970, London: Society for Nautical Research.

Bathe, Basil W., et al. *Visual Encyclopedia of Nautical Terms Under Sail*, New York: Crown Books, 1978.

BBC News South West, *Tallow Tales*, Nov. 18, 2005.

Beattie, J. M., "Sir John Fielding Public Justice: The Bow Street Magistrate's Court, 1754–1780," in *The Law and History Review*, vol. 25, no. 1, spring 2007.

Beeston, Sir William, "A Narrative by Sir William Beeston of the Descent on Jamaica by the French," in *Interesting Tracts Relating to the Island of Jamaica*, St. Jago de la Vega, Jamaica: Lewis, Lunam, and Jones, 1800.

Biddulph, John, *The Pirates of Malabar, and an Englishwoman in India Two Hundred Years Ago*, London: Smith, Elder, 1907. Also available at www.gutenberg.org/etext/11399.

Blair, J.S.G. "Sir Henry Morgan," in *Oxford Dictionary of National Biography*, Oxford: Oxford University Press, 2004.

——, "Sir John Pringle," in *Oxford Dictionary of National Biography*, Oxford: Oxford University Press, 2004.

Blake, Nicholas, and Richard Lawrence, *The Illustrated Companion to Nelson's Navy*, Mechanicsburg, Pa.: Stackpole Books, 2005.

Bosworth, Joseph, and T. Northcote Toller, *An Anglo-Saxon Dictionary*, Oxford: Clarendon Press, 1898. Also available at http://beowulf.engl.uky.edu/~kiernan/BT/Bosworth-Toller.htm.

Botting, Douglas, *The Seafarers: The Pirates*, Alexandria, Va.: Time-Life Books, 1978.

Boxer, Charles R., *The Dutch Seaborne Empire: 1600–1800*, New York: Alfred A. Knopf, 1965.

Brebner, J. B., review of *The British Post Office: A History*, by Howard Robinson, in *Political Science Quarterly*, vol. 63, vol. 3, New York: Academy of Political Science, 1948.

Brewer, John, *The Pleasures of the Imagination: English Culture in the Eighteenth Century*, New York: Farrar, Straus and Giroux, 1997.

Brezezinski, Richard, and Richard Hook, *The Army of Gustavus Adolphus I: Infantry*, London: Osprey Publishing, 1991.

Buchan, William, *Domestic Medicine: Or a Treatise on the Prevention and Cure of Diseases by Regimen and Simple Medicines*, second ed., 1772, New York and London: Garland Publishing, 1985.

Buckley, F., and G. F. Buckley, "Clock and Watchmakers of the 18th Century in Gloucestershire and Bristol," in *Transactions of the Bristol and Gloucestershire Archaeological Society*, vol. 51, Gloucester, 1929

Bucknill, J.A.S., *Coins of the Dutch East Indies: An Introduction to the Study of the Series*, London: Spink & Son, 1931.

Bugler, Arthur, *H.M.S. Victory: Building, Restoration & Repair*, London: Ministry of Defense (Navy)/HMSO, 1966.

Burgess, Robert F., and Carl J. Clausen, *Florida's Golden Galleons: The Search for the 1715 Treasure Fleet*, Port Salerno, Fla.: Florida Classics Library, 1982.

Bushnell, Amy Turner, *Situado and Sabana: Spain's Support System for the Presidio and Mission Provinces of Florida*, New York: American Museum of Natural History, 1994.

——, "Republic of Spaniards, Republic of Indians," in *The New History of Florida*, Gainesville: University Press of Florida, 1996.

Cabrera, Brian J., *Drugstore Beetle, Stegobium paniceum (L.) (Insecta: Coleoptera: Anobiidae)*, Gainesville: University of Florida, Institute of Food and Agricultural Sciences, Fact Sheet EENY-228, revised 2007. Also available at http://creatures.ifas.ufl.edu.

Carson, Edward, *The Ancient and Rightful Customs*, London: Faber & Faber, 1972, and Hamden, Conn.: Archon Books, Shoe String Press, 1972.

Chapman, Fredrik Henrik af, *Architectura Navalis Mercatoria*, Mineola, N.Y.: Dover, 2006; a reprint of the 1768 edition.

Chartrand, Rene, text, and Francis Back, color plates, *Louis XIV's Army*, London: Osprey Publishing, 1988.

Chartrand, Rene, and Donato Spedaliere, illustrator, *The Spanish Main 1492–1800*, Oxford: Osprey Publishing, 2006.

Clark, G. N., "War Trade and Trade War, 1701–1713," in *The Economic History Review*, vol. 1, no. 2, London: Economic History Society, 1828.

Cole, W. A. "Trends in Eighteenth-Century Smuggling," in *The Economic History Review*, vol. 10, no. 3, London: Economic History Society, 1958.

Cordingly, David, *Life Among the Pirates: The Romance and the Reality*, London: Abacus, Little, Brown, 1995.

——, *Nicholas Pocock, 1740–1821*, Annapolis: Naval Institute Press edition of Conway Maritime Press edition for the National Maritime Museum, 1986.

Cox, David, abstract, "A Certain Share of Low Cunning– The Provincial Use and Activities of Bow Street Runners, 1792–1839," in *Eras Journal*, fifth ed., Melbourne: Monash University, Nov. 2003. Also available at http://arts.monash.edu.au/eras/cfp.htm.

Crocker, Glenys, *The Gunpowder Industry*, Princes Risborough, UK: Shire Publications, 1986.

Cunnington, C. Willett, and Phyllis Cunnington, *Handbook of English Costume in the Eighteenth Century*, London: Faber and Faber, 1957.

Dana, Richard Henry, *Two Years Before the Mast*, Anne Spence, ed., New York: Barnes & Noble Books, 2007.

Daunton, M. J., *Progress and Poverty: An Economic and Social History of Britain 1700–1850*, Oxford: Oxford University Press, 1995.

Dear, I.C.B., and Peter Kemp, eds., *Oxford Companion to Ships and the Sea*, Oxford: Oxford University Press, 1976, revised 2005.

Defoe, Daniel (or perhaps Charles Johnson), *A General History of the Pyrates*, Mineola, N.Y.: Dover Publications, 1999.

Dickinson, Jonathan, *God's Protecting Providence: Being the Narrative of a Journey from Port Royal in Jamaica to Philadelphia Between August 12, 1696, and April 1, 1697*, ed. by Evangeline Walker Andrews and Charles McLean Andrews, New Haven: Yale University Press, 1945.

Duffy, Christopher, *The Military Experience in the Age of Reason*, New York: Atheneum, 1988.

Dunn, Richard S., *Sugar and Slaves: The Rise of the Planter Class in the English West Indies, 1624–1713*, Omohundro Institute of Early American History and Culture, Chapel Hill: University of North Carolina Press, 1972.

Earle, Peter, *The Pirate Wars*, London: St. Martin's Press, 2003.

——, *The Sack of Panama: Captain Morgan and the Battle for the Caribbean*, St. Martin's Press, 1981.

Elliott, J. H., *Empires of the Atlantic World: Britain and Spain in America 1492–1830*, New Haven: Yale University Press, 2006.

Exquemelin, Alexander O., *The Buccaneers of America*, trans. by Alexis Brown, introd. by Jack Beeching, Mineola, N.Y.: Dover Publications, 1969.

Farr, Graham, "Severn Navigation and the Trow," in *The Mariner's Mirror*, vol. 32, no. 2, April 1945, London: Society for Nautical Research.

Ferguson, Niall, *Empire: The Rise and Demise of the British World Order and the Lessons for Global Power,* London: Allen Lane/Penguin Books, and New York: Basic Books, 2002.

Finch, William, in Robert Kerr, ed., *General History and Collection of Voyages and Travels,* vol. 8, Edinburgh: W. Blackwood, etc., 1813. Also available at http://books.google.com.

Forshaw, Joseph M., *Parrots of the World: An Identification Guide,* Princeton: Princeton University Press, 2006.

Galvin, Peter, *Patterns of Pillage: A Geography of Caribbean-based Piracy in Spanish America, 1536–1718,* American University Studies Series 25, New York: Peter Lang Publishing, 1999, 2000.

Gentleman's Magazine, London: Sept. 21, 1750, vol. 20, p, 426, online archive, Oxford: Bodleian Library.

Graham, Henry Gray, *The Social Life of Scotland in the Eighteenth Century,* London: Adam and Charles Black, 1906.

Graham, Thomas John, *Modern Domestic Medicine,* third ed., London: Simpkin and Marshall et al., 1827.

Grant, Michael, *History of Rome,* New York: Charles Scribner's Sons, 1978.

Green, Jonathan, *Chasing the Sun: Dictionary Makers and the Dictionaries They Made,* New York: Henry Holt, 1996.

Greenhill, Basil, *The Evolution of the Wooden Ship,* New York: Facts on File, 1988.

Grose, Francis, *A Classical Dictionary of the Vulgar Tongue,* Eric Partridge, ed., New York: Dorset Press, 1992.

Guy, Alana J., *Oeconomy and Discipline: Officership and Administration in the British Army 1714–1763,* Manchester: Manchester University Press, 1985.

Hammond, J. R., *A Robert Louis Stevenson Chronology,* London: St. Martin's Press, 1997.

Harland, John, illus. by Mark Myers, *Seamanship in the Age of Sail,* London: Conway Maritime Press, 1985/1985; Annapolis: Naval Institute Press, 2006.

Hartley, Dorothy, *Lost Country Life,* New York: Pantheon Books, 1979.

Hattendorf, John B., "Benbow's Last Fight," in *The Naval Miscellany,* vol. 5, ed. by N.A.M. Rodger, London: Publications of the Navy Records Society, vol. 125, pp. 143–206; Allen & Unwin, 1984.

——, "John Benbow," in *Oxford Dictionary of National Biography,* Oxford: Oxford University Press, 2004.

Haythornthwaite, Philip, and Bryan Fosten, *Frederick the Great's Army 2: Infantry,* London; Osprey Publishing, 1991.

Hibbert, Christopher, *The English: A Social History 1066–1945,* London: Paladin/Harper Collins, 1988.

Hoffman, Paul E., *The Spanish Crown and the Defense of the Caribbean, 1535–1585: Precedent, Patrimonialism, and Royal Parsimony,* Baton Rouge: Louisiana State University Press, 1980.

Hoon, Elizabeth Evelynola Hoon, *The Organization of the English Customs System 1696–1786,* Newton Abbot, U.K.: David & Charles, 1968.

Hopkins, Alfred F., *Equipment of the Soldier During the American Revolution,* Morristown, N.J.: Regional Review, National Park Service, 1940. Also available at www.cr.nps.gov/history/online_books/regional_review/vol4-3g.htm.

Hughes, B. P., *Firepower: Weapons Effectiveness on the Battlefield, 1630–1850,* New York: Charles Scribner's Sons, 1975.

Jarrett, Derek, *England in the Age of Hogarth,* New Haven: Yale University Press, 1986.

Jones, Philip D., "The Bristol Bridge Riot and Its Antecedents: Eighteenth-Century Perception of the Crowd," in *The Journal of British Studies,* vol. 19, no. 2, 1980.

Jordan, Louis, *The Coins of Colonial and Early America,* Department of Special Collections, University of Notre Dame, South Bend, Ind. Also available at www.coins.nd.ed.

Jupp, Peter, *The Governing of Britain 1688–1848: The Executive, Parliament, and the People,* Abingdon, UK: Routledge, 2006.

Kaye, Theodore P., "Pine Tar; History and Uses," in *Conference Proceedings: Third International Conference on the Technical Aspects of the Preservation of Historic Vessels,* San Francisco, April 20–23, 1997.

Kelly, Jack, *Gunpowder: Alchemy, Bombards, & Pyrotechnics: The History of the Explosive That Changed the World,* New York: Basic Books, 2004.

Kemp, Peter, *The History of Ships,* New York: Barnes & Noble Books, 2002.

Kentley, Eric, *Boat,* New York: Eyewitness Books, Dorling Kindersley/Alfred A. Knopf, 1992.

Kenyon, J. P., ed., *A Dictionary of British History,* New York: Stein and Day, 1983.

Kilby, Kenneth, *The Cooper and His Trade,* London: John Baker, 1971.

Konstam, Angus, *Blackbeard: America's Most Notorious Pirate*, Hoboken, N.J.: John Wiley & Sons, 2006.

—, *The History of Pirates*, New York: Lyons Press / Mariners' Museum, 1999.

Konstam, Angus, and Tony Bryan, *The Pirate Ship 1660–1730*, Botley, UK: Osprey Publishing, 2003.

Konstam, Angus, David Rickman, and Giuseppe Rava, *Pirate: The Golden Age*, Botley, UK: Osprey Publishing, 2011.

Labat, Jean-Baptiste, *The Memoirs of Père Labat*, translated and abridged by John Eaden, introduction by Philip Gosse, Cass Library of West Indian Studies No. 8, London: Frank Cass, 1970.

Lambert, Andrew, *War at Sea in the Age of Sail*, London: Cassel, 2000.

Langford, Paul, *Eighteenth-Century Britain: A Very Short Introduction*, Oxford: Oxford University Press, 1984.

Langham, James, "London's Old Bailey," in *Journal of Criminal Law and Criminology*, vol. 39, no. 6, pp. 778–781, London: March–April, 1949.

Laughton, Sir John Knox, "John Benbow," in *Dictionary of National Biography*, Leslie Stephens and Sidney Lee, eds., New York: MacMillan, 1908.

Lavery, Brian, *The Arming and Fitting of English Ships of War 1600–1815*, Annapolis: Naval Institute Press, 2006; reprint of Conway Maritime Press edition, London, 1987.

Lazenby, Richard, in *Pirates of the Eastern Seas (1618–1723)*, by Charles Grey, Port Washington, N.Y.: Kennikat Press, 1971; reprint of 1933 edition.

Letley, Emma, ed., *Treasure Island*, by Robert Louis Stevenson, Oxford: Oxford University Press, 1985.

Lewis, Matthew, *Journal of a West India Proprietor*, intro. by Judith Terry, Oxford: Oxford University Press, 1999.

Little, Benerson, *The Sea Rover's Practice: Pirate Tactics and Techniques, 1630–1730*, Washington, D.C.: Potomac Books, 2005.

Little, Bryan, *The City and County of Bristol: A Study in Atlantic Civilization*, London: T. Werner Laurie, 1954.

Macarthur, Antonia, *His Majesty's Bark Endeavour: The Story of the Ship and Her People*, Sydney: Angus & Robertson / HarperCollins, 1997.

Macdonald, John, *Memoirs of an XVIII-Century Footman*, New York: Harper & Brothers, 1927; new edition of the 1790 edition, published as *Travels in Various Parts of Europe, Asia, and Africa*.

Macey, Samuel L., *Clocks and the Cosmos: Time in Western Life and Thought*, Hamden, Conn.: Archon Books, 1980.

Macinnis, Peter, *Bittersweet: The Story of Sugar*, Crow's Nest, N.S.W., Australia: Allen & Unwin, 2002.

Manucy, Albert, *Artillery Through the Ages*, National Park Service Interpretive Series, History No. 3, Washington, D.C.: U.S. Government Printing Office, 1962.

Marquardt, Karl Heinz, *The Global Schooner: Origins, Development, Design, and Construction 1695–1845*, Annapolis: Naval Institute Press / Conway, 2003.

Martin, Harold H., *Georgia: A Bicentennial History*, New York: W. W. Norton for the American Association for State and Local History (Nashville), 1977.

Massie, Alastair W., "Henry Hawley," in *Oxford Dictionary of National Biography*, Oxford: Oxford University Press, 2004.

McCusker, John J., *Essays in the Economic History of the Atlantic World*, Abingdon: Routledge, 1997.

—, *Rum and the American Revolution: The Rum Trade and the Balance of Payments of the Thirteen Continental Colonies*, vols. 1 and 2, New York: Garland Publishing, 1989.

McGrath, Patrick, ed., *Bristol in the 18th Century*, Newton Abbot, UK: David & Charles, Bristol Historical Association, 1972.

McMullen, Drew, Christopher Cerino, and Jamie Trost, *Sultana: A Guide to the 1768 Reproduction Schooner*, Chester Town, Md.: Sultana Projects Inc. and the National Park Service, 2002.

Mehew, Ernest, "William Ernest Henley," in *Oxford Dictionary of National Biography*, Oxford: Oxford University Press, 2004.

Meide, Chuck, *The Development and Design of Bronze Ordnance, Sixteenth through Nineteenth Centuries*, Williamsburg, Va.: College of William and Mary, Nov. 2002. Available online.

Monod, Paul, "Dangerous Merchandise: Smuggling, Jacobitism, and Commercial Culture in Southeast England, 1690–1760," in *The Journal of British Studies*, vol. 30, no. 2, Chicago: University of Chicago Press, April 1990.

Morgan, Kenneth, *Bristol & the Atlantic Trade in the 18th Century*, Cambridge, UK: Cambridge University Press, 1992.

Morris, Roger, *Atlantic Seafaring: Ten Centuries of Exploration and Trade in the North Atlantic*, New York: McGraw-Hill, 1992.

Mowl, Timothy, "The Evolution of the Park Gate Lodge as a Building Type," in *Architectural History: Journal of the Architectural Historians of Great Britain*, vol. 27, Cardiff: SAHGB Publications, 1984.

Mui, Hoh-Cheung, and Lorna H. Mui, "Smuggling and the British Tea Trade before 1784," in *The American Historical Review*, vol. 74, no. 1, Washington, D.C., American Historical Association, October 1968.

Newton, Arthur Percival, *The Colonising Activities of the English Puritans: The Last Phase of the Elizabethan Struggle with Spain*, New Haven: Yale University Press, 1914. Also available at http://books.google.com.

Nicholls, F. F., *Honest Thieves*, London: William Heinemann, 1973.

Niemeyer, Lucien, and Drew McMullen, *Schooner Sultana: Building a Chesapeake Legacy*, Centreville, Md.: Tidewater Publishers, 2002.

Ogilvie, A. M., "The Rise of the English Post Office," in *The Economic Journal*, vol. 3, no. 11, 1893, London: Royal Economic Society.

Pack, James, *Nelson's Blood: The Story of Naval Rum*, Annapolis: Naval Institute Press, 1982.

Palmer, Roy, ed., *The Rambling Soldier: Military Life Through Soldiers' Songs and Writings*, Harmondsworth, UK: Penguin Books, 1977.

Parry, J. H, *The Spanish Seaborne Empire*, New York: Alfred A. Knopf, 1966.

Parry J. H., and P. M. Sherlock, *A Short History of the West Indies*, London: St. Martin's Press, 1968.

Pawson, Michael, and David Buisseret, *Port Royal, Jamaica*, Kingston: University of West Indies Press, 1974.

Peace Corps Guide, *How to Make Soap*, http://peacecorps.mtu.edu/soap_making.html.

Perez-Mallaina, Pablo E., *Spain's Men of the Sea: Daily Life on the Indies Fleets in the Sixteenth Century*, Baltimore: Johns Hopkins University Press, 1998.

Picard, Liza, *Dr. Johnson's London*, New York: St. Martin's Press, 2001.

Plumb, J. H., *England in the Eighteenth Century (1714–1815)*, Harmondsworth, UK : Penguin Books, 1950.

——, *The First Four Georges*, London: Collins Fontana Library, 1966.

PortCities Bristol project, a consortium of projects led by the National Maritime Museum, Greenwich, under the title *PortCities UK*. Available at www.discoveringbristol.org.uk.

Porter, Roy, *English Society in the Eighteenth Century*, London: Penguin Books, 1990.

——, *The Greatest Benefit to Mankind: A Medical History of Humanity*, New York: W. W. Norton, 1997, 1999.

——, ed., *Cambridge Illustrated History of Medicine*, Cambridge, UK: Cambridge University Press, 1996.

Powell, J. W. Damer, *Bristol Privateers and Ships of War*, Bristol: J. W. Arrowsmith, 1930.

Prebble, John, *Culloden*, London: Book Club Associates/Martin Secker & Warburg, 1973.

Prest, Wilfred, *Albion Ascendant: English History 1660–1815*, Oxford: Oxford University Press, 1998.

Preston, Diana, and Michael Preston, *A Pirate of Exquisite Mind: Explorer, Naturalist and Buccaneer: The Life of William Dampier*, New York: Walker, 2004.

Price, Richard, *Alabi's World*, Baltimore: Johns Hopkins University Press, 1990.

Price, Richard, and Sally Price, "Maroons Under Assault in Suriname and French Guiana," in *Cultural Survival Quarterly*, Jan. 31, 2002, vol. 25, no. 4. Also available at www.cs.org/publications/csq/csq-article.cfm?id=1401.

Quinion, Michael, *Port Out, Starboard Home, and Other Language Myths*, London: Penguin Books, 2004.

Rankin, Nicholas, *Dead Man's Chest: Travels After Robert Louis Stevenson*, London: Faber and Faber, 1987.

Rediker, Marcus, *Between the Devil and the Deep Blue Sea: Merchant Seamen, Pirates, and the Anglo-American Maritime World 1700–1750*, Cambridge, UK: Canto/Cambridge University Press, 1987.

Ritchie, Robert C., *Captain Kidd and the War Against the Pirates*, Cambridge, Mass.: Harvard University Press, 1986.

——, "William Kidd," in *Oxford Dictionary of National Biography*, Oxford: Oxford University Press, 2004.

Robinson, John Martin, *Temples of Delight: Stowe Landscape Gardens*, London: National Trust/George Philip, 1990.

Robson, Brian, *Swords of the British Army: The Regulation Patterns, 1788 to 1914*, revised edition, London: National Army Museum, 1996.

Rodger, N.A.M., *The Command of the Ocean: A Naval History of Britain, 1649–1815*, New York: W. W. Norton, 2005.

——, *The Wooden World: An Anatomy of the Georgian Navy*, New York: W. W. Norton, 1986.

Rogozinski, Jan, *A Brief History of the Caribbean from the Arawak and Carib to the Present*, New York: Plume / Penguin Putnam, 2000.

——, *Honour Among Thieves: Captain Kidd, Henry Every, and the Story of Pirate Island*, London: Conway Maritime Press, 2000.

Romans, Bernard, *A Concise Natural History of East and West Florida*, Kathryn E. Holland Braun, ed., Tuscaloosa: University of Alabama Press, 1999; new edition of New York first edition of 1772.

Rushby, Kevin, *Hunting Pirate Heaven: In Search of the Lost Pirate Utopias of the Indian Ocean*, New York: Walker, 2001.

Sainsbury, Noel W., "The Two Providence Islands," in *Proceedings of the Royal Geographical Society of London*, vol. 21, no. 2 (1876–1877).

Sedley, Stephen, "In Judges' Lodgings," *London Review of Books*, vol. 21, no. 22, Nov. 11, 1999.

Severn, Bill, *The Long and the Short of It: Five Thousand Years of Fun and Fury Over Hair*, New York: David McKay, 1971.

Shorter, Edward, "Primary Care," in *Cambridge Illustrated History of Medicine*, Cambridge, UK: Cambridge University Press, 1996.

Singer, Steven D., *Shipwrecks of Florida*, Sarasota: Pineapple Press, 1998.

Skowronek, Russell K., and Charles R. Ewen, eds., *X Marks the Spot: The Archaeology of Piracy*, Gainesville: University Press of Florida, 2006.

Sloane, Hans, *A Voyage to the Islands Madera, Barbados, Nieves, S. Christopher, and Jamaica*, etc., London: printed by B. M. for the author, 1707–1725.

Slocum, Joshua, *Sailing Alone Around the World*, notes and intro. by Dennis A. Berthold, New York: Barnes & Noble Classics, 2005 edition of the first edition of 1900.

Smith, Frederick H., *Caribbean Rum: A Social and Economic History*, Gainesville: University Press of Florida, 2005.

Smollett, Tobias, *The Adventures of Roderick Random*, Oxford World's Classics, Oxford: Oxford University Press, 1999.

Smyth, Admiral W. H, *The Sailor's Word-Book: An Alphabetical Digest of Nautical Terms: London, 1867*, Algrove Publishing Classic Reprint Series, Almonte, Canada, 2004.

Sobel, Dava, and William J. H. Andrews, *The Illustrated Longitude: The True Story of a Genius Who Solved the Greatest Scientific Problem of His Time*, New York: Walker, 1998.

Souhami, Diana, *Selkirk's Island: The True and Strange Adventures of the Real Robinson Crusoe*, New York: Harcourt, 2001.

South, John F., *Household Surgery, or Hints on Emergencies*, London: G. Cox, 1852. Also available at http://books.google.com.

St. Clair, William, *The Door of No Return: The History of Cape Coast Castle and the Atlantic Slave Trade*, New York: BlueBridge, 2007.

Steel, David R., *The Elements and Practice of Rigging and Seamanship; Illustrated with Engravings*, London: D. Steel, 1794.

Steele, Ian K., *The English Atlantic 1675–1740: An Exploration of Communication and Community*, Oxford: Oxford University Press, 1986.

Stembridge, P. K., *The Goldney Family: A Bristol Merchant Dynasty*, Bristol: Bristol Record Society, 1998.

Stevenson, Robert Louis, *Treasure Island*, intro. by Emma Letley, Oxford: Oxford University Press, 1985.

——, *Treasure Island*, Puffin Books, London: Penguin Group, 1994.

——, *Treasure Island*, ed. by Wendy R. Katz, Edinburgh: Edinburgh University Press, 1998.

——, *Treasure Island*, intro. and notes by Angus Fletcher, New York: Barnes & Noble, 2005.

Swearingen, Roger G., *The Prose Writings of Robert Louis Stevenson: A Guide*, Hamden, Conn.: Archon Books, 1980.

Tannahill, Reay, *Food in History*, New York: Stein and Day, 1973.

Taylor, Duncan, *Fielding's England*, New York: Roy Publishers, 1966.

Thomas, Hugh, *The Slave Trade: The Story of the Atlantic Slave Trade 1440–1870*, New York: Simon & Schuster, 1997.

Thornton, John, *Africa and the Africans in the Making of the Atlantic World, 1400–1800*, second edition, Cambridge, UK: Cambridge University Press, 1998.

Trevelyan, G. M., *England Under Queen Anne: Blenhein*, London: Longmans, Green, 1930.

University of Bristol, Department of Extra-Mural Studies, *Wrington Village Records*, 1969.

Van Dantzig, Albert, *Forts and Castles of Ghana*, Accra: Sedco Publishing, 1980.

Watson, Harold Francis, *Coasts of Treasure Island: A Study of the Backgrounds and Sources for Robert Louis Stevenson's Romance of the Sea*, San Antonio, Tex.: Naylor, 1969.

Weigley, Russell F., *The Age of Battles: The Quest for Decisive Warfare from Breitenfeld to Waterloo*, Bloomington: Indiana University Press, 1991.

Wilkinson-Latham, Robert, *Swords in Color*, New York: Arco, 1978.

Wood, Peter, *The Spanish Main*, Chicago: Time-Life Books, 1979.

Zacks, Richard, *The Pirate Hunter: The True Story of Captain Kidd*, New York: Hyperion, 2002.

Zahedieh, Nuala, "'A Frugal, Prudential and Hopeful Trade': Privateering in Jamaica, 1655–1689," in *Journal of Imperial and Commonwealth History*, vol. 18, 1990, London: Routledge / Taylor & Francis.

——, "The Merchants of Port Royal, Jamaica, and the Spanish Contraband Trade, 1655–1692," in *William and Mary Quarterly*, third series, vol. 43, no. 4, Oct. 1986.

——, "Sir Henry Morgan," in *Oxford Dictionary of National Biography*, Oxford: Oxford University Press, 2004.

Further Reading

A General History of the Pyrates, by Daniel Defoe (or perhaps by a Captain Charles Johnson, whose identity remains elusive; scholars disagree on whether Defoe wrote the *History* under the Johnson name, or whether there was a Capt. Johnson), Mineola, N.Y.: Dover, 1999. First published in 1724, the *General History* is a basic, much-used source. This Dover Publications edition, annotated by Manuel Schonhorn, is particularly useful because of the commentary provided by Schonhorn on the sources used by Defoe/Johnson.

The History of Pirates, by Angus Konstam, New York: Lyons Press/Mariners' Museum, 1999. Includes voluminous maps that go well with the text, written by a specialist on the subject.

The Oxford Companion to Ships and the Sea, by I.C.B. Dear and Peter Kemp, Oxford: Oxford University Press, 1976, revised 2005. A handy reference source when reading about ships and the sea.

The Pirate Wars, by Peter Earle, London: St. Martin's Press, 2005. An excellent and readable account of the pirate wars through the centuries by a historian who knows the subject well.

The Sack of Panama: Captain Morgan and the Battle for the Caribbean, by Peter Earle, New York: St. Martin's Press, 1981. An excellent and readable account by an experienced historian who knows both the Spanish and the English archives.

The Sea Rover's Practice: Pirate Tactics and Techniques, by Benerson Little, Washington, D.C.: Potomac Books, 2005. The kind of book you would wish you'd had if you were going to be a sea rover in the 1600s and 1700s.

The Wooden World: An Anatomy of the Georgian Navy, by N.A.M. Rodger, New York: W. W. Norton, 1986. Mariners passed easily between the naval and merchant services, and Rodger delivers a fine introduction to life in that world as it was during the decade when the *Hispaniola* sailed to Treasure Island.

Image Credits

Scenes from the story are illustrated by Louis Rhead, from Robert Louis Stevenson's *Treasure Island*, Harper & Brothers, New York, 1915. Rhead was a poster artist whose work appeared in the top magazines in the early 1890s, and he later became a book illustrator. In addition to *Treasure Island*, he drew illustrations for Stevenson's *Kidnapped*, Daniel Defoe's *Robinson Crusoe*, and James Fenimore Cooper's *The Deerslayer*.

p. vii. Bristol. Clipart.com.

p. viii. Image of Henry Morgan. Wikimedia Commons.

p. ix. Admiral John Benbow. Etching based on portrait by Sir Geoffrey Kneller. Courtesy of the Granger Collection, New York.

p. x. Chain shot and cannon. Clipart.com.

p. xi. HMS *Victory*. Postcard published by Max Ettlinger & Co. Courtesy of the editor's collection.

p. xii. Ship rigging. iStock.com.

p. xiii. The *Sharke*, draught by Karl Heinz Marquardt. Courtesy of Karl Heinz Marquardt.

p. xiv. 19th-century brigantine. From R. J. Cornewall-Jones, *Ships, Sailors, and the Sea*, 1894.

p. xv. Sugar mill. iStock.com.

p. xvii. The port of Bristol. Clipart.com.

p. xviii. Map of the Caribbean World of *Treasure Island*. Created by Andrew Murphy.

p. xxi. Advertisement. *Felix Farley's Bristol Journal*, 11th–18th September 1756 © Bristol Central Library.

p. xxiii. Longitude and latitude. Wikimedia Commons.

p. xxvi. Silver coin "cobs." From Alan K. Craig, *Spanish Colonial Silver Coins in the Florida Collection*, Gainesville: University Press of Florida, 2000. Reprinted with permission of the University Press of Florida.

p. 25. Shaking out a reef. Reprinted from *The Young Sea Officer's Sheet Anchor*, with permission from Algrove Publishing Limited.

p. 26. A boatswain's (bosun's) call or whistle. iStock.com.

p. 28. George II. Courtesy of the Granger Collection, New York.

p. 32. Lugger. From D. R. Steel, *Steel's Elements of Mastmaking: Sailmaking and Rigging*, 1932. Courtesy of the editor's collection.

p. 35. Sextant. Clipart.com.

p. 43. Cutter. From D. R. Steel, *Steel's Elements of Mastmaking: Sailmaking and Rigging*, 1932. Courtesy of the editor's collection.

p. 51. Compass card. From D. R. Steel, *Steel's Elements of Mastmaking: Sailmaking and Rigging*, 1932. Courtesy of the editor's collection.

p. 58. W. E. Henley. Wikimedia Commons.

p. 59. Admiral Edward Hawke. Wikimedia Commons.

p. 59. Royal Navy frigate. Reprinted from *The Young Sea Officer's Sheet Anchor*, with permission from Algrove Publishing Limited.

p. 63. A ketch, snow, and sloop. From *Liber Nauticus*, by Dominick and John Thomas Serres, 1805.

p. 63. Figurehead. From Henrik af Chapman's *Architecturea Navalis Mercatoria*, 1768, bicentenary facsimile edition, London: Adlard Coles Ltd., 1971. Courtesy of the editor's collection.

p. 76. Ship detail. From Henrik af Chapman's *Architecturea Navalis Mercatoria*, 1768, bicentenary facsimile edition, London: Adlard Coles Ltd., 1971. Courtesy of the editor's collection.

p. 78. Capstan. From *Liber Nauticus*, by Dominick and John Thomas Serres, 1805.

p. 83. Detail of illustration of the *Sharke*. Courtesy of Karl Heinz Marquardt.

p. 84. Helm detail of the schooner *Halifax*, draught by Harold M. Hahn. Courtesy of the family of Harold M. Hahn.

p. 87. Corso Castle. Etching by Johannes Kips, 1732. Courtesy of the editor's collection.

p. 96. Captain William Kidd. Portrait by Sir James Thornhill. Wikimedia Commons.

p. 104. Blocks. Reprinted from *The Young Sea Officer's Sheet Anchor*, with permission from Algrove Publishing Limited.

p. 104. Rudder detail of the schooner *Halifax*, draught by Harold M. Hahn. Courtesy the family of Harold M. Hahn.

p. 106. Chains. Photo of the schooner *Sultana*, The Sultana Project, Inc. Courtesy of the editor's collection.

p. 108. Gig. Courtesy of the Granger Collection, New York.

p. 121. Clove hitch. Clipart.com.

p. 124. Union Jack flag. From R. J. Cornewall-Jones, *Ships, Sailors, and the Sea*, 1894.

p. 129. The Duke of Cumberland. Wikimedia Commons.

p. 145. Jolly Roger flag. iStock.com.

p. 173. Detail of illustration of the *Sharke*. Courtesy of Karl Heinz Marquardt.

p. 190. Detail of illustration of the *Sharke*. Courtesy of Karl Heinz Marquardt.

p. 202. Detail of illustration of the *Sharke*. Courtesy of Karl Heinz Marquardt.

p. 208. A vessel on her beam ends. Reprinted from *The Young Sea Officer's Sheet Anchor*, with permission from Algrove Publishing Limited.

p. 221. Marlin spike. Reprinted from *The Young Sea Officer's Sheet Anchor*, with permission from Algrove Publishing Limited.

p. 226. Drawing of hanged man. *The Gibbet*, by Thomas Rowlandson, 1756–1827. Courtesy of the Yale Center for British Art, Paul Mellon Collection.

p. 260. Coins. From Denis Diderot's *Encyclopédie, ou dictionnaire raisonné des arts et des métiers* (1751–1772). Courtesy of the Granger Collection, New York.

p. 264. Full-rigged ship. Clipart.com.